CW00472352

THE ̶ ̶ ̶ ̶ ̶ ̶
AFFAIR

A brand new totally unputdownable and utterly emotional
WW2 historical novel

VICTORIA
CORNWALL

Love In War Book 1

Choc Lit
A JOFFE BOOKS COMPANY

Choc Lit
A Joffe Books company
www.choc-lit.com

This edition first published in Great Britain in 2023

© Victoria Cornwall

This book is a work of fiction. Names, characters,
businesses, organizations, places and events are either
the product of the author's imagination or are used
fictitiously. Any resemblance to actual persons, living
or dead, events or locales is entirely coincidental.
The spelling used is British English except where fidelity to
the author's rendering of accent or dialect supersedes this.
The right of Victoria Cornwall to be identified as author
of this work has been asserted in accordance with the
Copyright, Designs and Patents Act 1988.

Cover art by Cover art by Nebojša Zorić

ISBN: 978-1-78189-606-8

CHAPTER ONE

5 January 1943, Cornwall

'Binoculars! I need the binoculars!'

Charlotte ran to the wheelhouse and grabbed the trawler's only pair — a cumbersome Victorian relic but which nonetheless had razor-sharp vision.

'What is it?' asked one of the crew as she emerged and pushed past him.

'I'm not sure.' She positioned herself on the starboard side, feet firmly apart. 'But I'm determined to find out.'

Charlotte braced herself against the rise and fall of the deck and lifted the lenses to her eyes. She frowned, grumbled under her breath and peered through them. Everything was blurred.

Slowly, carefully, her cold fingers rotated the focus wheel of the binoculars. Suddenly the dark surface of the North Atlantic emerged into sharp detail. On any other occasion it would have brought a smile to her face but not today. Her eyes narrowed in renewed concentration as she began a methodical search of the surface for the object she thought she had seen.

Under normal circumstances dawn was her favourite time of day as it revealed the world graciously, surreptitiously, silently, yet in plain sight for all to see. Its soft light brought character to the squabbling gulls and added interest to the white-crested waves and the faint dark shapes slipping in and out of the water. But nothing was normal now. Cornwall and its surrounding sea were at war and danger was all around. Now all these elements worked against her, causing too many distractions and twists on reality. She *had* seen something. Hadn't she?

Her conviction began to drain from her body. Whatever it was had gone, swallowed up in the mass of moving currents. Disheartened, she lowered the binoculars, but continued to watch the water, silently frustrated with herself for losing sight of the object.

'What did you see?' shouted her father from across the deck.

She wiped a salty strand of hair from her face. 'I'm not sure. It was probably nothing, but I'll just keep watch a little longer, just in case.'

She returned to her search, scanning the choppy water with the forensic intensity that had the rest of the crew smiling into their nets. After all, they had seen the skipper's daughter watch the sea a million times before, lost in her daydreams, so they saw nothing different now. Charlotte ignored them, unable to shake the feeling that evil was lurking out there and hiding among the dark surface shadows.

Charlotte watched the noisy gulls repeatedly clutch at the very same suspicious shadows with their claws. Even now, with all her experience on the water, she still questioned if those dark shapes were really phantoms of mystical marine creatures, rather than the shadows cast by the fat sun rising above the horizon. At times she even felt like that herself — only half-complete, half-existing, always yearning for something yet not knowing what. She was going to try teaching French, but she already knew it would not satisfy her. One day she hoped the real purpose of her life would emerge just as the dawn had done moments ago, surreptitiously, covertly, silently, as if the answer had been there all the time.

Her wandering gaze caught on a symmetrical shape fifty yards from the starboard side, bobbing in the water like a drowning man. She watched as its finer details emerged, just as the gulls and the waves had done through her binoculars only minutes before. Her stomach churned with foreboding. The sprouting metal spikes confirmed she had been right to be concerned — it was a rogue mine that had broken free from its cable, drifted away from its minefield and had entered the trawling grounds.

'Mine! Starboard side!'

Her father's small crew immediately abandoned their tasks and looked in the direction she was pointing. They rushed up against the bulwark for a better view as the deck rose and dipped beneath their feet. Her father was the last to arrive carrying a cherished memento he'd brought home from the Great War in his hand — his German Luger. He had never used it, declaring that he would when the time was right. It appeared that time was now.

He planted his feet firmly apart, lifted his gun and searched the water's surface.

'Where is it, maid?'

Charlotte pointed again. 'Over there. Fifty to a hundred yards . . . maybe less.'

'I'll try to shoot it, but if it keeps drifting this way it will soon be too close to detonate.' He blinked away the saltwater spray pummelling his face, muttered irritably, took aim and fired. To the disappointment of all those onboard, there were no satisfactory explosion or chink of metal on metal. A collective groan circled the crew as they realised the skipper they all so admired had missed. Her father swore, hurriedly apologised to his daughter for swearing, and took aim again.

'We could speed up and try to move out of its path,' suggested Davey, the youngest and most inexperienced member of the crew.

Her father shook his head. 'Nay, we have several hundred feet of net behind us. We don't know how long the mine's cable is and I don't want it catching on our wires.'

He fired again and missed. 'Blasted Nazi gun!' he cursed as he examined the firearm in his hand.

'Let me have a go,' suggested Charlotte.

Her father grudgingly handed it to her. 'You do have a steadier hand and a sharper eye than me.' He turned to his crew. 'It's my age, you see. I'm not as I was.'

Charlotte took aim. 'Rubbish,' she said as she steadied her aim. 'You are the sharpest man I know.' She threw him a smile. 'You just need to wear your glasses.'

'What's the use of wearing glasses at sea?' he argued back. 'They'll only get covered in spray.' It was a disagreement that had lost its heat long ago, having been repeated so many times. Now it had become a bonding tease, albeit set on a foundation of truth.

Charlotte rolled her eyes, took aim and fired. The bullet impotently pinged off the metal. They all groaned in unison again.

'Well, that's answered that question,' stated her father as if they all knew what he had been thinking.

'What question?' asked Davey.

'If a bullet will explode a mine at a safe distance.' They all nodded knowingly and gloomily stared at the mine. Charlotte's father proudly addressed the crew. 'My daughter has never picked up a gun before, but she tried and still hit it. We'll find another way.' A sudden swell brought the mine several yards closer, reminding them that time was not on their side.

Her father turned to one of the crew. 'Kill the engine. The rest of you, get the boat hooks and deck brooms. If it comes too near we'll edge it around the front of the boat and wait for the tide to carry it away before we move off. We might lose some of our fish, we might have to cut the net free, but there is no use having a good catch or net if there is no boat to haul it in.' The crew scattered, accepting it was the best they could do, under the circumstances.

Moments later they were ready, each member of the crew armed with a hook pole, deck broom or something similar in their hand. They watched in silence as the mine moved towards them on the crest of a wave, then appeared to stall, before moving forward again. The closer it came, the quicker any hope that it would simply pass them by dwindled. They leaned over the side of the boat and held out their poles in readiness. The poles were heavy and the waiting never seemed to end, each wave bringing the mine closer, then dragging it away, before bringing it even nearer to the hull of the boat.

Suddenly, the mine was upon them, strangely taking them all by surprise despite them having watched it approach. They scrambled to get the best position and leverage, desperate to prevent it hitting the side of the hull. The mine nudged against their poles and brooms as they took it in turns to take the lead and guide it along the side of the boat towards the front and away to the open sea on the far side. At times the waves changed course, twisting and turning the mine in the surf and they scrambled to regain control, time and time again. Their spirits were rising and falling dramatically as they finally realised the closer they came to the bow, the lower the water line was.

'We won't be able to reach it,' shouted Charlotte, who was the first to admit she could no longer stretch her arms far enough to maintain contact with the mine.

Her father called for the rope ladder. Charlotte was horrified.

'What are you going to do?'

'I'm going over.' He threw one end of the ladder to a member of his crew. 'Secure it well or it will be the last you'll see of me.'

Charlotte grabbed his arm. 'Don't! Send someone younger. I'll go!'

He shook her off. 'I'll not order a member of my crew to do something I'm not prepared to do myself.' He threw the ladder overboard and looked back at her. 'Sometimes risking your life is the right thing to do. Only a fool doesn't know when that is. And I'm no fool!'

The trawler rose and fell sharply as she watched her father climb over the side, his thick gnarled fists grasping each rung of the wet twisted ladder, each rung straining beneath his portly weight. The crew leaned over the bow and shouted encouragement, but Charlotte remained silent, inwardly fighting all the conflicting emotions churning inside her. Anger. Fear. Pride. Resentment that someone else had not offered to go in his place. Hopelessness. What would she do if he was injured or drowned?

Her father drew level with the water's edge, the grey sea licking at his boots like a hungry animal. 'Pass me a pole!'

A pole was duly passed down to him. He grasped it, his knuckles already grazed and bleeding from being bashed against the hull during his descent. Charlotte watched as he awkwardly manoeuvred the long pole into position. Once it was anchored securely under his arm, he reached towards the tumbling mine with grace and gentleness, as if he was feeding a garden bird. A cheer went up as he began to apply pressure and the mine began to once again glide towards the bow.

All appeared to be going well until her father's boot slipped from the ladder, causing him to dip unceremoniously under the cold water where he was in imminent danger of being lost at sea. Her father's sudden disappearance ignited a gasp from the faces above him. Yet his stubbornness, belief and motivation to finish the job shone through, and a hand suddenly appeared from the choppy waves and grasped a rung on the ladder. He slowly, methodically began his ascent, his body dripping and his expression as determined as before. The fall was not his last. Time and time again he had to reclimb the slippery ladder after a fall, re-anchor his position and reach out to the mine. Charlotte watched with tears in her eyes, her father's bravery and determination burning an enduring memory in her mind and heart. Each time he reappeared from the water, her confidence in him grew and although her body still trembled with fear, her pride in him was fierce and was the stronger emotion of the two.

Eventually the mine floated wide of their boat to roam free in their wake, fortunately just missing their net wires where they broke the surface. Relief, made all the sweeter by their previous anguish, flooded the crew as their skipper's grinning face appeared above the bow. He climbed on board to rapturous applause and a circle of congratulatory back thumping, but all the men made way for Charlotte as she threw herself into his arms. They hugged, her father's cold, soaked body chilling hers but she didn't care. If she had her way she would never let him go again.

Her father was the first to break away. 'It's all right. I'm not going anywhere. Let me breathe.' She smiled and let him go, glad that Davey had arrived with a warm blanket to wrap around him. They turned to watch the mine in silence as it floated away and for the first time she realised her arms were still throbbing from the effort of wielding the pole over the edge of the boat.

'It's time the war ended,' said her father.

It wasn't her father's words, but the melancholic emotion behind them that made Charlotte look up into his bearded face. It had been prematurely aged by over two decades of sea winds yet he had continued to battle the sea day after day. The sea did not defeat him, but this war had caused far more worry than anything he had previously faced at sea. He was looking tired, and tiredness made one vulnerable.

He indicated the mine receding into the distance, floating away on a new journey to somewhere else. 'A mine like that will kill all on board a fishing trawler one day.'

The gravity of his prediction sent a shiver through her. They had come so close to being blown to smithereens — next time they might not be so lucky. If she hadn't chosen to stand on that side of the boat . . . If she hadn't chosen to admire the view . . . Life and death balanced on a wire of chance at the best of times, but the war had taken any illusion of control and turned it on its head.

'Perhaps we should do something else and find safer work on land,' she suggested.

Her father shook his head. 'I prefer the sea to being on land.'

His reply did not surprise her. His experience of the first war had ensured he never wanted to spend more than a week on land again. 'I have spent too long living in the mud of the trenches,' he had once said when she had suggested it before. 'Never again will I be bound to the land. I need to feel the freedom of being at sea.'

Her father looked around, sensing something in the air. 'Time we got back to work. Start up the engine, Davey. I feel the weather will turn in the next few hours. We might be able to shoot a few nets before the squall arrives. By then we will be safely tucked away at home.' He turned to his crew. 'Okay you lazy lot, let's catch ourselves some fish. I want everything ready by the time I've changed out of these wet clothes.'

Thirty minutes later, her father gave the order to haul in the net. The crew immediately obeyed, their compliance born from a deep trust in the aging, experienced skipper, not just from his position. The winch was set in motion and the net wires grew taut and rose out of the sea, followed by the swinging otter-boards which kept the net open beneath the water.

After much creaking of cables and rope, the net emerged full of fish, their heads and tails butted up against the netting. The bulging net was swung over the deck, sagging with its contents and dripping with water. Charlotte efficiently untied the bottom. The catch spilled out onto the floor of the boat, flipping and flopping as they flooded around their boots. The net was set aside and the baskets were placed in position. The crew began to sort them, their speed and efficiency a testament to the number of times they had done it before. Haddock, skate and plaice were the main catch for today, and soon they were gutting and stowing them on ice as they resorted to idle chatter, teasing and black humour which kept their spirits high. Even her father's shooting skills became the butt of their jokes, but he took their teasing in good humour and finally admitted that Charlotte was a better shot than he.

Charlotte glanced up at her father's crew as she gutted the fish alongside them. They were all smiling at her and she found herself smiling too. She loved them all like brothers, every foul-mouthed, smelly, cigarette-smoking one of them. They treated her like one of them, not even censoring their bawdy conversations in her presence when her father was not there. She had learned a lot listening to their bragging, confessions and insecurities, sometimes more than she wanted to know, but she would not have wanted it any other way. She would do anything for them and their families, as she knew they would for her.

When the fish were safely stowed away, the unwanted fish and entrails were shovelled overboard for the gulls to fight over. The final job was to scrub the deck down with large, bristled brooms before preparing to shoot the net again. The bad weather had held off so the whole routine was repeated for the next catch. By the time they scrubbed the decks down for the final time the dark clouds had begun to gather. Her father had been right — a storm was on its way.

The homeward-bound command was finally given by her father and the trawler began its journey home to Newlyn Harbour. They had not seen land for five days and were glad when its harbour walls and the familiar hillside, stacked with quaint cottages, appeared in the distance. They waited patiently off the coast for the signal to approach and enter the sheltered waters of the harbour.

'It's time you have some days off,' said her father quietly as they studied the assortment of boats gathering to seek shelter from the approaching bad weather. Among the local boats, easily identifiable by the reference numbers and letters painted on their sides, were Belgian fishing boats who had sought sanctuary at the beginning of the war. The fishermen had arrived with their families, and had quickly settled in the community, catching fish and helping to feed the country they had found refuge in.

'I was going to ask if I could. A woman has replied to my advert in the paper. She wants a teacher for her son. I'm meeting them tomorrow. He might be my first student.'

'Just when I make a fisherman out of you, you are going to become a French teacher.'

Charlotte laughed. 'Only in an informal sense.'

'You have the quick mind of a teacher. You should think about training to be one. I've always wondered what you'd be doing if you had stayed at school.'

'There is not a lot of demand for French teachers in Cornwall. Besides, I can't see myself ever leaving you.'

Her father chuckled softly. Their gazes met, both content that in this time of war when her friends were working on the land or in factories helping with the war effort, she was happy to stay with him at sea. If her mother hadn't died, she wondered if she would have loved him as much as she did now. She stared at the little fishing village in the distance. Years ago, when her father returned from his trips, he would have had his wife waiting for him, with a hot meal on the stove and a warmed bed for him to sleep in. How suddenly that had all changed.

She was almost fourteen and in her last year at school, when her mother had died. Highly intelligent, she had always excelled at school and her teacher hinted she was destined for greater things, but her mother's early death from breast cancer had shattered those hopes. Her mother, who hated a fuss, had kept her illness a secret. Charlotte, who had prided herself on noticing things, had not noticed her mother's forced smiles and loss of appetite until it was too late. She had covered her fear well.

To make matters worse, Charlotte's own adolescent body began to change at the time of her mother's death. Painful buds began to erupt on her own chest, making her both mortified and terrified that she might be dying too. One of the most feminine parts of a woman's body had hosted her mother's killer and now it was turning on her. Loathing her life and her body, and with a father who was absent for days at a time, she became rebellious and disruptive in and out of school. Finally, her father was forced to face his daughter's grief as well as his own. On hearing of another disruptive episode, he had walked into her school and in a calm, decisive tone, informed the headteacher that he was taking his daughter out of education. The headteacher of the school did not resist. Charlotte was almost school-leaving age and he wanted the peace.

From that day on, until she reached adulthood, her father took her on every fishing trip with him. Charlotte expected to hate it, but there was no room for poor behaviour on board when everyone had to rely on one another. It was a lesson she quickly learned, despite her best attempts to fight it. However, the unpredictability and danger of every trip made her value life in a way she had not before, and seeing the ocean, in all its moods, somehow normalised her own volatile swings. The sheer physical work and finding her sea legs proved to her that her body was more resistant than she thought and working alongside an all-male crew, who were instructed to treat her as one of them, in a strange way made her appreciate her own unique feminine skills and characteristics more.

Her father had had many sisters, so he was not ignorant of a young girl's needs, but his matter-of-fact attitude and explanations, using the lives and deaths of the mammals, birds and fish around them, took the fear out of what she was facing and for the first time since her mother's death, she no longer felt alone. Her relationship with her father had been distant for most of her childhood, thanks to the nature of his work, but this new regime quickly changed it into a bond that even a sheet of paper could not slide between. During those early years she had learned more about her father, and about herself, than she had ever envisaged she would when she first arrived. She was grateful that he had awkwardly stepped up in her time of need. She knew it had been difficult to have a wayward teenager on board, disrupting the ship, but he had stuck it out and made her a better person for it. Today she was a strong, confident twenty-three-year-old woman. Her loyalty to him was fierce, but it was her love for him that kept her by his side now.

Finally, the signal came for them to enter the harbour. It was time to leave those turbulent memories behind once more — memories that were losing their ability to inflict pain with each year that passed. The trawler's engine roared louder and began to propel it through the water. They entered the harbour and were greeted with its distinct smell of fresh fish, drying crab pots and seaweed which clung to the harbour walls. Charlotte watched the vibrant green moss of gutweed and the dull greens and browns of wrack seaweed pass by, their limp branches coming to life as the tide rose to lift them. When they had left, some of the walls had been draped with nets in preparation for tanning, but now the nets were gone, safely stored to be used another day. Charlotte found herself sighing inwardly. It was the little things like this that made the harbour familiar but everchanging.

Her father slowly eased the trawler alongside the dock, where a truck waited for them. In no time at all, their cargo was transferred onto the waiting truck and driven away. Most of the crew disembarked, while her father remained on board to moor the trawler safely. Charlotte bid them all farewell as each man retrieved and lighted a cigarette which had been safely tucked behind one ear for much of the day. Charlotte smiled as they waved her goodbye through the wisps of smoke, before going their separate ways.

She collected a small package from the wheelhouse and slipped it in her pocket.

'For Fizz?' asked her father.

'Of course,' she replied with a smile. She watched her father light up his pipe, a habit he had when his boat was safely moored. 'How do you know?' she asked suddenly, as if her father's words had been troubling her, yet until that very minute she had not realised.

'Know what?' he asked through a cloud of fresh pipe smoke.

'You said that sometimes risking your life is the right thing to do and only a fool doesn't know when that time is. How do you know?'

Her father sucked on his pipe, each one feeding the embers to a burning frenzy. Eventually he removed it from his lips and looked at her, his brows low over wrinkled eyes, his irises as clear as a summer's day. 'You'll know, Charlotte. You'll just know.'

Charlotte would have questioned him further if it was not for the gravity of his voice which held such conviction and truth that it rendered doubts useless. She was now convinced she *would* know, should there be such a time, which in reality was probably highly unlikely. She smiled and headed for home, too, walking the narrow streets which threaded away from the harbour to where they lived. Her father remained on board under the guise of preparing for their next trip, but in reality she knew it was to enjoy some peaceful time alone with his boat. He would follow her later, with what was left from their food provisions, when he was ready. As always, her neighbour's cat was waiting for her on the doorstep, her loud motor-like purr reverberating throughout her body as she began to wind around her legs like a snake.

Charlotte disentangled herself and tickled it under its chin. 'Hi, Fizz. You always seem to know when I'm coming home.' She carefully withdrew the package from her pocket and unwrapped the brown paper to expose the slivers of fish inside. She left Fizz to her meal, as she carefully stepped over her crouching body and went inside, gently shutting the door behind her. It wasn't until the following afternoon that she stepped outside again. The woman who had entered the cottage, smelling of fish, wearing shapeless seafaring clothes and in desperate need of a bath, had now transformed herself — after a long soak, many hours of sleep and much indecision on what to wear.

She nervously smoothed the lapels of her mother's best coat as she emerged from her father's cottage. From her neighbours' interest, the coat was, perhaps, a little too stylish for Cornwall, but she hoped it would give the illusion of class and education to make up for her lack of formal qualifications. Charlotte raised her hand in greeting to her nearest neighbour, who returned it with a wave of her own. Charlotte smiled at her. She wished she had received as much interest in her advert as she was getting from the villagers, but with only one reply so far, this meeting meant far more to her than she cared to admit to anyone but herself.

CHAPTER TWO

Charlotte paused at the door of the tearoom to allow her eyes to adjust to the dim, cosy interior. It was quiet, with one grey-haired man sitting alone at Churchill's table, the nickname for the place setting for two by the wall. Above him hung a string of miniature Union Jack bunting, carefully strung between a picture of weathered fishermen gathered around a large swordfish and a nicotine-stained painting of Newlyn Harbour. Behind the counter stood Mrs Wilson's young daughter, who looked as if she wanted to be anywhere but serving in the tearoom on a winter's afternoon.

'Where's your mother?' asked Charlotte.

'She's out. Gone to get some washing soda.' Emily stood awkwardly behind the war-fund box, looking everywhere but at her customer. She had not yet acquired her customer service skills and appeared unsure what to do with her own hands. Charlotte felt her embarrassment. The young girl's body had begun to blossom into a woman, but Emily didn't have the confidence to be proud of it yet. *Teenage years!* thought Charlotte. She was glad she'd left that phase of her life behind.

'I'll just take a seat. I'm meeting someone and I'd like to wait for them to arrive before I order a pot of tea.' The girl shrugged, voicing no objection so Charlotte made her way to the back of the tearoom.

Square wooden tables with mismatched sturdy Victorian wooden chairs greeted her, inherited from the original owner of the tearoom. The tearoom ownership now stretched across two generations, but they were considered mere custodians by the locals as the building had a far longer history and tie with the community in one form or another. The building belonged to Newlyn — the owners merely gave it life and a new identity for a short while. Charlotte chose a small table with two chairs near the back of the room. It was quieter here and would provide the perfect space to talk to her prospective first student. She passed the older man on her way through. Although it was common in the small fishing village to acknowledge one another with a slight smile or tilt of the head in such circumstances, particularly when you are the only other customer, he did not. Instead, he kept his head bowed, reading the local newspaper with the fingertips of one hand lightly resting on the handle of a half-finished teacup.

As she sat down, Charlotte looked around and realised it was the only table with a small vase of flowers on it. The old sideboard, behind the counter, had new objects displayed on it since her last visit. The Art Deco lampshades, which hung from end to end, had seen better days, two holding dust and one even sporting a crack. The wooden-framed picture of the king, hung on the wall nearby, and was better cared for than the shades if the faint beeswax polish and shiny surface of the frame was anything to go by. Charlotte checked the clock on the wall. Her prospective student should arrive at any moment. She hoped they would not be late as it would not bode well for their future relationship.

The gentleman got up from his table, said something quietly to Emily and began to walk in her direction. As her table had no adjacent doors to exit the tearoom, Charlotte expected him to quickly realise his mistake and turn around, but to her surprise he stopped just in front of her and offered her a friendly smile.

'Miss Bray?'

Charlotte blinked. 'Yes.' To her surprise he pulled out the chair opposite. Charlotte braced herself. 'I'm sorry, but you can't sit there. I'm expecting—'

'Martha Roberts and her son William. I know.' He sat down and made himself comfortable.

Charlotte felt her heart sink. It appeared her first student had cancelled and he was about to deliver the news.

'Are you going to tell me they can't make it?'

He smiled. 'No, I'm not.' Just at that moment Emily arrived with a tray laid with a pot of steaming tea, a small jug of milk, matching teacups and a silver teaspoon in each saucer. The latter rattled loudly against the porcelain as Emily placed them on the table with trembling hands. Charlotte repositioned her empty cup in front of her for want of something to do.

'Thank you, Emily.' Charlotte watched her silently as she returned to the counter. When they were alone again, she returned her gaze to the man. He was rounded in the face, but not overweight, with a neat but full moustache and round, metal-framed spectacles. He was smartly dressed, with a tie, shirt and jacket, but on closer inspection she noted it was a superior quality than local folk wore even at Sunday service. The awareness he was a little different to most men piqued her interest and suddenly realisation dawned.

'I've seen you before.'

'You have?' He seemed impressed. He pointed to the pot. 'Do you mind if I pour?'

'Please do. And yes, it was eight days ago, when I was boarding my father's trawler.' He did not respond as he carefully balanced the silver tea strainer on her teacup and began to pour. Charlotte narrowed her eyes as she stared at him through the rising steam. 'You were standing on the harbour. You wore a long coat and hat.'

'Well remembered.' He stopped pouring, lifted the tea strainer and placed it on his own cup. Carefully and precisely, he proceeded to fill his own. A stream of amber liquid poured from the spout for a second time.

'And again yesterday, in the road outside my house. At least I think it was you. You were walking towards the harbour at the time so I could be mistaken.'

'You were not mistaken.' He placed the teapot down and lifted the small jug. 'Milk?'

Charlotte nodded. 'I was expecting to meet a mother and son, so I feel a little misled.'

'Yes. I'm sorry about that.'

To her surprise, he did appear genuine in his apology.

'But would you have met a strange man?'

Charlotte raised an eyebrow. 'Yes. There is no need to fear meeting a stranger, whether a man or a woman, if it is done in a safe way. My father knows I'm here and I'm in a public place with a witness.' She looked over at Emily, or at least where Emily should have been. He followed her gaze, before returning it to her with a glint of amusement in his slate eyes.

'Your witness seems to be taking a break. But you are right, you have nothing to fear from me. Although, may I offer a good tip for future meetings.'

'Which is?'

'Sit at the table by the window and door, so people can see you and you have a quick exit. Better still, take the chair closest to the exit, so your new student does not block your way if you feel he or she is a bit of an oddity.'

Charlotte was impressed by his advice. She took a sip from her tea, studying him over the brim of her cup as she did so. He intrigued her. The gentleman had a quick mind and might be quite fun to teach.

'You have made some good points. I will bear them in mind next time.'

'May I introduce myself, as I realise I have not yet done so. My name is Stuart Garland.' He offered his hand and Charlotte tentatively shook it above the small flower display.

'I expect you would like to know my credentials,' Charlotte said. 'I assume you saw my advert in the newspaper.'

'I learned of the advert, and you are right, I would be interested to know about your ability to speak French.'

Charlotte cleared her throat. 'I am half-French, half-English. My mother was born in Marseille, in the south of France.'

'Yes, I know of it.'

Charlotte was impressed. Most people in Cornwall were ignorant of the south of France. It was Paris, the northeast border and, of course, Dunkirk which were more familiar to them, learned through reading the paper, watching newsreels and the distorted, crackling voices speaking to them through their wirelesses at home.

'My mother moved to Paris when she was a teenager and later met my father when he fought in the Great War. They married and settled in England when the war ended.'

'Very romantic.'

Charlotte felt her cheeks warm, unsure if he thought she was rambling — yet he did not seem uninterested.

'I am telling you this because when my father was at sea, which was days at a time, my mother would speak to me in French. I have always been able to speak both French and English.' She felt a sense of achievement to see the respect in his eyes.

'You were right. It was me on the harbour when you left on your trawler. Fishing is a different world to teaching French. Do you think you will be able to commit to teaching?'

'Oh yes. Most definitely.' The words were right, but the tone was too forced. Charlotte was annoyed with herself. He had highlighted her only doubt. Could she leave all the uncertainty, excitement and physical work that both exhausted, yet thrilled her, behind? Would she like the predictability and normality of teaching one-on-one? She realised she was getting too far ahead of herself and made a concerted effort to believe what she was doing was right. 'Besides, teaching is just a sideline for now. I hope to build the number of students up and, perhaps, when the war is over, I will be able to concentrate on it more fully. In the meantime, I will continue to help my father out.'

She suddenly realised he had learned a lot about her, but she still knew very little about him. How had that happened?

'Mr Garland, may I ask why you want to learn French?'

He carefully placed his cup in the saucer and looked up at her. 'I don't.'

Charlotte frowned. 'Then why are you here asking about French lessons?'

He needlessly straightened the delicate teaspoon lying in his saucer. 'I haven't been asking about French lessons.'

Charlotte was about to disagree, but as she searched her thoughts for the evidence to quote back to him, she realised, a little belatedly, that he hadn't.

'Then you have me at a disadvantage. What exactly is it that you want?'

Mr Garland looked behind him as if to confirm they were still alone. 'I work for the War Office. We are looking for people who can speak fluent French. Your advert was brought to my attention. To put it bluntly, Miss Bray, we need people like you and I would like to offer you a job.'

'Oh!' Her high-pitched reply was all Charlotte could think of to say. For a bilingualist, it felt woefully inadequate.

'Of course, it would mean you will have to leave Cornwall.'

Another 'oh' escaped her lips. This time she felt a little more deflated at the prospect of leaving her home.

'You will be paid, of course.'

'Where would I be stationed? London? I assume it would involve translating communications.'

Mr Garland dropped his gaze as he repositioned his teacup away from him. It no longer formed a barrier between them and she wondered if she should read something into it. That he was earnest? Determined? Trustworthy?

'Something like that,' he said noncommittedly.

'I need to think about it.'

He sat back in his chair and stared at her. 'I understand.'

'It would mean leaving my father, and he needs me. We have a trawler. I am part of his crew. We catch fish to feed the country.'

'I know.'

Of course he knows, thought Charlotte. He had been watching her and had probably made his own enquiries about her. He would not offer such a job to just anyone. She felt both special and unnerved all at the same time and needed some time to consider his proposal.

'I see that you need some time to think about it.' He searched his pocket, pulled out a blank card and scribbled a telephone number on it. He turned it over so the numbers were hidden and slid it slowly towards her. She stared at it, but did not pick it up. 'And when you have thought it over and made your decision, ring this number. Your country needs you. You can serve it by catching fish or by working for us.'

Charlotte felt the urge to defend her father's work. 'Fishing is dangerous. Not everyone can do it.'

He looked at her, withdrew his wallet and placed some coins on the table without breaking his gaze away.

'If Germany invades England, fishing will be the least of your worries.' He stood and began to rearrange the collar of his coat in his preparation to leave. 'The pot of tea is on me.' He tilted his head in her direction and placed his hat on his head. 'Good day, Miss Bray. It has been a pleasure to meet you.'

He left the tearoom before she had a chance to say goodbye, leaving her in a state of shock and questioning if their conversation had really occurred. She stared at his card on the table for several minutes before reluctantly picking it up and turning it over.

The numbers were written in a slanting hand, but the depth of the pen was deep, showing confidence in what he was writing. She smiled at her thought process. Her father often said she was always reading too much into everything — perhaps this proved he had a point. Yet watching people and trying to analyse peoples' thoughts by their less obvious behaviour was fascinating to her. It was like trying to solve a puzzle, and she loved puzzles. Ultimately it could reveal what was really going on in their heads and to have the key to that information made all the difference on how to respond. It challenged her mind, and she liked challenges. However, despite her little quirk, Mr Garland had taken her completely by surprise. She had surmised he was a retired widow on a rare visit to relatives in the area, who normally balanced his time at home between Home Guard duties, gardening and searching the obituaries for old friends. It seemed some people were not who they appeared to be.

She came to a decision and slipped the card into her pocket, with a resolve that she would not be calling him. It was nice to be asked, but she couldn't envisage leaving her father. She was all he had since her mother had died and it would break his heart if she were to leave him now. Let someone else sit in a dreary office in London and translate piles of papers. She couldn't be the only person to speak French in England.

Confident in her decision, she rose from the table just as Emily returned. Poor Emily. She looked just as fed up and awkward as she did when Charlotte had entered several minutes ago, yet things felt quite different for Charlotte now. Her world had shifted slightly as an opportunity she had never expected had been opened to her. However, today she had learned something about herself. Charlotte Bray, who had been wondering if there was something more for her in life, when finally presented with an opportunity had preferred the status quo and declined to take it. The offer had unsettled her as it had placed doubt in her mind about her current contribution to the war effort. If that solid belief could change in a blink of an eye, what else could?

* * *

Charlotte decided not to tell her father about the meeting. She knew him too well. He had long-held a concern that he might be holding her back in life. 'Your mind is too clever to be hauling in nets,' he often said. His pride in her 'clever brain' was nothing new to her and something he was keen to promote whenever the opportunity arose.

Charlotte smiled at the memory of just such a moment when she opened the door of their home. She had expected to find him snoozing by the window, with a newspaper open on his lap and his pipe by his side, but his favourite chair was empty. The air was absent of the aroma of his afternoon tobacco and the house was unusually silent. He must have gone out, she thought as she slipped off her mother's coat and hung it on the hook by the door.

She left the card in the pocket, knowing her father would not find it there. If he saw it, he would naturally question her about it and she would have to tell him the truth about the man's offer. She didn't want her father to worry needlessly about it. She had endured his watchful, furrowed gaze too many times after her mother had died, despite her reassurances that she was fine. She didn't want to provide another reason for him to worry about her again. They were a team, just the two of them, and she saw no reason for anything to change.

A newly delivered envelope, written in her cousin Anne's familiar hand, lay on the doormat waiting for her. Charlotte smiled. Her father never picked up the mail. She enthusiastically opened it, always delighted to hear her cousin's news. Anne's polite enquiries after her father's health were routine but still warmly welcomed.

How the war has changed things! I now spend my days repairing Spitfire wings and take some pleasure in leaving my mark on the repair. To think those very same wings will carry a brave fighter crew to Germany only days later!

Did you hear about Sam? Our aunt had thought he was dead, but it seems he was captured and is now a prisoner of war. His letters are few and far between, but they are chipper and he often praises the Red Cross. Without them he thinks he would be in a sorry state. Unfortunately, his girlfriend, the one I told you about, was unwilling to wait to find out if he was alive or dead and found another man in the meantime. I hope the news did not distress him too much. He must feel so alone out there on foreign soil.

Hark at me spreading all doom and gloom. At least the Americans have joined the war and we now have hope where there was almost none. Billy and I wave to the American bombers when they fly over Falmouth. They often return in a sorry state.

For the rest of the letter Anne reminisced about their childhood meetups, an event their parents meticulously planned each summer for the cousins to spend time together. Memories of their parents lounging in the sunshine, pretending to guard the half-eaten picnic and watching them chase one another across the soft sandy beach filled Charlotte's mind until she could almost smell the seaweed and feel the grains of sand in her toes.

We built the largest castles with the deepest moats! Dear Sam was so determined we could fill them with water, but alas it was never meant to be. If he still has the determination he had as a child, I am sure he will make his way back to us again. Oh, for those carefree days again, when war was only a distant memory that our parents had to endure.
All my love to you, Charlotte.
Your loving cousin, Anne.

Charlotte smiled as she tucked the letter carefully back into the envelope and placed it gently on the mantel for her father to read, before noticing another note by the clock. She immediately recognised her father's poor, unsteady hand. She picked it up, unfolded it and read his short message inside. He had heard there was good fishing to the north of the Scillies and his nose told him the weather would be calm for the next five days. He would see her in six days but left her the note so she didn't worry. In the meantime, he wanted her to enjoy some extra time off and he would always love her. Of course, this was the message Charlotte read between the lines, but in truth her father was blunter.

Out fishing north Scilly. Weather good. Back in six. Dad.

Charlotte carefully replaced it by the clock. The stew she'd planned to cook for tomorrow would now last her three days instead of one. The less time cooking gave her more spare time. She could spend it compiling a new advert for the newspaper or creating some posters to promote her French classes. She should feel happy with this unexpected opportunity. So why did the days now seem to endlessly stretch out before her?

An hour later she was rummaging through her mother's books. Some were stored beneath her bed in neat piles. A fine film of dust covered many, which was testament to how long they had been neglected. Many were fiction novels, sent to her mother long ago by distant relatives who had disappeared through time. Charlotte was able to converse, read and write French easily, but reading a novel in French would be good practice. To have the opportunity to immerse herself in the language with the complete absence of English thinking was something she hadn't done for a while. It would keep her mind occupied while she waited for her father to come home. She reached deeper, searching for her favourite book which had been pushed to the far side and against the wall so her father would not find it. Her fingers grazed its cover, along with the embossed title, *L'amant de Marseille.* She slowly withdrew it from under the bed, held it in her lap and smiled. It had been several years since she had opened the pages of *The Lover of Marseille,* but it felt like only yesterday. The plot was emotional, the characters intriguing, but it was the sensual descriptions of lovemaking that would ultimately prevent a British translation. She allowed the open pages to pass beneath her fingertips. The lovemaking scenes had both taught her things and set her up for disappointment, as her only experience with a soldier home on leave had fallen short when compared to the passion felt by the lovers in this book. One can but hope she would not be so disappointed next time, she thought, as she climbed onto her bed and settled down to read it one more time.

CHAPTER THREE

'Bonjour, Monsieur Lesieur.'

'Please, call me Pierre, and I am happy to speak in English.'

'Thank goodness for that. My French is appalling at the best of times.'

The two men shook hands and Pierre took the seat offered to him. The wooden chair had a wicker-weaved back and creaked under his weight, but it was surprisingly comfortable. He settled into it and expected the British officer opposite him to do the same. However, a cup of tea seemed to be more important as he went to the door and asked his secretary to bring them a tray.

'I do hope Mrs Billingsworth is treating you well,' said the officer as he returned to his chair behind the desk.

'She is.'

The officer smiled. 'She is a marvel, isn't she?'

Pierre thought of the no-nonsense landlady with the stern face and draconian rules, who rented her rooms to guests who appeared and disappeared at odd times, day and night, yet asked no questions.

'Yes, she is quite a marvel,' he agreed, less enthusiastically.

A tray, laden with a teapot and two matching cups and saucers, arrived carried by a pretty, young woman. Silence fell as she efficiently poured a measure of milk into the two empty cups and filled them to near the brim with steaming, hot tea. Mesmerised by her actions, Pierre found himself still gazing at her as she left the room.

The officer offered him his cup with a steady hand and a perceptive gaze.

Pierre knew he had been caught staring and felt instantly guilty for doing so. 'I thought she looked new to the job,' he lied.

Should he try to explain how long it had been since he'd appreciated a woman's appearance? He read the unspoken message in the officer's eyes and realised the officer knew only too well how he felt. They would have done their research.

Pierre smiled and took the cup. This was the first time he had met Major Davies, but the man had yet to introduce himself, leaving the nameplate on his office door and desk to do it for him.

'I hear you have just arrived in England,' the major said. 'How was the journey?'

Pierre recalled his time hiding in the damp ditch of a hedge, waiting for the weather to break and listening for the sound of a Lysander's engine softly roaring above. When the plane had finally arrived, he'd emerged from his hiding place and hastily lit the makeshift landing lights that ran along the empty farmer's field. Within minutes the plane had landed and taken off again, and he was lying exhausted inside its outdated, but nimble body, deeply in debt to the 138 Squadron who had secured his escape from his homeland, France.

'It could have been more comfortable,' he replied, smiling sadly.

'I am sorry to hear that your network had to be disbanded.'

'It is difficult to survive when two of the members have been arrested by the Gestapo.'

'Who do you think betrayed you?'

'That I don't know.'

'Yet you got away. You were lucky. Luck seems to follow you around. This is the second time luck has been on your side.'

Pierre moved in his chair. For some reason it no longer felt so comfortable. 'Or bad luck. *Needle* was the second network I have been involved in which had to be disbanded. I am beginning to get a complex.'

Both men gave a hollow laugh, the humour of the joke tainted by the blood of those who had died as a result of the betrayal by one of their own.

'Don't. Being a Special Operation Agent and running a successful network in occupied France is dangerous work. Take wireless operators, for example. They seem to be only lasting six weeks before they are discovered. Do you want to continue?'

Pierre didn't need to think about his answer and replied immediately, 'Of course.'

'Then I will arrange for you to be parachuted into another part of France in a couple of weeks. In time we will have a new circuit up and running again.'

Pierre nodded in acceptance. It was what he had hoped for. There was nothing more important to him than the liberation of France and he was keen to play his part in achieving that goal.

The major got up from his chair. 'While you are here, I want to show you something.' He unlocked his filing cabinet and opened the top drawer. Pierre watched him carefully withdraw a roll of paper and roll it out on the floor. It was almost three yards long and half a yard wide. Pierre approached and his eyes widened as he realised what it showed. Stretched out in front of him, in the finest detail, was the Normandy coastline, from Cherbourg to Honfleur. Pierre crouched before it, studied it for a moment and indicated to areas on the map with a casual wave of his hand.

'Are these what I think they are?'

The major nodded, smiling smugly. 'Yes. Machine gun nests. Barbed wire defences. Minefields. Block houses.'

Pierre looked up, astonished. 'Where did you get this?'

'An agent escaped to England in June. He brought his family with him. They were being hunted by the Gestapo.

He also brought this with him. He had been given it while he was in France. Apparently it was wrapped up as a parcel and tied with string.'

'It must have been stolen from the Germans.'

'If it is genuine.'

'It looks it.'

'But we can't know for sure and if we are to rely on it for any planned invasion, we need to know it is accurate.'

'Is this why you wanted me to come to England? To see it for myself?'

The major nodded.

'And you want me to find out if it is accurate.'

'Confirmation of these defence positions would be helpful.'

Helpful, thought Pierre. It would be *vital*.

'Do you fancy exploring the north coast of France while we organise a new team for you?'

Pierre stood up and smiled. 'Funny you should say that. A few weeks walking in the fresh coastal air might be just what I need.'

'The Germans may not be too keen on sightseers.'

'Then I have no choice but to make sure that I'm not spotted.'

They exchanged knowing smiles. 'But for now, you need to rest,' said the major. He looked at him through his eyebrows. 'Although, we may call upon your French skills while you are here.' In response to Pierre's enquiring look, he added, 'We have some new recruits arriving next week. If they pass their initial interviews here they will be sent for preliminary training.'

'Training in what?'

'Oh, you know. The usual sort of thing.'

Pierre could guess and it would range from translating and decoding to agent work in the field.

'I want to identify between those who can speak French like a native and those who only claim they can.' The major sipped his tea and returned the cup carefully back to its saucer. 'It's a little less exciting than you are used to but—'

Pierre parried his concern with a wave of his hand. 'I've had enough excitement for the time being. All I need now is a good bed, food and rest. Just send word to my landlady when you need me.'

They studied the map for some time, Pierre knowing his access to it was limited and he must commit as much of it to memory as he could. However, it was made clear he was not required to duplicate it — only record and report what he observed so they could compare the two. After much discussion, it was decided this mission was best done on his own. The less people who knew about it the better. After completing it, he would be given instructions to meet up with a new team. This time he would be the organiser and in control.

As they shook hands, Pierre felt a stir of unease sweep through him. He had experienced the same feeling before and it always left him questioning if he would ever see the people he met in England again.

* * *

Pierre emerged from the headquarters of the SOE and looked around him. He had found locating the building difficult, as by its very nature, it was not well advertised. Many, even high-ranking officials, were unaware of the SOE's existence so it was natural that its headquarters on Baker Street, despite its height, would appear no different to the properties on either side. It blended in well. Just another townhouse which happened to survive the relentless bombing campaign of 1940–41, hiding behind a misleading name plaque with the words The Inter-Services Research Bureau.

The streets of London had been disorientating, which added to his difficulty in locating the building. Navigating any foreign city was not easy, but London was even more so. In some parts, large areas were wasteland where once a street had stood, the foundations and unsupported brick walls now the only evidence that there had been a street at all. The ruins reminded him of damaged skeletons, and the foundations resembled footprints where life had once stood.

Yet other parts appeared largely untouched by the carnage, particularly historical and significant architecture. It was as if Hitler himself had given an order to preserve those buildings so he could claim them for his own. Yet life was carrying on, just as it was in occupied France. People bought things, laughed, loved and went out to be entertained. It was the only thing they could do — carry on and keep going.

Although some barren land had been turned over for allotments, the main parks remained open to the public. From noon onwards, the parks would swarm with Londoners who had chosen to escape their offices and eat their lunches outside, despite the winter temperatures. Among them mingled uniformed soldiers from every rank and service of the Armed Forces. They could be found everywhere in London, on leave or on duty, their casual body language, or their focused mindset, the only way to identify if they were on or off duty.

This life was the new normal. If it was not for the barrage balloons keeping the city safe from low-flying bombers, or the soldiers, or the communal feeding canteens, or the destruction, or the missing iron railings, or the lines of children helping with salvage campaigns, one could forget there was a war at all.

He paused to watch a small group of boys and found himself looking at one in particular. He was no more than ten years old and was bubbling with excitement at having found a treasure among the rubble of a largely cleared bomb site. He showed his friend. The rest of his friends crowded round to inspect it. It was no more than a broken copper pipe, but it was the perfect length for a make-believe gun and instantly became a prized possession. It was put to good use and they chased one another around the dusty mounds of earth, laughing and shouting as they killed one another, then quickly rose from the dead. Their laughter was uplifting and he found himself smiling too, with the strange urge to join them and try to capture the time when he was an innocent child too . . . until their innocence reminded him of another young boy. Suddenly it was too painful to hear their laughter and see their smiles. He turned and briskly walked away, unable to look back. Even in England, it seemed, he could not forget.

He shook himself and made a concerted effort to push the boy's face to the depths of his mind. *Concentrate on the here and now and pretend that nothing has changed*, he told himself as he turned in the direction of his lodgings and made a determined effort to ignore the sandbags filled with earth and the windows crossed with tape on either side of the narrow road.

Dusk began to fall on the city, slowly plunging it into darkness as every light in every street, on every sign and framing every building were extinguished. It was hard to stay positive in the face of such bleakness, because although the lack of light made London a little less vulnerable in the dark, its inhabitants inevitably felt the most isolated as the city tried to sleep. Even Leicester Square and Piccadilly disappeared in the darkness, silently waiting for the war to end and for their time to shine again. No matter where he was in the world or what city he was in, he always hated the night-time as the dark hours left him alone with his festering regrets.

Pierre was greeted on the steps of his landlady's house by the solemn gatekeeper herself, her arms folded across her ample bosom.

'I told you to be home by ten. I don't want to be up all night waiting for guests to return. My lodgings are respectable.'

Pierre frowned and looked at his watch. To his surprise, the day had disappeared. He must have been walking for hours and had not only lost his bearings, but his track of time as well.

'Please accept my apologies,' he mumbled.

She stood aside and allowed him to enter the hall. 'First time in London?'

He nodded. To his surprise she smiled at him.

'It is often the way. You are not the first to come here and just walk and walk without the fear of being questioned. Have you eaten?'

Had he? He shook his head.

'I'll bring you a cup of tea and something to eat. But remember, I have rules. No women. No noise. No drunkenness—'

'And be home by ten. I understand. I won't do it again.'

Pierre climbed the stairs lined with hideous wallpaper and went to his room. It was small and basic but had some minor comforts that were welcoming and strangely reassuring. A crocheted blanket, a Home Sweet Home embroidered picture and a chamber pot hidden under the bed. He lay down on the hard mattress and rested his arms behind his head. His body felt weak. His mind ached with all the details. It was exhausting to be a liar and no one knew that better than Pierre Lesieur.

CHAPTER FOUR

Charlotte woke with a sense of unease. There was nothing to indicate that the day would be any different from any other. It was true, the sky was filled with low-hanging, grey-edged clouds, as if another winter storm were brewing, but Newlyn Harbour itself remained the same as always, busy in a quiet and methodical way. She strolled down the steep narrow road which led to the harbour and stood for a while watching several men, some wearing flat caps with a cigarette permanently set at the corner of their lips, working quietly on their boats. There was always something to do, whether repairing or preparing. It was constant, necessary and meant the difference between life and death.

Today was the day her father said he would return home. It was also the first time in her life she was unable to eat breakfast. Was there a connection between the two? She headed towards the harbour wall, hoping the fresh, salty wind would blow her concerns away. An hour later, her concerns had grown. Her father was late. Soon the same concerns began to show in the faces of her father's friends who approached her one by one. *Have you heard from your father? No, have you? No, we haven't heard from the* Lottie's Charm *since yesterday evening. Maybe he had a wireless breakdown?* They sidled away from her, heads

34

down, looking anywhere but at her, but she had seen the grief in their eyes. Using a breakdown of the trawler's wireless was just a hopeful excuse. Those who understood the sea knew that no one had used wirelesses at sea since the war began as messages could be intercepted and used to attack. They all knew something terrible had happened, just as she knew it now. The wives and mothers of her father's crew began to arrive at the harbour. They had been waiting at home, as they always did, but had grown concerned that the men had not yet returned. Her presence on the quay had at first reassured them, but when they discovered she had not gone with them they looked to her for news instead. It was painful to not be able to reassure them that all was well.

A Belgian trawler crew, who had made Newlyn their home, brought the news they had all dreaded. Debris had been spotted north of where *Lottie's Charm* was last known to be fishing. Little was left of the trawler — just a few splintered planks of wood had been spotted as they were buffeted by waves. If part of the hull had been left intact, it had long been dragged down by its full nets. The amount of floating debris indicated that a great tragedy had occurred in the area and it had probably taken the lives of the crew on board. A crowd had gathered around the trawler as some broken planks of wood were transferred from the deck to the quay. Charlotte was drawn to the semicircle of men and women who were studying what was in front of them. She elbowed her way to the front and saw the damaged planks of wood on the ground. On several were the scattered words *Lottie's Charm* painted in sea blue.

Davey's mother began to scream, her heartfelt anguish raising the curious seagulls nearby. Another woman began to cry and was led away, as several men's voices began to break under the strain.

'A freak accident?' asked someone.

'Did the engine blow up?' asked another.

At last, someone voiced what they all suspected. 'More likely a rogue mine. There's plenty about.'

A murmur of agreement circled the people who had remained.

Someone nearby echoed her father's words. 'It's time this war ended.'

Charlotte looked up, hoping to see his familiar face, but it wasn't him. How could it be? He was lying at the bottom of the cold, black sea, if what was on the ground was proved right.

'It was only a matter of time before one blew up a boat,' said Tom Cobb, a skipper of another boat. He realised she was there only when their eyes met. His eyes were already brimming with unshed tears, for the crew of any local boat was as close as family to him. Suddenly, the sadness in his gaze made everything real. Too real. Charlotte turned and pushed her way through the increasing crowd, sympathetic murmurs and distraught relatives of her father's crew. She couldn't bear the sympathy of some, or see the pain of others, for she feared she would fall apart if she dared to stop.

She walked away, her spine ramrod straight, as her last memory of the *Lottie's Charm* crew played out in her mind — laughing, teasing and waving her goodbye beneath a cloud of newly lit cigarette smoke. It was only when she reached the sanctuary of her home and saw her father's abandoned glasses on the sideboard did she allow herself to fall apart. Gasping for air between each howl of anguish, she sank to the floor and felt her heart break.

* * *

There were no individual funerals, just a simple service of remembrance for all the crew on board. Charlotte left the service for the wives and mothers of the crew to arrange. She wanted the crew's relatives to choose the hymns and eulogies in the hope it would help them with their grief. She may be the skipper's daughter, but there was no rank to bereavement. Her grief was private, so much so that she wrote to Anne suggesting that as fuel and transport were limited, Falmouth was so far from Newlyn and there was no body to bury, she would understand if they did not attend. She was somewhat relieved when Anne replied within days. They would dedicate their own local service to the seafaring life her father led, she wrote, intuitively understanding that the service and seeing other family members grieving, would not help Charlotte in hers.

The tragedy of the *Lottie's Charm* was felt by everyone. Even Fizz, her neighbour's cat, appeared to grieve, spending the days leading up to the funeral sitting forlornly at the end of the garden and meowing loudly whenever the smell of fish wafted up from the harbour. Yet she did not go down to the trawlers begging for food, as if she felt the fish would not taste as good if it was not caught by the crew of the *Lottie's Charm*.

On the day of the funeral, the boats remained in the harbour so the village could attend the funeral service. The church could not accommodate all the mourners, so many were left to sing hymns and pray outside, standing shoulder to shoulder, along the gravel path or scattered among the graveyard stones. And despite the singing, the heartfelt eulogies and the carefully selected readings, it was her father's words she heard and which kept running through her head. *It's time this war ended. It's time this war ended.* It was all she could hear or think about.

The service over, the villagers slowly made their way to the village hall for the wake. She spoke to every bereaved family but had no appetite to eat or drink. Although she politely accepted their numerous condolences in return, as soon as she could she escaped outside and began walking away with no plan in mind. She had not slept for days and had spent her time either wandering around the house or lying down, staring into space. It felt as if life no longer had a purpose. There was no father to care for. She had no boat to fish. She had no one to live for. What was the purpose when all seemed so bleak?

Yet all that changed when her fingers brushed against the stranger's card in her pocket. Suddenly, everything fell into place. Feeling its sharp corners was one sign in what she now saw had been many. Her father's repetitive words running through her head. A stranger asking for her help. This card reminding her that her skills were desperately needed. She inhaled deeply. It felt for the first time that she could actually breathe again. She had always felt half-complete as if she had yet to discover the real purpose of her life. She had thought it was teaching, but she had been wrong. The card that was barely touching her fingers was the key to her destiny. She could end the war, just as her father had wanted, or at least play a part in it. It was the first time since his death that she knew what she must do and nobody could stop her.

Charlotte heaved open the heavy, red telephone-box door and searched for some pennies in her handbag. A passing child, innocent of the pain of grief, pressed his grimacing face up to the glass, flattening his nose to a blanched mass. She shooed him away and he ran off laughing, looking to make mischief elsewhere. She turned her back on him and focused on the telephone. Although her hands were shaking as she lined up the pennies on the shelf, her mind was clear and her heart determined. She lifted the black receiver from its cradle, inserted all the pennies, dialled the number on the card and cleared her throat as she waited. The clipped tones of a woman answered, not the man she had met in the tearoom on the quay. The voice had taken her by surprise, but she quickly rallied and pressed the button to answer. Her heart began to thud in her chest as the coins rattled through the internal workings of the telephone.

'Hello. My name is Charlotte Bray. I can speak French and I want to help to defeat Hitler.'

CHAPTER FIVE

It was not long before Pierre received word that the new recruits had arrived and his services were required. It was the news he had been waiting for as he was now eager to return to France. He was greeted by an efficient woman who did not give her name. He provided his and she required no explanation, having been well briefed. Within a few minutes he was assigned an office and was interviewing the new recruits with the sole purpose of testing their French skills and submitting a report on his findings.

Pierre studied the list of potential recruits. Most were men, although there were three women listed at the bottom, as if they were added as an afterthought. He was given little information about each one but he quickly guessed which recruits had a background in the armed forces as he could spot them as soon as they entered his office. Their manner and knowledge instantly separated them from the rest and he made a note for his report that it would be beneficial for their future if they were able to disguise it in some way. However, to Pierre's surprise, there were many who were civilians with no combat experience at all. They were wide-eyed, nervous and appeared ignorant of the true nature of why they were there.

Some of the potential recruits had French ancestry or at least some knowledge of France, but all could speak French and had a steely determination to succeed in the interview to help with the war effort in any way they could. He respected them for their ambition but would not give them an easy ride. Understanding and speaking the French language could mean life or death to others if not the recruits themselves and he did not want to be the one who did not challenge them enough at the start.

As the British armed forces had no roles for women in combat, he assumed the three women would play a role in translating wireless messages and remain on British soil. Two were dressed in a uniform and had been transferred from the Auxiliary Territorial Service. The last one on the list was a civilian and wore a practical skirt, blouse and cardigan. The clothes would not turn heads, but he couldn't help thinking that the woman wearing them would.

The day had been long, and boredom and hunger had set in. There was only so many times a man, unused to sitting behind a desk all day, could hold a conversation with a queue of strangers and not exchange a single piece of personal information. It was against advice, but it left conversations bland, repetitive and lacking true substance so when an adventurous winter moth, with fringed pale grey wings, settled on his desk, his gaze was drawn to it again and again. Perhaps its rescue was why his last interviewee lingered in his mind for several days afterwards as he was able to concentrate on their conversation which ended up more stimulating than the ones that had gone before.

He only knew her as a number, but her sudden appearance, before he had a chance to call for her, had resulted in her walking in on him as he attempted to coax the moth off his sheet of paper and onto the outside window ledge and infinite freedom. The way she carried herself as she walked towards him and her well-balanced features set her aside from the others immediately and decisively. If it was possible for a woman to look French, she had those characteristics. Fine bone structure and well-defined arched eyebrows reminded him of a high-fashion model that adorned the type of magazine popular in Paris. Her brown eyes had depth, and her olive-toned skin and initial broad smile reminded him of southern France, where the people were known to be friendly and spent much of their time outside. She had short, dark hair which curled behind her ears, and had an athletic, energetic appearance. Her first words to him suggested that she would be motivated by a challenge rather than succumb to it.

'I hope you are not thinking of jumping,' she joked.

He had replied gruffly, and in response she had raised a haughty eyebrow as if she had expected better from him. In that moment he inexplicably chose to make it particularly difficult for her by speaking French quickly and quietly, to the extent of mumbling, and looking away at key moments so it would be hard to catch each word. Why he chose to be so tough on her, he had no idea. Yet, as soon as he denied it to himself, he knew the answer all too well. Not too long ago, he had thought of jumping. Suicide jokes quickly lose their humour when you have come close to those depths.

'Sit down. I don't have all day. We are only to converse in French.' He sat down and turned in his chair, opening and shutting several drawers on the pretext of looking for something. 'I expect you are tired of waiting. It's been a long day so we'll miss the formalities.'

Her reply was quick, clear and of an exemplary standard. 'I'm not tired of waiting and I wasn't expecting any.'

He shut the last drawer and looked up into her direct gaze. He lost his train of thought.

'Any what?'

'Any formalities. You must be tired of introducing yourself.'

His eyes narrowed. Was she scolding him or sympathising with him? He indicated for her to sit down, which she did. He quickly looked through his records about her which was barely one line.

'Congratulations on passing the initial interview. You are seeing me so I can assess your French skills.'

She crossed her legs, which caught his eye and made him glance up before he could help it. He found himself staring right into her beautiful but determined eyes.

'There is no need to explain. I understand what is expected of me.' Her eyes crinkled at the corners. 'I questioned your previous interviewees to prepare for my turn.'

Pierre sat back in his chair. He was intrigued. There was no need to play games regarding mumbling his words. He had a feeling she saw right through him and it made not one bit of difference to her. Her French was too good.

He smiled without humour in return. 'And what did you learn?'

'They said you looked bored.'

His smile faded. Stern, intimidating, intense. He could take those descriptions, but bored? It made him sound lazy and lacking in some way.

Her eyes darted to the clock on the wall. 'And as it is getting late, I would guess you are probably hungry too.'

For an insane moment, he wondered if she could read his mind. He clenched his teeth at the very thought.

'I have either amused you or annoyed you. I apologise. I am not used to being in London yet.'

'What I am feeling doesn't matter,' he countered.

'Oh! That's terribly sad.'

Her full lips curved in a slight smile and for a moment he had difficulty dragging his eyes away from them. He had a feeling she was teasing or testing him, he wasn't quite sure which.

He straightened in his chair and cleared his throat. It was time to take back control — which, to his annoyance, meant he had lost it at some point.

'You speak French well. Are you French?'

'My mother was.'

'Was?'

'She died several years ago.'

Silence descended as if she was waiting for him to respond. He allowed the silence to stretch between them to see her response.

Her gaze wandered across his desk. 'Usually, people offer some sort of sympathy. I'm glad you didn't bother. Expressed sympathy seems less valid when the death is of a stranger and happened years ago.' She shot him an enquiring glance. 'Don't you think?'

He did think. Words were easy to serve out, actions were what really mattered, and as her mother had died years ago, there was nothing he could do to help.

'But of course, you might have done it on purpose to make me feel uncomfortable.'

He narrowed his eyes. 'Why would I want to do that?'

'So that I lose confidence and fail somehow—' she indicated the notes in front of him — 'and you can write it down in your assessment of me.'

She was good. Intelligent. Observant. And her French was so good that he'd forgotten she was British.

'Were you trying to make me feel uncomfortable? Is that a tactic you use?'

'Does it matter?'

'It matters a great deal. I'm here to learn. I should learn to recognise it when it is used.'

'Yes, I did.'

He'd learned that people found silence uncomfortable and most felt the need to fill it. Often they ignored the natural, inbuilt filters in their hurry to fill the dead air. Secrets were exposed. Confessions were made. Confidences were shared. What drove him to use it in this circumstance, he wasn't sure. He steered the conversation back to the task in hand.

'Have you family in France?'

'My mother's family still live there, but we lost contact with them a long time ago. She came from Marseille.'

He stretched his legs out in front and crossed them at the ankles. He had been right — her Mediterranean looks came from her mother's side.

'My mother moved to Paris when she was a child.' Pierre nodded in acceptance. Her story explained why her dialect

43

was classic Parisian French and did not have the rhythm and speed of the Marseille dialect. He shook himself inwardly. Her French was so good that he was even assessing her dialect.

'What will you do if you don't get selected?' he asked.

'I don't know. Volunteer in some other way to help with the war effort. I can't go back to catching fish at sea.'

He laughed, but abruptly ceased when he realised she was quite serious. 'You worked on a ship?'

'We prefer to call them trawlers,' she replied gently as if correcting a child.

He fell silent as he tried to imagine her battling the Atlantic and hauling in a catch of fish. Even in sea waders and deep-fishing gear, she still held the allure that could turn a man into a gawping pubescent mess — if they allowed it.

'Why did you stop?' He answered his own question before she had a chance to. 'Ah . . . I understand. I suspect the comfort of an office is more desirable than being on a trawler.'

'It's not that. I have no trawler, crew or skipper to go back to.'

Her reply raised more questions than it answered and he couldn't stop himself from wanting to know more about her. He realised then that he'd crossed his own line about not wanting to learn about the personal circumstances of an interviewee. It was a timely reminder to remain guarded about his own circumstances and not give away too much about himself.

'Why not?'

'Because they were blown up by a mine a week ago.'

Silence stretched between them again. This time it was he who found it painful. Death could be so sudden and final when a bomb was involved. Suddenly, he felt ashamed of his earlier conduct and subsequent laughter.

'I'm sorry,' he said, still unsure if the tale she had just spun him was true. On the face of it, a woman trawling for fish seemed ludicrous, yet if any woman could battle the sea, this one could.

Her brown eyes darkened even further until they were almost black. 'Thank you,' she said quietly. He wondered if she really meant it, given their earlier conversation. He straightened in his chair and decided to change the topic to safer waters.

'What does your father do?' he asked as he looked at the column of interviewee numbers in front of him. He glanced up when she didn't reply. 'Well?'

'He was the skipper on the trawler.'

He noticed her swallow hard — a sure sign of stress — and there was a light sheen to her eyes now. So, it was her recent bereavement, not the loss of her job that drove her to volunteer. Grief was not a good reason to turn one's life upside down, but it was a common one. Hadn't he done just the same?

'What do you know about France?' he asked, purposefully changing the conversation.

'My mother often spoke of it. She told me more about Paris than her earlier years in the south of France.'

Pierre rested back in his chair. 'What did she tell you?'

He watched her as she dropped her gaze and her brow furrowed as she searched her memory. 'She told me that she sold cosmetics. She said she would ride her bicycle for miles, carrying samples in her basket and knocking on people's doors.'

He scribbled a note of it beside her number.

'What else did she say?'

'That Paris was always busy with cars and buses . . . and horse and carriages.'

He was relieved to see that the sheen in her eyes had disappeared. 'There are no horse and carriages anymore.'

The woman looked at him briefly. 'There were when she lived there.' The frown deepened. 'She spoke of lots of fountains.'

'Show me a city that does not have them.'

'And the vehicles are driven on the right.'

'Details that are widely known.'

Her frown deepened a little more as she tried to remember. 'She spoke of parks—'

'But you cannot recall a name?'

Her lips thinned in a tight line, then miraculously softened into a smile. She had remembered something.

'One was called Bois de Boulogne!' He could see from her delight that her mother's tales were coming back to her. 'She loved going there. It had a lake edged with tall trees, where swans and cygnets swam up to the water's edge to feed on the bread thrown by Parisians walking in the park. She said it was one of the largest parks in Paris and was popular with courting couples as it had rowing boats.'

Pierre found himself nodding as he had once been on one of those boats as a younger man, trying to look capable but failing miserably to the delight of his first date.

'And there was another park . . . what was it called . . .' She tapped a hand on her thigh as if it would help somehow. 'Pac Monceaux! Mother considered that one the prettiest. Artists, with big moustaches, would sit by the lake wearing straw boaters and painting on rickety easels. She said they would always be surrounded by a huddle of children who found it fascinating to watch the painting emerge.'

She uncrossed her legs and sat forward, as if to concentrate. He almost mirrored her but checked himself just in time.

'She talked of mobile ice-cream carts and that every restaurant had a speciality. There was one speciality she particularly remembered — caviar and pancakes!' She smiled at him. 'Sounds dreadful.'

Before he could reply she was back with her mother again, listening to her idle reminiscences. He wondered if she was finding the experience comforting in some way as her face had a faraway look that made you want to just sit and watch it.

'She used to say that the French took the time to enjoy life. They would indulge in—' — she mimed quotation marks in the air — 'an *aperitif hour* at their favourite café.

More customers would sit outside than inside. The pavement would be filled with rows of tightly packed customers at small round tables, with everyone dressed in their best as they chatted and sipped cool drinks in the sun. The waiters served the drinks on silver trays, wearing long white aprons and bow-ties, while pastries were served by stylish waitresses with large polite smiles on their faces.'

Pierre allowed her to continue, for she appeared lost in her world as if she was walking the streets of Paris at that very moment rather than sitting in an office with him, with only one small window for natural light.

'Newspaper, cigarettes and flower stalls line the pavements. The flowers are so cheap that it's not extravagant to buy fresh flowers every day. Boot shiners, gendarmes . . . with their white baton sticks.'

She tilted her head meaningfully towards him as if parting with some confidential information. 'My mother always said they were very courteous to her.'

Oddly, he felt pleased that she was back in the room with him and watching Paris from a distance again. 'Who? The boot shiners or gendarmes?' he asked, half smiling.

'Both. And the morning air, outside the bakeries, would be filled with the sweet aroma of yard-long sticks of freshly baked bread that required no wrapping but a good set of teeth to cut through the crust. She spoke of the opera house and that city life did not stop at midnight.'

'Place de l'Opera?'

'Yes! She said the traffic outside was constant but inside one experienced the most magnificent music in the world.' She sighed as if she had just heard the orchestra for herself. 'And she said the streets were very clean as the street cleaners spent their days following the water wagons and brushing water along the gutters and into the drains. And there was always something to see on the Seine, whether boats or lines of fishermen, in cloth caps, who—' she laughed softly — 'never seemed to catch anything. Are there still bookstalls along the Seine?' He nodded. 'Do customers still spend hours searching the books before buying one? Mother said that some customers were known to read an entire novel without buying and the stallholders didn't seem to mind.'

'That I don't know.'

'My mother said things were different in Paris. Hurried, busy, but there was always time to enjoy what life had to offer.' She looked up and he realised her eyes were sparkling. 'I would love to see it one day and walk where she walked. It is hard to lose someone that you love, isn't it?' She paused. 'But I think you have experienced that already.'

Pierre had spent the last few minutes walking through her mother's memories with her. In his mind he had been beside her, marvelling at the towering Place de l'Opera, hearing the laughter in the park and recalling the taste of pancakes and ice cream with an enthusiasm he had not felt in a while. Memories untainted by the constant presence of German troops. Thanks to this woman, for a brief moment they had not existed and he was able to enjoy the city as he used to only a few years ago — but her last remark had ruined all that.

'I don't know what you mean.'

'Yes, you do. I think you have lost someone close to you. Maybe even more than one. And it was sudden.'

He gripped the pen in his fingers a little tighter. 'Why do you say that?'

'When I spoke of my crew being blown up, there was a moment your gaze dropped to your right. I've noticed people often do that when they are remembering something.'

'I could have remembered I didn't buy bread.'

'If that was the case, you would have shown some expression of frustration not deep sadness. You didn't do that when I spoke of my mother's death, but when there was more than one and it involved a sudden loss . . .' Her eyes widened slightly. 'Have you lost your parents too?'

'I wouldn't tell you if I had.'

'I'm usually—'

'Right? Maybe. Maybe not. You'll never know if you were on this occasion.'

He shuffled his papers to avoid seeing her hurt expression. Her observational skills were outstanding, if a little disconcerting. Her wish to help with the war effort was commendable, but if she thought she could use it to visit Paris, she was naïve, if not foolish. It was unsafe. Especially for an Englishwoman. France was the last place she would want to be.

He straightened in his chair. 'Paris has changed. It is not the same as when your mother was there. I think I'll end the interview here.'

'You will?'

He ignored the confusion on her face and the question that followed.

'How did I do?'

'My opinion will be in my report, but a visit to Paris should not be your priority.'

'I never said it was.'

'Thank you for coming. Close the door on your way out.'

He knew it was a brutal way to end the interview, but it was necessary. If not to save her from outlandish ideas of exploring Paris as if she was on holiday, to save himself from wanting to be the man who showed her its delights.

After she'd gone, he wandered over to the small window, stretching his back and hoping to seek some fresh air. At the open window he looked down on the London street below before his gaze finally came to settle on the moth on the ledge. He watched its shimmering closed wings being gently buffeted by the breeze as it slowly turned around to face him. It did not seem deterred by its rescuer's presence, as it determinedly began an ascent over the window's frame and back into the room.

* * *

'Pierre Lesieur? I'm Major Roger de Wesselow.'

Pierre looked up in surprise and realised he was no longer alone. He immediately stood and shook hands with the man who had just entered his office. The timing could not have been more perfect. His reports were completed and he had just sorted the candidates out from worst to best.

'How were the interviews?' asked the major. He did not sit down, but remained standing, which told Pierre he should stand too.

'They went well. I have made detailed reports on each candidate.'

The major, his hands clasped behind his back, allowed his gaze to wander over each file on the table. Black-and-white photographs of the candidate's faces, attached by a paperclip, stared back at them from each report.

'Thank you for stepping in. Barbara usually assesses the candidates' French. She's only a teenager, but a godsend to us. She'll be back next week, but I really needed to get things moving.'

'Happy to help.'

'When are you off?'

'Tomorrow night.'

The major met his gaze. 'So you are probably keen to enjoy your last evening and get a good night's sleep.' Pierre nodded. 'Well, I won't keep you longer than necessary. Good weather and pilots don't hang around. Parachuting in?'

'Yes, sir.'

'Good, good. Fastest way.'

The major returned his attention to the photographs. 'I'll read your reports when you are gone, but how would you summarise each one in a few words?'

Pierre jabbed at the first photograph. 'His French is appalling. Unable to hold a conversation and his understanding is equivalent to a schoolboy who has played truant most of the time.'

The major raised an eyebrow. 'Shame, but best to find out now and not waste our time.'

'These men are good.' He pointed at several photographs in quick succession. 'They will need to work on their pronunciation to disguise their accents, but practice will help.' The major nodded. In unison, the men moved around the table. 'These four are good. Very good. So are these two women. They are keen and should do well.'

'Excellent. Excellent. And what about that one?' The major pointed to the woman with the dark brown eyes and full lips.

'Her French was flawless. She has the appearance of coming from southern France, but her dialect is pure Parisian.'

'Sounds like she would blend in easily if she was sent to France.'

Pierre looked up sharply. 'I thought only men were used as agents.'

'They were, but things have changed recently.'

'May I ask why?'

'The British are known for not sending women into combat, which is exactly why we should.'

Pierre frowned. He felt sick. He hadn't realised the women were going to be treated the same and he'd already passed two. A wireless operator lasted only six weeks before they were caught. Interrogation, torture and death usually followed.

'She has a good theoretical knowledge of the capital and pre-war Paris life,' he added slowly, hating every word he spoke. He realised that at some point he had picked up her file. Her black-and-white photo stared back at him. He glanced up to find the major looking at him with a curious expression on his face.

'How did you find her . . . as a person?'

Pierre thought for a moment.

Beautiful. Charming. Sexy.

'She's sharp and quick-witted.'

Funny. Inquisitive.

'She's also observant.'

And unforgettable.

'But she has recently suffered several bereavements which could make her a liability to her network and as well as to herself.' Even as he spoke he felt he was betraying her in some way, but he wanted her to be on the top of her game if she was used as an agent. It would help her survive any posting — and yet he still feared it was not enough. 'I also think she might be using the opportunity to visit Paris so she feels closer to her dead mother. That's not a good reason and, in my opinion, it's extremely naïve.'

'She rated very highly on her preliminary interview.'

Pierre faked a smile. 'It doesn't surprise me she did well and she *is* good.' He dropped the woman's file down on the table with a soft thud. 'But I don't think she's ready yet. Her father and all the people she worked with died last week. Grief can make things complicated.' He realised the major was still watching him with the same curious expression as before. 'She might become unstable under stress. However, I am confident she would make an excellent translator based in England.'

'We need women like her in France.'

Pierre could still see her photograph pinned to the folder lying open on the desk. If he recommended her and she was killed, he would be the reason the spirit and sparkle would morph to the blind gaze of death. 'If her acceptance was delayed by a year.'

'That's a long time.'

'Six months. If the war is still on, she could be reconsidered then.'

The major nodded thoughtfully. 'Yes. Well . . . we'll see about that. Time is a luxury we can ill afford. We have all lost someone we know or love.'

The major's last words on the woman continued to linger in Pierre's mind long after he returned to his lodgings. The woman had already impressed the SOE and the majority of his own report had supported those initial findings. She was fast becoming a viable candidate to work undercover in occupied France. It was a role that was shrouded in the utmost secrecy and he did not relish temporarily playing a part in selecting the candidates. Sending a woman into a job where she could be dead in two months jarred against the natural protective instincts of any decent man. A muscle worked in his jaw as he lay on his bed staring at the mottled ceiling above. He should have been made more aware why he was assessing the women. It was bad enough knowing what they intended for the men, but he hadn't seen the new changes coming. He felt blindsided. None of the women had fought in combat before, they would be ill-prepared for what was in store. They probably hadn't even been told why they were being interviewed.

He moved restlessly on the bed. He should have made more of her recent bereavements. Grief could manifest in a variety of ways and was often delayed. He had no evidence it would happen to her, of course, but if he could delay her recruitment as an agent a little longer, she may settle into a translation job on British soil instead and decline the position when next offered. The war may even end in six months. He tossed the lumpy pillow aside and rested the back of his head in the crook of his arm. In reality, peace seemed improbable, as improbable as the woman refusing to go.

He thought of the other two women he had passed and his stomach churned with regret. They were ignorant of their true fate, just as their families and friends were. They knew nothing of what was in store and his burden was that he knew too much. He was unable to put things right as his positive assessments had been eagerly accepted and were now impossible to withdraw. Even so, he was glad he had raised concerns on at least one of the three women. He'd been responsible for one woman's death in the past — he did not have the appetite to be so again.

CHAPTER SIX

Charlotte's heart missed a beat as she recognised the man walking briskly along the busy London pavement. She hastily rubbed the dirty glass of the window. Despite only being able to see the back of his head as he walked away, she would still recognise that arrogant Frenchman anywhere. Realising the bus was about to pull away from the stop, she shouted to the driver to wait and waded her way through the feet and bags lining the gangway, politely ignoring the groans from the miserable commuters.

She jumped down from the steps and followed him with no real plan in her head about what she was going to say to him. But she *had* to see him again — even if it was only to vent her anger at him. How dare he report that her recent bereavement made her unsuitable and her selection should be delayed. He wasn't a doctor! He knew nothing about her. Her father's death only made her all the more determined.

His strides were long and measured as he increased his distance from her, weaving among the pedestrians with a grace and agility that reminded her of a dancer in a Hollywood musical. He crossed the street several times, taking her by surprise and confidently dodging cars and buses as if there was no danger at all. Charlotte followed more cautiously as she was still acclimatising to the sheer scale and noise of the capital city, yet two cars still blew their horns at her in anger. London could be overwhelming at times, and Charlotte had to admit that sometimes it felt as if every one of her senses were under attack from something new and strange. However, she remained determined to speak to him and would pick her moment, choosing it carefully at a time that suited her.

She followed him for a full five minutes before he suddenly turned around, walked towards her and stole the opportunity for himself. His chest was flat against her face before she realised what he'd done. As she stepped back, she left a slanting lipstick mark on his white shirt and was aware of faint notes of his aftershave up her nose. She looked up into his accusing dark eyes.

'Are you following me?'

His English grammar was impeccable, although heavily accented. Hearing him speak in her own language presented another side to him, one that intrigued her as much as the other had done and acted like a truth serum.

'Yes.'

Her honesty appeared to surprise him as much as it did her.

'What do you want?'

'Information.'

He turned to leave. 'That I can't give.'

She followed him, walking briskly to keep up with his long strides.

'You don't know what it is yet.'

He frowned and shoved his hands deeper into his pockets. 'It may surprise you to know that I don't want to know.'

'You don't like me very much, do you?'

'I don't know you and you don't know me so that is quite a statement you have just made.'

'I'm right, though, aren't I?'

Without losing momentum, he took her arm and guided her away from the busy streets and down a narrow side road.

'I don't take kindly to being followed, if that is what you mean.'

He let her go and looked around him. She copied and looked around, too, as it seemed the thing she should do. He had taken them down a narrow alleyway, where the tall buildings on either side cast the cobbled road in shadow. The rhythmical dripping sound of water and a scurrying noise could be heard, but despite several doors leading off the road and being in the heart of London, they were quite alone.

'I didn't plan to follow you.'

'You got off a bus and followed me for almost half a mile.'

Charlotte was impressed. 'You saw me get off the bus?'

'No, but I saw you on it.'

'That was very observant of you. There were a lot of people on that bus.'

'But only one making herself conspicuous by standing up and rubbing the window like a demented—'

Charlotte frowned. 'I knew it! You don't like me. It was you who told them that my father's death could make me unstable.'

'What I feel about you does not matter.'

'But that's where you are wrong. The death of my father has nothing to do with my ability to speak French.'

'My assessment was accurate.'

'How can you jump to such conclusions when you don't know me?'

'My assessment is only one of many you will have to go through.'

Charlotte clenched her jaw. He was avoiding taking the blame. He was deflecting. She was right.

'You were there to assess my French, not my mental health. You attempted to ruin my chances!'

'I did not. I merely raised concerns about your recent bereavement. Although your behaviour today has raised even more concerns.'

'What behaviour?'

'You have made a spectacle of yourself in the street, highlighting a relationship that should be confidential.'

'What relationship?'

He indicated to her then himself in turn with a wave of a finger. '*This one.*'

She copied his hand movement. 'There is no *this one.*'

The man was not only arrogant, but he was also daft in the head. Her thoughts must have showed on her face as he took her firmly by the arm and walked her further down the narrow side road.

'Don't flatter yourself that there is any relationship other than a working one.' He noticed the lipstick stain on his shirt for the first time. 'And, thankfully, that one is coming to an end soon.'

She scowled as she watched him attempt to remove the stain but just make it worse. A thrill of pleasure ran through her to know the shirt was ruined.

'It's ruined,' she stated needlessly.

'I know.' He threw her a glance. 'Your lipstick isn't the first to end up on my shirt. A shirt can be replaced.'

She bristled at the implication as she imagined his shirt discarded in a bin along with several others. Did nothing bother him? Nothing would if he knew he had the upper hand.

'What gave you the impression that I was unsuitable?'

'On the contrary, I said you would make an excellent translator.'

Charlotte studied him through narrowed eyes. He seemed genuine. The muscles in her shoulders began to relax. She allowed herself a smile of relief. 'I thought you'd failed me. Then why did they follow up my interview with you with intense questioning about my family and crew dying?'

'Because I said you aren't suitable to be an undercover agent while you are still grieving. I suggested they delay it. Grief can eat a person up. It takes time to—'

'Undercover agent?' The ground seemed to move beneath her feet. 'Do you mean a spy?' A little shaken at the revelation, her smile faded. 'They thought I could be a spy?'

'I didn't say a spy.'

She ignored him, her mind wandering back to the elderly man in the teashop. 'He didn't say anything about spying. I had no idea what I was being assessed for. No one did.'

'Who is he?'

She shook her head. 'It doesn't matter.'

'Well—' he glanced at his watch — 'if you have finished your interrogation, I need to be somewhere. Do me the courtesy that if you should ever see me again, treat me like a stranger you have no wish to get to know.'

He walked a few steps before turning back. 'Are you all right on your own? You shouldn't stay here too long. Get back to the main street and public transport. It will be safer there.'

She didn't move and just kept looking at him. 'Why didn't you think I would make a good spy?'

He sighed. 'I never mentioned the word spy. Do we have to talk about this now?'

'You have just implied I should never speak to you again. Now seems to be my only chance to ask. Why didn't you?'

He looked around him as if searching for an answer. 'I told you, you have just lost your father.'

She lifted her chin. 'There is a war on. Everyone has lost someone.'

'You are naïve.'

'Rubbish.'

'You are standing in a dark alleyway with a man you don't know.' He opened his arms. 'I rest my case.'

She studied him. He was lying. 'What is the real reason?'

He sighed. 'Do you know the life expectancy of an agent?'

She shook her head.

'Believe me when I say that it's not long. You have a better chance of surviving a little longer if you are alert—'

She frowned. 'I am alert.'

'Keep your emotions in check—'

'I do keep my emotions in check.'

'—and are not grieving for a family you've recently lost.'

Her lips tightened. He had a point, but he also didn't know her very well. Losing everyone and everything might make her a better spy.

'It's dirty, it's dangerous and you'd witness things that you'll never get out of your head again. Someone who has lost everyone they love only a few weeks ago may not be able to face such horrors.'

'I could.'

'And peoples' lives will rely on you not falling apart.'

'Why do you think I'm naïve?'

His laugh was hollow. 'Because you think you can relive your mother's life by seeing the sights in Paris as Nazis patrol the streets. This is a fantasy and living a fantasy doesn't keep you alive.'

'You are being unfair. You asked me what I knew about Paris so I told you. I didn't know I was being interviewed to be an undercover agent. The War Office said they needed people like me to help win the war. I wasn't told more than that. I would make a *good* agent.'

'No, you wouldn't.'

'I noticed you in the crowd and followed you, didn't I?'

'And continued to follow me without realising that I was aware I was being followed.'

'That can be improved with training and had no bearing on your decision to fail me.'

'I didn't fail you. I delayed it and suggested you were more suitable elsewhere. You talk about spying and secrets as if you are talking about the weather. What if someone heard you?'

'No more than you.'

'I never used the word *spy*,' he snapped again.

'You used the word *agent*. And besides, our conversation today is irrelevant to the interview. I think I would be good at working undercover in France.'

She noticed him brace himself. 'Now don't get silly ideas in that pretty head of yours.'

Silence fell. His confession that he thought she was pretty annoyed her intensely, but also flattered her.

'Don't patronise me,' she said quietly. 'I think you're better than that. I'm not afraid to die.' She noticed him wince.

'You should be. If not for yourself, for your loved ones.'

'I have lost everyone who loved me.'

'Then find someone else.'

He attempted to leave but she stepped in his path. 'I'm not afraid of risking my life for my country. Many people do.'

'I know. Many people do and many people die.'

'You say my bereavement is my handicap, but to me it's not. Grief affects people in different ways. Some crumple and find solace in the bottom of a bottle, others build barriers so they don't feel such pain again . . .' She saw the slight rise of his chin as if to parry her words away. '. . . but my grief is no handicap to me. It drives me now and makes me want to do whatever it takes to help end this war. Even if it means risking my own life.'

'And it will mean that if they still decide to choose you.'

'And I will be ready. My father once said I would know when it was the right time to risk my life.'

'That time is not now.'

'What better time than when we are at war?'

He inhaled deeply. 'I would not want that for you.'

She let their words hang in the air between them. Despite the lack of sunlight, a slight shadow coloured his cheeks. Charlotte firmly believed that if he was a man who was prone to blushing, he would be blushing now. It was time to put him out of his misery, snatch his confession from the air and restart the conversation again.

'Ultimately, it won't be your decision to make.' She tilted her head to one side. 'What if my intention was for you to see me?' she asked.

He frowned. 'What do you mean?'

She slowly walked towards him. 'What if I knew I was at a disadvantage and would never catch you up? After all, I was on a bus. By the time I got off I knew I would be several seconds behind you. I also knew my strides would never keep up with yours.'

He looked decidedly uncomfortable at this new change in tack. 'What are you trying to say?'

'That I might have gambled that a handsome man's interest might be piqued as to why a woman with a "pretty head", even if it is filled with "silly ideas", was following him. His arrogance, his need to discover why, would be his downfall and he would eventually challenge me.'

He stepped closer, his hand cupping her elbow so he could turn her face towards the only source of light — a narrow beam of sunlight filtering through the high-pitched roofs around them. His voice was gentle, but the words were not.

'You are lying.'

Charlotte tilted her head to the other side as if she was studying a specimen of interest. 'Perhaps I rubbed the window to attract your attention, walked as fast as I could to keep up, but when that failed, I ensured several cars beeped their horns at me as we crossed the roads. Only an idiot would not notice the culprit of so much commotion. I don't think you are an idiot. Do you?'

'You did that on purpose?'

'Maybe.' She carefully eased her elbow away from his cupped hand and smiled a little more broadly. 'Maybe not.' She rubbed her elbow to bring an end to the tingling his handprint had left there. 'But isn't that the mark of a good undercover agent? The enemy must never really know what they are up to?'

The man, whose name she did not know and may never learn, suddenly grasped her upper arms. Her breath caught in her throat at the intensity of his gaze and the strength in his fingers. In that moment she did not know if he was going to strangle, shake or kiss her. Part of her wanted to close her eyes and hope for his lips, the other part did not trust him one bit.

She returned his intense stare until he finally released her.

'You will thank me one day,' he grumbled under his breath as he began to walk away.

'The War Office approached me. Remember that when I arrive in France,' she called after him. 'They saw something in me even if you don't.'

He did not respond, which was just as hurtful as his curt dismissal the last time they'd met.

She remained where she stood, angry at herself, but most of all at him. 'You still don't think I would be good enough, do you?'

He paused. 'No.'

'Why not?'

'Because a person needs to be ordinary, forgettable and go unnoticed if they are to work undercover.' He looked at her over his shoulder. 'And I knew within the first second of you entering that interview room, you could never achieve any of those.'

There it was again, that uncanny knack he had of offering a compliment wrapped up in an insult. Such throwaway gifts had the power to steal her breath away and leave her more confused than ever. But she quickly rallied.

'Perhaps I am only unforgettable to you. That is your problem, not mine or anyone else's. Besides, an intelligent woman knows how to use such traits when needed. If I possess them, which I don't think I do, they can be an advantage too.'

'Did you do all those things to make sure I noticed you?' he asked as if an afterthought.

His head was bowed as he waited for her answer. She could see that the poor man's ego had been dented. Let him suffer a little more. It was her turn to take back control.

'I'm not telling you.'

'Why not?'

'Because a good undercover—'

'—agent leaves the enemy never really knowing what they are up to,' he finished for her. He smiled. 'Is that what I am to you? The enemy?' Before she could reply, he added, 'I hope you will never need to learn what makes a good agent, but I think you will do all you can to achieve it. If you are selected . . . I hope they teach you well. Be a good student. If you don't, it may cost you your life and that of all those around you.'

He turned and walked away, leaving the shadows of the alleyway and stepping out into the bustling street. She hastily followed him, but by the time she had reached the main street's pavement, the Frenchman, with all his arrogance, faint aroma of sophisticated aftershave and rare fleeting smiles, was gone.

Charlotte rested her back against the building behind her. The street was full of people, but unlike Newlyn, she knew no one. Everyone had somewhere to go or someone to see. Everyone but her. A dark cloud of loneliness engulfed her and suddenly she felt more isolated than on the day of her father's death. Once again she felt as if she was on the outside of normal life, where the ability to feel true contentment was too far out of her reach. It would explain why she was already missing the Frenchman's company. She would rather be arguing with a stranger, than be left alone to remember her grief.

* * *

Pierre returned to his lodgings, both stimulated and mad as hell at his chance encounter with *that* woman. She as good as said she wanted to risk her life in France! He began to pack his meagre belongings as he muttered angrily to himself. Death wasn't heroic and the fallout was painful, he should know. He had told the major that her French was flawless — surely they would not fail to use her skill in some way on home ground. 'We'll see . . .' the major had said. He wished he'd never agreed to help them out.

He threw the few things he had into his rucksack, muttering under his breath as he did so. He'd only been drafted in to assess the potential candidates' French because he'd happened to be in England and they trusted him. The female candidates were better and keener than even some of the men and he'd been happy to recommend them until he learned the truth. None of the candidates really knew what job they were being assessed for. If they'd really known, their keenness might have withered like a neglected vase of flowers. However, she had remained keen even after he'd told her — if not keener — and he had the feeling she would continue to try her utmost to pass the selection process to not only play a part in winning the war but to also spite him.

The idea lingered, as did the memory of her face, which had a habit of appearing at odd moments when he would least expect it. He vacated his lodgings and travelled to the airfield deep in thought. On arrival he settled down to wait for night to fall so he could make the return journey to France. As the hours ticked by, he realised the memory of her refused to fade. Their highly charged encounters, that strangely left him wanting more, kept replaying in his head. The woman, he concluded, was difficult to forget . . . if he ever managed it at all.

* * *

The order confirming that his drop was on schedule finally came. The weather had remained calm and there was a full moon, the two key factors pilots hoped for to aide with the accuracy of a drop. Pierre emerged from the aircraft hut and watched the Lysander plane taxi into position. He knew from experience that the plane lacked comfort and space, but it was nimble and able to evade being spotted easier than most. He was eager to climb on board and waited impatiently to be told that he could. Soon he would be on the short flight across the Channel. Finally, he was going home.

* * *

The French countryside appeared beneath him in the moonlight. As always, he felt his heart swell in his chest at seeing it

again, with its scattering of quaint villages and large sprawling towns and cities. He thought of all the families lying
asleep in their beds, oblivious to the plane above them.

Three white lights, arranged 100 metres apart in a line,
marked out a temporary runway. A duplicate light at one end
indicated the direction downwind. The pilot must have spotted them, too, for the plane climbed and turned to approach
the area again. Pierre positioned himself, ready to jump, the
speeding night air ready to tear his words away from him
should he attempt to converse with the pilot. The signal
was given and he dropped into the roaring slipstream which
pummelled his cheeks and ears until his parachute finally
opened. The roaring stopped and all fell silent but for the
creak and flutter of his parachute above him. It was oddly
peaceful and slow, considering one was floating towards the
earth with only limited control.

He approached the ground at speed. He was about to
land in occupied France, a land of false liberty, but in reality
no better than a prison. A country where one could live, but
not feel alive. Sleep but not rest. Be free to roam, but have
every movement watched, checked and questioned. France,
a country that both demanded its liberty but also waited for
salvation. A country that both obeyed and resisted the arms
of the Third Reich. *His* France. Viva la France! He was finally
home.

CHAPTER SEVEN

11 February 1943

Wanborough Manor exuded Elizabethan charm from its warm, red-brick walls and country setting to its latticed windows and tall chimneys. Situated in a rural village in the heart of Surrey and straddling the North Downs rocky ridge, known as the Hog's Back, it was the perfect home for a rich, English gentleman. Charlotte studied the building and its location. Grand, stylish and admirable, but not overly so, it still retained a sense of British humbleness so the villagers could be proud of its presence rather than rebel against it.

Before the war, Wanborough Manor would have been considered an unlikely setting for the headquarters of a training course, yet this was wartime England and it no longer seemed unusual for the War Office to requisition grand houses to help in the war effort. Charlotte suspected that many of the biggest decisions of the war happened behind the walls of enchanting properties, just like this one, and only the people at the top seemed to know the whole truth of what was going on at any given time. Even now, after several interviews, a French assessment and an unplanned heated argument that had revealed that some roles involved undercover work, Charlotte still hadn't been officially informed what role *she* was about to train for.

The organisation who had selected her was referred to as *the Firm*, but other than that she knew very little and was not encouraged to ask for further information. The Firm was a secret organisation — so secret, in fact, that after she was informed she'd passed the preliminary interviews and had been selected to go forward for further training, she would henceforth be known by another name throughout the course. She had also been instructed to not share details about herself with the other trainees. Charlotte was now to be known as Colette Pascall — at least for the time being. Could this be the agent training the Frenchman had tried his best to sabotage her selection for?

She nervously smoothed down the skirt of her First-Aid Nursing Yeomanry uniform. It felt strange to wear a uniform that had no bearing on her future role, but as she was a civilian with no military background, the Firm accepted it as an appropriate uniform for the circumstances, as it was not worn by any of the military services and provided a good cover story to tell friends and relatives.

She had been told that the training syllabus she was about to embark on would identify her skills and strengths so they, whoever *they* were, would know how she could be used for the war effort. She looked about her. Several soldiers from the security branch of the intelligence corps were patrolling the area, making the whole situation seem rather surreal, like a Hollywood thriller. Suddenly it all felt rather serious and no longer an adventure. What would her father say if he could see her now? Would he be proud or think her a fool? Whatever he might feel, she could not shake off the feeling that this place, and whatever it might lead to, was where she was meant to be. All those years looking out at sea and feeling there was something more . . . She didn't feel that anymore. Her life was already a far cry from trawling fish.

She tightened her grip on the leather handle of her small suitcase as she recalled the Frenchman's words of advice.

I hope you will never need to learn what makes a good agent, but if you do . . . I hope they teach you well. Be a good student. If you don't, it may cost you your life and that of all those around you.

Her firm knock on the wooden door exuded more confidence than she felt. A woman opened the door and introduced herself as Mrs Sanderson. Her duty, Charlotte was informed, was to take care of the female trainees. If Charlotte had any problems, Mrs Sanderson would do her best to sort them out. She showed Charlotte to her accommodation, which was no more than a bedroom located in the attic. There were to be ten trainees in the cohort, she was informed. There were two more women who would have a room along the corridor, the rest were men and would sleep elsewhere. The living room downstairs was available for them to gather in the evenings and the cupboards were well stocked with light entertainment such as board games and cards.

'You must abide by the strict security rules while you are on this training course,' said Mrs Sanderson. 'You must remain on the grounds unless you have special instruction to leave or are accompanied. You must not disclose to anyone, at any time, that you have been here or to any other subsequent training schools. If you should meet someone you recognise from your time in training, you must not show that you know them unless you are on official business. Any questions?'

Charlotte shook her head.

'Do you have any identity documents in your possession? Ration cards? Paybooks? Anything that shows who you are?'

Charlotte searched her handbag and handed over what little she had.

'Do you have anything else, such as firearms, weapons, cameras or notebooks,' asked Mrs Sanderson as she looked through Charlotte's ration book.

Charlotte shook her head. 'No.'

'How much money do you have?'

'Money?'

'You cannot keep more than £5 in value.'

Charlotte tried to recall what she had last seen in there as she opened her purse. 'I don't have that much on me,' she replied truthfully as she searched through her coins.

'That's all right then. If you need any more you must let me know.' The woman walked to the window. 'Any letters must be handed to us in a stamped, unsealed envelope for censoring. Try to avoid giving details and do not mention your letters are censored.' She turned to look at Charlotte. 'You will be provided with a postal box for an address. Do not use the address of any training establishment. Your letters will be posted from London so your location will remain secret.'

'Can I receive mail?'

'Yes, but they will also be censored by the Administrative Officer. Telegrams can only be sent in an emergency, but they must go through us for censoring first.' She slowly walked to the door, with Charlotte's documents still in her hands. 'You are not allowed to use the telephone here or in the area. If urgent communication is needed, let me know and I will arrange something.' She turned to face her. 'Do you have any questions?'

Charlotte's mind raced and she thought about Anne. 'I would like to write one letter to my cousin. I will tell her that I have volunteered as a member of the First-Aid Nursing Yeomanry and I will be too busy to write for a while. Would that be all right?'

Mrs Sanderson nodded. 'Anything else?'

'No, I don't think so.'

Mrs Sanderson offered her a gentle smile. 'It's a lot to take in, isn't it? Quite a shock to the system. Just try to remember that you are not on your own while you are here.' She awkwardly patted her arm. 'Make yourself at home, my dear,' she said quietly, before walking efficiently away with the few documents that proved Charlotte's identity. From now on, Charlotte realised, Charlotte Bray was no more.

Charlotte suddenly felt quite alone. Her fellow trainees would be complete strangers, from different backgrounds, who probably had far more experience in life than she did. She teased her bottom lip with her teeth as she silently admitted that coming from a small coastal village in Cornwall gave her little worldly experience to call upon. It had taken all her skill to navigate the underground of London. She approached the closed door of her room and rested her forehead upon it. There was no going back now.

* * *

It was soon made clear to Charlotte and her fellow trainees that the course they were about to embark on would be different from any training attended by a civilian before.

'The Organisation's purpose is subversion,' said the top instructor on the first full day of their training. 'As potential agents, we are going to provide you with the skills and knowledge required to achieve four main objectives. The first is to damage the enemy to a maximum extent through sabotage, such as by hampering or damaging their military armoury — their production of it — and their ability to distribute it.'

The instructor walked across the room with slow, measured steps. Charlotte watched from her desk in the third row, wondering if the other students felt as she did — on the precipice of something extraordinary.

'The second objective,' said the tutor, turning on his heel and retracing his footsteps, 'is to put strain on the enemy by placing pressure on their resources and diverting their manpower.

'The third is to undermine the morale of the occupied forces and their collaborators. The final objective is the opposite . . . to raise the morale of the population who wish to be liberated. If they have hope and believe in something, they will remain strong and defiant.'

He began writing furiously on the blackboard, speaking quickly as he did so, underlining titles and slashing rudimentary arrows across the smooth, chalk-dusted surface, to various key points.

'Sabotage can be passive resistance, such as non-cooperation within the law. The aim is not to be arrested, but make the occupiers feel alien and have no right to be there.

'There is industrial sabotage.' He underlined the subtitle, breaking his chalk in half as he did so. 'This means damaging, wasting and delaying . . . or reducing the rate, capacity and quality of their military production.' He discarded the broken piece of chalk on the table. 'There is also minor sabotage, such as blowing up bridges, electric transformers etc., or major sabotage, such as destroying major railway lines.

'Finally, propaganda can be both our friend and our enemy. We will show you how to use it as the former and recognise and ignore it as the latter.' He placed his chalk down in the wooden gutter that ran along the front of the board, brushed the chalk off his fingers and turned to face them. He stood with his hands behind his back, his shoulders braced and his feet slightly apart as his gaze passed over the class. He lifted his chin slightly. 'You are in training to be agents for the Organisation.' His gaze settled on Charlotte. 'Only the best will remain at the end of it.'

* * *

A well-constructed syllabus timetable provided the plan for the next few weeks. There were ten trainees in all and the cohort was named 27X. Charlotte wondered if this meant they were the twenty-seventh group to attend the training at Wanborough. According to Mrs Sanderson, they were only the second group to contain women. It was quite a responsibility, but Charlotte and the only other two women, Isabelle and Jeanne, welcomed the accolade. If they hoped for more details of their predecessors' fate, they were quickly dashed. Such information was strictly classified, Mrs Sanderson informed them. Instructors were only told what they needed to know to train them. After they moved on, they no longer existed to them. So Charlotte, Isabelle and Jeanne asked no further questions about their predecessors, realising it was now up to them to prove their worth and be as good as their male counterparts, as their success would keep the door open to other women who wished to serve their country in the future.

All the instructors were from a public-school background and had some former experience in the army. Everything the trainees did, including their attitude, was observed and assessed and reported back to Major de Wesselow.

After breakfast, the trainees embarked on cross-country runs, which left them both exhausted and energised. Next was basic weapon training, map reading, unarmed conflict and an introduction to demolition. Charlotte found it was a conflicting experience to want to help France yet be taught skills that would damage its infrastructure. The wireless operating and coding lessons seemed more logical to Charlotte, although in truth she was more skilled at setting explosives. It seemed a cruel twist of fate that despite being bilingual and proficient in using her father's radio at sea, she could not master the skills required to send simple short messages. She was reassured that some of the trainees were quicker to learn than others and that no one was classed as failing at this stage, but the Frenchman's opinion that she was not ready yet still lurked behind every task like a foul smell.

'Our lessons were only elementary. Try not to fret,' Isabelle reassured her one evening as she finished dealing the well-worn pack of cards in her hands. They sat alone in the cosy well-furnished room, just the two of them, the other recruits preferring to listen to the wireless in the lounge next door.

Charlotte slid her dealt cards from the table and fanned them out in her hand. The game of Whist had become their firm favourite and although it was better with a team of four, two could also play. It also provided the perfect moment to voice her concerns, rather like a religious confessional box in a large Catholic Church, and before she realised what she had done, Charlotte had confessed the humiliation she had felt at failing the wireless task. They both knew that everything they did was noted and documented, which gave each task a gravity that was not widely voiced.

'They are testing our capabilities, that is all,' soothed Isabelle again, her gaze quickly scanning her own cards. She glanced up at Charlotte. 'They want to see if we are good enough for specialised roles. Exploding things might be your forte.'

She smiled reassuringly, which was infectious and Charlotte reluctantly smiled too. 'My mother used to say if there was something to be broken, I would break it.' She sighed. 'I shall just have to prove myself in other ways. Perhaps push myself forward to get noticed. I don't want to fail again.'

Isabelle laid her first card with a confident flourish. 'I am sure they have noticed you already, Colette. Most of the men on the course already have.'

Charlotte rolled her eyes. She had no desire to impress just any man, unless he had the badge of instructor, of course.

French speaking and culture lessons were the easiest for Charlotte and came as a respite from the more demanding parts of the training regime which was both confidence destroying and confidence building all at the same time, yet the most positive thing to develop came from the card game with Isabelle. From that moment, their tentative friendship began to strengthen and when Jeanne later joined them, Charlotte realised with a growing sense of relief, that she no longer felt so alone.

She did not know their real names, a vital detail that helped form an invisible barrier that both separated and protected them. However, not being allowed to share personal information did not stop her surmising who they really were.

On first impressions, Jeanne was quietly spoken, appeared quite naïve and was a little too trusting, and Charlotte wondered if she had spent much of her life volunteering for worthy causes at her local church. However, as the days had gone by, snippets of one's past experiences were inevitably shared, despite the restrictions on personal details. The revelation that Jeanne could speak both French and German and had once lived a mysterious year in France as a muse to an artist was both surprising and intriguing. It also taught Charlotte a valuable lesson: to never take one's appearance as an indicator of one's character. Isabelle, on the other hand, was the complete opposite.

Tall, thin, with a long face and prominent teeth which gave her a permanent happy expression, Isabelle's appearance completely matched her persona. From her clipped English accent and the mention of her father's wine collection, Charlotte suspected she came from a wealthy family. Her appearance and chipper aristocratic phrases always bolstered the spirits and gave the impression she was up for any challenge. She had high energy levels from morning to night and made no secret that she wanted to "beat the bloody Hun", as she said it often enough. Yet, despite her no-frills bluntness, she had a kind heart and took on the role of leader of their little group with a velvet glove. Not that they needed a leader, but Isabelle wanted the role and fitted it perfectly.

Every minute of Charlotte's day was both physically and mentally dedicated to the training, but the night was her own. She relished the solitude her bedroom offered her and she could allow her body to recover from the day's trials without fear that someone may consider her too weak to complete the course. As her bedside clock ticked away in the darkness, her mind truly belonged to her again, free from calculations, study and memorising. In the darkness she could indulge her thoughts where she wished. Sometimes she would return to the Cornish countryside, with its lush green meadows, babbling brooks and the warm scented air of rural life. Sometimes it was the unpredictable open sea and the safety of the compact wheelhouse, her father's presence by her side, as together they watched erratic waves crash over the bow in yet another rising squall. But often, uninvited, it was the Frenchman's dark, brooding face that came to mind and it was only then that she allowed herself to finally fall asleep.

CHAPTER EIGHT

16 February 1943

Pierre opened his eyes — or at least he tried to. The bruising had increased since he had gone to sleep and now the poorly lit cell could only be viewed between two narrow slits. He had lost track of how many days he had been there. He wasn't even sure if he cared anymore. But that was what they intended — to disorientate and break one's morale before the true interrogation began. The dehumanising treatment had started soon after his arrest, his treatment swinging from good to bad in the blink of an eye, along with good food, then slops, and sometimes, no food at all. At times he had been given a little freedom, only to have it snatched away when he was locked up in solitary with little light or fresh air to fill his lungs. It was the first time he'd found himself in such deep trouble — and it probably wouldn't be his last.

He had been arrested for using binoculars on the north coast of France. He had prepared for the possibility and had memorised the bird species of coastal France. Mediterranean and Sabine's Gulls, Savi's Warbler and the rarer Balearic Shearwater. His interrogator's eyes soon began to glaze over as he rattled them off. They had found nothing else incriminating on him, but his attempt to dispose of the compact binoculars as they approached was deemed suspicious enough for interrogation. They wanted a confession from him, but he wouldn't confess no matter how many times they beat him.

What the guards didn't know was that he had a secret weapon which he carried in his mind. She was half-French, beautiful and owned a smile that a man would do his utmost to earn. Although he had only met her twice, he could still recall every detail of her face. At first he ruminated over their last meeting, when their argument had swung wildly from protection, to insults, with teasing somewhere hidden in between.

Over the last few days his memories had mellowed the frustration, despair and anger he had felt in that dark alleyway. What he had seen as naïvety had really been courage. What he had viewed as lack of comprehension had, in fact, been stoicism. He thought he was protecting her, but his actions only fed *his* need, not any need she had displayed. She was using her grief to motivate her, whereas when he'd experienced such raw emotion it had torn him in two and still scarred him to this day. What would she say if she walked into this cell now and saw him like this? Would she be encouraging? Soothing? Lambasting? Constructive? Probably all four. He would have smiled, if it did not hurt so much. However, he knew she would use all she possessed — her courage, her stoicism, her determination — to succeed and prove her adversaries wrong. And so would he.

Sometimes, his imaginings of her would wander to a more pleasant and indulgent scenario, where his passion for the woman's body was matched by her own, but they were only fleeting, comforting and acted as a salve to the unpleasant surroundings and unpredictable nature of his torture. She probably did not give him a second thought, but thinking of her and what she was capable of achieving helped in more ways than he cared to admit. No wonder she felt blindsided when he had not recommended her to continue.

He braced himself at the sound of the warden's footsteps tap-tapping towards his room, the keys nonchalantly jingling in his hands like a warning bell. Although the warden was friendly, Pierre still didn't trust him an inch. A friendly jailer was all part of their box of tricks to get him to confide or confess — a friendly staff member, a bully interrogator and another who was clear, concise, but relentless in his questioning. Sometimes he thought the friendly one was the most dangerous of them all. When one was beaten and alone, a kind word and an understanding look had the power to break down the defences.

He was escorted out of his cell and taken to a room he had not been in before. The light at the far end was blinding, its spotlight angled straight at a vacant wooden chair. His chair. Despite its length, the room was stifling hot and for once he was glad they had stripped him of his shirt, jumper and coat. He was encouraged to move forward with repeated shoves, which he did despite every bone in his body aching. It was a relief to finally sit down despite being tied to the chair. He was left alone as the two main interrogators stayed at the other end of the overly long room.

They spoke in German, not filtering what they said. Why would they? Their prisoner only spoke French or so he had said. It was a lie. His German was faultless. Although their sentences were broken, on the whole snippets of words and phrases carried the length of the room easily. They spoke of someone called Sturmbannfuhrer Kieffer, who was going to be based in Paris and was expected to visit today. Pierre thought he heard the word double agent but wasn't sure. They spoke of their partners and what they had for tea. One was to be married soon, although he wasn't sure which one. The conversation had just begun to bore him, when it turned to him. How they would approach the interrogation. How bruised and battered he looked today. They laughed, made a joke about raw meat, then laughed again.

Suddenly, someone else entered the room. He tried to twist round to look and caught a glimpse of who it was. The translator had arrived. He was another reason he had told them he could only speak French as using a translator slowed down the interrogation and gave him time to think.

He listened to their footsteps approach from behind. One pulled up a chair and sat down, a packet of biscuits in one hand, a steaming beverage in the other. His stomach betrayed him and rumbled loudly. The interrogator smiled in victory and carefully placed the mug on the floor, selected a biscuit and began eating it, knowing that his prisoner had not had a meal in twenty hours. Pierre had met him before and had named him interrogator Number One.

Interrogator Number Two stood on his other side, his uniform crisp and sharp, his hands behind his back.

Number One started first, each question and answer translated back and forth. 'Who are you?'

Pierre had answered the same question a hundred times. He had the urge to tell them where to stick their question, but he knew it would not help. *Remain calm, clear, precise. Speak firmly and slowly. Convince them you are an honest civilian. Avoid replies that might lead to further questions.*

He cleared his throat, which felt sandpaper dry. 'Pierre Lesieur.'

'Where do you come from?'

'Paris.'

'What were you doing at Le Touquet?'

'Taking some time away from Paris.'

'You had binoculars? Binoculars are prohibited.'

'I didn't know.'

'What were you looking at?'

'I was birdwatching.'

'Why?'

Pierre lifted his gaze to meet his interrogator. 'I like birds.'

A lengthy set of questions on where he had been, how long he had been there and where he had stayed followed. Pierre answered truthfully, knowing each guesthouse owner was oblivious to the real reason he was there. Interrogator Number Two took over.

'We know you are up to something. We have you under surveillance.'

Pierre stared at the ground. If they really knew, he would not be alive right now. Number Two kicked his chair, making him jump.

'What were you looking at?'

'Gulls.'

The man slapped his face hard.

'What were you looking at?'

'Gulls.'

Another slap.

'We have your wife and child. What were you looking at?'

Pierre's cheeks stung from his beating and his eyes began to smart. They must have found his photograph and were trying to scare him. 'I was looking at seagulls. Just seagulls.'

The interrogation went on for what seemed like hours. He felt exhausted, hungry and every limb hurt, when they brought out a tub of water and forced his face into it. Every vein and artery in his body screamed for oxygen and soon he was fighting the hands that pushed him beneath the surface. Finally, violently, they pulled his face out and allowed him to breathe. He gasped, hungrily sucking in the air. This was a new type of torture and he knew it was one that could end in his death.

'What is the name of your hotel in Paris?'

'*Fleur de Lis*.'

'Are you part of the Resistance?'

'No.'

'Why were you in Le Touquet?'

'I was taking time away from the hotel.'

His head was pushed into the water again, snatching his ability to breathe before he had a chance to fill his lungs. The little vision he possessed was taken from him as he was thrust into a distorted world of strong light bending in moving, bloodied water. *Don't panic like last time. Keep calm. Think of something pleasant.*

The woman's face came to mind again, with soft dark curls and teasing arched eyebrows. She spoke of Paris as if she had been there, yet in reality she had never set foot in the city. He felt his pulse slow as his mind's eye remembered every feature of her face. Once again his pleasant fantasy allowed him to control how her chocolate brown eyes looked up at him and glinted, as her shapely lips formed words to entice him to kiss her.

His head was yanked back into reality by his hair, leaving the woman's face in the surreal world under the water. He sat back in his chair, gasping for breath and a little shocked that he had conjured up her face to help him get through the near-drowning torture.

'Sturmbannfuhrer Kieffer has arrived,' said one of the interrogators. 'Send this one off to a camp.'

Pierre lifted his head. If he was sent to a camp he would be no use to anyone. 'I want to speak to Sturmbannfuhrer Kieffer. Alone.'

'You speak to us!' shouted Number Two, incandescent with rage.

'I'll only speak to Sturmbannfuhrer Kieffer. If you won't let me, what I know will die with me.'

* * *

Sturmbannfuhrer Kieffer sat behind an enormous desk, studying him in silence. It took a great effort for Pierre to remain standing, but he had no intention of collapsing on the expensive carpet. He wondered if Kieffer's study of him was taking in the bruises on his body or questioning why his interrogators had dressed him in recently laundered clothes. He wouldn't blame him — he questioned it himself.

Sturmbannfuhrer Kieffer sat back and rested his hands on the arms of his wooden chair, idly rolling the tip of his middle finger with his thumb as if testing the sensitivity of it.

'You want to look at me?' he asked.

Pierre nodded. Sturmbannfuhrer Kieffer's French was understandable, but the accent and grammar were diabolical.

'What is it you want?'

'I want to do a deal.'

'What is deal?'

Pierre licked his cracked lips and tasted the metallic tang of dried blood. He changed to German. 'I want to do a deal. I hear you are being transferred to Paris soon.'

Kieffer stopped rolling his fingers. 'You speak German.'

'I am half-German.'

'You didn't tell my men that.'

'They didn't ask.'

The officer sat forward, his interest piqued. 'What deal?'

'I own a hotel in Paris.'

'I know. We checked out the few answers you gave us. We also know more than you've told us. How is your wife?' he mocked with a humourless smile.

'I want it protected,' said Pierre, ignoring his last comment. 'I will wine and dine your officers at excellent rates.'

'You have no choice about what we do or where we dine. Have you forgotten that we are in charge of France?'

'And in return . . .' Pierre paused, allowing it to hang in the air between them.

'And in return what?'

'I will supply you with important information. A network fell in northern France some time ago. I was a part of that network. I can use my knowledge to get valuable information.'

'What makes you think I won't shoot you where you stand?'

'Because you are clever enough to know that if you kill me now, the supply of useful information will stop before it begins. Keep me alive. Work with me. Protect my hotel. And you will have a steady stream of information that only you will have. You will get the glory and be a valuable asset in your new post in Paris and I will keep my life and my living.'

Kieffer's eyes narrowed as his mind worked with the possibilities.

'What makes you think I need your help?'

'Because your investigations take up valuable time but having someone on the inside sending you information . . . well . . . that is a different matter.'

Kieffer's chin lifted. Pierre could tell that the revelation of his German heritage had surprised him. From the interest glinting in his eyes, there was a real chance he might agree.

'Do we have a deal?' he prompted.

Kieffer studied him for a full minute over the steeple of his fingers. Finally, he offered him a chair.

'We have a deal.'

CHAPTER NINE

At the end of the final week the successful trainees were informed of the next stage in their training by Major de Wesselow himself. He stood at the front of the room, surveying the seated trainees one by one.

'You have all successfully passed your preliminary training,' he said, smiling briefly. 'That is no mean feat. In fact, this is the first group we have had where everyone has continued on to the next stage and that is something to be proud of.' He walked a few steps, to consider his next words . . . or was it to ensure they could all see him . . . or leave them time to think on their achievements so far. Charlotte wasn't sure, but she was sure Major de Wesselow was. The class waited in silence. It was as if the room itself held its breath.

'Your training, so far, has been basic,' he continued. 'Your success means that you are considered suitable to receive more in-depth training as agents with the aim of sending you to live and work in occupied France.' He walked again, allowing his words to sink in. 'The next stage of your training is to prepare you to do this undercover, so you can carry out specific tasks for the war effort and not be identified by informers . . . or the Gestapo. It will be highly dangerous and the risk of being tortured, imprisoned or killed, possibly all three, is high.'

Charlotte released the breath she had been holding. Pierre had told the truth — it had not been just a ploy to scare her. His words were followed by a heavy silence. The major nodded as if to confirm to himself that his warning had been clear and had been duly received.

'What tasks, Major de Wesselow?' someone behind Charlotte asked.

'Sabotage, communicating by wireless, carrying messages. When the time comes you will be appointed a mission.' He braced his shoulders and thrust out his chin. 'Churchill wants us to set Europe ablaze, and that is what we have been attempting to do . . . from the inside.' He began his measured steps again. 'Now . . . if you don't wish to carry on, it is best to voice your decision now. If you decide to leave, we will send you for debriefing and you must forget what you have learned so far.' He turned to look at them squarely. 'But if you want to serve your country, we will prepare you as much as we can. The next stage is paramilitary training. You will start on Monday . . . at Arisaig House, in Scotland.' He loudly tapped the map on the wall with his pointer. 'Here. On the west coast. You have the weekend to get there. Training starts 9 a.m. sharp.' He added dryly as an afterthought, 'And don't be late.'

* * *

Charlotte, Isabelle and Jeanne travelled to Scotland together by train. It was their first time across the border so they sat in silence, content to watch the rural, agricultural hills of the southern uplands give way to the broad valleys and mountains of the central lowlands. They changed trains at Glasgow and headed north, leaving the bustling station behind to pass through leafy countryside, vast salt marshes and picturesque lochs where deeply forested islands broke the surface like large recumbent prehistoric animals.

Eventually the train left the swathes of pine and spruce behind to travel through a desert of peat bogs before the familiar backdrop of natural glens returned, surrounded by majestic sleeping mountains and wandering grazing Highland cattle.

Much of north Scotland had been sealed off and required a permit to enter. They arrived at Fort William and waited for the permits to be checked, worried that they would not arrive before dark. Eventually they were allowed to proceed and Charlotte, Isabelle and Jeanne settled into their seats, comforted by the knowledge that they had almost reached their final destination, a remote railway station called Beasdale.

Although their journey through Scotland had gifted them with breathtaking scenery, this final stage was the most beautiful of all. It was varied and everchanging, travelling along the banks of vast, deep blue lochs, wide open glens and windswept wild mountains. Finally, the train slowed, sending them into a frenzy of suitcase gathering. Soon they had disembarked onto the platform at Beasdale, exhausted, a little anxious, but in love with the Celtic land.

A car was waiting for them and the latter part of the journey was a narrow road, lined by tall sturdy conifers, which offered only glimpses of water and the barren mountains beyond.

'That's Loch nan Uamh,' said their driver, as if pre-empting a question he had been asked a thousand times before.

The sprawling Victorian house, peppered with numerous dormer and tall windows, was waiting to welcome them into the forecourt. On first impression, the building appeared quite mysterious with its many angles, as if hiding secret entrances behind grey brick corners. It was, however, truly magnificent and held its own against the backdrop of high mountains, the surrounding trees and the deep swathe of grassland which led right down to the water's edge. Sheep grazed idly on this vast grassy path, giving an air of normality to an otherwise clandestine location. Charlotte could see that this was the perfect setting for what was in store for them — isolated, hidden and with the perfect terrain to test physical fitness and learn new skills. It now became clear to Charlotte why this part of Scotland had been isolated from the rest. Its remoteness, wild terrain and numerous isolated country houses which made is so unique and beautiful, provided the space, secrecy and accommodation for military and specialist, clandestine training.

* * *

Their love affair with Scotland, born from its breathtaking landscape viewed on a sunny day, was somewhat muted over the days that followed. Spring arrives late in the Highlands, they were told, as they watched the dark clouds approach from the west and linger for most of their stay. The days thereafter were often wet, always damp, with temperatures that plummeted to below freezing at night resulting in disturbed sleep and cold toes. However, just like Cornwall's weather, it was also unpredictable, suddenly giving way to windows of sunshine with no warning at all. Sometimes they would wake to find the tips of the mountains covered in white snow or hail, which gave them a Nordic freshness which was untouched by mere mortals.

* * *

'Today you are going to learn how to kill silently and quickly. Forget gentlemanly conduct. Forget taking prisoners. If you are in danger, it is kill or be killed,' barked the combat instructor. It was an unusual skill to learn after lunch, when the stomach was full and the body was sluggish. Yet here they were, surrounding an instructor on the lawn of a grand house.

He produced a knife. 'Taking prisoners is foolhardy. They are a handicap and a danger, as they will turn on you any chance they get. It is best to kill them and move on.' He pointed the tip of his knife to each trainee agent with a glide of his hand. 'Kill them quickly so they do not suffer. If your enemy is injured, that is to your advantage as it means you can kill them easier. Remember, if you leave them injured, they can report your existence and it will be you receiving a bullet from the Gestapo. And that's if you are one of the lucky ones.' He looked around at their faces. 'I want a volunteer.'

Charlotte immediately volunteered but was ignored. He pointed his knife to another recruit and all eyes turned to the person he had indicated. Charlotte only knew him by his first name, or at least the one he had been given — Francois. From his physique and knowledge, she suspected he had been in the army. 'You! Come here. Quick!'

Francois obediently jogged towards the instructor and waited for further instructions.

'If you have experience in boxing, forget those rules. The knife—' he held it up unnecessarily, turning it as if to prove the blade had two sides — 'is silent, deadly, easy to hide and hard to defend against . . . unless you have a firearm or can run as fast as a rabbit.' A soft ripple of laughter swept around the circle.

When did I start finding humour in killing someone? thought Charlotte, as she realised she had laughed too.

'I will teach you to be able to use it with both hands, passing it from one to the other. How to use your free hand to parry or open up the vulnerable abdominal area.' He poked Francois in the eye with a finger and as Francois' hands sought to comfort the pain, the instructor pretended to stab him in the stomach. 'Gravel, flour, anything to hand can be used, or simply slashing the face with your knife. All will provoke the instinct to protect and soothe, leaving the stomach unprotected to be stabbed.'

The demonstration was slick and well executed. The instructor had chosen a trainee with prior fighting experience and a strong physique for a reason. If he could show how easy it was to disarm and kill him, it would prove the tactics worked.

'Of course, there are no rules to say that you have to face your opponent.' He indicated for the trainee to turn around.

'Slitting the throat from behind, or if you can't reach, stab here and here. These wounds will penetrate the lungs enough to incapacitate him so you can finish him off.'

He swapped his knife with a gun, as if he were simply changing an item of clothing. 'If you are armed and want to search someone, kill them to do it.' He demonstrated how, aiming his gun and pretending to shoot twice rapidly. 'It may not always be convenient to kill. In that scenario, order them to lie down.' He indicated the floor with his gun and Francois obediently lay prone at his feet. 'Order them to stretch their arms out in front.' Francois obeyed. The instructor raised his gun even higher. 'And crack them on the head with the butt of your rifle.' He performed the action. Everyone winced at the force he used. They opened their eyes to discover the accuracy of the instructor's skill had ensured the butt of the rifle had stopped just short of Francois' skull. Francois' face was notably paler when he was ordered to stand up. The experience had not only shaken the former soldier, but the civilians who had watched. For the first time, they realised their own mortality. It was an experience they must accept if they were to progress through to the next part of the course.

The course intensified. Long treks and early cross-country runs, over tough terrain, became a regular part of the syllabus. Compass, map-reading and weapon training intensified. Shooting at targets progressed to fast-moving dummies, hung by winches, being propelled at speed towards them. Charlotte volunteered to be the first to try everything. Her keenness became a standing joke among the recruits, a joke she slowly become aware of but chose to ignore. If standing out from the crowd meant she would be sent to France, so be it.

* * *

'Shoot twice, in quick succession, to kill,' said the instructor as he handed out Colt 45s and 38s. 'The *double-tap* technique will ensure they are dead.' By now they were two months into their training. Now, the instruction on how to kill was accepted without comment, as if he had advised nothing more sinister than to use less bathwater or drink less tea. A disused train was supplied by the railway company to practise demolition and it seemed only logical to learn how to derail a train even if that meant killing all on board. Success was to be celebrated. Death was inevitable.

Charlotte stared at the gun in her hand and finally acknowledged that at some point she had changed without knowing it, as a result of each new challenge and skill learned. She no longer saw herself as the Cornish woman who came from a long line of fishermen. Now she was an undercover soldier, a secret agent, who accepted the unthinkable and was willing to risk her life to maintain her country's freedom. Dying did not scare her. She now believed that her life so far had led her to this calling and she could not shy away from it now.

Every skill learned, every lesson attended, continued to be observed and reported back. As the days passed, their minds became sharper, their bodies became fitter and their reactions became quicker. So it came as a shock when her instructor asked to see her and informed her she was too gung ho.

'I thought enthusiasm was to be admired, sir.'

'But not reckless volunteering for things you are not yet equipped or trained to deal with. It has been reported to me that at every opportunity you are the first to step forward before you know the full extent of the task.'

Charlotte felt as if she had been slapped in the face. 'But I thought that would be viewed as a positive trait, sir.'

'Not when things should be assessed first.' He tapped his fingertips together to some unknown tune as he leaned back in his chair and studied her. 'Reckless volunteering comes with a risk and can put others in peril. To pass this course one must first understand the task, assess how it can be completed, be able to recognise one's own limitations — either physically, in training or experience — and be prepared to change how one tackles it accordingly. At the moment your determination overshadows the basics.' He saw her confusion. 'One should not run towards a fire with the aim of putting it out if one has not thought to pick up the bucket of water first.' The officer looked at her through his brows. 'Reckless enthusiasm can risk lives.' Being told the head instructor wanted to see you in his office was not an invite any recruit wanted to receive, so when Charlotte was informed at breakfast, her heart had sunk and she'd been unable to eat anything since. Yet, despite her shock, his words rang true. She had been so busy trying to prove her ability that she had missed the bigger picture. Why had she not realised? The Frenchman came to mind. He had sowed the seed that she would not be able to cope and every task had seemed an opportunity to prove him wrong. And by doing so, she had raised concerns.

She straightened and grew an inch taller by doing so. 'I shall do better, sir.'

'I am sure you will try. The thing is, is trying enough?'

Charlotte realised quickly that making promises would not be enough for this officer. 'I have learned many things during my training. The most important lesson I have learned is that I have more to learn and will never stop learning. Being informed I am too gung ho is one of those lessons. I was keen to prove myself, sir, but I see that being a good agent is not about proving oneself. It is about doing the job well.'

To her relief, it appeared she had found the right words to say as the officer slowly nodded his head. 'I have read your reports. You have reached good grades and on paper you will make a good agent, but a reckless agent is a dead one and will put other lives in danger. Tomorrow is the last day of the course here.' The corner of his lips curved in a wry smile. 'I shall look forward to hearing how you *don't* try to prove yourself, yet still pass the task set.'

* * *

Charlotte returned to her room, lay on her bed and stared at the ceiling above her. Isabelle and Jeanne's voices carried through the walls from the corridor outside. Despite their laughter and gossip sounding inviting, she didn't have the will to join them tonight. Why were things going wrong? She was so determined to succeed, yet somehow her efforts ran the risk of her failing, and she didn't know what to do about it. She had not had to prove herself for years as each member of her father's crew had accepted both her strengths and weaknesses as she did theirs. But these instructors were strangers. They didn't want to see her weaknesses, yet if she only showed how brave and determined she was, they saw that in a negative light, too. Gung ho? She had never been called gung ho in her life! Tears of frustration stung at her eyes. Perhaps the Frenchman had been right — she was not ready to make a good agent. Didn't her tears prove that? She angrily wiped them away. *No!* she argued back to herself. His righteous opinion still rankled and she was even more determined than ever to prove his words wrong.

* * *

Thick fog sat on the top of the mountain ranges, threatening to sink lower and engulf the party of ten recruits, two instructors and much of the valley and neighbouring loch. The twenty-mile route was ill defined but the start and ending point was non-negotiable. Failure to finish the course in time, which would take them over some of the steepest highland ranges and boggy ground without a map, would mean an automatic disqualification. However, all were prepared and carried their rucksacks filled with essentials proudly on their backs. It was not long before their mood grew sombre as the gaps between them lengthened. Some walked in pairs, while others struck out confidently on their own. As much as Charlotte wanted to depend on no one and complete the task by herself, she realised quite quickly Isabelle was struggling. She had woken with a temperature, and as much as she had tried to ignore it, she was lacking her usual energy and was beginning to lag behind. Charlotte fell back to join her.

'How are you feeling?' she asked tentatively.

Isabelle shook her head. 'Not good. You go on without me. I don't want you failing because of me.'

Charlotte did as she suggested, but soon felt uneasy about leaving her friend behind. The fog was thickening and although she could hear distant voices, the others were no longer in sight. She retraced her steps, found Isabelle and fell into step beside her again.

'We'll do it together or not at all. Besides, I can't leave you now. What if you collapse?'

'At least you will be free of me. I'll just sit and blow my whistle and hope help comes.'

'I doubt they will hear you. The wind is blowing in the opposite direction and will blow the sound away. Even if they do hear you, I'm not convinced that they will be able to find you. The fog is too thick. Stay here. I'm just going to climb a little higher to get our bearings. Perhaps the fog is clearer up there. I'll be back in five minutes. Don't move.'

She helped Isabelle to sit down on a rock and began trudging up the steep incline, but the visibility was no clearer. The muted sounds of the others had already receded, carried off by a rising wind which had grown stronger with each elevation they had gained.

Charlotte tilted her head and listened. There were no birds, all having gone to seek shelter from what she suspected was an impending storm. In the distance, towards the coast, she could hear the lapping water of the nearest loch, and the faint jingle of deck chains coiled up in a bobbing boat. Suddenly, the distinct sound of earth and stones tumbling down a mountainside snared her attention and her thoughts returned to Isabelle.

'Isabelle! Was that a landslide? Are you all right?'

She carefully retraced her steps, keeping the faint sounds of the loch to her left as she made her way back to where she had left Isabelle. The rock was still there, but some distance away, a new rocky ridge had appeared, where oversaturated earth had grown heavy and swept the rest of the terrain downwards, possibly taking Isabelle with it. Charlotte called her name again as she neared the edge. At first she did not see her, but the fog briefly tore apart and revealed Isabelle, not moving, with a badly grazed face.

Charlotte was about to slide down to her, when she realised the freshly exposed ground was too friable and treacherous under foot to hold her without help. She reached for her rucksack, tore it open and dragged out the rope they'd been given. It was too short for hill climbing, but if she secured it to the rock and reached Isabelle, she could tie hers to it and guide them both downwards to more stable ground.

With well-practised fingers she secured one end around the rock and began to walk herself backwards down the slope. Several times her boots slipped on the earth, forcing her to fall on her stomach and cling to the steep gradient. As soon as the sliding earth settled around her, she slowly regained her stance and, step by step, began her descent towards her friend again.

'Stay still!' she called out when she saw Isabelle begin to stir a few yards below her. To her relief she saw her slowly nod and open her eyes.

Charlotte reached her and carefully lay beside her just as Isabelle quietly said her name.

'Hello, chum,' greeted Charlotte softly as they stared into each other's eyes. She noticed a bruise forming above Isabelle's right brow and her right cheek was scratched and pitted with dirt and gravel. 'You poor thing. You look like you have been boxing.'

'You should see my opponent,' whispered Isabelle. She winced in pain.

Charlotte nodded and continued the dark humour. 'I did. They had to carry him off on a stretcher.'

Isabelle smiled through bruised lips. 'Good. I didn't like the way he looked at me.' Her smile faded. 'How are we going to get out of this, Colette?'

Charlotte retrieved Isabelle's rope and began to efficiently tie it to her own. 'We are going to walk down to the bottom. I think I can see firmer ground down there.'

'I'm so sorry. I've ruined it for you.'

Charlotte shook her head. 'It doesn't matter. If they throw us both out, they can't be that good at selecting agents, can they?'

Isabelle's eyes began to close.

'Don't go to sleep on me now,' Charlotte teased, successfully hiding the concern she felt for her friend's health. 'We have a hill to descend.'

Isabelle forced her eyes open, slowly reached for her friend's hand and gently squeezed it. They looked at each other in silence, both knowing there was no need for words to express her gratitude or acknowledge the peril they both faced.

'Are you ready?' asked Charlotte gently. Isabelle nodded and together they attempted to find a foothold on the friable slope. Testing their balance briefly, they began their descent together, anchored against the steep gradient by their joined ropes.

Isabelle, weakened by her illness and still dazed by her fall, also struggled with a painful leg, which made each step anything but smooth.

'Lean on me,' suggested Charlotte. 'We are nearly there. Just a bit further.'

Their progress was slow, although careful, but Charlotte soon realised their combined ropes would still fall too short.

'The firm ground is still too far down. We'll try another way. I want you to keep hold of this rope. I am going to take the end and walk sideways to the firmer ground, taking the end with me. When I am there, you can follow me by holding onto the rope like a rail.'

Isabelle was horrified at the thought. 'You might start to slide.'

Charlotte looked at the expanse that in reality was only five yards, but still far enough. 'I know, but we can't stay here all day. Don't let go of the rope. Promise me.'

Isabelle nodded. 'I promise.' She clutched it against her chest. 'I'm ready.'

Charlotte nodded, turned and began her journey, crawling on hands and knees across the earth and rock expanse. As she gained ground, several stones and rocks dislodged and began to roll and tumble, like meteor showers, down towards the loch below. At one point Charlotte slipped too, tightening the rope between her and Isabelle and forcing her friend to lurch forward. They both froze, allowing the tumbling earth and stones to settle once again, before they dared to breathe and Charlotte could set out again. At last, she reached firm, sweet smelling, grassy turf and clutched onto it for another anchor before she heaved herself upon it. Bracing herself against the rope with heels dug deep into the earth, she encouraged Isabelle to follow, which she did, using the rope as a safety line and guide until she fell upon Charlotte in gratitude and relief.

'Hugs and celebrations for later,' Charlotte laughed as she eased her friend away. 'We still have a course to complete, and if you feel well enough to come with me, I have an idea on how to do it.'

* * *

'When someone is injured you should call for help.' The same officer who had reprimanded her the day before sternly waited for her reply.

'The wind was blowing in the wrong direction, sir. They would never have heard the whistle.'

He indicated the file on his desk. 'This report says you used ropes, which was foolhardy without an experienced instructor. You could have fallen.'

'If we had fallen, sir, it would not have been the fault of my knowledge of ropes. I know about knots.'

'You do?'

'Yes, sir. I used a round turn and hitches knot for the rock and a zeppelin bend to secure both ropes together. They are foolproof and I have been using them for years.'

The officer frowned. 'In what capacity?'

'Am I allowed to discuss it, sir? I thought we were not meant to discuss personal things.'

The officer moved uneasily in his seat. 'I am not sure I wish to hear it either.' He made a show at looking at the report again. 'It says here you both finished the course. How did you do that with an injured recruit?'

'I heard the sound of a boat on the loch. The rules stipulated that we were to get from A to B by a certain time, but it did not say how. I therefore thought it was permissible to sail around the coastline and disembarked at point B. We arrived first, sir.'

'By an hour.'

'Indeed, sir.'

'You do realise you are the first recruit to do such a thing.'

'That surprises me, sir. However, I thought it was for the best as a storm was coming.'

'So the others found out. They were a soggy mess when they arrived. How did you know? The weather report did not predict it.'

'My father could sense it on the wind, sir, but it was the birds who told me.'

'How?'

'Their absence. It was one of the first things I noticed. Along with the fog, of course.'

'Am I going to have an irate boat owner knocking on my door looking for his boat?'

'No, sir, I returned it.'

'What did your instructors say to your innovative arrival?'

'They were surprised but thankful.'

'Thankful?'

'That they did not have to walk back. The storm was getting worse, sir, so I offered to sail them back to the manor which cut their journey by almost two hours. They were rather wet already and by that time were keen for a hot meal.'

The officer pushed her file away and stood up. For the first time their eyes were almost level and she thought she saw a hint of amusement in their depths.

'I don't know whether to reprimand you for not following orders or congratulate you for showing teamwork and exemplarily assessment, planning and execution during an unforeseen predicament.'

'I would rather it was the latter, sir.'

'I had a feeling you would say that.' He finally allowed the smile in his eyes to reach his lips.

It gave her the confidence to ask after Isabelle, who she had not seen all morning. 'May I ask a question, sir?'

He nodded.

'Can Isabelle continue on the course?'

'Your concern for your teammate is commendable. She needs a couple of days of rest and recuperation, but she finished the course, which were the rules . . . thanks to you.' He braced his shoulders. 'You did well. Now go and get yourself something to eat. Your training in Scotland might have come to an end, but there are still more skills to learn yet.'

'Then I can stay?'

'You can stay, and between me and you, I have a funny feeling you might end up being the best of the lot.'

Charlotte saluted, stiffly turned and left, careful not to show any emotion on her face until she stood outside his closed door. Alone, she allowed herself a broad smile and looked up to the ceiling, silently thanking her father for teaching her everything he knew.

* * *

On the last day of their time in Scotland, the thick heavy cloud and sporadic wind, rain and fog, which had been their constant companion throughout their stay, gradually melted away to reveal the breathtaking scenery which had welcomed their arrival. Their time in Scotland had passed in a blur of new experiences and as Charlotte watched the wild mountains and glens pass by her train window, she felt a sense of regret that she had not had the chance to get to know Scotland and its people better.

* * *

The Ringway Parachute Training School, near Manchester, was their next stop. They arrived to the sight of olive-brown Dakota planes coming and going from the vast airfield, while large, draughty hangars housed those in need of repair and maintenance. Seemingly confident paratroopers walked the grounds and, for a moment, Charlotte's self-confidence melted away. These men had joined the RAF, whereas she had never even been in a plane. However, as 27X were led into one of the hangars, she realised the interior had been specially designed to equip paratroopers with the skills and confidence required to complete their first jump. Somehow the rigging, platforms and equipment, and the small huddle of training groups in different parts of the hangar, were comforting to see as she had spent the last few months learning new skills, with different equipment under experienced instructors.

They learned flight drills, how to wear and check their equipment and how to land on the ground correctly. Their head for heights was tested by candidates being hung from winches and cranes suspended from one-hundred-foot towers. The skill and dedication of the RAF instructors helped enormously, gradually building the confidence of the fearful amateurs and teaching them the techniques to jump from a plane and descend to earth safely. Charlotte even began to find the process fun. It turned out she was not the only one.

'Who wouldn't want to swing from platform to platform and learn to tumble as if they were a child in a playground?' said Jeanne breathlessly as she was strapped into a harness for the fifth time. She was right. Every member of the group was eager to have another go, running from one end to another like teenagers on some wild adventure.

However, Isabelle, Jeanne and herself quickly realised they were viewed as oddities, as women were usually packing chutes not learning to use them to drop behind enemy lines. The parachute instructors had been ordered to treat them the same as the men, and they did for the most part. Everything the men were instructed to do, the women were instructed, too. Orders were orders and must be obeyed, after all. Yet, the occasional glance still leaked from the instructors' innermost thoughts, along with the politer, softer tone they always used when talking to them individually. There were other subtle differences that were indiscernible to the other recruits, but the women noticed them — every slight, every curious look, every surprised reaction — for they had experienced the very same ones for most of their lives. It gave them the reason to succeed in what was a male-dominated training facility. They did not want to be different from the men, and in order to achieve that, they had to be better. It made her realise that Pierre had done none of those things when assessing or arguing with her. He had talked and argued with her like an equal. Perhaps he had known she had the stamina and confidence to take it and give some back in return.

Ultimately, they had to undertake several jumps from both balloons and planes. Each experience was both terrifying and exhilarating and each time Charlotte landed, she fell in love with the firm ground all over again. As her final jump came to an end, she knew she had proved to her instructors, and to herself, that she had the courage required. She saw it in her reflection in the mirror, felt it in her heart and saw the respect in the eyes of the new intake of novice RAF recruits as they arrived to start their training.

Their time at Ringway was short, it was yet another experience they would never forget. Jumping from a plane would always be fraught with dangers and no one could guarantee that their jump would be successful. This shared experience, with its possible macabre outcome, bonded their training group like no other lesson so far because they understood each other's intense anxiety and exultation as they undertook their jumps, with only a look and without uttering a word.

* * *

The final phase of their training was on the 7000-acre Beaulieu Estate in the New Forest. The estate was home to numerous secluded country mansions and schools scattered throughout the estate. Eleven schools were equipped to prepare them for the covert life they would have to live in France — essential training, they were told, if they wanted to stay alive.

One of the schools was simply a building which had been changed substantially to reflect a typical French house with the aim of familiarising trainees who had yet to step onto French soil. Other lessons included political propaganda, burglary, forgery, picking locks and personal security. They were taught how to maintain a cover story and withhold information under interrogation. What to do if they suspected they were being followed. How to disguise themselves using simple techniques which were no more complicated than changing how their hair was parted. They undertook mock training scenarios, which lasted two to three days and sometimes, unintentionally, involved the local police force. They also honed their skills in specialist areas. The men mainly worked on sabotage and organising, while the women trained as couriers and wireless operators. It was one of the rare times they were treated differently and took advantage of their natural skills and appearance. Or at least it was meant to. Halfway through the training, Charlotte was relocated to the men's specialism. It appeared that sending messages in code remained her weakest skill.

As the course came to an end, they were finally introduced to an array of gadgets that were both ingenious, yet remarkably simple, for they looked like everyday objects but ultimately were not. A folded map in the heel of a shoe. A compass in a button. A camera in a matchbox. A saw blade on the buckle of a belt. A smoking pipe which concealed a pocket knife. They had learned so much in their time together and tomorrow they would be sent to separate holding flats to wait for their final briefing. Their time was upon them and there was little they could do about it now . . . even if they wanted to.

* * *

Their last night together was a sombre affair. There was no wine to toast their success at completing their training for they were wiser now, if only a few months older, and understood the reality of their situation. At the beginning they had known little about what they had been chosen to do. How naïve they had been then, thought Charlotte, as she looked around the room at Isabelle and Jeanne. Perhaps the Frenchman had seen that in her at a time when she'd been blind to it. Yet she, and these two women, were determined to undertake any mission given to them to the best of their ability, as the Organisation had placed their trust in them and they must not let them down.

'Well, it has been jolly fun,' said Isabelle lightly as they sat around a table drinking cups of steaming tea. The library was a popular place for the cohort to congregate in the evenings to talk, play cards or throw darts, but tonight they were the only ones. Now it was silent, as the other members had either gone for a walk or returned to their rooms to pack.

Charlotte smiled brightly, but her mock joy did not reach her eyes. 'Yes, it has been quite a journey. We may not see each other again after tomorrow.'

'And if we do meet again when we reach France, we will have to pretend we don't know each other.' Jeanne reached across the table and they all held hands. 'I hope you will know that inside I will be saying hello.'

Charlotte gently squeezed their hands. 'Yes. Me too.'

Isabelle swallowed and nodded.

She stared at their entwined hands. 'We should agree to meet up when the war is over . . . for old times' sake,'

'That would be nice,' said Jeanne.

Isabelle took charge. 'That's a wonderful idea. We will be able to reminisce about our training together. It will be the only time we can as we have signed the Official Secrets Act and won't be able to talk to anyone else about it.'

'Perhaps by then we can tell each other our real names,' said Charlotte. They squeezed hands, each one desperate to know now, but willing to sacrifice that knowledge in case they were tortured to reveal it.

'As it's the month of June, how about we meet on the first Saturday in June, one year after the war has ended?'

'Sounds wonderful,' said Jeanne.

Charlotte smiled with difficulty. 'Where?'

'Why, where it all began of course!' said Isabelle. 'We must meet at the entrance of Wanborough Manor! At noon.'

And so, it was excitedly arranged and often referred to during their last evening together. It gave them something to look forward to and a reason not to sever their bonds completely. For a few hours, they chose to ignore all that could happen between now and then, which fed their hope that they would be victorious and still be alive on that sunny day in June, one year after the war had come to an end.

CHAPTER TEN

Charlotte watched the cohort of 27X leave, one by one, from the window of her final accommodation. Their partings had been innately British, wishing everyone good luck with a stiff upper lip and a firm shake of hands. They had spent weeks learning to live as French civilians, yet in these last moments their true selves would not be hidden. She didn't know their real names, yet she felt she knew some parts of each one more intimately than their closest acquaintances. For some reason she was asked to stay behind. Unlike the others, who would receive their final briefing at their holding residence, she would receive it here. Why she should be singled out from the others was intriguing to say the least.

A knock on the door startled her and she looked up to see the captain of the Air Liaison Section. 'How are you?' he asked. His soft enquiring gaze told her his question was genuine which threatened to open a floodgate of concerns she'd, until now, kept to herself. However, they both knew that showing such weakness would not be appropriate right now.

'I'm looking forward to doing my job, sir.'

From the slow nod of his head, it appeared he both respected her reply but was also saddened by it. He looked about him. They had been given a small comfortable room for their meeting. The door was firmly shut and the house staff had been instructed to leave them alone. It was just her and him now.

'This is a nice room. Comfortable. Reminds me of home.' He looked at her. 'Do you know why I am here?'

'To brief me on my mission and accompany me to the airfield, sir.'

'Not exactly. I won't be taking you to the airfield. You will be returning to Cornwall.'

Charlotte's heart sank. 'I'm not going to France?'

He sat on the sofa and settled himself into the cushions. 'But I can do this, sir. I know I can.'

He signalled for her to sit down, too, as if she hadn't spoken. She tried again, reluctantly sitting down as he had requested her to do, although in reality she was too upset to keep still.

'At the beginning of my training I was unsure, but not now—'

'You *are* going to France . . . just not by parachute.' He opened the briefcase. 'We have another method of getting you into occupied France. It's a little different, a little more arduous, but I think you are the perfect agent to take it on. But more of that later.' He withdrew a file of documents and placed it on the table. 'First, I must brief you on your mission.' He searched his pocket, withdrew a small case no bigger than a button, and carefully positioned it next to the file. Charlotte stared at it. The documents were intriguing, but it was the case that held her attention as she knew it was the cyanide pill she had heard about.

She had often wondered when and how the capsule would be given to her. She hadn't expected it to be given by a gently spoken man. How quickly her life had changed over the past few months. Her father would not recognise her now. When was the exact moment that started her on this road to madness that could turn death by cyanide into a plausible, even preferable, method to end her life?

Yet she had known the answer before she even finished asking herself the question. It was in the early hours of a wintery morning, somewhere on the Atlantic, where the wind and sea ruled, seagulls scavenged from trawlers and the rising sun shone a soft flickering light on a spiked metal forewarning of what was to come. Moments before, she had questioned why she felt half-complete and if the reason why would reveal itself one day in the future. Within days, her father was dead and what remained of his body was doomed to ride the tidal stream for decades to come. Her father's death had brought her to this moment. He had said she would know when it was right to risk her life and he had been right. She had no doubts when she had made that call to help end the war. In a funny way, it was as if the call was her destiny as she had not felt as if there was something missing in her life ever since.

'Are you ready to carry on?' he asked gently, wrenching her thoughts back to the here and now.

Charlotte blinked and looked at him, unsure how long he had been waiting. She nodded stiffly.

He smiled. 'Good. First let me fill you in on your new identity. Here is a file on your background, family, job, etc. Read it, memorise it and burn it.'

His instructions refocused her thoughts. He smiled as he handed her the file.

'The pill is always a shock. I like to take it out first so the agent has a chance to get used to it before I leave.' He tapped the file in her hand. 'Your new name is Mademoiselle Marie Veilleux. Code name Adele.' He withdrew a slightly larger box from his case and placed it on the table next to the pill case. 'And here are a few personal objects with your new name engraved on it to provide some authenticity.' He waved a finger at it. 'I think there might be a bracelet and ring in there. The sort of jewellery a woman of your age would wear.'

Charlotte tentatively opened the box. One was a necklace, rather than a bracelet, with a message from fictional loving parents. The other was a ring with her new initials entwined with another's.

'Who is CF?' she asked.

'You will learn from your file that he was a past boy-friend, nothing more important than that. Died before the war from an illness. It's all in the file. These little background details add authenticity to your new identity.'

She picked up her forged identity card. Marie Veilleux. She was no longer to be called Colette. Strangely, she missed the trainee already.

He withdrew a map from his case, stood and unfolded it onto a nearby table. He glanced at her over his shoulder, expecting her to follow him, which she immediately did. It was no surprise to see that the detailed map showed northern France and the English Channel.

'We have networks all over France. Their role is to encourage and aid resistance against the German occupation of the country by gathering intelligence, supplying groups, sabotaging transportation, communications and industrial facilities. The number of members in each network are small, but there are many networks. Each network, or circuit, is highly effective and dedicated. You will join the Pointer network, which is currently in the process of being set up. Several networks have recently been disbanded and Pointer is helping to fill the gap.' He glanced at her. 'Networks being disbanded is an occupational hazard, I'm afraid.'

Disbanded? Did he mean no longer required or had they been discovered? If it was the latter, she wondered where the men and women were now. She focused on the map, biting back the question. The less she knew the better.

He indicated to an area on the map. 'We have an agent in Paris. He says there is an important meeting coming up in one of the hotels there.'

'Which hotel?'

'The one he owns. He will tell you more about it when you get there.'

Charlotte was intrigued. What sort of man owned a hotel and risked it all by being an agent?

The captain continued to brief her. 'There will be many German dignitaries and officers attending. It may be an opportunity to obtain some information.'

'What information?'

'Anything of interest. Movements of troops. Plans. Ammunition factories. We don't know yet what we might get our hands on. That is Pointer's mission. That is your mission. We want Pointer network to obtain the information and radio it back to London. We will send back your next steps and supply you with the necessary ammunition.'

'I am not going to be a courier or a wireless operator?' To her relief, he said no.

'We felt you were better at the more physical rigours involved with sabotage. Pointer needs a new member who is good with explosives. They already have a wireless operator and we already have couriers in the area.'

Couriers had no base but went from network to network. Working as a member of a network suited Charlotte better. After all, she had worked with a tight team of men for years. She noticed his steady gaze on her. Of course, he already knew that and the knowledge had helped him select her role.

'It sounds like we won't know what we are looking for until we find it.'

'For an agent to be of most use, they must be flexible. It might be the only thing between success or failure. Which reminds me.' He withdrew another small box from his pocket. 'This is Benzedrine to keep you alert. And that one . . .' he finally named the pill in the case on the table '. . . is cyanide.' He picked up the case with the rubber cover and turned it carefully with his fingers. 'When your situation is at its bleakest, bite down on this pill. You will be dead in fifteen seconds. It is best to kill oneself rather than share information that will result in the deaths of many.'

He offered it to her as if it was no more harmless than a blueberry. Charlotte reluctantly took it.

'I will sew them both into my clothing.'

'Has your clothing arrived?'

'Yes. The Organisation has done an amazing job.' Whoever had made her outfit had done their research. The clothes were from French designs and had French labels inside.

He nodded in agreement and held a small package out to her. 'I want you to deliver this too.'

'What is it?' asked Charlotte.

'Two crystals for their wireless.'

She took the small package. It was light, small and would be easy to carry.

'They've had problems sending messages so we are sending replacements. Now we will discuss how you will get there.' Their heads came together to study the map again. 'The whole of the north coast has been declared a prohibited area. This area stretches twelve miles inland. Sea routes across the Channel are compromised as it is almost impossible to land agents anywhere along the coast now. We are still leaving supplies along here to be picked up later, but for the time being this method is not suitable for dropping off agents. However, there is still a way using fishing boats. Tomorrow you will return to Cornwall.

'Accommodation near the Helford River has been secured for you to rest in. The details are in your file. A boat will take you to the Isles of Scilly where it will be disguised as a Breton fishing boat. At the allotted hour it will take you as far as here.'

He vaguely pointed to an area at sea, north of France. 'Here you will meet with a flotilla of French fishing trawlers and will change boats. They will take you to here.' His finger slid across the map to a small coastal port in Brittany. 'Waiting for you will be a member of the Resistance. He is the organiser of Pointer, and known to us. You will travel to Paris together and he will provide you with safe accommodation.' He finally looked up at her. 'I suggest you get a good night's sleep tonight. You have a busy day tomorrow. Any questions?'

'My clothing will give me away.'

'You will be supplied with fishing clothes to wear over your skirt and blouse for the journey.'

'Does the file provide me with an occupation?'

'We had much discussion about that. We felt your looks suited something to do with fashion and your flawless French and confidence in conversing could also be utilised. We decided on a salesperson.'

'A salesperson?' It took all her effort not to sound disappointed. She only knew two salesmen. They visited Newlyn with a van crammed with products and she wouldn't trust one word that came out of either of their mouths.

'We know your mother sold cosmetics when she was younger and living in France.'

'Yes, she did. She often spoke of it, although I never saw her as a salesperson.'

He smiled. 'But she was.'

'Yes, I suppose she was. I like to think she was more professional than the ones I've met.'

He chuckled silently. 'We think it is best to have your background as close to something you already know. Deep-sea fishing is not believable.'

'But true.'

He smiled, kindly. 'Nevertheless, a job as a cosmetic salesperson is more suited and will provide a good cover story should you be questioned while travelling. The cosmetics were dropped some days ago. They will be waiting for you at your new residence in Paris.'

'How will I know the person who will meet me?'

'He will ask you about the fishing and you will reply, "It can always be better. The fish grow slow in dark waters." He will reply, "Then we must light up the sea."'

Charlotte watched him fold up the map.

'I will leave this map with you but destroy it along with your file before you leave. When you board that boat tomorrow, I want you to be thinking in French and speaking French. *Be* French or someone will betray you.' He shut his briefcase and looked at her. 'How are you feeling now, Mademoiselle Marie Veilleux?'

Charlotte considered the question. This time she would be truthful as this might be the last time she would see him again.

'I feel scared . . . determined . . . but ready.'

He nodded slowly at each word. 'Good. Those feelings will help you during your time in France. Being gullible, distracted and incompetent would not.'

'If I felt like that, I would not admit to it.'

He smiled. 'Which is also the right thing to do. I usually give my trainees a tot of rum before they jump. It helps a little, I think. I won't be with you in body when you board the boat, but I will be with you in spirit until your return.'

He left as quietly as he had arrived and she wondered who he would be briefing next. Every member of 27X was about to leave for France, arriving separately and without fanfare, in the dead of night. She hoped they would all stay safe and well, knowing in her heart that should she meet them or be asked about them, she would have to deny she knew them at all. But at least she would see Cornwall again and have the chance to absorb its colours, smells and views to lock away into her heart for one last time. She looked at the small box containing the cyanide pill. Should she face the bleakest of times, she would think of her home and imagine herself there. Walking the coast of Cornwall would be a comforting memory while she bit into the pill that would silently kill her.

CHAPTER ELEVEN

Helford River always looked beautiful in June, with its over-hanging oak trees, deep blue waters and sheltered creeks which meandered deep into the countryside. The water teemed with life despite its peaceful ambience. Birds scavenged for food above the tidal surface, while oysters and other underwater wildlife thrived beneath. Locally owned boats, of all sizes and characters, bobbed upon the surface in peaceful silence, as if waiting for their owners to return when the war was over. Just beyond Port Navas Creek entrance was a stretch of water which was particularly protected from the easterly winds. Hidden in peaceful seclusion, away from too many prying eyes, was moored the Inshore Patrol Flotilla waiting to carry out the next clandestine operation.

Charlotte arrived early and was directed to a sixty-foot trawler, where a crew of eight was waiting for her. Despite being painted grey, she recognised the trawler immediately.

'That's a Newlyn boat,' she remarked after the skipper introduced himself as Sub Lieutenant Townsend.

The skipper was impressed. 'That's observant of you, considering it spent some time half submerged in Newlyn Harbour.'

'A heavy storm damaged it,' said Charlotte, somewhat comforted that it would be a Cornish fishing boat taking her to France.

'And we commissioned it. There is a distinct lack of boats with a reliable engine needed to cross the Channel. Parts are not easy to come by these days. It was extremely difficult to get hold of a British diesel, but we did it in the end.' He looked at her. 'I'm sorry. You don't want to hear about my problems.'

'On the contrary. I understand more than you think about trawlers and their reliability problems.'

'Don't tempt me or I will spend the trip talking about *all* of the difficulties we have faced.' He smiled. 'What do we call you?'

'Marie Veilleux.' His handshake was firm but friendly and Charlotte immediately liked him. He had a shock of dark curly hair, a pipe clenched between his teeth and a calm enthusiasm that could bolster the spirits of any downhearted crew.

Another man approached. He introduced him immediately. 'This is Sub Lieutenant John Garnett. The rest of the crew are not from the forces. They are fishermen.' Charlotte smiled. No one understood the sea or fishing boats like a fisherman. She knew she was in safe hands now. 'We have one Breton in case we are caught. I suggest you spend your time talking to him in French. It will help prepare you for when you land. I'm afraid the rest of the crew's French is verging on non-existent.'

The trawler, loaded with mail, money and equipment, and its crew set off within the hour with Charlotte on board. Initially, their route followed the line of the Cornish coast. Charlotte watched the everchanging view in front of her, as quaint coastal villages, rocky cliffs and quiet secluded coves came and went as if they were on a scenic conveyor belt. It was as if Cornwall was displaying its wares to her in a vain attempt to tempt her to stay. She sadly wondered if she would ever see it again.

Soon, Cornwall was behind them, no more than a distant memory swallowed up by the receding horizon. Despite it being a clear morning, the choppy waters and cross-winds of the Celtic Sea eventually forced her to seek warmth below deck. Despite no fish on board, the smell of previous catches forcefully greeted her as she entered the confined space. She learned from her Breton friend, that despite many attempts to rid the boat of the potent odour, the smell had still lingered, much to the annoyance of one crew member who found it difficult to tolerate. He would not elaborate, but Charlotte soon noted that Sub Lieutenant Townsend was the only one to remain above deck, in the fresh air, for the entire trip.

The Isles of Scilly was a cluster of small islands and it was only a few hours later that they slowly emerged in the distant haze. Less than thirty miles off Land's End, its temperate climate, unspoilt islands and tropical vegetation gave the initial impression it had been untouched by the war. As they entered the sheltered waters of the islands, Charlotte could see that life there, although probably hard at times, was simpler and calmer. But then she saw the numerous pillboxes lining the coastline, barbed wire scarred the beaches, a fighter aircraft came into land as they approached, and waiting in the sheltered waters of the largest island, St Mary's, was a British warship. It seemed Churchill was adamant that these small islands should never be invaded as they could provide a stepping stone for an enemy invasion of the mainland.

Yet, despite the military presence, she suspected that beneath the surface, life continued as normal and the community spirit remained strong. What would they think of the comings and goings of this grey painted boat?

'They suspect we carry torpedoes to shoot at submarines and we have not told them otherwise,' replied her Breton friend when she asked him in French. 'It is best they do not know our real reason for being here. They watch us come and go, but they do not question us, and leave us alone. They understand whatever we are up to is for the good of the war effort.'

Their trawler made its way slowly towards the second largest island, Tresco, and put down anchor in New Grimsby harbour. It was here the crew planned to spend the next few hours repainting the boat and transforming it into a Breton fishing boat. Charlotte took the opportunity to explore the small island and spent the next two hours roaming the Stone Age settlements, rugged outcrops and sandy beaches of Tresco, being careful to avoid the shooting ranges and training areas of the soldiers stationed in the area.

She returned to watch the final touches to the trawler being applied. The Newlyn boat, with its navy grey coat, had blossomed into a brightly painted Breton fishing boat. The hull, bulwarks, deckhouse and masts were now painted in a combination of bright blue and green. A new registration number and Breton name had been painted in white on the hull, and as this information was a closely guarded secret until they were with the French fishing fleet, the crew were in the process of covering their identification numbers with canvas. They had painted French flags at the waterline, a requirement, she later learned, for all French fishing vessels under the new German regulations.

Finally, her transport was ready and they had received no message to abort the transfer. Charlotte, from her viewing place on the harbour, wondered for the first time since arriving back in Cornwall, if she was up to the task ahead.

* * *

By the time they set out on their journey the sky had clouded over and there was a light mist forming over the water. The change in weather was taken as a positive, as the nights were short and although cloud could provide some cover and clear skies often provided uninterrupted views, both also could be detrimental to a safe journey into German-held waters.

They left Tresco and headed south, towards the most western rocky islet of the Isles of Scilly, Bishop Rock. From there they were escorted by three RAF Beaufighter planes, who took turns protectively circling above them with wide graceful arcs. At ten o'clock, just as the sun set in the west and under a golden glow of its dimming light, their RAF guardians dipped their wings in farewell and returned to base. Now they were alone at sea and had to complete their journey unprotected. The RAF had flown as far as they could — to fly further would draw attention to the disguised fishing trawler.

The equivalent of no man's land at sea lay ahead, a vast stretch of water sandwiched between British waters and German-occupied territory. Their little French fishing boat, with only one Frenchman on board and no viable excuse to be sailing so far south, was on its own with no more than a disguise, the cover of night and a thickening mist which was settling around them.

The crew took turns to look out for German patrols, but they were all insistent that Charlotte stayed below deck and tried to sleep. An agent that arrived with dark circles under her eyes was bound to raise suspicions, they told her. Charlotte understood their logic. There was no guarantee she would be able to find a place to sleep for several days, so rather than be stubborn and stay on deck, she went below to rest.

* * *

The rise and fall of her surroundings and the strong odour of fish mixed with warm porridge oats reminded her of where she was before she opened her eyes. She checked the light outside. It was morning and a bowl of porridge had been placed on the nearby table. She ate it and immediately joined the rest of the crew on deck. The mist had dissipated and she was informed by her Breton friend that they were twenty miles west of the island of Ushant. They followed the western coast of France, passing the headland of Pointe du Raz by midmorning. A fleet of French crabbing boats was spotted in the distance. Did they change their route and give them a wide berth or continue as planned in a straight line? Their skipper decided on the latter as it would raise suspicions if they changed their course.

They passed the boats, close enough to see the French crews' weathered faces, but not close enough to damage their catch. Although they showed no aggression or betrayal, it was still a relief when the crabbing crew lost interest and returned to their tasks.

They continued, passing through the waters of Baie d'Audierne, with its coast of golden sands and enchanting, white villas reflecting in the bright morning sun.

On several occasions, German bombers and reconnaissance seaplanes were spotted above them. The crew could do nothing but hope and pray that if they had been spotted, they would be deemed too unimportant to follow up. Just as they thought they were leaving, one reconnaissance seaplane circled back and flew over again, before arcing away inland. There was much discussion as to what could have caused the change in route, but it was generally felt that if they had been spotted as an enemy, the plane would have radioed the encounter back, not returned inland.

They had almost forgotten about the encounter when a German armed convoy was spotted heading their way.

'Shall we give them a wide berth?' Garnett asked Townsend, as Charlotte joined them on deck.

Townsend continued to study the ships through his binoculars, before finally lowering them, deep in thought. He looked at his crew who had gathered around him. They were all dressed as hardworking fishermen, with woollen hats, jumpers and wellington boots. His eyes settled on Charlotte, who was dressed no differently and could be easily mistaken for a man.

'They will have already spotted us. We don't know if the pilot informed them about us.'

'It would seem heavy handed to send out a convoy to check us out,' said a crew member.

'But if they were heading this way anyway . . .' said another.

Sub Lieutenant Townsend made up his mind. 'We'll stay on course. It worked before. We can only hope it will work again.' He turned to his crew. 'Look busy. I want them to think we are here to catch fish.'

The crew set about preparing to drop a net. The armed convoy of German ships bore down on them, their massive bulks sending a ripple of waves in their wake. Townsend kept his course, passing so close that, once again, they could see the faces of the German naval crew as they passed. Charlotte noticed one was watching them through binoculars, so she turned her back and began to untangle some rope. Fortunately, the man's interest was short-lived and the convoy passed by, leaving their French trawler rising and falling violently in its turbulent wake.

They continued their journey towards the Glénan Isles. These fishing grounds were busier than any that had gone before. Nimble French tunny boats, larger trawlers and brightly painted fishing vessels, not unlike their own, fished the waters as seagulls waited to scavenge on the fish guts thrown back into the sea. Their crews paid them little attention, much to their relief. They continued to their rendezvous, just off the Glénan Isles. The cluster of islands surrounding sheltered waters, reminded Charlotte of the islands she had left behind.

The next hour dragged by. The rendezvous time came and went and hope was fading that her transfer would happen at all. They had received no message of cancellation, so they continued to pretend to fish as the minutes turned to hours. Eventually, a boat bearing all the characteristics of the vessel they hoped to meet appeared on the horizon. It made a steady approach, each characteristic becoming clearer the closer it got.

Hardly daring to breathe, Charlotte watched as the skipper signalled to identify himself. Almost immediately the correct reply was received back. All indications confirmed that it was them, but even so, handguns were made ready, just in case it was a trap. Within minutes, their boats sat side by side and any fears of entrapment quickly disappeared as packages and mail were rapidly exchanged. Charlotte was the last to jump on board. The transfer had taken weeks to plan, countless people to carry out and multiple vehicles, boats and planes to execute. On the British side, the transfer was now complete, carried out in a hurry that lasted no more than five minutes.

The feelings of relief and fear, that she had successfully boarded a French boat but that there was now no turning back, were almost overwhelming in their contradiction. All there was left for her to do was to thank the British crew and her Breton friend, who had had made it possible for her. Her thanks to them was hurried, but came from the heart, and she could only hope that they all understood her French. From their cheerful waves and poorly spoken French goodbyes, she believed they did and found herself almost crying as she left her new friends behind.

CHAPTER TWELVE

The quiet port of Doelan, on the south coast of Brittany, consisted of a narrow estuary, two guarding lighthouses and sloping banks of pretty houses to welcome exhausted fishing crews home. The quiet seclusion and calm waters of the port were the perfect place for Breton boats to seek shelter from rough winds and its beauty, which had been effortlessly preserved by its inhabitants, was a welcoming sight for crews on their return. Fresh fish was sold directly to the people along the old harbour walls, capturing the very essence of French culture where much resolve was put into choosing the finest fish to cook.

Pierre had arrived the day before. He spent most of the day drinking coffee — black due to the shortage of milk — in its harbour-side café and waiting, waiting, waiting for *the Emilienne* to arrive. He braced himself as the fishing trawler finally entered the narrow estuary and slowly manoeuvred into place by the quayside. He hoped he would be able to spot the crew member who knew nothing about fishing, but to his surprise, every crew member appeared confident and skilled in their duties, unloading their catch onto the quayside without the need of direction or commands. Identifying the agent was going to be tougher than he first thought.

He wandered over to the view the catch. Gutted fish, their eyes bulbous and their mouths gaping, lay neatly in baskets lined up along the harbour wall. He pretended to be interested.

'How was the fishing?' he asked one of the crew.

'Good. The weather was fair.' The crew member left to collect some more fish, oblivious that his reply was not what he wanted to hear. He asked another with the same unsatisfactory response so he waited some minutes before another crew member arrived. This one was slighter in stature, but he was still able to heave the basket full of fish into place as if it weighed half its appearance. He straightened some fish, as if their appearance would fetch a better price, before turning away. Pierre asked him the same question before he had a chance to walk away. There was a slight pause, before he replied.

'It can always be better. The fish grow slow in dark waters.'

Pierre braced himself at the sound of the woman's voice. It was unexpected, yet strangely familiar. She was about to walk away when he realised he had not replied.

'Then we must light up the sea.'

She halted and slowly turned to meet his gaze. Dark brown eyes looked up at him from beneath a worn woollen hat. Although her hair and curves were hidden beneath baggy masculine clothes, he knew it was *her*. His heart lurched in his chest. He had a feeling that things were going to get a whole lot more complicated from now on.

He dragged his eyes away from her and looked about him. The small port was busy, despite its size. 'Wait a minute, then follow. I will be waiting for you.' He turned and walked away in the opposite direction from the harbour, aware of her steady gaze burning a hole in the centre of his back. Turning left along a road lined with houses, their shutters brightly coloured and unique to each house, he waited at the top of the hill, casually leaning against a wall. Eventually the agent appeared. She quickly spotted him, so he continued casually walking along the narrow road as if he had all the time in the world. Eventually he reached his destination and waited for her to find him. He did not have to wait long.

He indicated for her to follow with a jerk of his head as he opened a small, concealed door in the side of a house. He had found the entrance to the poorly lit basement the day before. The house appeared to have been neglected and empty for several years and it provided the ideal place for an agent to discard their disguise.

'You can take your clothes off here,' he said as he searched for the low hanging light. He turned it on. The bulb flickered feebly before emitting a dim glow. 'I assume you have something on underneath,' he said, turning to discover she was already pulling the woollen jumper over her head to reveal a blouse, half-unbuttoned and showing a glimpse of her breast. 'They kept you on the course then.'

She ignored him as she slipped her arms free of the sleeves.

'I was expecting a man.'

Her head popped out from the jumper's neck.

'Well, as you can see, I'm not one.'

Her face still glowed from the sea wind and her hair was tousled as if he had just made love to her. He clenched his jaw as he stared at her.

'I told them I needed someone good with explosives.'

'And you got that.'

'You won't get special treatment. I won't have time to look after you.'

'Good.' She must have seen how those words surprised him. 'You look disappointed? Does it concern you to have a woman on your team?' Unfazed by his sullen glare, she redid the buttons of her blouse and proceeded to wriggle out of her trousers and boots. She pointedly looked at him and raised an eyebrow as she set her old clothes aside.

It was only then he realised he had not answered.

'I don't like being surprised.'

'I'll try to remember that.' Despite the promise, she didn't sound as if she really cared if she surprised him again or not.

'What do I call you?'

'Marie Veilleux.'

'Do you have papers?'

'Yes.'

'A cover story?'

'Of course.'

'Am I going to ever learn it?'

'Depends. Do you really want to know?' She gave an accusing glare of her own, with her hands on her hips and a little breathless from either the exertion or the excitement . . . he wasn't sure which. He allowed his gaze to trail her body. The British were a sly lot. They had dressed their agent in a blouse and skirt that accentuated her small waist, rounded hips and pert breasts. This woman didn't even need to open her mouth to use her sex appeal to help her out of a sticky situation with a German soldier, particularly if he didn't have his wits about him. She just had to smile and wriggle those hips of hers, or arch her back provocatively . . . or feign interest in every word he uttered.

'Yeah, I want to know,' he said, surprised at the liquid sound of his voice.

She straightened. 'I sell cosmetics, hence this ridiculously fashionable outfit. It would have been better if they'd given me trousers.'

'No, it wouldn't.'

She looked up, surprised. 'Why?'

'Because a draconian law left over from the revolution bans women from wearing trousers unless they have permission from the local authority. It's poorly enforced but it's better not to raise suspicions by asking.'

She thought for a moment. 'Then I'll get myself some culottes instead. I can't run around in this skirt.' He almost admired her determination to surpass any hurdle placed in her way. Almost.

'Did my cosmetics arrive?'

'They should have arrived in the latest drop.'

Her hands fell from her hips. 'You don't know?'

'I have been busy, on another mission. We are travelling back to Paris together. Are you hungry?' Without waiting for a reply, he withdrew a parcel and offered it to her. 'Here.'

She looked at it but didn't take it. 'Only if you eat with me.'

He realised he was hungry and reluctantly nodded. He opened the package, tore the baguette in two and offered one half to her. They ate in silence, watching each other over their crusts of bread.

'It doesn't have to be difficult,' she said. 'Between us, I mean. I know you don't like me.'

'I've never said that.'

'You don't have to. It's written all over your face.'

He frowned.

'There. Right there.' She pointed to his forehead. 'I could plant a row of potatoes in that furrow.'

He almost laughed . . . almost. He shoved the last piece of bread into his mouth and chewed in silence as he watched her.

'What's your name?' she asked.

'Pierre Lesieur.'

'Hello, Pierre.'

They had been talking in French since her arrival and she'd not made a mistake yet. Even her greeting had the French warmth of friendship. She deserved to be praised for completing the tough training. He knew the failure rate was high yet her arrival proved that she had graduated. Yet . . . he had the distinct feeling she didn't need his praise.

'I won't let my father's death affect me, Pierre.'

'I don't think you will have a choice if it suddenly does.'

'You sound like you talk from experience.'

'We had better leave.' He brushed the crumbs from his hands, ignoring her last words. 'There's a train leaving Lorient in a couple of hours.'

'How are we going to get there?'

'Can you ride a bike?'

She followed him as he made his way deeper into the basement.

'Yes. Why?'

He retrieved two bikes from the shadows. 'Because I bought these yesterday and I hadn't planned for an alternative if you couldn't.'

* * *

He led the way, keeping a steady pace that was both speedy but did not leave her behind. On occasion, he glanced over his shoulder to check she was close behind. To his surprise, she always was. He grudgingly respected her physical fitness, but still resented having her as an agent. She had spent most of the war in a county barely touched by it and this was her first mission. He had been hoping for someone with a little more experience.

They approached La Laita estuary, which he had planned to cross by boat before heading inland towards Lorient to board the train for Paris. The presence of the Wehrmacht in the distance slowed his approach to a stop. Marie arrived at his side.

'German soldiers?' she asked quietly.

'Yes.'

'Will they give us trouble?'

He clenched his jaw. Her inexperience was already showing through.

'You have lived with them for some time now,' she continued. 'It is not an unreasonable question to ask.'

'Isn't it? I've not lived with them by choice.' He realised he was being unfair and he should enlighten her. 'In the beginning they praised our architecture, our art and our city. "Paris is beautiful," they said. "Every soldier must visit this wonder at least once in their life." But soon things changed.

'They stifled our press and radio. They took over our hotels, theatres and restaurants. They defiled our grand architecture with their Third Reich banners and replaced French signs with German ones. Paris had been gifted to them on a silver platter and they took it and still wanted more. The politicians should have known it would never be enough.

'Now they send our men to work in their factories and fight in their army. Their earlier pretence of friendship fooled those who were there to protect France. Now they are aggressive and resentful. Their false promises that were written on paper have been burned to ashes long ago.'

He realised he had spoken too long, spilling his guts in his attempt to incise a fetid boil. 'Will they give us trouble? you ask. Of course they will! They have been doing that ever since they set foot on French soil. Why should they stop now?' He felt her watching him and looked down at her. He frowned. 'But I think you know this, already,' he added more quietly.

'I knew the facts, but I could only imagine the heartache behind them. Hearing what you have just said . . . well, now I feel that I know some of that too.'

For a moment he could not drag his eyes away from hers. She appeared genuine, even sympathetic. He despised sympathy. She knew nothing of what really broke his heart.

'You don't believe me?' she asked, her gaze searching for something in his eyes. His soul perhaps? She wouldn't find it.

'It doesn't matter what you feel. It doesn't matter what any of us feels. Feeling is a luxury we can't afford.' He searched his pocket for his papers. 'Get your papers ready. They will want to see them. Lorient has become a U-boat base so the port will have a heavy military presence.'

She looked about her. Finding that they were quite alone, she suddenly turned on him. He discovered that she had quite a temper when she wanted to show it.

'I know you don't want me here. You have certainly made no secret that you would have preferred a man.'

'I said I was *expecting* a man.'

'Well, I have news for you . . . I am not the first female agent and I won't be the last. I am here now, so you better make the most of it. Let me know when you have grown up enough to cope and perhaps we will make a good team.' Without waiting for a reply, she rode off on her bike, did not look back and cycled straight towards the Wehrmacht patrol. For the first time in his adult life, he could not think of a word to say.

By the time he caught her up, the soldier was already looking at her identity papers. She looked a little nervous, but not overly so. It would not be the first time they would be checked and at some point the fraudulent papers would need to be tested, but he hadn't expected it to be so soon. He had hoped by travelling inland, they would avoid the more concentrated patrols along the coast, but it seemed the initial test of her papers could not be delayed. The soldier glanced from one to the other. He asked her where she was going in German, but she didn't understand. Pierre did.

'She is travelling with me. We are going to Paris.'

The soldier looked at him. 'Why?'

'I own the *Fleur de Lis*.'

The soldier stared at him.

'It is a hotel. A favourite of the German army. I am surprised you do not know it. It has featured in *Pariser Zeitung*. I believe that is the newspaper German soldiers enjoy reading. The exchange rate favours you. You should pop in when you are next in Paris.'

The soldier returned Marie's papers to her and offered his hand for his own. He handed them over and watched in silence as the soldier studied them.

'This hotel of yours—' he said, as he casually studied his paperwork — 'is a long way from here.' He lifted his gaze and stared at him.

'Too far. No doubt the staff will be running amok in my absence.' He glanced at Marie. 'Which is why I am bringing this lady back with me this time. A mistress on the other side of France is very inconvenient.'

A smile formed on the soldier's lips and he returned his paperwork. 'The *Fleur de Lis*. I shall look forward to visiting it when I am next there.'

They did not speak again until they reached the station. Lorient was a strategic target for Allied bombing, due mainly to its concentration of U-boats. However, bombing was inaccurate and many buildings, including the town itself, had suffered great damage. It was a sombre journey and it was only when they were on the station platform, did Marie express her surprise that he could speak German and asked him to translate what he had said to the soldier. Needless to say, she was furious at the role he had given her.

'You said I was *what*?'

'Do I need to repeat it?'

'Is your imagination so limited?'

Her whispered indignation made him want to laugh. 'I thought it was very imaginative. The likelihood that we would ever become lovers is unthinkable.'

She folded her arms. 'It would never happen!'

'Never.' He glanced at his watch. 'I just used the advantage of having a woman on the team.'

'If you think labelling me as your mistress is the only advantage of having a woman on your team then you have even less imagination than I first thought.'

The distant engine of a train suddenly exploded in an echoing roar around the station platform.

He decided to ignore her insult. 'Our train is here.'

'I can see that!' she snapped as she stepped forward to the platform edge.

Steam billowed from beneath the wheels as the train came to a screeching halt. He took her arm and retreated them both away from the steam invading the platform.

'I think we should call a truce,' he said, allowing her to shake his hand away. 'We will only attract attention if we are seen bickering all the way to Paris.'

They stepped aside to allow the passengers to disembark.

'And I think you should start taking me seriously rather than view me as an impediment,' she snapped under her breath.

Pierre began to lose patience. 'Are you usually this difficult?'

'No . . . I can be a lot worse if I'm crossed.' She abandoned him and stepped into the carriage. He hurriedly followed before someone else took his place. He followed her until she found a quiet seat by a window.

'Am I allowed to sit here?' he asked as if she had a choice. He sat down when she didn't reply.

She was mutinously staring out of the window, her usually soft lips in a firm, pressed line. She had a little furrow between her two shapely brows. He had never appreciated a woman's eyebrows before, but Marie's were the perfect frame to her dark brown eyes. Beautifully arched, they added to her facial characteristics that suggested both arrogance and innuendo. His heart lurched to his throat when he realised those sultry brown eyes were staring right back at him. When had she turned her head?

Thankfully, the platform guard blew his whistle and diverted her attention. The train began to slowly depart the station, quickly breaking out into the countryside and they both resorted to staring at it through the window in stubborn silence. The invisible, but palpable tension remained between them for the next hour as their train travelled across northern France, pausing only at the main stations along the route. By the time they reached Le Mans, they were covertly glancing at one another, but the cat-and-mouse game only stoked his resentment of her and, he suspected, her resentment of him.

'Are you going to ignore me forever?' It was the closest he could bring himself to breaking the standoff.

'I am not ignoring you. Ignoring you would not be a very grown-up thing to do . . . it is as bad as sulking.' Her accusative glance was as sharp and deadly as a knife. Her choice of words reminded him of her earlier suggestion — that he should grow up and accept he had a woman on his team. Although he didn't appreciate the inference that he was sulking, she did have a point.

The train pulled into the next station, pausing for longer than at the others. It seemed a timely rest stop to start afresh.

'When we reach Paris, I will introduce you to the others and where you will stay.'

She primly tilted her head in gratitude. 'Thank you.' To his surprise, she stood, smoothing down her skirt and tugging at her jacket with quick movements of her hands.

He frowned. 'Where are you going?'

'I think I will just stretch my legs for a minute. I suspect they are loading supplies. I won't be long.' Her suggestion was concerning, yet he felt a sense of relief when she had gone. Their self-imposed silence may have ended, but there was still something between them that put him on edge.

It wasn't long before the reason for the delayed departure became known. Six high-ranking German officers, wearing crisp uniforms, an assortment of elaborate insignia and accompanied by an entourage of obedient soldiers, boarded one of the earlier carriages. Soon the train began to move out of the station, spitting and hissing as it pulled away. Marie had yet to return. He waited a little longer, torn between showing his trust in her to return without detection, yet naturally concerned for her safety. He finally gave in to his basic instinct to protect and went in search of her. He passed through two carriages before he found her. She was bracing herself against the movement of the train, attempting to pass the high-ranking officers who had blocked her path with their splayed legs. It was as if she was caught in their booted net, its sinister intent disguised as jovial banter. Although every nerve in his body was alight with the instinct to go to her aid, converse with the officers in German and extract her from their circle on the same pretext as before, he tightened his jaw and held back.

The soldiers near the windows were standing, watching the new entertainment with hungry voyeurism in their eyes. Occasionally, they burst into laughter at a joke or comment made by their superiors, keen to show their loyalty even if it was to the detriment of Marie's character. In turn, their responsive audience only fed the six officers' enjoyment and their teasing of Marie intensified. A hand slid up her thigh, causing Pierre to grit his teeth but he held back, noticing that the officer with a smirk of contempt on his face also held a gun in his hand. The gun rested nonchalantly on his thigh and Pierre had no doubt that this man was capable of killing someone with as much indifference as he held the weapon

129

in a crowded carriage. Marie's eyes fleetingly caught Pierre's. Although she was careful to show no recognition, he knew instinctively that she had just told him to stay back.

He gripped the carriage doorway and watched, noticing for the first time that she was more in control of the situation than he had first thought. She did not pretend to understand what they were saying but laughed innocently when they did. This amused the officers, as not everything they were saying was for a lady's hearing, yet it allowed them to be lulled into a false sense of her innocence. One attempted to speak in French. His French was poor, almost unintelligible, but her reaction of delight and praise, puffed his chest out in pride. As they smiled and raked their appreciative gazes over her, each one diverted by her flirtatious innocence, she casually, one by one, stepped over their splayed legs and eased herself past their uniformed bodies. She was almost past them when suddenly the smirking officer with the gun stood up, walked towards her and blocked her path entirely.

Pierre's throat dried. He recognised the type of man he was. Arrogant, controlling, uncaring. It was not Marie's charms that had brought him to his feet, but his need to be the centrepiece in front of his peers. He was *that* boy who would stamp on a butterfly to show off to his friends. Such boys grew into equally flawed men who were unpredictable, unreliable and dangerous to know.

Marie's gaze lifted to Pierre's as the officer pointed his gun to the V-neckline of her blouse. She had recognised his type too. Silently, she told Pierre to stay where he was. If he intervened and won, the battle as a whole would be lost. All the German soldiers in the carriage would turn on them both.

He clenched his fist as he watched the barrel slide like a seductive finger to her breasts. The jovial banter around them instantly died to an icy silence, but for the sound of the relentless rattle of train tracks beneath their feet. The officer leered at her, seemingly feeding on the unease that had enveloped them. Yet Marie showed neither fear nor contempt for the man staring down at her. Instead, she sought the officer who had attempted to speak French earlier.

The officer stood and spoke harshly, telling the soldier to put his gun away and not spoil their day. As others agreed, he saw he was outnumbered and eventually he lowered his gun. Grudgingly, he sat down to the relief of all around, as Marie threaded her way past the remaining splayed legs to the safety of the corridor and Pierre.

Teasing, threat and physical assault, it seemed, had its boundaries, too, thought Pierre. The boundaries were indefinable and could never be relied upon, but it seemed there were boundaries, nevertheless.

CHAPTER THIRTEEN

Pierre leaned forward in his seat. 'We are here.'

The sign for Montparnasse train station came into view. Charlotte breathed in deeply, savouring the fullness in her lungs. She had finally reached the city where her mother grew up and always secretly grieved for, despite her best attempts not to show it.

'I'll introduce you to the others tomorrow. We meet in a house in the country, but we will need to take another train out of Paris to get there. It's been a long day. I'll take you to your apartment where you can catch up on your sleep.'

'Do I look tired?' she asked.

He ran a hand over the stubble on his chin. 'You hide it better than I.'

'Then you must rest too.'

A humourless smile curved his lips. 'Later. I have been away from my hotel for too long. I need to show my face. I trust the manager with my life, but an owner needs to be around occasionally or questions will be asked.'

The platform was crowded with strangers in a hurry. Charlotte followed Pierre closely as he stepped down from the train and into the cacophony of conversations, trundling wheels and announcements. They made their way through the bustling crowd to the back of the train where Pierre arranged for the unloading of their bikes.

'Petrol is in short supply. The German army have priority,' Pierre needlessly explained above the noise. 'Now everyone travels around Paris by bicycle.'

As they left the bustle of Paris's busiest station, Charlotte noticed the Eiffel Tower in the distance, but managed to stop herself from showing her excitement. She was meant to be a Parisian and should take the view for granted.

'Can we go up it?' she asked quietly.

'Only if you are a German officer. It's not open to the public anymore.' He stared at it in the distance before adding sadly, 'Besides, it is not the same as it once was. They have defaced it with their flag and banner, covered its base with barbed wire and now greet people with primed machine guns.' His voice softened. 'Come back when Paris is liberated, and we will go up it together.'

Their eyes met and she wondered if he had meant the invitation. She had not seen him this way before — as a man she could discover the delights of Paris with. Since that telephone call all those months ago, she had been too busy trying to prove her worth, too focused on the job in hand, too busy hiding from the grief of her father's death. How better to hide from it than to replace her old life with her mother's earlier one and attack those that had killed her father? Yet . . . at this very moment, she almost forgot that she was an agent who had been trained to kill.

She felt heat rise from her breasts to her neck. For the first time she let herself see his expressive hazel eyes and dark lashes that accentuated the intensity of his lingering gaze. And in that slow languid moment, she wondered how different things would be if they were simply two people visiting Paris in the summer. In that parallel universe, she could dare to surrender to her desire to lean into his body, rest her head upon his shoulder and stay for a while in silent acceptance of his suggestion — and in her wild fantasy he would welcome it.

He cleared his throat noisily and she tore her gaze away from him. 'We better be on our way. Stay close behind. There are more bicycles than vehicles, but it is still easy to get lost.'

They travelled northeast, along wide, straight avenues, lined by tall, blanched buildings with stone-carved balconies and railings. On first impressions, Paris appeared normal, bustling with people all with something to do. It even had the air of a holiday destination, with cafés full, shops busy and newspaper stands selling papers.

But first impressions rarely last long. Evidence of its occupation slowly emerged, growing all the more sinister as each new sign made itself known as they cycled through the streets of Paris. Government buildings were adorned by German flags, prices were high and shortages were evident from the carefully arranged shop window displays to lines of customers for bread. If the headline title, *Pariser Zeitung*, was anything to go by, the permitted newspapers were in German too. A queue trailed out of City Hall where, Pierre told her, allotted food coupons were distributed depending on age.

'The food coupons are inadequate and many are starving,' explained Pierre. 'The black market thrives here but be careful who you trust. Only our *visitors* eat well.'

The word "visitor" was spat out with contempt but used with the knowledge they were entering an area more frequented by France's occupiers. This part of Paris was beautiful and drew an abundance of uniformed soldiers to the area where they were enjoying the afternoon sunshine, appreciating the sights of Paris and eating and drinking at its quaint cafés and elite restaurants, which probably only thrived, thought Charlotte, thanks to their links to the black market or German army. Yet, despite living side by side, there seemed little contact between the Parisian citizens and the soldiers, as they each strolled down the street and rested at fountains individually or in groups. However, Charlotte's astute observation was not fooled and she soon noticed one Frenchwoman searching for her neighbours' twitching curtains before welcoming a uniformed soldier inside her home as if he was her lover. Charlotte found this revelation of occupation particularly difficult to accept. If she felt her anger rise, how must Pierre feel?

Charlotte's observant mind continued to forensically take in her surroundings. Each nuance should not be new to her if she was to fool those around her that she was a Parisian. She noted the lack of leather in the shoe shops and softly remarked upon the rubber and canvas shoes. Pierre quietly told her leather had long ago been diverted to make boots for the German army. Occasionally they would come across large posters in big red-and-black lettering, announcing, and at the same time celebrating, the mass executions of French resistance fighters as a warning to those who might be tempted to fight back. Sometimes the posters were graffitied with a large Churchill V sign, but many were left alone to exhibit their grim news until they weathered in the elements.

'The majority of French people are *Attentistes*,' said Pierre as they rested before one such post. 'They are just keeping their heads down and waiting for the war to end. Perhaps in their heart, waiting for another country to save them for their own government did not. Whatever happens, they will fall in with whatever side wins. I hate them for not doing more, but I also understand. Sometimes it takes all one's energy to just survive and the fear of death is too great to fight back.'

Charlotte was beginning to understand this strange limbo the French people had found themselves in. Although the restaurants were busy, she realised it was all a facade. The customers smiled and the meals were served outside on the pavement, just as her mother had described, but the meals lacked meat and fresh produce and the coffee was probably more chicory than not. It was the perfect setting for a black market to thrive, smuggled in through the back door from outlying farmers hoping to make a profit, under the noses of paid-off French police officers. No one could be trusted, yet to survive, one had to trust. It was a constant conflict of tension that at any moment could snap . . . with good cause or by mistake.

Pierre had been right — although vehicles were present, they were greatly reduced and the streets teemed with bicycles. In a surreal moment, rural France met urban France as they spotted a horse and cart meandering down a Paris street under the control of a bent old man. His stoop gave the appearance of carrying the weight of two world wars upon his shoulders and his sombre defeated expression gave the impression that he had endured this all before. Perhaps he had even seen the German occupation coming long before his government had opened their eyes.

Paris, for all its vibrancy, also lacked young, and fit older men. The young had been sent to fight, the older transferred to factories in Germany. Only the very young and the withered were left behind. Pierre stood out, his athletic physique drawing the eyes of the women around him. Even some officers noted his presence, although his confident low-key confidence made them doubt their initial concerns. As they travelled northwest, the streets became narrow, lined by tall buildings which threatened to block out the sun. Another turning and they were heading towards the rustic charm of eastern Paris, with its crowded, exquisite architecture, narrow passageways and secret courtyards. Hidden away, a few streets beyond, lay one such narrow road. Pierre climbed off his bike and Charlotte followed, content to push her bike along the final enclosed walkway. Here, the sound of Paris became muted. The narrow road opened into a cobbled courtyard, surrounded by tall buildings on every side, each one adorned by vibrant green trailing ivy. One of these apartments was to become her new home, hidden from the prying eyes of the Gestapo, yet with neighbours who were able to see her every arrival and departure. She had finally arrived. Her new life as a Parisian was about to begin.

Charlotte followed Pierre to one of the doors where he withdrew two keys from his pocket and unlocked it with one of them. The communal hall was poorly lit, but clean and tidy, she observed, as she followed him up the stairs. He paused at one of the doors on the corridor and handed her the keys.

'This one is yours.' He stepped aside and watched her unlock it.

'Are you testing whether I am able to use a key?' she asked as she pushed open the door.

'You seem unsettled. I would have thought you were used to being observed. Your training was full of it.'

'I don't know what you mean,' she replied absently as she walked around her new home. The room was basic, but adequate, with a small kitchen area and even a bathroom. 'I don't think people find me so interesting that they have to stare.' She trailed her fingers along the small table and looked at their tips. They were clean. She glanced up. 'Do you?'

He was leaning against the wall, his ankles casually crossed and his arms folded. 'Do I what?'

She looked out of the window. A gutter ran down to the ground. It was old and not adequately secured to the wall.

'Find me interesting.'

She walked to the bathroom and looked out of the window. She had to crane her neck, but there was a rusty ladder. It stopped five feet from the ground but six bolts secured it firmly to the exterior wall.

'I think any man would find you interesting.'

She looked over her shoulder to find him staring at her bottom. He quickly looked away as she withdrew her head from outside the window and turned around. She had a feeling he was doing it just to test her.

'Just when I was beginning to like you, you are right back to being an arrogant chauvinistic pig.'

He chuckled. She had been right.

'Are the escape routes to your satisfaction?' he asked.

'One is better than the other, but at least they are better than none.'

He levered his weight away from the wall with a backward push of his foot. 'I have filled the cupboards with some basic provisions. Enough for a day or two until you are more settled.' He reached into his pocket and gave her some food coupons. 'These will tide you over until I can get some more.'

She flicked through them. 'Are they real?'

'No, forged, but they are indiscernible from the real ones. At least, I cannot tell.'

She glanced up at him, unsure if he was trying to put doubt in her head or trying to reassure her. She concluded that if there was a risk, he would not have given them to her.

'There is also enough food in the cupboard for the first few days . . . to allow you more time to acclimatise to Paris life.'

She inclined her head towards him. 'Thank you.' She pointed to the package on the table. 'Is this for me?'

He looked at it. 'Yes. It's the package that was dropped a few days ago.'

She tore open the brown paper and was in the midst of examining the contents, when an old woman arrived carrying a letter for Pierre. They had a brief conversation in hushed tones outside her room. He returned, shut the door behind him and tore open the letter.

'Who was that?'

'She lives downstairs. Her name is Madame Chastain and she is harmless,' he replied as his eyes raced across the letter. 'Forgetful . . . but sweet.' As an afterthought, he added, 'She is an Attentiste and is ignorant of our true reason for being here.' He lifted the page with a flick of his wrist. 'This is from my hotel manager. The officers' meeting has been brought forward to tomorrow. The guests have been arriving all day. They will dine tonight and stay overnight.' He checked his watch. 'I have to get back to the hotel. They are high-ranking officials and will expect to see the owner.'

'Is the meeting tomorrow the same one that London spoke of?'

He nodded, troubled. 'I have arranged to meet the rest of the network tomorrow. By the time we meet with the others, the meeting at the hotel will be over and the guests about to leave. Any important documents will go with them. I had hoped we could work out a plan to secure the documents with the rest of the network.'

Their eyes met for a moment.

'What time is the meal tonight?' asked Charlotte clearing her throat.

Pierre looked at the letter. 'It's at eight. The meal will last two hours. After that I will have no control over their movements. They may stay and get drunk or return to their rooms.'

'Do you think they will leave their documents in their rooms while they eat?'

'Yes. They enjoy dining with fine wine so the evening will be for leisure and entertainment. The next day they will focus on the war. I have seen it many times before.' His eyes narrowed as he realised why she had asked the question. 'But it would be an ideal time to search for any information.'

'How many rooms will need searching?'

'At a rough guess . . . ten.'

'Then I will have twelve minutes from the beginning of each search.'

He considered her suggestion as he carefully folded the letter in his hand. He shook his head. 'No. It's too dangerous.'

'But, Pierre, it is why I am here.'

'I can't let you do it. There is not enough time to search and move on to the next room.' He shoved the letter into his pocket.

'It is not about having enough time to search. It is about searching in the right places. A cistern lid left askew. A bedspread corner lifted up.'

'You think you can do it?'

'Don't you?'

'If you're caught, you will be tortured . . . even executed.'

She wanted to shout and scream that she'd just spent months training for this moment, but she had a feeling becoming hysterical would not change his mind. She began searching the cupboards.

'Would you like some coffee?' She held up an empty cup as a peace offering.

Troubled, he shook his head. 'I should be going. I have to inform London of the new development.'

She ignored his reply and began searching the cupboards again. She found the coffee. 'I think I will.' She filled the kettle and placed the cup carefully beside it, the slow familiar ritual holding his attention as she hoped it would. The silence gave them both time to consider the situation.

She leaned her back against the sink as the kettle came to the boil. 'Can you bring the meeting with the network forward?'

He shook his head. 'It will take time to get a message of the change of time to each one by courier.'

'This meeting of German officials at your hotel . . . is it common?'

'We have officials dining and drinking too much all the time,' said Pierre as he stared at the floor, 'but it is rare to have one of their meetings at the hotel.'

'Sounds like too good an opportunity to miss.'

He threw her an irritable glance.

'All those important documents,' she mused, 'just lying unattended in their rooms while they get drunk. I wonder if there will be any secrets that could turn the war in our favour.'

'I know what you're doing.'

She raised an eyebrow. 'I don't know what you mean.'

'You know exactly what I mean.' He raked a hand through his hair. 'If you insist on doing this—'

She turned off the kettle. 'I do.'

'Then you will need someone to look out for you. I can't do it. I have to attend the meal to ensure they are happy and occupied.'

'I can do it alone.'

'You can't. You need someone to keep a look out.'

She walked towards him. 'I won't need anyone if they think I'm staff. If I'm disturbed, I'll use the excuse of cleaning the room to explain why I'm there.'

'An excuse they may not accept. These are high-ranking officials. They are suspicious of everyone and care for no one.'

'Then I can't waste time. We are fortunate to have received this package in time. They told me I would be provided with cosmetics samples for my daytime occupation — and a camera. It will come in handy for tonight.' She pulled back the brown paper to reveal the contents of the package. A single, small compact camera lay amid the wrapping.

Pierre stepped forward to take a closer look. 'Does it have a film?'

'Only one roll.' She showed him the reel.

Pierre picked it up and began examining it. 'You will have to be selective on what you photograph. How many photographs is in a roll of film? Ten? Twelve?'

'Not enough, but it is all we have.'

He nodded solemnly. 'We have no choice, do we? They will be gone by this time tomorrow.'

Charlotte took the camera from him. 'No, we don't. We can't wait to involve the rest of the network.'

He nodded again, deep in thought. 'I will keep an eye on them during dinner to ensure no one leaves the table, but once the meal is over it will be harder to keep them downstairs without raising suspicions.'

'I will need a uniform.'

'I'll leave one by the back door.'

'Draw me a map of the hotel.'

Pierre found a pen and they both sat down at the table. He quickly drew a rudimentary sketch of the rear of the hotel. 'The back door is here. I will leave it unlocked. There is a cupboard here — you'll find your uniform on the bottom shelf. Behind this door is a cleaning trolley.' His pen stabbed the map two doors from it. 'This is an elevator, use it to get to the top floor. The ten rooms are along this corridor.' He scribbled down the number of the floor. 'You'll need keys. I will leave spare ones on your uniform. Twelve minutes for each room. No more. Do you have a watch?'

She shook her head.

He unbuckled his. 'Have mine.' He fastened it around her wrist, his fingers grazing hers. Their eyes met briefly again. For a fleeting second she saw the man who had offered to show her the sights of Paris. Then just as suddenly as he had appeared, he disappeared again behind his stern expression. He began to scribble some letters and numbers down on the envelope.

'These are the coordinates of the hotel. Do you think you will be able to find it?'

Charlotte compared the coordinates to a map of Paris supplied along with her cosmetic samples. 'Yes, seems easy enough to me.'

'Good. This is the time and coordinates of where we are meeting tomorrow.'

She checked the map again. 'It's quite far from Paris.'

'Is that a problem?'

'No, of course not. Will we travel together?'

'I can't.' He stood up. 'I have things to do first but will meet you there later.' He rapped a short beat on the table — two slow knocks, a pause, followed by two in quick succession. 'Knock like this and they will know you are one of us.' He reached for her wrist. She stood as he gently tilted it so he could check the time. 'I must leave. The staff will be on edge. Nazi dignitaries have a habit of doing that.' He looked up and their eyes met. He let go of her wrist. 'Here,' he mumbled as he offered her the envelope defaced by his scribblings. She reached for it, but he didn't immediately let go. 'Good luck, Mademoiselle Marie Veilleux, or whoever you are.'

He released the envelope, in effect releasing her, and went to the door. He paused with his hand on the doorknob. 'No heroics. And don't get yourself caught,' he said quietly. 'I am only just getting to know you and I have a distinct feeling I have only just touched the surface.'

Before she could reply, he'd already left, leaving her staring at the open door alone.

* * *

The *Fleur de Lis* hotel towered above her, stretching into the sky with proud defiance against all its near neighbours.

Possibly one of the grandest hotels in Paris, it was located on the long stretch of the Rue de Rivoli and had the uninhibited grandiose, arched facade, size and opulent decadence to make it the ideal hotel for the German army to enjoy. From the upper floors, guests could overlook the Tuileries Gardens, the River Seine and be within walking distance of the Arc de Triomphe at one end and the largely empty Louvre Museum on the other. She had imagined a small hotel, squashed between fading buildings around a small courtyard catered by bustling cafés. His ability to walk around Paris as a fit healthy young man, largely unquestioned by officials, became clear. He hid in plain sight, hosting their dignitaries while he conspired against them in the dark.

A small narrow path off one of the side streets took her to the entrance of a similar secret courtyard to her new residence. This area was more utility in nature. It lacked flowers and what plants were there had long ago been neglected. A bin for discarded wine bottles and several rubbish bins lined one side, while a solitary cat weaved its way among them looking for scraps. She waited in the shadows to survey the scene. There were many doors, but Pierre had told her to take the left one. It was more discreet, he had said, usually used for deliveries rather than staff. The area was quiet, the staff possibly too occupied with preparing a lavish banquet. She glanced at Pierre's watch. She only had five minutes to get to the executive landing and to start searching the rooms. Carrying out a final visual search of the area, she crossed the courtyard and slipped inside.

It was just as Pierre had described — the cupboard, the uniform, the keys. She changed quickly, found the cleaning trolley and located the staff elevator. She was about to press the button to open the doors when the elevator sprung into life and she realised it was descending, possibly with someone onboard. Just as she began to retrace her steps and hide, she heard female voices behind her. She had a choice, face the person in the lift or face the people behind her. She made the decision to stay, concluding that one usually looked forward when exiting an elevator rather than at someone standing to the side. She lowered her gaze as a pair of men's legs came into view. The elevator stopped and the porter inside slid the metal concertina door and outer rails open before walking away. She pushed her trolley into the confined space and hurriedly shut the outer and inner door, catching a glimpse of the two women who had been chatting amiably behind her and had yet to notice her. She breathed a sigh of relief as the elevator jerked into life and started its ascent.

She was relieved to see a deserted corridor in front of her as the elevator came to a smooth stop. The walls were adorned by paintings and lavish lighting, marking it different to the ones she had passed along the way. She parked her cleaning trolley between two doors, so it would not be too obvious which room she was in, yet would provide a good excuse if she was discovered. Within seconds she was inside. The room was beautifully decorated, spacious and neat, offering every comfort to the elite of France. She looked at Pierre's watch, noted the time and hurriedly began searching the room. Where does one begin searching when the treasure is unknown to you as no one knew the size or amount of the documents they needed to find? The discarded wallet left on a table? She rushed to it. Nothing, only money, family photos and receipts. Each one a snapshot into the officer's life. The drawers? She frantically pulled on each handle to reveal only neatly folded clothes or empty spaces. Under the bed? It was a childish place to hide something, yet if one did not expect to be searched . . . She skidded to her knees and found it as disappointing as the other places.

She entered the bathroom, with its casually left personal toiletries showing the vulnerable side of the guest. Tablets for indigestion. A well-worn toothbrush that desperately needed renewing. Despite his impeccably neat bedroom, he was still a flawed man. She had found nothing and her time was up. By the time the second hand had hit the twelve-minute mark, she was entering the neighbouring room and starting her search all over again.

The search became more frustrating the longer it went on. These officers had arrived with little as they did not intend to stay long. She had taken photographs of a couple of letters she had found, but knew one was too personal while the other, although formal, lacked any real information. By the time she unlocked the last bedroom, she was despondent but still on time. A quick cursory glance up and down the corridor, and within seconds she had slipped inside, quietly locking the door behind her. She slipped the key into her pocket and began frantically searching. Several minutes had passed before she saw the leather briefcase beneath the luxuriously draped window. For the briefest of moments, she could not breathe or move. This is what she had been looking for.

She knelt, dragged it to her and set about opening it. The flap was secured by two locked silver latches. She removed a pin from her hair, bent it to the right shape, entered the lock and slowly turned it, testing the resistance and changing the angle accordingly. She pushed it in a little deeper and the resistance gave way, turning the lock with a satisfactory quiet click. She repeated it on the other lock, learning from the first to achieve it in half the time. She sat back on her heels, silently amazed that her training at picking locks had worked in the field, before sliding her hand inside, slowly withdrawing an assortment of papers. A formal letter. A map. A list. Another list. A telegram. A packet of cigarettes. She retrieved her small camera and began taking photographs.

Aware she was taking longer than the other rooms, she checked Pierre's watch. To her horror she realised that at some point it had stopped. Unsure what time she had left, she captured the last item to film with the aim of leaving straight after. It was then that she first heard the footsteps outside. They were steady and measured, not hurried and panicked, but they were approaching, nonetheless. She quickly gathered all the papers, shoved them back into the briefcase and pushed it across the carpet to sit beneath the curtain. The footsteps paused at the door, as if the person outside was searching for the key. She had no time to debate how the curtain had looked when she found it, she only had enough time to scramble underneath the bed.

She watched a pair of shiny boots enter and slowly pace the room. She had been trained to kill, but she had not expected the likelihood to present itself so soon after her arrival. Her mind began to race. She had no excuse if he found her under the bed with a camera on her. Her eyes darted away from his pacing boots to skirt the room at the level of the carpet. What was available to her? The curtain had a silk cord. Did she have the height and strength to strangle him? A glass jug was on the table. A jug, with a broken edge, would make a basic, but lethal weapon. The suitcase was another, if swung hard enough, but could she get the height to knock him out? From the size of his boots he was tall. She rehearsed the scene at a frantic speed in her head. She'd stab his eyes with her fingers, smash the jug and cut his throat. Could she do it? Could she watch the life ebb from her victim's eyes? Her heart began to drum so loudly she feared he could hear it too.

The pacing slowed. She watched his boots walk towards the edge of the bed, shining in the light. Then she heard the sound of him withdrawing his gun and placing it carefully on the bedside table. Securing that gun, if the need arose, would be her priority now.

While her mind raced, he seemed to lack the energy or motivation to do much at all and she began to fear she would be trapped there all night. He lay on the bed, fully clothed and booted, his body forming a depressed shape in the mattress above her. She could hear his breathing and hoped he couldn't hear hers. She had been ready to kill, while all he wanted to do was rest. She waited for the steady breathing of sleep, but he still appeared unsettled, irritably moving an arm or a leg as if in a desperate bid to seek comfort. Then a soft rap on the door stiffened his body. The man lying above her answered in German. Charlotte found his voice oddly unthreatening. There was no curt demand or sharp retort, just the ordinary voice of an ordinary man.

The door opened and a conversation in German ensued. From the tone, the new arrival was concerned for his friend, his voice quiet and gentle, his presence unhurried and relaxed. The officer appeared to warm to his unexpected guest, even welcoming his company. It took several minutes, but eventually he swung his feet off the bed and sat up. Another brief conversation and Charlotte saw the shoes of his companion, for that was what it sounded like, enter the room too.

She froze again when she recognised Pierre's voice, speaking German. She should have been relieved, yet she couldn't help feeling surprised at the ease with which the two men spoke. She had initially thought they were friends, but surely that would be impossible. The man on the bed suddenly stood. With his weight gone, the mattress suddenly lifted too, providing her with more space to move if she needed. She watched his boots cross the room as the sound of a match was struck. The potent aroma of cigar smoke infiltrated the air as the two men talked in an unhurried casual manner. At one point they quietly chuckled as the air grew thicker with their cigars.

Charlotte's knees began to stiffen as the minutes ticked by. Neither man seemed to be in a hurry and appeared to be enjoying their time alone and away from the entertainment downstairs. Eventually their conversation came to a natural close. The officer retrieved his briefcase and followed Pierre outside, their conversation reigniting again as he slowly turned the lock in the door.

Then she was alone, hiding in the deafening silence of a smoke-filled room, feeling as if she had witnessed something she should not have as she listened to their receding footsteps and quiet laughter fade away down the corridor of the *Fleur de Lis* hotel.

CHAPTER FOURTEEN

Charlotte checked her map and concluded that, although she was still in the Ile-de-France province, she was now in the historic region of Hurepoix. Paris, with its many buildings and secret courtyards, lay northeast and only a short train journey away, yet Pierre's coordinates had brought her to this isolated three-storey house, surrounded by fields of bright yellow rapeseed.

She had almost missed the house as the short lane leading to its entrance was concealed by a cluster of dark green trees. The house itself was charming and tranquil, although a little neglected as its modest window boxes had been invaded by trailing weeds long ago. However, the open shutters, the solitary cat sunbathing on the stone steps and the array of hardy potted plants on either side of the steps, was both restful and welcoming. The isolated building, hidden away in rural France, was the perfect façade for the Pointer network to meet in secret. She knocked, as instructed, and was quickly greeted and welcomed in by a stocky middle-aged man.

He looked over her shoulder as she entered. 'Were you followed?'

She shook her head and was shown into a room with a large stone fireplace, plenty of natural light and four men sitting around a table dismantling handguns. They briefly glanced at her as they continued their firearm checking and cleaning.

'I'm Bernard,' said the man who had opened the door. 'He's Raymond. That one is Gérald. And this good-looking one is Sully.' Charlotte's gaze slid across each face, locking away their weary-lined features so she would not forget them.

'I'm Marie. Pierre is going to be late.'

She placed the package she had been secretly carrying all this time onto the table, glad to finally deliver it.

Bernard jerked his head towards it. 'What's that?'

'Crystals for your wireless,' she said, taking a seat. She could feel their wariness dissolve around her as Raymond reached for it and tore it open.

'About time!' he said, showing them to the others. He smiled at her and she could not help smiling back.

She withdrew the camera and placed it on the table too. 'Can anyone develop photographs? The meeting at the hotel was brought forward so we had to search the rooms last night. I found a briefcase full of documents and took as many photographs as I could. I don't know if there is anything of use.'

Gérald reached for it. 'I can. How many did you take?'

'I don't know. As many as I could before I ran out of time.'

He turned the camera in his hands. 'It's a Minox. Made in Latvia. The British must be buying their spy cameras from them now. If you have used the whole film, there should be eight photographs.' Her concern that he might damage the film inside instantly melted away. This man knew about photography.

'He is our forger,' explained Bernard. 'He is used to developing photographs.' They watched Gérald leave the room with the camera cradled in his hands as if it were a delicate bird. 'He will be gone for some time. Would you like some coffee?'

Charlotte felt the tension in her shoulders drain away. For the first time since leaving her lodgings this morning, she felt in safe company.

Bernard noticed. 'It's not easy travelling through France when you are carrying something that could get you killed. We have all been there. Sit and rest a while. Now is the time to enjoy a hot drink and some conversation.'

Charlotte smiled as she accepted the chair offered. 'Coffee would be lovely. Thank you.'

A pleasant time followed as she got to know each man. The main members of the Pointer network were welcoming, no doubt helped by her introductory gift of vital equipment and potential secret information. However, despite their friendliness, each one held a barely suppressed feeling of frustration that they could not do more or act quicker to liberate France.

After a few minutes, Sully came to sit beside her. He had been quiet, content to listen to his colleagues' frustration and taking no part. However, Charlotte soon discovered his initial reserve was not down to shyness. In fact, Sully was probably the most confident of them all, as his character was calm and considered, which was exactly what she needed right now.

'Can I get you anything more to drink?' he asked as he pulled out a chair.

'No thank you, I've had enough.'

He sat down next to her. 'I'm afraid our coffee is not as good as it used to be. It's been a long time since I've drank good quality coffee.'

She smiled. 'Although excellent company can make anything taste better.'

He laughed and looked around him. 'Not the company I keep. Are you with us for long?'

'I don't know. It depends when London calls me back. How long have you been doing this?'

'Long enough. My last network fell. Pointer is a new start.' He leaned back in his chair. 'I would rather spend my time doing other things.'

'Like what?'

'I fancy having a small farm one day.'

He didn't look like a farmer. 'Really?'

'Yes.'

'Have you any experience?'

'I have never done it in my life.'

She laughed.

He smiled. 'You don't think I can? I think it will be easy. A few goats here—' he waved a hand to his right — 'a few pigs there.' He pointed to something in the distance. 'A few cows in the shed on that hill over there.'

She pretended to look at his imaginary shed. 'No chickens?'

'You think I should have chickens?'

She nodded in earnest. 'Most definitely. No farm is complete without chickens. Where will you get your eggs?'

'I thought a shop.'

'The shop is too far away. You live in the countryside now.'

His eyes softened and he smiled another smile just for her. 'I hadn't thought of that.'

They stared at one another in silence as the others chatted around them. She found him intriguing, with a roguish curve to his smile and teasing eyes that widened as he waited for her replies.

'Did you parachute in? It's an unpredictable and dangerous way to arrive.' His interest in her appeared genuine. His conversation was refreshing, but most importantly, he treated her as an equal. If she had not been trained to conceal her identity, she could easily imagine sharing every detail of her life with him before it grew dark outside.

'You know I can't tell you that, other than it was successful.'

'And for that I am thankful,' he replied softly next to her ear.

Gérald returned.

'Were you able to develop the photos? Is there anything of importance?' she asked.

He helped himself to some coffee. 'They are drying. It's hard to tell at the moment. The room is dark and the details on the documents are small. A few more minutes and we will be able to examine them with a magnifying glass.'

'May we look?' asked Sully, pre-empting her own request. After giving reassurances that they would keep the room dark, Gérald agreed that they could.

* * *

The room smelled of chemicals and was lit by a low-wattage, red bulb, which cast a meagre light and the power to only highlight the outlines of the dark shapes in the room. As her eyes became accustomed to the darkness, Charlotte could see a row of photographs pinned to a line of string cast over several shallow trays. She walked along the line, hoping to see something exciting, but Gérald was right, the light was so poor and the print on the documents too small, that it was impossible to see any details without a good light source and spyglass.

'What do you think of Pierre?'

The question caught her by surprise. 'I don't know him very well. I only met him a couple of days ago.'

'But you have known me for less time and I would like to think you have an opinion of me by now.'

She saw Sully smile in the glow of the red light. She found it infectious and smiled back.

'Yes, I have an opinion of you.'

'Favourable, I hope.'

'It is . . . for now.' She heard him chuckle as she looked closer at one of the photographs. 'Why does it matter what I think about Pierre?' she asked, turning to look at him again.

'To see if I have competition.'

'How can you have competition when there is no prize to be won?'

Sully tilted his head to one side. 'Is that a warning to me to stop flirting with you?'

She took another step along the line of photographs and feigned interest in the next one, yet keenly aware he was waiting for her answer.

'I wasn't aware we were.'

Sully laughed. 'I need to brush up on my skills if the woman I am attempting to flirt with doesn't realise that I am.'

She raised an eyebrow. 'That is not for me to say. Besides I have known you for such a short time, which is a little early for flirting.'

He shrugged. 'War speeds things up. There is little reason to wait too long when time is so precious.'

Silence fell between them. The smell of the chemicals seemed more potent and began to claw at her throat. Sully was right, war did speed things up, but his talk of flirting still felt a little out of step with the normal way of things.

'There is something about Pierre . . .' he added more seriously. He left the name in the air to linger, his silence telling her more than the words he'd just spoken.

'You don't trust him?' she asked, surprised.

'I didn't say that.'

'You didn't need to.'

'It is hard to trust someone whose second tongue is German. It's even harder to trust someone who appears to enjoy their company.'

She paused. Sully had voiced her own concerns and she was tempted to talk candidly to him, but instead, she pressed her lips firmly shut. After all, she had only just met him. Instead, she turned to look at the last photograph.

Sully came to stand behind her. 'Perhaps I should have kept my concerns to myself.'

'Perhaps . . . perhaps not.'

Sully lowered his voice. 'It would be best if you didn't mention what I said to the others.'

She nodded curtly.

Sully moved a little closer. 'I can trust you, can't I?'

It was a legitimate question to ask yet it still felt off to her and she couldn't understand why. She was usually good at reading people, but Sully was harder than most, and if his concern about Pierre was right, it meant she had read Pierre wrong too.

She sidestepped and turned to face him. 'This is a little intense,' she teased. 'Of course, you can trust me. I trust you.'

'Is this a private party or can anyone join in?'

Charlotte jumped at the sound of Pierre's voice coming from the shadows of the door.

'How long have you been there?' asked Sully.

'Not long enough, it seems.' He emerged into the red light, which highlighted the deep furrows between his brows, giving him a devilish appearance. His gaze travelled along the line of photographs. 'I've just arrived.' His eyes finally settled on her. 'Congratulations, Marie. It appears you were successful. Good work.' But despite his compliment, he didn't look happy.

Charlotte had the sudden desire for fresh air, but to get it she would have to pass close by him. The thought made her stay where she was and endure the fumes.

'We won't know until we have had a chance to examine them,' said Sully.

Pierre looked Sully up and down with a cursory glance. 'Which is why I have interrupted your little party. Gérald thinks they should be ready. He's just finishing his cigarette and then he'll be here. I thought you would want to know.'

* * *

Charlotte stared at the eight photographs on the table. There was a letter confirming the meeting at the *Fleur de Lis* hotel, several with detailed lists of tanks, planes and ammunitions and their intended destination, a diagram of a flying missile titled V1, and a map of northern France which was too small to decipher. One photograph was too blurred and the final one was a document that no one could make sense of. It was all rather disappointing.

'I should have been more discerning. I just photographed the first ones I could get my hands on.'

Sully patted her hand. 'You did your best.'

Pierre's chair scraped back noisily as he gathered the photographs. 'They may come in useful one day.'

'I can't see how a shopping list, a diagram and a map will be helpful. I have a map already. I shouldn't have wasted time photographing it. I was disturbed.' She looked pointedly at Pierre and saw her meaning dawning on his face.

'You were under the bed?'

'Yes.'

'I saw your trolley but thought you'd left in a hurry.'

'You were meant to keep them downstairs.'

'And you were meant to be gone by then.'

Raymond dropped a map on the table. 'Fighting won't help. Let's look at a proper, more detailed map and see if any buildings, names or terrain can be linked to what we have found.' It seemed a logical thing to do so Bernard, Sully, Gérald and Pierre crowded round it, Charlotte's photographs temporarily forgotten. She picked them up and began going through them again with a magnifying glass. As she did so, she noticed the address on the list detailing the ammunition, tanks and planes.

'Vent Sombres. Is that a building?'

Bernard answered without looking up. 'No. It's an industrial facility. It makes cars.'

She lowered her magnifying glass. 'Have you been there lately?'

The men looked up at her.

Charlotte dropped the photograph on the table in front of them. 'I think the Germans have taken control of it. Probably since France fell. This order is for thousands of military vehicles and planes, suggesting it's been in operation for a while. And according to this,' she said, dropping the photograph of the diagram on the table too, 'it's going to start making V1s, too, whatever they are.'

'How do you know that?' asked Sully, taking the photograph of the diagram and staring at it.

'Because on the back of the V1 diagram was the same address as the order, only I didn't get a chance to photograph it.'

Pierre straightened. For a moment she thought she saw respect in his eyes.

'Looks like a flying bomb,' said Bernard as he took the photograph from Sully.

Raymond stabbed a finger on the map he'd been looking at. 'There it is! Vent Sombres. It's located near a small village not twenty miles from here.'

Pierre took control. 'We need to let London know.' He turned to Sully. 'Get a pencil and write this down. Pointer circuit now operating. Six-person team secure. Operation Rory completed. Potential military producing facility identified. Coordinates . . .'

He beckoned to Raymond. 'What are the coordinates?' Raymond read them out and Sully scribbled them down.

'Facility under surveillance. Report again in two days. Will need explosive drop.'

He looked over Sully's shoulder to check the message. 'Can you send it?'

'I will have to encode it first. It's a long message. I only have thirty minutes before the Nazis detect the signal.'

'Then break the message in two. Cut here . . . at the end of "Operation Rory completed". Find another safe spot and send the rest. You need to keep on the move.'

'I could do with someone to watch out for me.'

'Bernard will. He knows some morse if you are incapacitated.' He indicated Raymond and Gérald. 'I want you two to watch the facility. Note the movements of everyone and everything. If we get the go-ahead from London to blow it up, I want to know how to cause the maximum destruction but the least deaths. We must remember that the workers are French. They are likely to be on our side, despite what they are building.' Pierre looked about him. 'We'll meet again next week. Hopefully, Sully will have received a reply by then.' As if he had given a silent instruction, the men began packing up and leaving one by one. He turned to Charlotte. 'How will you utilise the coming days?'

'Live the life of the person I'm meant to be. Mademoiselle Marie Veilleux sells cosmetics and knows Paris well. I will sell cosmetics, shop, walk in the parks and drink coffee in the best roadside cafés. I'll peruse the books by the Seine and live my mother's life.'

'Are you reminding me of my own words?'

She was tempted to say yes, but the truth was, she wasn't. 'No, I'm no use to London if I remain a misfit who can be easily identified as a non-Parisian if interrogated. I need to build up my alibi and customer list. I need to have witnesses that will be able to vouch that I live in Paris. I need to learn what it is like to live in an occupied city. And I only have a few days to do it.'

He slung his rucksack over his shoulder, but there was respect in his eyes. 'I expected you to argue that I hadn't given you a job.'

'It would be foolish to delay building up my backstory. And you are not a fool.'

He paused at the door. 'You did well last night.'

'Thank you.'

He remained in the doorway but didn't look at her. 'I hope the glimpse into your mother's past life brings you joy. Don't let her absence make you feel sad.' He rested his hand on the frame of the door but still wouldn't meet her eye. 'Paris should be enjoyed and loved. When it is loved, it comes back to life.'

'I won't.'

'Lock up and put the key under the pot in the back garden when you leave. See you here in a week.' He paused again. 'And get yourself some of those culottes you talked about. You'll need to be able to run when you blow up that factory.'

He left before she could say goodbye, shutting the door firmly behind him. Only minutes before, the room had bustled with excitement and tension as their mission was finally revealed. Now she felt a strange sense of deflation as she stood alone in the deafening silence.

She slowly gathered her photographs, hid them under a floorboard and locked up the house. But as she cycled away, she could not shake off the feeling that something just wasn't right.

By the time she entered the suburbs of Paris, the vague feeling had lifted, and by the time she cycled into the heart of Paris, the noise, smell and culture had absorbed every niggling unease. She had a week to explore the delights and culture of Paris and build a fake life. At last she had the chance to see the city through her mother's young eyes. Isn't that what she had always wanted? Pierre had even encouraged her, which seemed unfathomable as only a few months ago he had railed against her desire to do it. Pierre had changed, unless he was just keen to have her out of the way? The niggling unease returned, the cause of which she had not quite worked out.

* * *

For the next few days, she cycled the streets of Paris selling cosmetics. She was greeted with a mixture of suspicion and relief, the former as a result of fear, the latter as a result that she represented normality in a time when nothing was normal.

The remainder of the week was spent walking in her mother's footsteps. She visited the Bois de Boulogne park whose lake was still edged with tall trees, but due to the limited food coupons available, the starving Parisians' generosity had severely waned and the once healthy swans looking for bread now looked scrawny compared to those of her mother's youth. She imagined her teenage mother first arriving in Paris and eventually leaving at eighteen after falling in love with her father. Her mother had said the park was filled with romance, but Charlotte suspected the number of courting couples had also dwindled since her mother's day. Their absence in such a romantic venue resulted in a sombre mood that could dampen even the brightest of smiles.

She visited the Pac Monceaux, which her mother had considered the prettiest park of them all. Artists, with big moustaches, still painted by the water's edge, but their paintings were dark and depressing, reflecting the creator's mood. The excited huddles of children that her mother had often spoke of were missing too, their parents too fearful to let them run wild while short-tempered German soldiers patrolled their streets. There were no mobile ice-cream carts or restaurant specialities, and although the morning air could still be filled with the sweet aroma of freshly baked bread, the long snaking queues reminded her yet again of the shortages and that soon the shelves would be bare. The opera house and city life, which, from her mother's lips, did not stop at midnight, were silent and dark by curfew. As for the bookstalls along the Seine — they still remained for the time being, although each book was scrutinised before it was allowed.

A constant line of old men fished in the River Seine to supplement their rations or the black market, whichever the need was greater for that day. Their presence reminded Charlotte she needed to acquire more rations, too, but it wasn't until her fifth day in Paris that she felt brave enough to join the long queue for food, acutely aware that the coupons burning in her pocket were fake. She had heard that forgery was punishable by death, yet she had no choice but to trust Pierre's reassurance that they looked real, as her small number of provisions were dwindling fast. The queue she had joined shuffled forward and she did the same, advancing one small precious step closer to the counter. The woman in front of her looked tired and worried, and the old man behind, weary and solemn. The novelty of communal waiting must have worn thin long ago.

A commotion in the street turned everyone's heads. Charlotte had noticed that Paris under occupation was an unusually quiet city. The cacophony of hawkers, street minstrels, performers, traffic and construction work had severely diminished since the booted occupiers had marched into their city. Due to such quietness, any loud noises, particularly shouts and screams, brought a nervous response from everyone around.

She could see that the French police had broken down a door on the opposite side of the street and were in the midst of dragging what appeared to be a priest outside. Yet despite the raised angry voices around him, the priest stood proud and erect as his fellow countrymen accused him of keeping "illegals" in his attic. Charlotte, unable to drag her eyes away, watched horrified as several young men soon emerged from the building with their hands on their heads. The men were herded out into the street, then pushed and prodded until they were forced to form a small huddle. The priest was made to join them, too. In the hope of raising their spirits, he began to say a prayer, his voice steady and loud above the Gendarmes' barking orders.

'They have found him out,' said the woman in front of her in the queue. She crossed herself with a well-practised slide of her fingers through the air. 'May the Lord welcome them safely and spare them any pain.'

'Hush!' said the old man behind Charlotte. 'Keep your mouth shut or someone will hear you and you'll be next!'

His warning angered the woman. 'You fool!' she spat. 'We are all going to be next!'

'Not if you keep your head down and do as they say,' grumbled the man under his breath.

'And I suppose that you think we should work with our oppressors too! Or perhaps you mean work *for* them—' her eyes darted to the Gendarmes ordering the men into a waiting vehicle — 'like those pigs over there! Do you think the Nazis can keep us under their thumbs so well without their help?'

Two people in front of the queue turned around and shushed her, too.

'You will get us all killed, you stupid woman!' hissed another.

The woman fell silent, to everyone's relief, and the queue shuffled forward again just as they had before. Outside in the street, the engine of the vehicle, unusually loud thanks to the absence of motor cars, sped off and then gradually receded into the distance with its terrified passengers inside.

Charlotte's stomach churned, her appetite fading along with any hope those men had. The truth was that the Paris her mother once knew no longer existed. She had hoped it did, but in reality, the facade remained but its soul was stifled. There was a genuine fear among its people that it may never rise again.

'Coupon!'

Charlotte blinked and realised that she had reached the head of the queue. She fumbled for her food coupons, selected two and slid them across the counter. The man who received them squinted through his glasses at them. His vein-threaded hands were gnarled with rheumatism and his lined expression looked as weary as the rest. One lens of his glasses was slightly chipped and had yet to be repaired, yet the eyes behind them were as sharp as his brain as they flitted across the markings to check the print. He looked up at her and half smiled as she felt herself blush. She would never know if he realised they were forgeries or not, but she would often wonder in the days that followed, why, after he fetched her allotted food items and slid them across the counter, he had felt the need to pat her hand before he sent her away.

* * *

Four days later, they were sitting around the same table again — at least everyone except Sully. They sat in silence, the time appearing to pass slower than normal as they waited to hear from London. Charlotte found herself glancing up at Pierre, imagining the responsibility he would have at planning the next mission. At least she was getting used to being in France. She had been in the country for only nine days, but her week building a fake life had been helpful as well as successful. She had a list of customers to memorise, had learned to navigate the city with ease and had purchased clothing more suitable for sabotage. She had been stopped only once, but a cursory look at her identification card and a couple of easy questions and she was on her way again.

Pierre looked up then and their eyes met briefly, as if he had seen her memory of talking to the officer. Caught looking, they both made a conscious effort to look away.

Finally, to everyone's relief, the secret knock came. Bernard rushed to the door to let Sully in.

'Well?' asked Pierre.

Sully handed him the decoded message. 'We have been given the go-ahead. Explosives are being dropped tonight. Coordinates are at the bottom.' He smiled and winked at Charlotte, a gesture that was not missed by Pierre, and settled into the seat beside her.

'We can start planning now. Raymond, Gérald, what has your reconnaissance discovered?'

Gérald unrolled a map he had drawn of the facility. 'We estimate there are at least two thousand French civilians working here. Raymond knows someone whose neighbour works there.'

Pierre looked at Raymond. 'Can you trust him?'

'Absolutely. He says they are the same workforce who used to make the cars. Interestingly, he said they still work the same hours as his neighbour is the caretaker and opens and shuts the factory.'

'Why is that important?' asked Charlotte.

Pierre returned his attention to the map. 'Because it will mean the factory is empty most of the evening and night. It gives us an opportunity to blow it up when there is no one inside.'

'Raymond and I have been watching the factory every day for the past week.' Gérald pointed to an area of the map. 'We know they leave at six in the evening and return at eight in the morning by this route. This area—' he swept his hand over an area of scribbles — 'is woodland. It made good cover for us to spy on them. We could hide here.' He pointed to another area. 'This is a fuel tank store. This area is the factory floor, held up by five pillars.'

Pierre pointed to the map. 'We could plant the explosives here, here, here and here. If we blow up each pillar, it will collapse the roof. We should also set the fuel tank store alight. A fire should do the rest of the work for us. I will pour a trail of fuel to the store.'

'How will we get in?' asked Sully.

Raymond withdrew a small, battered tin from his pocket and placed it in the centre of the map. The paint was worn in several areas, exposing the silver tin beneath.

Pierre jerked his head towards it. 'What's that?'

'My contact loves France and wanted to help. He was aware that his neighbour would have a set of keys so he visited him one evening on the pretext of borrowing a tool. He came home with the tool . . . and this.' He opened the tin with a twist of a penknife. They all peered in. Nestled inside was a bar of soap with the detailed impression of a key pressed into the bar.

'Bernard, can you make a key from this?' asked Pierre.

Bernard picked up the tin, smiling. 'Try stopping me.'

Pierre returned his smile. 'I hoped you would say that.'

* * *

Charlotte saw the strain of the operation drain from Pierre's face at the sight of the newly made key. He gave a boyish smile as he picked it up and turned it in the light. Bernard, Raymond, Sully and Gérald began to talk excitedly about the next stage of the plan. Taking no part in their discussion, Pierre's gaze finally lifted to meet hers over the key. Something inside her chest began to flutter erratically as the voices of the others faded into obscurity. She lowered her gaze to the key in his fingers and stared hard at it as his gaze heated her body to its core.

'When shall we do it?' she asked him quietly.

His answering silence brought a whole new meaning to her question, forcing her to look up at him again. Intense hazel eyes looked back at her, his smile fading as the key in his hand was forgotten by the both of them. His eyes lowered to her lips and turned the fluttering in her chest to a thundering beat. This exchange, with all the heat and intensity of molten lava, did not last long.

Perhaps realising the foolishness and danger of such an exchange, his gaze fell abruptly away. He dropped the key on the table and stared at it intently as he gathered his thoughts.

'First, we need to pick up the explosives,' he replied as if nothing had just happened between them. He stood up and walked away from the table to pour himself some coffee, spilling some as he did so. 'You lot should get yourselves something to eat and drink,' he added, ignoring the spillage. 'We have a long night ahead of us.'

If there had been a fragile thread of mutual attraction between them, thought Charlotte, he had severed it with the diplomacy of an angry bull.

CHAPTER FIFTEEN

The designated area for the explosive drop was no more than a field set next to a small area of woodland. It had been chosen because it was in a valley, but both areas had advantages and disadvantages. Dropping it in a field allowed easier recovery, but little cover. Dropping it in a wooded area made it harder to spot, but by its very nature gave excellent concealment. Drops were inaccurate at the best of times, and it appeared that tonight they were in the lap of the Gods — or at least the wind direction and the navigational skills of the pilot.

They arrived early and spread out throughout the area, at the same time keeping a look out for the local police, Nazis and the plane that was going to drop the explosives out of its hatch. The atmosphere was tense, the waiting unbearable and, despite the cover of darkness, the sky was clear and the moon far too bright for their liking, resulting in every one of their senses being on edge. A snap of a twig, a rustle of leaves, a distant cry of a fox, were all sounds they expected to hear, yet tonight they instantly set their hearts racing. Charlotte found herself gravitating towards Pierre — or was it him towards her? Whoever made the first move, eventually they were standing no more than a few feet away from each other.

Sully came over to join them. 'I think I might have heard a plane on the other side of the wood. I'm going to check it out.'

Pierre nodded and watched him leave. He surveyed the shadows and in the dim light and saw Gérald. Using hand signals, he informed him of Sully's search area. Gérald nodded and passed the message onto Raymond and Bernard. Gradually, a low rumble could be heard coming from the opposite direction. They searched the sky and saw a small, dark shape emerge from a distant cloud.

'This must be it,' said Pierre, turning on a light and shining it into the sky. The plane flew over their heads, then immediately circled back. Charlotte tracked it across the sky, afraid that if she blinked it would disappear. To her relief, an object with a fluttering white tail, was expelled from its belly as if giving birth. For a moment Charlotte thought she had lost track of it, until suddenly the small, white tail exploded into the perfect skirt of a parachute, slowing its descent so it swung gently down to earth.

Pierre cursed. 'It's going to land in the woods. Keep an eye on it!'

They both began to run towards where they had last seen it disappear into the canopy of trees. Pierre slipped a penknife from his pocket as they entered the wood, preparing to cut the explosives free if they were caught in the branches of a tree. The visibility deteriorated markedly as they moved deeper into the wood and there was no clear path to follow. The ground was littered with branches, broken twigs and sprawling roots. Every ditch and earth mound seemed to be waiting to trip her. Pierre slowed his pace until he eventually stopped.

'What's wrong?' she whispered. 'Germans?'

He lifted a finger to his lips. 'French police, I think,' he whispered.

She tilted her head to listen and heard, for the first time, male voices some way in the distance, directing a search.

Pierre grabbed her hand. 'We have to leave.'

She followed him back along the route they had just come from, but further voices ahead forced them to stop. They looked at each other. Pierre silently signalled a new direction. They began to run again, breaking contact intermittently if a gnarled trunk or a fallen branch came between them, yet wordlessly seeking contact again with their outstretched hands. Another voice, this time Bernard's. He was shouting, then cruelly silenced as if hit with a truncheon or the butt of a gun.

They ran for several minutes, until they came to the edge of the wood. A vast field stretched out before them, and they realised they had no choice but to break free from the woodland. Although the field gave little physical cover, it was dark enough that they could remain hidden, especially if they kept within the shadows of the hedge. If the pursuers continued to focus their search on the wood and did not use dogs, this route might just save them from arrest. They looked at each other. There was no need for words, a conversation or a debate, they understood one another and both agreed to the plan with a decisive nod of their heads.

They let go of each other's hands and Pierre led the way, occasionally looking behind him to check she was still with him. They ran, half crouching, along the line of the hedge, which took them over a shallow hill and down into a gently sloping valley. Nestled on the gradient was the shape of a farmstead and they headed towards it, knowing that the sprawling outbuildings would provide shelter and somewhere to rest.

They entered the seemingly deserted farmyard. The sheds, barns and outhouses were in various states of repair, with abandoned farm machinery and implements scattered around. The sound of grunting animals and the strong odour of pigs emanated from one. The heavy breathing and grinding of cud came from another. The third building was stacked with hay and would provide cover and somewhere to rest for the night.

'We'll leave before dawn,' whispered Pierre, pre-empting her next question.

Several feral cats appeared from between the stacks of hay, their eyes wide and unblinking as they watched them enter. One hissed, his spine arching high as his standing fur expanded his thin little body. Then suddenly they all scattered and disappeared into the night, leaving Pierre and Charlotte alone and surrounded by hay. The silence accentuated their rapid breathing. They had run for more than a mile and for the first time Charlotte realised how much her lungs were burning.

'Are you all right?' asked Pierre, concerned.

'I'm fine. You?'

'I will be when we are back at the house.'

She watched him return to the door of the barn. He held it ajar and looked out into the night.

'Are they coming?' she asked.

'I don't know.' He turned his head to look at her, his gaze briefly dropping to take in the whole of her. She thought she saw an internal struggle in his eyes and wondered what he was thinking. He opened his mouth as if to speak but thought better of it and kept the words back with a firm press of his lips.

She was about to ask him what he was going to say when he suddenly put his finger to his lips again. 'Someone is coming.'

'Police?'

He shook his head and tilted it to listen. 'Sounds like Germans.' He saw something and stepped back into the shadow of the barn. 'Yes, Germans. I think they have dogs.' He scanned the room for an alternative exit. 'We have to leave. Now!'

'Where? We are surrounded by open fields.'

'We have to. We can't hide. The dogs will sniff us out.'

'But if they see us running, they won't bother asking questions. They will shoot us in the back.'

Pierre raked a hand through his hair. 'You go and I'll distract them.'

'They'll want to know why you are here alone.'

'I'll take care of them.'

'You will be outnumbered. You won't stand a chance. *We* could kill them.'

He smiled at her suggestion. 'Yes, I think *we* could . . . but we won't. Several dead bodies will only highlight the fact that we were here. There will be others, and if they haven't found the explosives yet, they will search harder to find them.'

'Then we must hide and if they find us, we have to deceive them.'

She could tell that he knew what she was suggesting. Why else would a young couple be in a hay barn at night? They both heard the voices grow louder outside. It was now or never. He reluctantly nodded.

Not daring to look at one another, they began to strip, peeling off their clothes in such haste that an observer would think they were truly impassioned and desperate to be in one another's arms. It was all a façade, of course, Charlotte told herself as she stood awkwardly in her culottes and bra, with her coat, cardigan and blouse scattered at her feet. Her bra was new and French, so a little more flattering than a basic British style, but even so, she wondered how she would measure up to his previous lovers. Goosebumps prickled her skin at the sight of Pierre stripped to the waist. The top buttons of his trousers were slightly undone. A light smattering of dark hair ascended from his naval and across his chest, accentuating the moving contours of his muscles as he walked towards her. Her breath caught in her throat as her lips dried. This was her idea, yet now she was questioning if she was up to the task.

Despite his calm appearance, his words and self-imposed hands-off approach showed he was wondering just what the rules were. The voices outside grew louder.

'We had better kiss . . . or something . . . I suppose,' said Charlotte. She reluctantly placed her hand on his arm. The muscle moved slightly beneath her touch but he did little else. 'You better do something, Pierre. They'll be here soon!'

He put his hands on her waist but kept her at a distance. 'Look, this isn't easy for me either,' he muttered.

Charlotte looked up at him in surprise. She could see a real struggle in his eyes, but she didn't know the reason why.

'Is it so hard to pretend we are lovers?'

His breathing had deepened but he could not meet her eyes. His reluctance was putting their lives in danger. She would have to goad him into doing something, because they did not have the time for her to persuade him she would be fine.

'Oh, for goodness' sake, Pierre! Throw me on the hay and make love to me. What are you so scared of?' She thought of her favourite book, with its well-thumbed pages filled with passion, lying on her bed where she'd left it. 'I thought French people made great lovers!' she hissed. 'It seems I was wrong.'

His eyes widened, then darkened. He scooped her up, tossed her on the hay and launched himself on top of her.

His lips sought hers and they kissed, initially as if they were mere actors upon a stage. This charade did not last long. Lust and passion are natural instincts that lurk in the silence, waiting to blossom and build in strength when the opportunity presents itself. Such emotions have the power to silence doubts, fade the sights and sounds of the outside world and focus one's every thought on wanting more. They cannot be easily controlled — even when there is the desire to. And if the desire to control is momentarily forgotten, then another world is experienced where there is no need to hide their hunger for the other at all.

Every one of Pierre's kisses, whether deep or tender, chased and savoured every one of hers. Despite her earlier fears, they were equally matched, both in the strength of their passion and need. Every nerve in her body came alive. Every part of her skin yearned to be touched. Every arch of her body into his embrace had brought an aching groan to his throat. She had no doubt that they would have gone further if he had not been suddenly torn from her arms. Her need for him had become a physical ache, his breathless groans had told her he felt the same. Now, breathless and dishevelled, she almost felt bereft for the blissful experience she had felt and lost. The German officer was shouting at them, demanding to see their papers as she blinked and tried to shield her eyes from his torch.

She sat up, her trembling fingers searching her coat for her identity card. She was aware Pierre was trembling too, despite the defiant tilt of his chin and the gun pointing to his head.

The German studied her card, his eyes glancing up at her and back down to the document in quick succession. He began to question her in French.

'What's your name?'

'Marie Veilleux.'

'Are you married?'

'No.'

'Where do you come from?'

'Paris.'

'Address?'

'Apartment 2b, Rue de Florne.'

'Where is that?'

'Not far from the Place de la Bastille.'

She wondered if the officer was aware of the revolutionary history of the area. If he was, he chose to ignore it as he handed the card back to her and ordered her to get dressed.

'What is your occupation?'

'I sell cosmetics.'

'Where?'

'In Paris.'

'To whom?'

'Customers in their homes. I travel around.'

'I asked you who?'

She rattled off a few names, with their addresses, but her customer list was limited and she knew it would come to an end soon.

Pierre guessed her concern and began to speak to his captors in German. His voice was calm and cajoling, resulting in the gun pointing at his temple lowering slightly. He was asked a few sharp questions, which he answered immediately. A short silence followed. Pierre began speaking again, gently, sounding almost hypnotising in his casual delivery. Somehow he persuaded the officer to step a few feet away from Charlotte. She watched the two men together as she buttoned up her blouse. Pierre's quiet voice had brought out an equally quiet tone in the officer, so when he withdrew his wallet, the man showed no fear that he might be pulling out a weapon. Pierre withdrew a photograph and showed it to him. The officer looked at it, then over at her, a sly smile curving his lips. Whatever Pierre had shown him had convinced the officer that they were just lovers enjoying their time alone. As quickly as they had arrived, the two officers left.

Pierre pulled on his shirt. 'We better leave. Raymond, Sully and Gérald will hopefully be waiting for us back at the house.'

They left as Pierre dragged on his jacket, both walking quickly into the night and along the farm's rutted lane. By the time they reached the road, the farmhouse windows were alight, shadowy figures moving from room to room. Dogs began to bark incessantly from inside and outside the building. Charlotte feared for the family inside.

'They're searching the farmhouse. I hope they don't hurt them.'

'If they have nothing to hide, hopefully they will move on.'

'And if they do?'

Pierre did not reply. She knew then that he felt the burden of bringing the search party to the farm as heavy as she did and could only hope they brought them no harm.

* * *

When they arrived at the Resistance safe house, the building was cold and silent, telling them that the others had not returned.

'I hope they managed to avoid being caught.' Charlotte touched Bernard's empty chair. 'I hope he's all right.'

'They are resourceful. Bernard will have put up a fight, at least.'

A heavy silence followed. They were both concerned for Bernard, but to discuss his possible fate so early might nurture foolish plans. It was best to trust his ability to cope. All they could do was listen out for information and if the worst outcome came to fruition, they both knew that ultimately they'd have to pretend they'd never knew him. The latter, he knew, would be the hardest to do.

Charlotte's hand lingered on the back of Bernard's wooden chair. 'Someone must have betrayed us. How would they know we were there waiting for a drop?'

'They may have seen the parachute.'

'Or someone who knew told them. Can everyone be trusted?'

He glanced at her. 'Can anyone?'

'I'm serious, Pierre.'

'So am I.'

'Are you suggesting I shouldn't trust you or that you don't trust me?'

'I'm suggesting you should only trust yourself. The others say they trust me, but I know it's difficult for them to forget I'm half-German.'

The confession slipped out before he realised what he was saying. He'd often felt distant from the others, but seeing Sully and Marie so close the other day made him wonder if Sully was dropping poison into her ears. He tightened his jaw. He would say no more. Thankfully, Marie picked up on his mood and did not question him further.

They waited for an hour, playing cards to pass the time, before he looked at his watch again. He had hoped they would have returned by now.

'It's too late to go back to Paris now. We'll attract too much attention if we are seen walking through the streets after curfew.' He scraped his chair back and stood up. 'We need to lie low tonight and leave in the morning. There are rooms upstairs. We should get some sleep.'

'Won't the owner mind?' asked Marie as she packed away the cards.

'No.'

'How can you be so sure?'

'Because the owner is me.' He showed her the way to the stairs.

Sleep was the logical option, so she did not argue, and followed him. The steps creaked beneath their shoes as they slowly ascended to the first floor.

'And the cat?'

'He's not mine.'

'Is he a stray?'

Pierre paused and looked down at her, his eyebrow lifting slightly. 'I prefer to think of him as an adventurer.'

Her curious expression told him that she was still trying to work him out. What sort of man mused over the daily life of a scavenging cat yet could be so cold to her at times? Well, he had news for her: he was trying to work that one out too.

His physically fit frame dominated the confines of the stairs as he looked down at her. Her physicality was the opposite to his in so many ways, yet sometimes such opposites were created to one day answer the call to become one. In that moment, he heard that call loud and clear as it sizzled between them. He'd had a glimpse of what it could be like from their time in the barn and it had been hard to forget it ever since. However, she either did not hear it or chose to ignore it as her steady gaze did not waver from his. He turned away and continued up the stairs, stopping to push a door open with one hand and stepped aside to reveal a vacant bedroom.

'The bed is made up. It might need a bit of airing, but it is better than sleeping on hay.'

She stepped past him and into the room. She gave a cursory glance around, then turned to face him. His gaze dropped to her lips and he was instantly reminded of their earlier kisses.

174

'I still think someone must have betrayed us,' she said. 'What do you know of the others?'

'I have known Sully for less than a year. Gérald and Bernard have always been reliable. Raymond is a newcomer but I don't doubt him for a moment.'

He was finding it difficult to drag his gaze from her lips as he spoke. Just as he tried, she began teasing the bottom one with her teeth. For a few seconds it mesmerised him.

'But there must be—'

'Did you enjoy it as much as I did?' he asked suddenly.

'Enjoy what?' she asked quietly.

He stepped closer and rested one arm on the doorframe above her head.

'Our kiss in the barn? I think you did.'

She pulled her coat tighter about her. 'I was acting.' She looked away. 'The room looks cosy. Do you stay here often?' She chose that moment to study a long-forgotten picture on the wall next to him.

He looked around the room that he had never considered cosy in the past. 'I was acting too . . . in the beginning. And yes, I used to stay here a lot.'

'And then what happened?'

He looked at her. 'I wasn't acting anymore.'

The tone of his voice had changed without his bidding. Now it held hints of seduction that had been building in his veins since the barn, and probably long before that. If this concerned her, she did not step away.

'I meant, why did you stop staying here?' she asked.

He didn't want to talk about the house. Now he had finally admitted it to himself, he wanted to talk about what was happening between the two of them. His hands slid around her waist and with the merest of pressure turned her to face him.

'Were you acting?' he asked again.

'I'm . . . not sure.'

Her answer surprised him. 'You aren't sure?'

'I don't remember.'

He frowned. How could she not remember? 'Are my kisses that forgettable?'

She shrugged. 'It was a stressful situation. Stress can block out a memory.' He saw her wince at her own excuse. She was lying. It gave him hope that he was not as forgettable as she claimed.

'Perhaps you could do with a little reminder.'

She raised an eyebrow. 'And what is it I'm supposed to remember?'

Although her lips were not smiling, there was a definite sparkle in her eyes now that he had not seen before. He had the feeling that she was teasing him this time. Or perhaps she was challenging him to reveal his own thoughts first. The chasm between them that had been created from a difficult start, no longer seemed so vast or impossible to cross. To his surprise, he realised he was ready to take the first step. It would either bring them closer together or he would fall headfirst into it.

'You're supposed to remember that the softness of our first kiss ignited a passion that you did not know existed. And that each kiss, although more delectable than the last, only left you hungry for another.'

'Go on.'

'That you still marvel how those kisses had the power to consume you so that only how you felt . . . and how you pleased the other . . . mattered.'

He watched her throat ripple as she swallowed.

'It could be, Pierre, that I have nothing to remember.'

His hands slowly fell from her waist. He knew he was out of practice, but did she really feel nothing? She began fiddling with her hair, as if she would rather have a comb in her hand than him standing in front of her talking of their kisses.

He lifted his chin. 'I think that you are denying what you felt.'

'You think a lot of yourself.' She began to take an interest in the buttons of her coat, undoing them slowly one at a time and seemingly unaware that her remark had cut far deeper than she had probably meant.

'I think a lot about *you*.'

His confession shocked them both. It had escaped like a frustrated stray cat escaping the confines of a locked room. He had never felt so vulnerable in the silence that followed.

Her fingers stilled and she looked up at him. 'Do you?'

He shrugged, unable to resist the urge to retreat a little. 'There have been times when you have entered my thoughts.'

'You make me sound like a shopping list.'

'You still haven't answered my question.'

'I have. I told you that I was acting. I'm a good actress.'

'I don't believe you are *that* good.'

'I am.'

'Then show me.'

'How?'

His head moved closer so there was less than a breath between them. 'Kiss me again.'

He heard her breathing become shallower. 'We shouldn't.'

'Shouldn't what?'

'Kiss. Agents shouldn't kiss.'

'We already have.'

'But not properly. Not when there is no need to.'

He noted the change in her tone. It had softened and held a whisper of breathlessness. He was encouraged.

'Is that what your training taught you?' he asked, this time welcoming the huskiness in his own voice.

'My head is telling me that we shouldn't kiss.'

Her words mirrored his own usual sentiments, which reminded him he was acting out of character. The realisation sobered him. 'You are right. My head usually barks the same instructions.'

They nodded in agreement, yet neither of them moved.

She tilted her head and looked at him. 'Are you going to listen to it?' she asked.

He moved closer. 'I should, but I don't want to.' He could not resist the urge to lightly brush the backs of his curved fingers along the sleeve of her coat. 'Are you?' His body responded when he heard her soft sigh, but he came no closer. 'Be truthful,' he whispered. 'Remember, we have to be able to trust one another.'

'I should listen to it . . . but . . .'

He moved closer and lifted his chin so that her soft curls passed silkily across his lips.

'But what?' he murmured.

'But I have a need to . . .'

He traced the line of her jaw with his fingers and felt her lift her face to his.

'Kiss me?' he asked.

'Yes. Kiss you.'

'Me too.'

Her lips touched his before he could finish the last word. It was as fervent as the ones before, stealing his breath and every other thought from his mind.

Another kiss, more sensual than the last followed before they finally broke apart.

He traced the line of her jaw with his fingers again before finding a home for them in the curve of her neck.

He looked down at her. 'I didn't plan this.'

'I know.'

'It's probably the stress of nearly being caught.'

'Yes. Possibly.'

'Is it bad that I don't want it to stop?'

She reached up and kissed him. 'It would be bad if you did.'

He lifted her off the ground and as he kissed her, walked deeper into the room. Several more kisses followed as he lowered her to the floor, each one as hungry as the last. She rested against the bedstead to anchor herself, her lips flushed and swollen from his kisses. He could still taste her and seeing her lips so ripe and inviting only made him want to seek more. They stood looking at each other, both already a little more flushed and breathless than before.

He returned to the door to close it but turned to face her before he did. 'Perhaps we should stop before it goes too far.' Stopping wasn't what he really wanted, but once the line had been crossed . . . 'There will be no soldiers to drag us apart this time.'

Marie smiled at him, her hair already tousled from his caressing fingers.

'Good.'

It was all the encouragement he needed. With a backward kick of his heel, he closed the door and crossed the space between them. Their hurried passionate kisses formed an intimate dance of their own making, both not wasting a moment to draw breath until they fell onto the bed. They were alone, they were hungry for love and there would be no turning back now.

CHAPTER SIXTEEN

Charlotte woke to sunshine breaking through the curtain and warming her face. She stretched. Her limbs felt weak, her body deliciously sated and her mind at peace. She smiled and turned her head to see the reason for this calm euphoria. Pierre was sleeping beside her, his breaths deep and steady. His tousled head, the naked curve of his back, the sheet tangled about his legs and waist, were exquisite reminders of numerous moments of passion she had experienced throughout the night. The author of her favourite book had not lied — a man and a woman could feel such passion as he had described. She smiled as she recalled those moments. Her fingers raking through his hair, his body rising above hers, their entwined limbs moulding and rolling as they kissed and caressed, his resting body looking at hers until they had wordlessly decided to do it all again.

She wanted him again now, desperately. However, she could see he was tired. It would be selfish to wake him now. She crooked her arm under her head and stared up at the ceiling. They had been lucky to escape last night. If Pierre had not talked his way out of the situation, they may have been captured, possibly like Bernard. Talking to Germans seemed to come naturally to him, which was impressive to fake when they had turned his life upside down. She had heard it for herself on several occasions, even believing he was a friend of one as she hid under the hotel bed. It had been a shock to discover the voice belonged to Pierre. It could have so easily have gone wrong that day if he had not persuaded the German to leave, enabling her to escape. Particularly as she should have finished her searching by then . . . If it hadn't been for the watch stopping. Pierre's watch.

She frowned and looked at him. Her training taught her to always question. Nothing was always as it seemed — her instructors had hammered that home. Did Pierre know his watch would not keep time? If he didn't, why did he bother going to the hotel room to coax the officer away? Only he hadn't, had he? He told her himself he thought she was already gone. So why did he go to the hotel room at all? Perhaps he had gone to check if she had been caught. She shook the thought from her head. It was absurd to believe that Pierre might have set her up to be captured. It had been her idea after all . . . yet he *had* given her a watch that failed. Someone had betrayed them last night and, as always, Pierre had walked away free. Was that why he was reluctant to play her lover in the barn? Did he know that in reality he was in no danger and it was not needed? When she had brought up the subject of betrayal, he refused to believe it. When she had brought it up again, he had changed the conversation to their kisses. Was he trying to divert her or silence her? He had succeeded, if that was his aim.

Yet, he had not been unkind since her arrival. He had found her a place to stay and had shown an interest in what she did outside of Pointer. Was that good or was it to know where she was and keep an eye on her?

He *is* half-German. It must have been difficult to choose sides when both sides of your heritage were at war with one another. Why did he decide to fight for the French? It was a question she hadn't asked. Would he have told her if she had?

His last network had been betrayed. Was he the common cause? Had he dismantled that one and was now trying to dismantle another?

Yet he was the organiser. If he wanted to betray them, he could have had them all arrested the other night as they sat around the table, planning. She looked around the room. It was a fine house. His house. Everyone knew what happened to houses used by the Resistance and networks — they were burned to the ground. Perhaps Pierre feared that would happen to this one and wanted the arrests to take place elsewhere.

Pierre moved his arm in his sleep. His muscles flexed and glided beneath his tanned skin as he did so. The movement was a dance of beauty and strength that could leave one breathless. And he had left her breathless, as she had him, many times last night. She turned her head away to try and block those delicious memories out. Her gaze fell on his wallet. What photograph had he shown the soldier which made him smile at her and let them go free?

She slipped from the bedsheets, picked up his wallet and eased the photograph free from the inside pocket. A beautiful woman and a child with smiling eyes looked back at her. The boy was no more than ten years old but there was no doubt in her mind that he was Pierre's son. The woman had a ring on her finger, and her arm round the boy. Pierre was married. How had she not wondered about that before? The conversation in the barn became clear. In his gentle persuasive voice, he had cast her in the role of his mistress again, telling the officer that the only place he could meet her was away from his house. A mistress would come more readily to mind than the role of a girlfriend, fiancé or spouse if you had a loving wife already waiting for you at home. A role that would demand less commitment would not grate on his conscience so much. His lie had worked — again. The soldier's smug smile now made sense. Pierre was married with a child and she had helped him betray them. She wanted to die, or leave — or kill him. In that moment she really didn't know which.

She needed air. Yes — fresh air. By the time Pierre would wake, she would be long gone, travelling by whatever means she could, on the road back to Paris and as far away as she could get from him.

* * *

Pierre opened his eyes as the door closed behind her. He listened to her footsteps descending the stairs, cross the hall and then heard the back door softly open and close. He did not follow. He could only guess where she was going. She had been right to question if someone had betrayed them. He had secretly been thinking the same thing, but how could he discuss it with her when he'd seen Sully, his main critic, share so many quiet conversations with her? Now that he had silently watched her rifling through his belongings, he began to wonder if she had only voiced her concerns to divert the suspicion away from her. He had been confident he could trust her, if not Sully, but now he wasn't so sure. He thought last night was something special, that she had wanted to make love as much as he had, but perhaps she had tricked him so she could search his things? He covered his eyes with the crook of his arm. At first he had tried to deny his attraction to her. He hadn't been ready to open that door as he knew the feelings of guilt would be too much to bear. He should have held the line.

His fingers began to hurt and he realised he was clenching his fist too hard. He slowly unfurled his fingers before they slowly closed once more. His reluctance had been real, he recalled, but impossible to fight forever. Those moments in the barn had given him hope that perhaps there was no guilt to feel. Last night was the same because he believed that Marie was special and his wife would understand. Now, in the cold light of day, he had watched the woman he had held search his things and he saw every tender moment between them with a different, clearer lens. He had been a fool. He had betrayed his wife. He had cast the love he had for her aside to sleep with a woman who thought nothing of searching through his things as he slept. The guilt of his betrayal felt ruthless and painful, just as he had feared. Yet somewhere in that swirling mix was the hurt of Marie's betrayal too.

He clenched his fist tight again as he closed his eyes firmly to block out the world. He had told Marie no one could be trusted. He had not thought he couldn't trust her. Everyone lied to survive, it seemed, including himself.

CHAPTER SEVENTEEN

It had been two days since Charlotte had left Pierre sleeping. She had returned to her lodgings, undertaken a mandatory search of her room to ensure it had not been searched while she was away, and had been sulking ever since as she waited for the Pointer network to reconvene. Initially, Madame Chastain had hovered around like a concerned hen with her chick. It was sweet of her, but despite her well-meant enquiries as to the cause of her glum face, Charlotte had resisted confiding in her elderly neighbour. She didn't understand why she was feeling this way so how could she explain it?

Pierre being married should not hurt her so much. After all, there was never going to be any future for them together. At any moment their cover could be blown and the Germans could find them. And even if they survived the war, one day she would be recalled to London. His betrayal of his marriage vows was his problem to overcome. She was just someone who had got temporarily duped and dragged into the middle of a faltering marriage. Yet she felt as betrayed as if she was his wife. Her heart suddenly went out to the woman in the photograph who was oblivious to what a rat he was. It was a mess, but although she was tempted to tell his wife everything, she realised that was not sensible — not when she was an agent trying to blend in.

She pushed the half-eaten bowl of soup away from her and stared out of the window. Two days she'd wasted and she was still swinging from feeling enraged to pining like a lovesick teenager. She mustn't let him affect her so. She wasn't the only woman in the world who had fallen into bed with a man and had come to regret it. For heaven's sake, she hardly knew the man and wasn't even sure if she liked him. True, he was handsome, dynamic and got things done — all appealing character traits. He also had a physique that was truly memorable with a softer side that was equally unforgettable. At times he was even quite the gentleman. She smiled at a distant memory. But her smile faded as she reminded herself that she had just discovered a whole new side to him — which included a wife and child. All this, on top of their failure to retrieve the explosives and mounting concern for Bernard. It had not been a good week.

She gave herself a mental shake. She couldn't do anything but wait for a message that would give the go-ahead for Pointer to regroup. But she had come to France as an agent and would rather put her initiative and skills to good use than wait for a message.

She had not intended to seek Pierre out. If this was her intention, she would have gone to the *Fleur de Lis* area to gather intelligence. Any information, no matter how insignificant, would be gratefully received by London if it helped the Allies to plan their attacks. She spent most of the day observing the comings and goings of the patrolling soldiers — where they gathered, what exits and entrances of their headquarters they used, where the artillery guns were stationed. She had eventually ended up in the Latin Quarter of Paris with its long winding picturesque streets and hidden courtyards.

However, despite her intentions, her thoughts would unwillingly return to Pierre time and time again. The sight, feel and scent of his body. The sound of his voice. His guttural sighs. The taste of his kisses. The taste of his skin.

Whether it was the same invisible force that had driven them into each other's arms or a grotesque joke played by someone up above, suddenly he was in front of her, walking briskly past a long queue of people lined up outside a poorly stocked bakery. The urge to follow was too strong to ignore.

He was dressed in a casual suit and hat, and in his hand he carried a bag. He appeared disinterested in the shops or the people, as if he had a specific destination in mind. She had not expected that destination to be a quaint café festooned in clinging ivy. He chose a table in the corner and sat down, declining to order as if he was waiting for someone. His wife, perhaps? Charlotte remained outside, intrigued to see who had brought him to this part of Paris. It was a full five minutes before she found out.

A high-ranking German officer walked briskly by her and entered the café, his shoulder nudging hers in his haste. He stood near the entrance and looked around, as if he owned the place. Charlotte retreated behind a wall, concerned that his entry would draw Pierre's attention to the door and in turn to her. Two deep breaths later, she tentatively edged towards the window again. Through the leaves of the clinging ivy, she watched Pierre's resentful gaze follow the officer across the room. At first he kept a low profile, as any agent should but, to her surprise, suddenly he stood and greeted the officer with a smile and offered him a seat. They both sat down at his table, ordered coffee and waited in silence as the waiter scurried over, served them and quickly left.

Charlotte watched, in shock. This must be an accidental meeting, she told herself, between a hotel manager and a frequent guest, and not a prearranged meeting. Under such circumstances, Pierre would have felt obligated to greet him. Yet, it made her feel sick to see them drinking coffee together. Was Pierre in danger? He had not mentioned this associate to the other members of Pointer. He had not mentioned this contact to her. He suspected that the other members were not fully at ease with having a half-German as their leader. Was this why he was meeting a high-ranking officer without telling them? Or perhaps what she was seeing only confirmed that Sully was right to feel uneasy. Was the real Pierre a double agent? If the latter was true, not only could she not trust him with her heart, but she couldn't trust him with the Pointer network either.

Her lips grew dry and her heart sank as she watched. Their conversation seemed easy as they drank their coffee, but it was when he opened his bag, withdrew an envelope and slid it across the table, did she admit that she could no longer fool herself about Pierre.

She stepped back and rested her head against the wall as the image burned into her mind. He was passing information to the enemy and that could never be explained away. She opened her eyes and discovered that her behaviour had attracted unwanted attention. Two German soldiers were approaching, their steady gazes focused solely on her. She had to remain there, as to leave would only heighten their suspicions. How long had they been watching her resting against the wall as if she had all the troubles of the world upon her shoulders? She had to think of a reason for her behaviour.

A baby began to cry. She looked down to find a child, no more than three months old, cocooned in a bundle of blankets with his little fists flaying. The mother was nowhere to be seen. Perhaps she had slipped inside the shop and left the cumbersome pram outside, as Charlotte grappled with what she had seen. Charlotte scooped up the baby just as the soldier reached her, and began to whisper endearments into its ear. Charlotte the agent had vanished, and in her place was a tired new mother with a fractious baby to console. Her new persona was enough. One soldier frowned and looked elsewhere; the other's eyes softened as if she had triggered some memory from his past. By the time they had reached her, she had been dismissed from their minds. By the time they passed her, it was as if they had not noticed her at all.

She sighed in relief, kissed the baby's head in thanks and was in the middle of settling him back in his pram when his mother returned. A few words of explanation and Charlotte was walking away, leaving a confused mother, a soothed baby and Pierre unaware she had seen him at all.

* * *

Madame Chastain was waiting for her, or at least she was repotting a plant at the front door, when she returned home.

'Ah, there you are, my dear. Pleasant walk?'

Charlotte nodded and smiled as she fished in her handbag for the door key.

'Such lovely weather.'

'Hmm, lovely,' replied Charlotte absently as she inserted the key into the lock.

'Oh dear! Oh no!'

Charlotte stopped before she turned it. Madame Chastain had begun to search the area around her plant pots with mounting distress.

'Is everything all right, Madame Chastain?' she asked the frail woman as she began frantically searching her apron pocket. Moments before, she had been happily planting, now she was on the verge of panicked tears.

'I have lost my glasses. I had them a moment ago. Oh dear! I can't see a thing without them.'

'The ones on your head?' asked Charlotte.

Madame Chastain straightened her arthritic back and patted her head with her blue-veined hands in search of them. She found them, lifted them from her hair and positioned them on her nose with a flourish, delighted she could see again.

'I am just an old woman. Take no notice of me.'

Charlotte smiled and opened the door.

'You had a visitor earlier.'

'I did?' Even now, after what she found out about Pierre, her first thought was that it might be him wanting to know why she had left without saying goodbye. 'Who?'

'A woman.'

Charlotte's heart sank a little at discovering it had not been Pierre. A thought struck her. It suddenly began to race. Had his wife found out they had slept together and come to confront her? A duped wife could be resourceful when searching for the truth.

'Were you planning to meet someone and you forgot?' asked Madame Chastain.

'I don't know who it could have been.' She entered the hallway and the old woman followed.

'A friend perhaps? She seemed very nice.'

Charlotte had the urge to shake her off. 'I expect it was no one of importance.'

Madame Chastain continued to follow. 'Everyone has some importance.'

Charlotte reached her door, unlocked it and stepped inside. 'I am a little tired, if you don't mind.'

Madame Chastain ignored the brush off. 'It's lovely to have friends. If you are lonely anytime, do pop down for a glass of wine.'

Charlotte smiled and slowly began to close the door.

'You remind me of my daughter. She's just had a baby.'

'How nice. I really have to go.' Charlotte eased the door shut a little more until she was talking through the crack. 'Goodbye, Madame Chastain. Take care.' She shut the door with a soft click and leaned against it. Madame Chastain was a lovely woman, but sometimes her incessant talking and scattiness could wear on the nerves.

* * *

An hour later Madame Chastain was at her door again, with who was apparently her previous visitor in tow. Charlotte had never set eyes on the woman before but intuitively felt she would not speak until Madame Chastain had been asked to leave. Even when they were alone, she did not utter a word, but just pressed a small note into her palm and walked briskly away. Charlotte retreated into her room and locked the door before she unfolded the message. It took a few minutes to decode it, but the message, although short, was clear and precise.

Meeting.
Pointer.
Saturday.
Operation Still On.

Charlotte carefully folded it, put it into her mouth and chewed the message to a pulp. It was time to face Pierre again. At some point she would have to confront him with what she had just seen. She swallowed the tasteless mass. If only all things could disappear so easily.

CHAPTER EIGHTEEN

Charlotte arrived late at the safe house and by the time she entered the kitchen it appeared that their plan was in full swing as the dining table was covered with primed explosives.

Pierre was the first to notice her arrival and the only one who did not greet her.

'Where did all this come from?' she asked.

Raymond offered her a seat with a jerk of his head. 'I found the explosives and buried them. Waited a couple of days then went back for them. You're late. We thought you weren't coming.'

'Pierre thought you weren't coming,' corrected Sully. 'I knew you wouldn't let us down.'

She smiled at Sully and sat down next to him. Pierre stirred in his seat.

'I wouldn't miss this. My train was delayed.' She avoided looking at Pierre. She hadn't expected to see him taking an active part by preparing explosives and it had thrown her a little.

Sully slid a Sten gun across the table to her. 'This needs to be checked.'

Charlotte reached for it. 'Has anyone heard from Bernard?'

Gérald tore the tape he had been using to wind around an explosive. 'They let him go, but only after a good beating.' He pushed the prepared explosive towards the end of the table and started preparing another. 'He's recovering in a safe house. Best he lies low for a while until he's better.'

Charlotte picked up the Sten gun. The submachine fire-arm was compact, crudely made and nicknamed the "plumber's nightmare" as it consisted of little more than metal tubes, bolts and springs, all with a tendency to jam. However, it could shoot up to 600 rounds a minute, spitting out shells from its belly to make room for more. Reliability relied on good handling and preparation, so she set about meticulously disassembling, cleaning and assembling it as if her life depended upon it, which it undoubtedly would.

'What's the plan?' she asked no one in particular. She had still avoided looking at Pierre despite feeling his eyes upon her.

It was Pierre who replied. 'It hasn't changed. Gain entry. Plant the explosives. Light. Leave.'

She should have known he would not elaborate. They had gone through the plan before, but it was good to know that nothing had changed. Now all they could do was to hang on until dark. In the meantime, they would prepare, pack and wait. The first two helped take her mind off things, the latter she would find intolerable, but not as intolerable as being so near the man who had made love to her only four days ago.

* * *

It was time to finally leave. They hitched their rucksacks, filled with explosives and detonators, over their shoulders in solemn silence and wished one another good luck. Pierre and Charlotte were the last to leave. He halted her by the crook of her arm.

'You left without saying goodbye.'

She stared ahead, acutely aware that the heat from his hand was burning through to her arm. 'I didn't want to wake you.'

'Did you decide that before or after you rifled through my pockets?'

She looked up at him. 'Did you decide to sleep with me before or after you ate breakfast with your wife and child?'

His eyes narrowed in disbelief that she had uttered such words. Realisation dawned on him. 'You saw their photograph.' His grip on her arm softened. 'It was after. Is that what you were searching for?'

'I don't need to explain anything to you.'

'You owe me an explanation or—'

'Or what?'

'I won't be responsible for what happens to you.'

She twisted her arm free from under his hand. 'I don't need you to feel responsible for me. I owe you nothing. You owe me nothing. Now, if you'll excuse me, I have a factory to blow up. Are you coming?' She raised an eyebrow at him. 'Or do you have better things to do?'

'Jealousy and sarcasm do not become you,' he ground out as he followed her outside.

* * *

They arrived under the cover of darkness and secured separate positions on the hill above the factory. The scattered bushes, rocks and trees provided excellent cover from where they could observe the factory, now emptied of its workers, and wait for the order to advance swiftly down the hill. Raymond and Pierre signalled that they were ready to approach and check out the site. Charlotte watched from her vantage point as their silhouettes crawled quickly along the ground. In no time, they reached the factory and began to circle the outer wall, checking the windows and outbuildings for any signs of life. The minutes dragged by, especially when they both disappeared behind the far side of the factory. Sully ran across the hill and joined her.

'How are you?' he asked as he settled behind the bush with her.

His question took her by surprise. 'I will be better when this is over,' she whispered noncommittally as she tried to concentrate on the factory below them.

'I just couldn't help noticing that there was some tension between you and Pierre.'

'Isn't there always tension between us?' When he didn't reply immediately she glanced over at him.

Sully's eyes softened in the moonlight. 'You don't need to lie to me, Marie. I know what he's like. I don't trust him either.'

Charlotte tried to refocus on the factory, strangely torn between telling Sully about Pierre's liaison with a German officer and feeling like she would be betraying him if she did.

Instead, she said, 'It's natural to be suspicious. After all, someone has already betrayed us.'

He raised an eyebrow. 'You sound on edge.'

She didn't reply. Of course, she was on edge. Wasn't he?

'Your silence is telling me all I need to know,' said Sully softly. 'He is half-German after all.'

Charlotte renewed the grip on her gun. Sully was being so understanding that it took all her control not to tell him everything. The burden of knowing had weighed heavily on her since seeing him in the café sliding the documents across the table.

She turned to look at Sully again and opened her mouth to speak, but nothing came out. Something in his eyes had stopped her. Moments ago she had seen softness in their depths, but now his pupils looked hard, sharp and cold. Perhaps it was the light. She refocused on the factory ahead.

'He is also about to blow up a German factory,' she reminded him without much conviction.

'What better cover for a spying agent? Who could suspect him then?'

Sully had a point.

'I don't know anything for sure.'

'But you do suspect *something*.'

'I suspect *someone*.'

'But you have reason to suspect *him* more than most. What has he done?'

Charlotte prepared to leave. 'We can't talk now. And I'm not even sure there is anything to discuss. I will tell you when I know for sure.'

To Charlotte's relief, Raymond and Pierre chose that moment to reappear and give the all-clear signal. Sully would have argued for more information, but it was time for them to advance. As they went their separate ways, Charlotte wasn't sure who had had the lucky escape — Pierre or herself.

They scurried down the hill, using the bushes and trees for cover. By the time they reached the factory, Raymond had successfully unlocked the side door and they all filed in, shutting it behind them.

The factory was cavernous. Large, barred windows ran the entire length and allowed the dim gloom of a fading moon to bathe the floor and the machinery laid out in front of them. The roof was held up by a skeleton of heavy girders, metal pipes and five massive pillars. Military vehicles and missiles, in various stages of completion, lined each side. Only a few hours before, the building had been productive, noisy and dangerous. Now it was silent, with shells of armoury waiting to be completed. Charlotte was amazed they had not placed guards to patrol it. This oversight or arrogance would be to their advantage . . . unless it was a trap. She exchanged concerned glances with Pierre, who appeared to have wondered the same thing. It seemed easy — too easy.

Using hand signals, Pierre pointed to each exit, identified which one was open and which remained locked. He delegated a pillar to each person, giving Charlotte the one closest to one of the unlocked exits. He took the one farthest away. There was no time to waste, and with a curt nod of his head, Pierre gave the go-ahead to start.

They ran to their delegated pillar, emptied their packs and began attaching the rectangular cyclonite explosives, covered in rubberised fabric, to the base of each pillar. Charlotte was attaching the detonator and fuse when Sully signalled with a soft whistle that he had heard something outside one of the unlocked doors. They instinctively picked up their guns and took cover behind their pillars.

Silence fell. At first Charlotte wondered if Sully had been mistaken. She was about to break cover when she heard the sound too . . . movement outside. Indistinct but there, nevertheless. She sunk behind the pillar again, pressing her back against it as she crouched on the floor. She heard the door move, as if it had been tentatively nudged from outside. Another creak and the door slipped from its latch and opened a little, squeaking loudly on its hinges. Charlotte, being the nearest to it, could hear soft breathing, almost panting, as if someone had been running. Footsteps, a pause, then a few more in quick succession. Whoever it was had entered the building and decided to come Charlotte's way. She lifted her gun in preparation to shoot them in the back if they walked by. She pressed herself up against the pillar, her face turned to the side from where she thought the intruder was approaching — only she wasn't sure. *Was it to her left? Was it to her right?* The footsteps came nearer. *Yes — right. Definitely right.* She lifted her gun and took aim at the height she thought the intruder would appear.

A fox padded into view, turned and looked at her with amber eyes. Realising he was not alone, the fox jumped and its hackles rose. In his desperation to flee, he turned and slipped, his claws desperately trying to find some traction on the concrete floor. Finally, he gained his grip and fled.

Charlotte rested the back of her head against the pillar and released the breath she had been holding. She had been ready to kill, just as she had been in the hotel shortly after arriving. She had wondered if that initial moment of self-confidence was as a result of just arriving in France and being keen to use her training. If she harboured any doubts, they were now set aside. She had still been willing to kill, even at close range and face to face, because her life and the lives of others depended upon it. She would watch her enemy's life ebb from his eyes and although she would have wished there was never a need for it to happen, she would still feel relief that it was them and not her. It was a poignant moment, as it was proof she was a different person to the one who grew up in the Cornish fishing port of Newlyn, and she wasn't sure if she liked who she had become.

Charlotte closed her eyes and took a few precious seconds to allow the feelings necessary to take a man's life to drain from her body. When she opened her eyes, she realised that Pierre was looking at her from across the factory floor.

'You okay?' he mouthed silently. She nodded. Pierre nodded that he believed her and signalled to everyone to continue.

The disturbance had set them all on edge, but they had no choice but to carry on. Within minutes they were ready to light their fuses, knowing that they only had a short period of time to escape and find cover.

Pierre checked everyone was ready and gave the order. The matches were struck in unison, making them sound oddly loud in the large factory. Focused concentration followed as they attempted to light their fuses. To Charlotte's annoyance, her fingers began to shake. She knew that if she failed to light it on the first attempt, she would not have the time to try again, but thankfully, her fuse burst into life with a satisfying fizz. Charlotte threw the match aside, grabbed her gun and rucksack and began to run. She heard running footsteps behind her and could only hope that they had *all* been successful.

She was the first to reach the door and pushed it wide open. The cold night air hit her hard in the face as she left the building. Running as fast as she could, she only looked back briefly when she began to climb the hill. The gradient was steep, quickly sapping her strength and making her lungs burn. Finally, she took cover behind a tree to rest, vaguely aware that the others were close behind. Sully, then Raymond, arrived and took cover nearby. They exchanged signals to communicate they were all right, which left two still missing — Gérald and Pierre.

The primary explosions detonated, shattering the windows into a cascade of razor-sharp shards. Charlotte edged around the trunk of the tree to see if it had weakened the structure of the building. The factory roof creaked and groaned like a wounded animal, and began to collapse slowly in on itself. A fire ignited inside, growing quickly in intensity, clearly visible through the broken windows. Silhouetted against the burning red glow, Charlotte saw Gérald and Pierre approaching. They arrived and took cover just as a secondary set of explosions ignited and thrust pillars of dense smoke into the sky. Everyone exchanged smiles. The fuel tank store had just blown up.

Debris began to rain down, lighting up the sky with falling ribbons of flames. Three more minor explosions followed in quick succession. By the time the final explosion reverberated throughout the surrounding area, the Pointer network was gone, stealthily scattering into the night as the local inhabitants awoke, their attention drawn towards the raging flames.

* * *

Charlotte collapsed on her bed, exhausted. Returning home had been a difficult journey. After hiding her weapon, she had carefully made her way back to Paris, lying low in the suburbs until the night-time curfew had lifted. She entered the city as an ordinary citizen, while her head was filled with the memories of the night. She desperately wanted to meet up with the others to debrief, but the risks were too high at the moment. It would only take one of them to be trailed and they would all be arrested in one swoop. And, of course, there was Pierre. She had not confronted him about his German contact, but her silence could not last forever.

She fell into a deep sleep and didn't wake again until mid-afternoon. Feeling refreshed, she washed, got dressed and was in the middle of brushing her hair when she heard German voices outside. She looked out of the window and down onto the courtyard. Several uniformed soldiers were standing around talking loudly. As she watched, one of them banged loudly on the door below her window. Charlotte dropped her brush and stepped back. Were they looking for her?

She listened as the soldiers entered and spoke to Madame Chastain. She looked out of the window again. There were still some soldiers waiting below, effectively cutting off the route to escape. Booted footsteps began to ascend the stairs outside her flat. She retreated to the bathroom. Who had betrayed her? Bernard? He had been interrogated and let go. Pierre? He had warned her that he wouldn't be responsible for what happened to her. Sully? He had disappeared when the explosives had dropped, effectively making himself absent when the Germans had arrived.

They banged on her door. She opened the window and eased herself onto the ledge outside. The door burst open as she lowered herself out of sight until she was hanging from the windowsill. A soldier in the courtyard spotted her and began yelling. She looked down to see a circle of rifles forming below her, rising in unison to aim right at her and she could hear an officer approaching the window from inside. The face of an officer appeared above her as she looked up. He looked back at her, then at his men on the ground, then back at her again. He smiled kindly — then spat coldly in her face.

She was pulled roughly into the room by three soldiers as the officer looked on, the flesh on her arms tearing against the window frame as she was dragged across its grating surface. Orders, in German, were shouted at her from all directions until whatever she did to comply seemed to be wrong and would ignite a fresh round of shouting.

Finally, she gave up trying to understand and knelt at their feet, her head bowed and her body trembling so violently that she could not have spoken if she'd tried. Her submission seemed to calm things for a moment and they set about binding her hands tightly behind her back, the act done so roughly that her shoulders burned with pain.

Then her head was pulled savagely backwards by her hair. The arresting officer stared down at her, taking a perverse delight in seeing his spittle still on her face. She did not recognise him and tried to remain calm, but her steady gaze only seemed to reignite his anger. He pushed her head away from him with a violent thrust and barked another heated command. His soldiers immediately sprang into action and hauled her to her feet. Half-dragged and half-pushed, she was shunted out of the room and into the hallway. For the first time in her life, Charlotte felt paralysed by fear. Every muscle and joint grew rigid with terror — not because her fate was unknown, but because it was becoming all too clear. She was going to die! But how? When? Was she to be executed on the pavement outside or endure long bouts of torture first?

She tried to walk but failed. Losing patience, they immediately dragged, kicked and bundled her down the stairs until she found herself lying on the pavement outside. Dazed and terrified, she looked about her. A small crowd had gathered, too fearful to come too near, and through her newly swollen eye, she thought she saw her landlady disappear behind her closing front door. The crowd dispersed as quickly as it had formed, everyone distancing themselves from the further violence that may or may not come Charlotte's way. Charlotte realised she was on her own and only fate would know what was in store for her now. Her only means of controlling it, her cyanide pill, was now lost to her. She'd sewn the single capsule into the lining of her jacket, which continued to hang limply on the back of her apartment door.

CHAPTER NINETEEN

Northwest from the Eiffel Tower, adjacent to the wide residential boulevard of Avenue Foch, was the Gestapo Headquarters. The three large buildings had been commandeered early during the occupation, the fifth floor of the middle one being the main interrogation centre for agents in and around Paris. It had taken Pierre a week to discover what had happened to Marie. His German and French contacts, diligently courted over the last four years, were his only source of help. He had to find out if she had been called back to London or arrested. It was with horror that he had discovered it was the latter.

He entered the building and was greeted by the commander himself.

'Welcome!'

Pierre inclined his head politely at his greeting. 'Sturmbannfuhrer Kieffer. I have been informed that Mademoiselle Marie Veilleux is here.'

'She is.' Hans Josef Kieffer led the way up the stairs. 'She is being held in one of the interrogation cells on the top floor. But first we must talk.'

Pierre's jaw tightened. 'Talk? Why? You promised me her release.'

'Even so, there is no rush.' Kieffer paused, looked down on him, and smiled. 'You do have time for a conversation, don't you?'

Pierre relented. It would serve no purpose to upset the German officer now, not after all this time. 'Yes, of course. Lead the way.'

He followed him up four flights of stairs and into his office. A large ornate desk dominated the room. Kieffer poured himself a drink and offered Pierre one. Pierre silently declined.

Kieffer lifted his glass in the tips of his fingers and walked around the desk, where he carefully placed it on his blotting pad so as not to mark the wood. He sat down and indulgently settled himself lower into his chair.

He levelled a steady gaze upon Pierre as if he was studying an exotic find. 'You know, your German is really very good. I can't detect an accent at all.' He sat behind the desk and indicated for Pierre to do the same. 'It makes life so much easier. We have a translator in the building, but I hate using them. Besides, as you will understand, his time is taken up with the interrogations.'

'I'm half-German, but you already know that.'

'Mother's side, isn't it?'

Pierre nodded.

'I hear she is related to Sturmbannfuhrer Hersche.'

'Distantly.' Pierre sat down and brushed a speck of dust from his trousers. He could feel Kieffer's steady gaze on him but refused to give him the satisfaction that he cared.

'You have been lucrative with information. Nothing particularly helpful, but true, nonetheless. We need people like you.'

Pierre wondered if his flattery was a precursor to informing him Marie was dead. His stomach churned at the thought.

He lifted his gaze to meet Kieffer's. 'I may have my father's name, but I am dedicated to the Third Reich.' His words brought a smile to Kieffer's lips.

Kieffer leaned forward in his chair. 'Your latest information has been very intriguing. We were expecting an invasion via Sicily, but the documents you've passed on to us indicate Sardinia and confirmed the information we intercepted a few months ago.'

'What information?'

'The corpse of a British major was found. He had a briefcase with some documents in it. They revealed the same detailed plan. We believed them to be authentic, but what you have supplied has confirmed it. We have deployed troops accordingly.'

Pierre indicated the bottle. 'May I have that drink after all?'

'To celebrate?'

'Something like that.' Kieffer gave a curt nod of his head, so Pierre got up and poured it himself. The longer he stayed, the higher the chance Kieffer may become suspicious. Conversations were always risky. They were like sieves, leaking multiple signs of mistruths. The quicker this interrogation cloaked in friendship was over, the better. He swallowed deeply before he turned to face the man sitting behind him.

'I need the woman released.' There, he had said it! He placed the glass carefully down on the table.

'That might not be possible.'

'You promised.'

'I have changed my mind. I believe she is in the Resistance.'

'Who told you that?'

'Her landlady.'

Pierre laughed. 'You believe that forgetful old woman?'

'That forgetful old woman, as you call her, has reported ten people so far. She is not as fragile as she appears.'

'Were they ten Resistance fighters or ten innocent people? How do you know if she didn't just report them out of spite?'

'Probably a mixture of both. We pay her in bread coupons.' Kieffer rested his forearms on the table.

'Is that what we have come to — a life for extra bread coupons? Perhaps the Third Reich should allow the French to eat more.'

'You know what they say — why have the vanquished better fed than their victors? Besides, I am not responsible for what people choose to trade with.' His eyes narrowed. 'What is this woman to you?'

Pierre returned his steady gaze. 'Where do you think I get my information from? Imprison her and you cut off my information line.'

Kieffer sat forward in his chair. 'Is she part of the Resistance?'

'Of course not.'

'Then where is she getting her information?'

'Where do you think?' Pierre let the words hang in the air. He didn't like to portray Marie as anything she was not. He'd done it too many times already and it always made his stomach churn. However, if it was going to save her life, then he would do it.

'Are you saying she has a boyfriend in the Resistance?'

Pierre swallowed the thought down.

A smile dawned on Kieffer's face. 'She thinks you are in love with her, doesn't she?'

'You are a clever man.' Pierre smiled at him and looked out of the window. 'She has a loose tongue. Her boyfriend tells her things. She tells me. What can I say? She's not too bright.' The insult left a bad taste in his mouth. Marie, or whatever her real name was, was the smartest woman he knew. He stared at the Parisians on their bicycles below.

'Are you sleeping with her?'

Pierre tightened his jaw. Their night of passion had been memorable and special and he wasn't about to hand it to Kieffer on a plate for him to imagine the details. The details were sacred and would always stay that way.

Kieffer laughed. 'Well, well. You are more callous than I first thought. She whispers sweet nothings in your ear and you come running to us.' Pierre had guessed Kieffer had a dirty mind and his conclusion had proved him right by his easy acceptance of his lies. However, despite it helping him gain his trust and Marie's release, he had had enough of degrading her character.

'Will you release her now? How can I trust you again if you break your word now?'

The wait for his answer seemed interminable.

Kieffer suddenly smiled. 'Yes! Of course! She wasn't talking anyway. She is stronger than she looks. A week of interrogation and she's not said a word. I was going to send her to Dachau, but from what you say, she is of more use to us if I release her. Follow me.'

Kieffer stood with an almost boyish flourish and led Pierre out of the room. He continued his monologue, as if he were providing a tour of Paris on a fine summer's day. He threw in some questions but answered them immediately himself without waiting for a reply. Pierre was relieved when they finally arrived at the top floor. Kieffer gave a curt order to the guardsman to set Marie free and immediately left without saying goodbye. Pierre suspected Kieffer had no wish to see the physical results of the interrogation methods he had ordered. Pierre waited, unsure if he was up to the task of viewing it as well.

The guard unlocked the cell and ordered her out. Marie slowly emerged into the light. She was dishevelled and badly bruised but was still able to walk. One trembling hand held onto the wall as if for physical guidance, but then she braced herself, inhaled deeply, and walked towards him with her chin lifted high. Her soft lips were cracked, her hands betrayed a slight tremor, but her soft curls still twisted endearingly around the frame of her face.

Mindful he was being observed, Pierre resisted the urge to tear the building down brick by brick and kill every man inside it. Instead, he simply took her arm and escorted her down the stairs. As they stepped into the street, he saw her wince and sag a little. She had shown courage and strength in front of her captors but she could not hide her discomfort from him forever. No longer able to watch her suffer, he lifted her in his arms, cradled her close and whispered hoarsely, 'It's all right, Marie. It's over, and I'm taking you home.'

CHAPTER TWENTY

Pierre had known Georges since he was a boy so it seemed only natural to close the door on his own office and seek his company. In the early years, Georges had worked for his father, rising through the ranks at the *Fleur de Lis* as a direct result of his excellent work ethic and loyalty. He had taught Pierre many things by his example and, in a way, quietly complemented the stern training his father had given him. When his father had died suddenly, the hotel passed to Pierre who, at that time, had been married less than a year. Inexperienced and still relatively young, there had been no man Pierre felt he could trust to help him run the hotel other than his mentor and friend, Georges Plourde. He might have been old enough to be his grandfather, but his mind was sharp, he held the respect of the staff and he treated Pierre as the son he'd never had. It was this father-and-son bond that Pierre subconsciously sought now.

Georges's pale blue eyes looked at him over his half-moon glasses as Pierre entered his office. 'How is she?' he asked, no longer interested in the scattered paperwork littering his desk.

Pierre thought of when he last saw Marie. Her bruised face had been in stark contrast to the crisp white pillow he had laid her head on.

'I'm told she's sleeping.'

'You look tired. You should get some sleep.'

'Not until I know she's okay.'

Georges beckoned to him to come closer and indicated a chair. 'She will be. Give her time.' He gathered the papers on his desk into an untidy pile. 'Have you heard? The Allies are attempting to take Sicily. If they are successful, it will be a major gain.' He looked up again and realised Pierre's mind was elsewhere. 'Pierre? You look worried. Do you think she told them anything?'

'No, I don't.'

'Did you think she would?'

'I didn't know. I caught her looking through my things. It was hard to fully trust her after that.'

'But now you do.'

Pierre realised he did and slowly nodded. 'I don't think she trusts me, though. She saw a photograph of Odette and Lucien in my wallet.'

Georges chuckled.

'You find that funny?'

'We have to find humour where we can.' Georges sat back in his chair and studied him. 'Why are you here, Pierre? You should either be in bed and catching up on your sleep, or with her. So why are you hiding in here?'

'I have a hotel to run.'

'You have me for that.'

'And she is sleeping in my bed.'

Georges chuckled again. 'You own a hotel, Pierre.'

'And?'

'You have a choice of beds to sleep in. It is no excuse.' He waited for Pierre to offer a better reason, but none came. He sat back in his chair to study him. 'I will tell you why you are here. It is because you cannot sleep while she is so unwell, but you don't have the courage to help her through it. Since you brought her here you have left her care to others.'

Pierre straightened in his chair. 'Steady, Georges. We might be friends but I am no coward.'

Georges wouldn't back down. 'Yes, you are. I believe you like this woman a lot. It takes courage to open yourself up to a woman again, particularly after what you've been through.'

Pierre shook his head. 'You don't know what you are talking about. I think you are becoming a romantic fool in your old age.'

'Ah, I must be close to the mark. You don't usually insult me.' He tapped his forehead knowingly. 'I know I'm right.'

'Why would you think I have any feelings for her beyond what is expected?'

'Because you made incessant enquiries about her disappearance.'

'That was because I didn't trust her.'

'You risked being discovered yourself and you did not stop until you found her. Then you bargained for her life.' He sat back in his chair and cradled his hands in front of his stomach. '*That* tells me a lot. A lot more than you are willing to share.'

'Congratulations,' Pierre said dryly. 'You should be a detective.'

Pierre hoped his sarcasm would end his friend's surmising, but Georges had warmed to the role.

'Yet, since you have brought her here you have handed her care to a cleaner and barely visit her.'

'She is more than a cleaner. Besides, barely visiting her hardly shows I have feelings for her.'

'But is evidence that you don't have the courage to admit it.' Georges's voice softened. 'Sit with her, Pierre. We both know it is what you really want to do. I'm tired of seeing you walking the corridors like a caged animal and getting frustrated with the paperwork on your desk. It's been three days now. Sit with her. Care for her. It is why you brought her here in the first instance, isn't it?'

'I brought her here as her neighbour is a treasonous witch disguised as a frail, kind woman.' He tapped his foot with impatience. 'I wonder how many extra rations she received for Marie's life. It doesn't help that I was the one who found that apartment for her.' He looked up to the ceiling and imagined Marie lying in the bedroom above him. Georges was right, he should be by her side.

'You are right.' He stood up. 'Thank you.'

Georges accepted his thanks with a smile. 'Be kind to her. The Gestapo are not known for their gentle ways.'

'I know. I've experienced their interrogation myself.'

'Which makes you the perfect person to help her now.'

Pierre knew he was right.

'When she is well she may be recalled to London. Her time in Paris might be coming to an end. Make the most of it, Pierre, while she is still here. I think you like her very much. It is all right to have feelings for a woman again. If you wait too long, it might be too late to tell her.'

* * *

Pierre carefully placed the glass of iced water on the bedside table, sat down next to Marie and watched her while she slept. How strange his life had become. He had a woman who was not his wife sleeping in his bed — a woman who'd risked her life to work alongside him. He knew almost every inch of her body yet knew nothing about her. He didn't even know her real name. He regretted not asking at the SOE training centre, although he doubted they would have told him. Marie wouldn't tell him now, even if she suddenly woke and learned that she owed him her life. Keeping it secret would have been drilled into her during her training. She had been taught to trust no one.

His chest ached with a desire to know more about her. How did she like to spend her time before the war? What was her family like? At least he now knew she was not a traitor, despite the hell the Gestapo had put her through. Why she had been looking through his pockets still gnawed at him. Perhaps she had just been inquisitive? It was a question he intended to ask when she was well enough to answer it.

Marie stirred and he braced himself, but she only turned her head and continued to sleep. He settled back into his chair, somewhat relieved. Nursing did not come naturally to him, but he wanted to try. The realisation he wanted to try surprised him and he wondered what his wife would say if she saw him now. Probably that it was about time he felt something in his heart.

His gaze wandered over Marie's face. The left side was bruised, but the right side looked perfect and as smooth as carved alabaster. Her lips were cracked and a little bloodied in one corner, but he could still imagine gently kissing them to wake her from a deep sleep. His gaze followed the way her hair curled behind her ear and grazed the delicate skin of her neck. Her chest rose and fell with a gentle steady rhythm. It would not be a hard task, he thought, to sit and watch her every move, offer her drinks when needed and help her to the bathroom should the need arise. How had he left the task to the hotel staff? Now, he suspected, he would argue with anyone who offered to take the role of carer from him.

* * *

It was another two days before Marie finally made a marked improvement. Although, he had helped her to the bathroom and fed her nourishing drinks, her exhaustion had robbed her of any desire to resist his support and do it for herself. But everything changed on the third morning of his care and within a few minutes of waking, he knew the independent Marie he had come to know had returned to him.

Her lashes fluttered, then slowly lifted. Her eyes widened when she recognised him.

'How are you?' he asked, gently.

She winced in pain as she struggled to sit up. 'Better . . . I think.'

'Lie down. You should rest.'

'You shouldn't be here. Your wife—'

'She is not here so don't concern yourself.'

She lay back on the pillows, more from exhaustion than acceptance of his reassurance. 'I don't want to upset her. What if she guesses we have slept together? She doesn't deserve this.'

He felt he owed her an explanation. 'My wife and child don't live here anymore.'

'I'm sorry. I didn't realise you were separated.' She looked genuinely saddened by his confession.

'You could have asked me if I was married rather than search my pockets while I was asleep.'

She had the good grace to blush. 'I wasn't looking for evidence that you were married.'

'Then what were you looking for?'

She didn't answer.

'It's not good for a man's ego to discover that after a—' he searched for the right words '—memorable night, the woman he has made love to is more interested in what is in his pockets than lying in his arms.' He raised an eyebrow in her direction and was pleased when he received a crooked smile in return.

'You are teasing me.'

'Perhaps. Perhaps not. Water?' She nodded. He placed an arm around her shoulders, cradled her to sit forward and was about to gently bring the glass to her lips when she took it from him.

'It's all right. I can do it.'

He gave her the glass and watched her struggle to drink with her tender mouth. A droplet escaped and she caught it with a finger before it wet her skin further. When she indicated she'd had enough, he took the glass from her and placed it on the table, and she settled her back onto the pillow. He returned to his seat, no longer surprised at how natural it felt to care for her.

'Thank you.'

'For what?'

'For taking me in when they released me.'

He waved away her thanks. 'It was nothing. I am still interested to hear your side of the story.'

'What story?'

'The one where you searched my clothes.'

She shrugged. 'I thought you were . . .' Then she frowned as if she had remembered something and pressed her lips together. Her reaction intrigued him.

'You thought I was what?' He watched her eyes wander away from him. She was hiding something. 'I have just rescued you from the Gestapo so I think you owe me an explanation.'

'I thought you were . . . working for them.'

'Who?' Realisation dawned on him. 'The Nazis?'

She nodded. 'And I think you still do.'

He raised his eyebrows. He hadn't seen that one coming.

'You gave me a watch that stopped.'

He moved uneasily in his chair. 'We have been over this.'

'You speak German.'

'Speaking German is not a crime. In fact, in this climate, it's a bonus.' He felt that he couldn't be angry as he had been just as suspicious of her.

'You have friends who are German.'

'Ah . . . that is where you are wrong.' He lifted a finger to emphasise the difference. 'I have *relatives* who are German.' Her eyes widened and he realised he had just made things worse. 'I have not seen them in years. Besides, not all Germans are bad. In fact, many are good, hardworking people who have found themselves caught up in a war they didn't see coming. They believed in Hitler's promises. I blame him and his henchmen for the war.'

'But you *are* half-German. You could have decided to side with the German side of your heritage.'

'I am also half-French.'

'I followed you.'

He sat up in his chair. 'You followed me where?'

'To a café in the Latin Quarter.'

Realisation dawned on him about what she might have witnessed.

'I saw you meet a German officer and pass over information. There is no point denying it.'

He shook his head and shrugged. 'Then I won't.' He saw a veil of disappointment in her eyes. 'Don't jump to conclusions. I didn't say that the information was of any *use*. At least not to the Germans.'

She frowned again, reminding him of an angry child. He resisted smiling. Did she realise that her face hid nothing when she was with him? He sobered. Distrust between them was too serious to ignore. It was time to trust her.

He stood up and began to wander around the room. His suite had not felt like a home for some time and he now realised he had not tried to make it so. He repositioned a lamp that was in the same style as all the executive bedroom lamps in the hotel. He glanced at one of the other bedroom doors. A better lamp was behind that door — with a lot of other things that were too painful to look at. He realised he should have cleared it all out a year ago. It was time to start afresh.

'I have been feeding them false information.' He felt compelled to correct himself. 'It *was* correct intelligence in the beginning, but I would deliver it too late and it would be of no use. However, it was enough to build their trust in me. Now I feed them disinformation about proposed tactics and plans.'

'Is London aware?'

He threw her a glance. 'Absolutely.'

'They didn't inform me.'

'No one in Pointer knows.'

'Do the Nazis know you are an SOE agent?'

He shook his head. 'The Gestapo believed you were connected to the Resistance, which is why they arrested you. Your sweet, elderly neighbour informed on you for the prize of extra food coupons.'

'Madame Chastain?'

He nodded. 'I feel somewhat responsible. I did find you the place to live. I think I have managed to persuade them you're not dangerous. I told them it would be more beneficial to have you free and alive than imprisoned or killed.'

'So, you are the reason they released me.'

'Yes.'

'And there was me thinking that I had beaten them. How did you convince them?'

'I said you were helping me, unknowingly.'

'Unknowingly?'

He ran his hand along the bedpost. 'I told them that I was romancing the information out of you. I told them you are in love with me.' He patted the bedpost awkwardly for want of something to do. 'It will only be a matter of time before they discover the truth.' He turned his focus back to her. 'You do realise what this means, don't you?'

Her chin thrust out and he saw that she did, but he voiced it anyway just so they both were clear.

'You have to return to England before they find out.'

'If I disappear, they will start asking questions. You should leave too.'

She had a point. But leave France permanently? Never. 'I can't. My hotel is here. France is my home.'

'And you have a wife and child.'

He thought of his son, Lucien, laughing and playing on their last holiday in southern France. It was time to be truthful about them as well.

'No, I don't. They died three years ago.'

His loss was her loss in that moment. She understood more than most how a loved one's death ripped a part of you away. He could see it in her face, but she was intuitive enough not to express it with a verbal condolence. He was suddenly reminded of their conversation when they'd first met all those months ago.

'You thought I'd experience loss. Well, you were right.'

'Not like this, Pierre. And not involving your child. When I saw their photograph . . . When you said they weren't here, I assumed they'd left you.'

'They did, in a way.' His throat felt thick with emotion. He stood up, poured himself a glass of water and gulped it down. 'It was me who told them to go.'

'You don't need to explain anything to me.'

He turned to face her. 'I think I should. I owe you an explanation.'

'Because we slept together?'

'Yes. I should have told you before, but I'm ashamed to say that my wife and son were the last things on my mind at the time. I wanted you and nothing else, no one else mattered. I'm sorry. I got carried away.'

'We both got carried away.'

'When you brought up the photograph at the meeting, I didn't tell you what had happened to them and I should have.'

'Why didn't you?'

'Because it was easier to not go there.'

'I don't understand.'

'Whatever was between us had already ended.' He raked a hand through his hair. 'I'd betrayed my wife . . . and for what? As I said, it was easier not to.'

'You did not betray your wife.'

'I *felt* I did. She was the reason I was reluctant to hold you in the barn. You would have been the first woman I'd kissed since I'd kissed my wife. Once I'd touched your lips, her last kiss would have been gone from mine. I know it makes me sound crazy, but that is how it felt. It felt as if she was watching me and waiting to see what I did. Yet, when we finally did sleep together, I didn't give her a second thought until the morning. When I realised that, it was hard. It felt like I'd betrayed her in every sense of the word.'

He sat in the chair, rested his forearms on his knees and stared at his hands cradled in front of him. Marie remained silent and he was thankful for that. He had just confessed what his inner voice had been berating him for ever since he had watched her leave the bedroom. Now he needed a moment, space, to gauge the fallout of his confession, both externally and internally. The seconds ticked by and nothing changed. He was still living and breathing and so was she.

He refocused to the here and now. The past was too painful to linger on too long as it only tore up the soul.

Perhaps this was the catalyst to start living in the here and now.

He looked up to find her staring at him with glistening eyes. 'I understand why you lost trust in me. You have seen me fraternising with the Germans. Yes, I am half-German, but I will never forgive the Nazis for what they've done to my family. I might smile and appear to be on good terms with the officers in Paris, but I am doing it for France, my wife . . . and my son who I will never see grow up.'

He stood abruptly and began needlessly folding a hotel dressing gown that hung over the back of his chair so he didn't have to look at her. Seeing his pain validated in someone else's eyes would be the undoing of him.

'I've treated you poorly,' he blurted out. He heard an exasperated sigh behind him.

'How do you come to that conclusion, Pierre?'

'I wasn't exactly welcoming when you arrived. I'm not proud of that. I also allowed myself to be carried away.'

'I was not a passive player, Pierre.'

'And I slept with you not only because I wanted to, but maybe to prove to myself that you did too.'

'I was not a passive lover, Pierre.'

A memory of her naked body against his came to mind. 'I know. However, I should have . . .' He felt himself floundering. 'I am the organiser of Pointer. I shouldn't have—'

'I was not a passive lover,' she repeated stubbornly.

'Perhaps I would feel less guilt if . . .' *I'd not known Odette since we were children.*

'If what?'

'I had . . . wined and dined you . . . been a little more romantic.'

'Do you mean planned my seduction?'

He almost laughed. Almost. 'If I had planned it, I would have had time to talk myself out of it. Sleeping with another agent is risky for the network.'

'And the heart?'

He glanced at her. He had a sneaking suspicion she was teasing him. 'It's too late now. What is done is done.' He dropped the badly folded dressing gown back on the chair where he had found it. She raised an eyebrow at it and he began to wonder if she knew his character better than he did.

'It's never too late for romance,' she said a little too cheerfully, considering his discomfort. 'My mother told me that Paris was the most romantic city in the world. It would be a shame to return to London and not experience that side of it.'

At first he thought she was teasing again, but when he looked at her, he realised she was serious.

'You've just been tortured.'

'I've been beaten, sleep deprived and starved, but I've had worse.'

'When?'

She looked at him sheepishly. 'I fell overboard when I was sixteen. The waves smashed me against the hull of the ship three times before I was rescued. I couldn't sleep or eat properly for two weeks.'

He stared at her in disbelief. 'Is there anything else I should know about you?'

'I fell off the harbour wall when I was ten.'

'It's a miracle you reached adulthood.'

'I think many in the village felt the same way.'

He found himself smiling. 'Will you ever stop surprising me?'

'I hope not.' She turned serious. 'You told them I am your mistress . . . again.'

'I'm sorry about that.'

She waved his concern away. 'I think we should be seen out and about together to prove your story right.'

A slight curve blossomed on her lips and softened her serious expression, making him immediately suspicious to what plan she was about to come up with.

'You should romance me in public.'

It dawned on him that this woman was not only beautiful, astute and brave . . . but she was also a minx.

'Of course, you may not be capable of being romantic.'

'You don't think I can?'

'I think *you* don't think you can.'

'Then I will have to prove myself wrong.' He frowned at what he had just said. *Prove himself wrong?* How had he been manipulated into playing a romantic lover when he had just confessed how bad he felt about sleeping with her in the first place?

'If it makes you feel more comfortable, look at it this way. You have just told the Gestapo that you are romancing me to get information.'

'I did.'

'Not very imaginative, I might say. You keep using the same excuse for us being together.'

He rubbed the back of his neck. 'I did say I'm sorry. It's my vivid imagination that keeps leading me to the same excuse.'

Her soft laughter made him smile.

She eased herself a little higher against her pillows. 'The Gestapo will be watching us initially. It might throw them off our trail if we behave romantically in public. It will prove you told them the truth.'

He had to acknowledge that she had a point.

'It would.' He began to warm to the idea. 'We could do that. Couldn't we?'

'It will be interesting.'

Interesting was not quite the word he would have used. However, the challenge was tempting. It would certainly relieve the guilt of not romancing her first.

'When will you feel able to get up?'

She wriggled her toes, bent her knees slightly and winced. 'A couple more days,' she replied quietly.

'That's settled then. In two days, when you are better, we will explore Paris together.'

'You make it sound like a project.'

He didn't turn around although he had a distinct feeling that she was smiling at him again. 'I need to prepare,' was all he could think of to say. He closed the door on what sounded like her gentle laughter and headed for his office, walking briskly along the corridors of the *Fleur de Lis* and barely noticing the hotel staff he passed. His mind raced with the situation he had got himself into. It was only when he reached his office door did he pause and reflect. Only then did he realise he was looking forward to sharing the delights of Paris with Marie Veilleux — and as for playing her romantic lover, well, he might be out of practice at that sort of thing, but in truth, he didn't mind at all.

CHAPTER TWENTY-ONE

Charlotte woke to find a fresh set of clothes and a bag laid out on the chair by her bed. On the bedside table was a breakfast tray with a single red rose. She eased herself up against the pillows. She hadn't expected Pierre to start his romantic seduction so early. In fact, she was a little surprised he had not found an excuse and avoided it all together.

The rose was a little unimaginative, but sweet. She lifted it carefully from the water, breathed in its fragrance and twirled it in her fingers, before carefully returning it to its miniature vase. She craned her neck to look at the clothes laid out for her and recognised they were hers. It was thoughtful of Pierre to have collected them from her now abandoned lodgings. Who would want to see Paris dressed in the same clothes she had been interrogated in?

She ate her breakfast, washed and looked at herself in the mirror. The swelling on her face was gone and her bruises had finally begun to turn yellow, which would be, she hoped, far easier to disguise. She turned her head this way and that as she silently thanked her instructors for preparing her for what her interrogators had meted out. Controlling one's mind and body, all helped withstand the methods they'd used, but she was nobody's fool. She knew that in the years ahead she would revisit that cell many times in her thoughts and nightmares. She wondered how the experience would show itself at unexpected times. Those thoughts scared her more than how she felt now, which was why she didn't want to think about it anymore today.

She rummaged through the bag. Thankfully, it contained her cosmetic samples, so she carefully applied them with gentle dabs. When she'd finished, she had to admit that she was pleased with the result. She inhaled deeply. She hadn't admitted to Pierre how scared she had been. To survive something like that made one appreciate things far more. Like Pierre. Like Paris. She wanted to make the most of the little time she had left to be with and enjoy them both.

Dressed, hair brushed, she stared into the mirror for the final time. Mademoiselle Marie Veilleux was ready to be romanced in Paris — only it was Charlotte Bray who stared back at her.

Her heart sank a little as she realised she had little experience of being romanced.

She had spent her adult life at sea, unfazed by fish entrails sliding across the deck or the coarse banter of fishermen. The opportunity for romance had been scarce and she had never actively sought it out. Her relationship with the soldier had been far too brief for any real romance . . . or at least she had never felt *romanced* by him. To be romantic, one would have to suspend any worries and just live for the moment — to accept the good and the bad in each new shared experience, to find the waiting to see one another again a silent torture. At least that was what *The Lover of Marseille* conveyed. But that was fiction. It was wonderfully, sensually, sensationally portrayed, but fiction nonetheless. What about the here and now? She recalled her trips to the pictures for inspiration.

If a couple were caught in the rain, they laughed and kissed. If they missed a train, they used the moment for a romantic stroll. If their shoes rubbed, they took them off and strolled barefoot along the pavement without a care in the world. She sighed. Films glossed over the damp chills from

221

wet clothes, the troubles caused by missing a train or the bleeding blisters on the feet. She turned a little to the right and a little to the left as she straightened out the creases in her dress. This was the first time she had worn it. She was pleased to find that it fitted well. At least she looked the part of a woman who loved romance. In the next hour she was about to find out if she was.

* * *

'Where are we?' asked Charlotte. They had come upon a canal, lined by shrubs and trees, which stretched lazily in both directions. Intricate cast-iron footbridges crossed the water at intervals, while a series of locks aided the rise and fall of the water level to accommodate the barges waiting patiently at their gates.

'We are at the Canal Saint-Martin. Napoleon commissioned it to bring water to Paris. Now *he* was a great lover.'

'You are referring to Napoleon's love for Josephine?'

'I am.'

'But they divorced, didn't they?'

He looked a little uncomfortable at her knowledge of history. 'Ah . . . but when he died in exile, her name was the last word on his lips.'

She leaned on the railing. 'I bet that didn't make his second wife or his numerous mistresses happy.'

He leaned on the railing beside her. 'Are you going to make it difficult for me to be romantic?'

She smiled. 'I'm sorry. I'll try harder to behave. Thank you for the rose. *That* was very romantic.'

'What rose?' asked Pierre as they pushed away from the railings and approached one of the locks. Both gates were closed and a lockkeeper, dressed in a jumper, trousers and a black beret, was frantically turning the lock handle. A torrent of water began to flow into the lower-level section, churning up the water in clouds of white bubbles, forcing the water to rise rapidly.

'The one on the breakfast tray.' When Pierre didn't respond, she realised what had happened. 'Oh . . . you didn't prepare the tray, did you?'

'No, I didn't,' he said, showing more interested in the lock workings than her.

The gate opened and a waiting barge moved through. Charlotte felt her cheeks redden and wished she were on the barge too. Anywhere but making a fool of herself in front of Pierre. She watched in silence as the barge worker methodically coiled a length of rope into a hoop and tossed it onto the boat's canvas cover. The chore reminded Charlotte of her father and his crew.

Pierre cleared his throat. 'Let's walk along some of the length of the canal. It is peaceful around here . . . and there are no German banners or police to remind us of their occupation.'

Pierre was right, despite the numerous slow-moving barges, with their rippling wakes, it was peaceful and beautiful. They walked slowly under the trees that lined the canal. On occasion, they climbed the steps of one of the narrow footbridges so they could soak in the view of the ribbon of water below. It was romantic and relaxing, although there was still a band of tension between them.

Charlotte decided to confront the atmosphere head on. 'We are not particularly good at being romantic, are we?'

'I'd like to think we are trying.' He smiled back, although she noticed that his smile did not reach his eyes.

'Perhaps we should stop . . . trying. We could just enjoy the day as friends.'

'Friends?' He stared at the canal, a deep furrow formed between his dark brows and she wondered what he was thinking. She knew she would feel less obligated and she hoped he would feel less guilt. He shrugged. 'If that is what you want. I must really be abysmal at being romantic.'

'I don't think that at all. I just don't think you are willing to show that side of you yet, and I am unsure if I would know how to respond to it. I think it will take the pressure off us both. I goaded you into it, but it didn't cross my mind that I would not be up to the challenge myself.'

'Up to it or just not interested?'

'Would it matter?'

'I think it would.'

She was about to ask why when he reached for her hand.

'Come on, let's get out of here. I want to show you Montmartre. I may not be able to show you a view of Paris from the top of the Eiffel Tower, but I can show you it from the steps of the Sacre Coeur Church.'

His hand remained in the air between them. Compelled to fill it with her own, she reached for it. It felt warm and fitted hers perfectly, yet their bodies touching seemed strange and awkward, which was absurd considering that they had done far more.

* * *

Charlotte fell in love with Montmartre. Many Parisian buildings were at least six storeys high, whereas Montmartre had kept its individual identity, born from its humble origins of an area of scrubland only fit for housing the poor. Today, Montmartre had become part of Paris, but the buildings' distinct architecture remained unique, and vastly different from their six-storey counterparts. Brick, picturesque houses had replaced the original shacks and were the perfect backdrop to the snaking, narrow cobbled streets. Over the centuries, Montmartre's quaint beauty had inspired poets, artists and sculptors to flock to the cheap lodgings and make the neighbourhood their home. Each one had left their mark in either paint, word or stone, sacrificing the comfort of a regular income to feed their creative compulsion.

Charlotte watched another generation of artists set up their easels to paint as she sat with Pierre and drank black coffee at one of the cafés which had spilled out onto the pavement. Many were elderly, too old to be considered for work in the factories by the occupied force, so their time painting was both a blessing as well as a compulsion, yet she was aware that the romanticised life of an artist was, in many cases, far from the reality.

'There are so many talented artists, yet so few are successful at earning a reasonable living from it,' she mused over the brim of her chicory-laden coffee, its nutty, woody flavour a tolerable, but not preferable substitute. 'Even some of the successful ones end up living tortured lives or die in poverty.'

Pierre stirred the liquid in his cup. He had not spoken in a while and she wondered what he was thinking. His voice was as smooth as liquid honey when he finally began to speak.

> '"*To bear so vast a load of grief*
> *Thy courage, Sisyphus, I crave!*
> *My heart against the task is brave,*
> *But Art is long and Time is brief.*
>
> *For from Fame's proud sepulchral arches,*
> *Towards a graveyard lone and dumb,*
> *My sad heart, like a muffled drum,*
> *Goes beating slow funereal marches.*"'

He glanced at her, a little embarrassed.

'It's lovely. Who wrote it?'

His hazel eyes darkened at her interest. 'Charles Baudelaire. He was a famous nineteenth-century Parisian poet. His works have inspired many over the years.'

'What's it called?'

'"Ill Luck". It's about a poet's constant struggle to be recognised as he journeys towards obscurity. Baudelaire would know. He was extraordinarily gifted, but he died young, in poverty and disillusioned with a world that was unwilling to publish many of his works during his lifetime. I can only remember the first two verses.' He fiddled with his teaspoon. 'I used to enjoy reading poetry before the war. I was fascinated how the rhythm of words could evoke so many emotions and images. How so much could be expressed in so few words. Every poet's voice is unique. Every poet's poem has its own story to tell.' He pressed his lips together as if he had shared too much.

'And what about now?'

'Now?' He laid the teaspoon down carefully by his cup. 'I haven't read a poem in years. It is hard to enjoy such pleasures when the darker side of life is the stronger force.'

Charlotte smiled. 'It must be the magic of Montmartre. It has inspired art for years, now it is working its magic on you.'

'Maybe.' He smiled at her and this time his eyes smiled too. His son, in the photo, had smiling eyes. She suddenly realised the earlier tension between them was no longer there. At some point it had melted away and left an opportunity for something else to form. It was exciting and slightly nerve-wracking.

'Where are you going to take me next?' she asked, eager to keep the mood light.

'The Sacre Coeur Church. We will be able to see all of Paris from there.' He finished his coffee and reached out his hand to her again.

This time it felt more natural to slip her hand into his. They strolled to the steps of the Sacre Coeur and climbed the steep steps of the hill together. The white-stoned church of exotic domes and intricate mosaics greeted them at the top. Charlotte was aware that the translation of Sacre Coeur was Sacred Heart. It was a romantic name and she wondered if the name was the real reason Pierre had chosen it as a place to visit, but as they arrived at the top of the hill, a panoramic view of Paris lay out at her feet just as he had promised. They admired it in silence for some minutes, standing side by side and hand in hand.

Pierre moved to stand behind her. 'Have you fallen in love with Paris yet?' he asked quietly. He was standing so close she could almost feel his breath on her skin. A shiver of pleasure raced through her body. 'Are you cold?' he asked, concerned.

She shook her head as she felt the warmth of his body behind her. If she wanted to she could easily rest backwards against him . . . if she dared, she thought.

'It is easy to fall in love with Paris. Tell me more about it. I want to know everything that you know.'

He rested his hand on her shoulder, as if to guide her, and quietly pointed out the major landmarks of the city, and sometime, somehow, unconsciously to her if not to him, she found that she had indeed leaned against his body for comfort, support and warmth. His arms folded around her body to welcome her there.

She sighed. 'It is as if I am looking down from the sky.'

'This is the highest point in Paris. It is said that our sacred heart is halfway between heaven and earth.' The sound of his voice was seducing and, in her foggy mind, full of sin. She felt her body inwardly melt at the images and memories it evoked.

'At this moment, I feel as if I am between heaven and earth,' she whispered, knowing every word of it to be true.

* * *

Bois de Boulogne had been one of her mother's favourite places. As they entered the large public park, she admitted to Pierre that she had already visited it in the days she'd decided to explore the city and build a background story to her identity. The visit had been brief, and as the park was so vast, she had seen little of it, but they had made a silent pact to be truthful so she felt it was only right to say.

'Did you take a ride in one of the boats?' he asked as he indicated a man who was renting them out.

'No.'

He glanced at her as the man approached. 'But you wanted to?'

'Yes. How do you know that?'

He slipped his wallet from his jacket in readiness to pay the man. 'You had a faraway look in your eyes when you told me about the boats in the park the first day we met. I assumed you would like to take a ride in one someday. So I arranged for the rental of a boat for the afternoon.'

'You remembered what I said at the interview? But that was months ago.'

He raised an eyebrow at her. 'It was not the only thing I remember. You were hard to forget.'

He left her then, keen to secure his booking. Charlotte watched him talking to the boatman. He had just admitted he had found her difficult to forget, but instead of taking advantage of the moment by flirting with her or kissing her, he had marched off. She realised it had not been the first time. The man had no idea that he was romantic. When he was, he either interrupted the moment or changed the topic.

She would have happily returned his kisses if he had taken advantage of the moment at the Sacre Coeur, but instead he had abruptly released her from his arms and suggested they move on to the next destination. He was either oblivious to how well he was doing, or unwilling to fully break down the wall between them.

He called out her name. 'He has a boat ready for us. It is time to ride the waters of the Lac Inférieur.'

She joined him and discovered that a bundle of food and what appeared to be lemonade were neatly packed into the bottom of the boat.

'I thought about arranging a bottle of wine, but I didn't know your preference and thought something more refreshing would be better.'

'You arranged a picnic for us!'

'It is more of a snack.'

He had done it again, downplaying and distancing himself from his romantic gestures. She wondered if he had really provided the rose on the tray after all. Was he afraid of rejection? She climbed into the boat and they spent a pleasant hour on the water, Pierre gently rowing while she lounged in the sun.

At times he rested too, content to watch a bevy of swans swim past or listen to the birds calling to one another in the trees.

Sometimes they sought refuge from the heat of the day and rested in the shadows of heavy, overhanging branches laden with leaves. It was at times like these, after they'd ate and drank their humble meal in contented silence, that they talked about life, poetry and music, and concluded that Bois de Boulogne was an oasis from the war, as at times it was impossible to tell that they were in a city at all.

They returned the boat to its owner and followed the narrow trails through the dense woodland to the Parc de Bagatelle, which was at the heart of Bois de Boulogne. Ancient trees of oak, pine, sequoias and cedars lined their routes as they explored the follies, little bridges, grottos and waterfalls of the park. The atmosphere was filled with the potential for romance and it was easy to be seduced by it. They eventually came across the small chateau and its exquisite fragrant gardens. They reminded Charlotte of England and she couldn't help thinking that her time in Paris would inevitably come to an end one day.

'I will never forget my time here with you.' The words escaped her lips before she had a chance to stop them. All day she had been aware Pierre had remained silent about his feelings for her, but she had not realised that she had kept her feelings about him quiet too. Now she had voiced them and she suddenly felt exposed to his teasing or rejection. She waited for him to reply, hoping he would agree, yet dreading he wouldn't. Finally, he broke the silence that seemed to stretch forever.

'Charles Baudelaire understood how we feel:

"Then I will dream of blue horizons deep;
Of gardens where the marble fountains weep;
Of kisses, and of ever-singing birds—
A sinless Idyll built of innocent words.

And Trouble, knocking at my window-pane
And at my closet door, shall knock in vain;

I will not heed him with his stealthy tread,
Nor from my reverie uplift my head;

For I will plunge deep in the pleasure still
Of summoning the spring-time with my will,
Drawing the sun out of my heart, and there
With burning thoughts making a summer air.'"

She met his gaze. His quietly spoken words stretched between them as if a taught cord joined them from heart to heart. He may have chosen a poet's words to hide behind, but she could see from the sincerity in his gaze that they had been carefully chosen. He may be a man damaged by grief, and bitter from war, but he had just admitted that he would always cherish their time together, *their springtime*, and revisit it in his memory time and time again, to help him get through any dark times ahead.

* * *

They headed for his hotel, hoping to reach it before curfew as they were eager to avoid unnecessary questioning from patrolling Germans. Their mood had slumped during their journey home. Every street corner brought them closer to the centre of Paris, where bold reminders of everything they had tried to forget throughout the day increased. Soldiers at checkpoints, swastika flags flying in the rising breeze, the grand architecture of Paris defaced by enormous banners supporting the Third Reich, queues for food and, finally, a temporary power cut which brought irate shopkeepers and café owners into the street.

In the confusion, Charlotte thought she saw Isabelle in the crowd. Their time in England and Scotland together seemed like a lifetime ago, yet she was confident it was her. She watched Isabelle walk towards her in the street, inconspicuous in the crowd shopping for essentials. Every part of her mind and body wanted to speak to her as she approached. Where was she staying? What name was she known by? How was she getting on? Instead, Charlotte remained stiffly by Pierre's side. Isabelle passed her without a backward glance, but the sweep of her gaze had momentarily jarred on Charlotte's face. Neither spoke, neither smiled, as she walked briskly by, but the flicker of recognition told them both they were silently saying *hello*.

'Are you all right?' asked Pierre, concerned her grasp had tightened.

She blinked away her sadness. 'Yes. I just want to get away from here.'

He took her arm. 'Come. Let's get back to the hotel.'

* * *

They were both relieved when the electricity flickered back on as they entered Pierre's hotel. She walked with him through the grand entrance, into the elevator and silently watched the floors pass through the metal, latticed doors as they ascended to his suite. As they stepped out into the corridor, it finally felt as if they were blocking out *that* world outside. He unlocked his suite door and stepped aside so she could enter. He handed her the key.

She looked at the gold tag with the name of his hotel embossed into the metal. 'I've enjoyed today.'

'Yes, I did too.'

'We must have walked for miles.'

'Yes, miles.' They fell silent. Pierre shoved his hands in his pockets and looked down the hall. She wanted to ask if he would like to come inside, knowing the invite would mean so much more.

He must have seen her hesitancy as he said, 'I have a room down the corridor so if you need anything, I'm not too far away.'

Disappointment turned her stomach, forcing her to admit that she didn't want their day together to end so quickly. She searched for something to say in the hope of delaying the inevitable. Pierre beat her to it.

'Are you tired?'

Her hopes rose. 'No, why?'

'It has been a long day and you are still recovering. I thought you might be keen for a rest.'

'No, I'm not tired . . . are you?'

His eyes darkened, their hazel depths disappearing behind centres of black molasses.

'No, I'm not tired.' He tilted his head to one side as he studied her. 'I have enjoyed today.'

'Yes, you said.'

'I mean *really* enjoyed it.' He withdrew his hands from his pockets and stepped forward until he was so close she could have wrapped her arms around him. He brushed her cheek with his lips as if it was the most natural thing in the world, and whispered, 'I've enjoyed it and don't want it to end.'

His nearness and softly whispered words sent racing heat through her body. 'I'm glad,' was all she could think of to say.

She felt his hand slip around her waist and rest in the small of her back. 'I have a confession,' he whispered into her hair.

'You do?' she murmured feeling as if she was drowning in his spell. Her lips felt more sensitive, her mind a little foggy and all she could think of was his touch and the faint aroma of his soap.

'I didn't prepare the tray, but I did pick the rose.'

Suddenly she felt a little breathless too. 'Why didn't you tell me this before?'

Another soft brush of his lips against her cheek. 'Because I was afraid you would think it was unimaginative.'

Had he read her mind? If he had, she was in trouble right now with all the wild thoughts racing through it . . .

'I would never think that,' she lied not wanting to break his enticing spell.

He kissed her neck. Another shiver, another ache rising deep inside her and crying out to be touched.

'And now what?' he asked.

'Now what?' she asked, finding it hard to concentrate. Needing a moment to take a breath, she rocked her head away from his next kiss.

'I am not expecting anything in return.'

She opened her eyes to look at him. 'In return? I'm not sure what you mean?'

He smiled at her. 'For my efforts at being romantic.' His eyes looked over her head and towards the room. The smile slowly faded as he stared at the slightly ajar bedroom door. Charlotte felt the enticing atmosphere of promise change in an instant. His body stiffened, as the softness in his features drained away. He stepped away from her abruptly, leaving her feeling suddenly lonely. She frowned, confused by his behaviour.

'Forgive me,' he said, politely. 'I have been too forward. This is where our cultures are different.'

'Different?'

'The English are too polite, too well-mannered, too cautious of the consequences. In France, we are more relaxed about these things. We are more open about our desire to make love, but I forgot where I was.' His eyes wandered around his apartment. 'This place is not the right place. I could never make love to you here.' Her quiet gasp brought his gaze back to her. 'I can see my honesty has shocked you.'

She frowned, confused. 'A little.'

He inhaled deeply before releasing it with a sigh of clarity. 'I have embarrassed myself. I was only thinking about what I wanted and not what was right. I think it is time I said goodnight.' He turned to go. 'Goodnight. I hope you sleep well.'

She watched him walk to his room and disappear inside. Perplexed, she closed her door and leaned against it as she tried to relive the last few minutes to untangle the conversation they'd just had. One minute he was kissing her, the next he was walking away. Now she felt unsatisfied, disappointed — even deprived now that he'd returned to his room.

We are more open about our desire to make love.

Was he suggesting she was uptight? Hadn't she already proved that she was anything but uptight?

She forlornly approached the bedroom, slipping her coat from her shoulders and dragging it along the floor with her fingers. She paused at the door to *his* bedroom and looked about her. She had not explored his apartment during her recovery. It dawned on her that this large hotel apartment was his home, the place where he had lived with his wife and son.

Curiosity got hold of her and she opened one of the bedrooms to find it stored with boxes of belongings as if in the process of being cleared out but things had never quite reached the door. An exquisitely expensive lamp protruded from one, but many of the lids were closed, although not taped. She lifted the lid of two boxes in quick succession. The contents confirmed what she had already guessed. His wife's clothes, lovingly folded, filled one. His son's toys were carefully stacked in the other, as if waiting for the moment when they would be needed again. The reason for his sudden change of mind became all too clear. Pierre could not bring himself to make love to her in the same apartment where he had lived with his wife and child.

She understood and then felt compelled to tell him so. She wrenched open the door, followed the long corridor to his room and banged on his door.

The door opened and she found herself staring straight at him. Her gaze automatically dropped to his chest as she realised that he had already stripped to his waist in readiness for bed. Vivid memories of trailing her lips across his skin came flooding back. She lifted her gaze to meet his.

'I understand what you were saying back there. I didn't, but I do now. I respect your decision, but you can't change the past, Pierre.'

He braced himself. 'I know.'

Her eyes wandered around the room he was in now. It was moderate but lacked personal belongings. It was not a home, but a room probably used for family guests when visiting Paris.

'We are not in your apartment anymore.'

'No, we are not.'

She stepped across the threshold, shut the door behind her and rested against it. 'I will leave if you want me to, but I just wanted you to know that I want you, very much, and I think you want me.'

'You are right to think that.'

'Soon I will have to leave. And I don't want to leave, Pierre. I'm afraid that if I go back to the apartment now, I am wasting an opportunity that I might live to regret.' She laughed nervously. 'You see, Pierre . . . the English can be open about their wish to make love too. We might find the words difficult to say, but the desire burns just as strongly.'

In the next instant, she had reached for him, or had he reached for her? Whatever happened occurred in a flash, wrapping them up in a whirl of passion and taking them straight to his bed. There was no need for confessions, apologies or righting misunderstandings. They both knew what they needed and they needed it now.

Their passion was heated, angry and driven, leaving a trail of discarded clothes on the polished wooden floor. There was no romance. This union was basic and needy, but it was what they both wanted and they were too impatient to wait. Soon they were sated, exhausted and quivering in a haze of spent tension. It had taken them both by surprise and they found themselves laughing as they looked into each other's eyes.

As the evening turned to darkness, they reached for each other again, their fierce youthful passion now replaced with softly spoken words and mature, languid exploration. Fingers trailed each other's soft curves and firm undulations as they talked of nothing too important. It was time for discovery of mind and body, to stir every sensation and make new memories that would last forever.

As time passed, it was inevitable that their fierce passion would revisit them again, hungry and growing in its demand for every desire to be fulfilled. They both knew their time together was coming to an end and they wanted every minute to last and be seared into their brain. As the city of Paris slept, their joint cries came unhindered and unashamed as they melted, then collapsed, into one another. Their hunger had only been temporarily satisfied and contented, Charlotte was sure, because she was now convinced her craving for Pierre would never die.

CHAPTER TWENTY-TWO

Pierre looked at Marie sleeping beside him. She lay naked beneath the white sheet, her short hair tousled as if she had been outside on a windy day. Her breathing was deep and slow, indicating she was lost in a world of dreams. He wondered what she was dreaming and if he featured at all. Marie had been the first woman he had slept with since his wife had died. It had left him burdened with guilt. Of course, the guilt did not bring Odette back, it just ruined the afterglow of a memorable night, and any budding relationship struggling to grow. So what use was guilt when it neither ceased grief or soothed it? He knew Odette would've wanted him to be happy, not mourn her forever. He'd resisted moving on, chosen to not move on. Meeting Marie threatened that plan. He had regretted her coming into his life. Now, as he watched her sleeping in his bed, he regretted it coming to an end.

He heard a soft knock on the door and got up to answer it. A female courier passing messages between networks handed him a note and quickly walked away. He closed the door and sat down at the dressing table to decode it, and had just finished when he heard Marie stir. He glanced up to find her looking at him, the white tangled sheets twisted around her body and clutched to cover her breasts.

He smiled. 'A little late to play coy.'

'It is never too late to play coy,' she teased as she rolled onto her stomach and rested on her forearms.

He reluctantly dragged his eyes away from her curves and tried to concentrate on the note in his hand.

'What are you reading?' she asked.

'The courier has just passed it to me. It sounds like Prosper network might be compromised. There have been many arrests.'

Marie sat up. 'What happens now?'

Pierre tossed the note onto the dressing table and sat back in his chair. 'It means that the Germans have probably been infiltrating the network for months. It won't be long before they learn about Pointer. We need to let the others know and arrange for you to return to England.'

'I don't want to go home.'

'And I don't want you to go either, but if I don't get you out of here, I know I will regret it for the rest of my life.'

* * *

The train station was busy. They passed through the routine controls without incident but remained vigilant as every major station had secret surveillance now and it was best to remain cautious. Yet, despite knowing all this, Marie suddenly turned to Pierre and said she needed to speak to someone.

'Who?' he asked, confused. 'Who do you know in Paris?'

'Don't look now, but I know the woman over there. The one in the brown coat. I saw her the other day but thought it best not to acknowledge her. Things have changed now, Pierre. I have to warn her.'

Pierre followed her gaze, disguised as vague interest in his surroundings, and instantly recognised the tall, dark-haired woman, with a ready smile and watchful eyes. She was reading a poster, but despite being British, her French language skills were excellent. He knew this because he had assessed them in London all those months ago.

'Is this wise?' He knew exactly what Marie wanted to warn her about, but here? Now?

'Please, Pierre. I'll regret it for the rest of my life if I don't. It's my only chance before I leave.'

She looked at him with beseeching eyes and he reluctantly relented with a curt nod of his head. He knew what it was like to live with regrets so how could he force it upon her?

'I must be mad to let you do this surrounded by surveillance.' He looked about him. 'I shall stop her or distract her, but any message must be fleeting. No long conversations. Promise me.' He caught at her arm. '*Promise me.*'

She smiled to reassure him, no doubt thankful for his help. 'I promise.'

They threaded their way through the crowd, concerned when their fleeting glimpses through the mass of travellers revealed that Isabelle had moved away from the poster. They searched the sea of faces, both aware that they would have to board their own train soon. A child ran past them, followed in hot pursuit by his worried grandparents. Two soldiers walked by, their large German Shepherd dogs straining at their leads as they barked ferociously at any passenger who encroached on their path.

Then they spotted Isabelle walking briskly to the exit, unaware of their presence and obviously eager to avoid the patrolling soldiers. Pierre overtook her and suddenly crouched to tie his shoelaces in her path. She halted in midstep, a little alarmed, until she saw Marie beside him.

'Gosh!' was all she could say, whispered on a breath of surprise and shock.

'Ssshh! Don't say anything more!'

Pierre glanced up and saw that Marie was looking at him but speaking to her friend under her breath. Reassured that it appeared little conversation between them was taking place, he returned his concentration to his shoes.

'Prosper about to fall. Many arrests. Pointer may be compromised too. Germans possibly infiltrating networks for months. Trust no one.'

A whistle blew loudly in the distance, a sure signal that no more could be said.

Pierre stood and took Marie's arm. 'We have to go. Our train is about to leave.'

He looked at the tall woman and saw that she had tears in her eyes. Her hand quivered, aching, no doubt, to reach out and touch Marie's arm to thank her for warning her, but thankfully, she resisted and remained silent. She turned and walked stiffly away as he guided Marie in the opposite direction.

'It's done. You have warned her. There is no more you can do.' Despite his reassurances, he felt it would be the last time he would see the tall, brave woman, who had risked her life to work in occupied France, and he had a chilling feeling that the woman knew it too.

* * *

Although the train was not crowded, Pierre preferred to stand by the carriage door, away from the other passengers and where they could watch the countryside hurtle by outside the window. Pierre braced their bodies against the moving carriage by resting one hand against the wall of the train and the other around Marie. They remained like this for much of the journey, silent and thoughtful, as there seemed little to say. What did one talk about, he thought miserably, when the end of their time together hurtled towards them as quickly as the passing trees outside?

Finally, the train came to a graceful halt at Marolle-en-Hurepoix station. They quietly collected their bikes from the back of the train and cycled out into the countryside of Hurepoix. The terrain was largely flat and they made good progress. Finally, they arrived at their destination — their rural safe house where the Resistance met. They parked their bikes and walked towards the house holding hands. They paused at the front door and looked at each other. They were members of the Pointer network again and their time as lovers must be put aside. He saw his own sadness reflected in her eyes that it had to be so. Together they slowly released their entwined fingers and their hands drifted apart.

Bernard and Gérald answered their knock, unaware of their pain, and welcomed them inside.

* * *

Pierre watched Marie select a potato and begin to peel it. He had told her there was no need for her to cook a meal, but she had insisted. Raymond was late and it would give her something to do while they waited for his arrival. When she began peeling the third potato, he put down his playing cards and joined her, preferring to be by her side than so far apart. They exchanged smiles as they began to peel the vegetables together. Bernard and Sully noticed but said nothing.

The aroma of the stew soon filled the kitchen. Raymond finally arrived just as she was about to share it out. She served the men and sat down at the table with her own portion but just picked at her food. Pierre knew she was disappointed that he had insisted she returned to England, but she understood his reasoning. She didn't like it, though. Looking up, she caught him staring at her and they exchanged fleeting, sad smiles again before she returned to pushing her vegetables around her bowl.

'I have a feeling you wanted us to meet for a better reason than eating stew,' remarked Bernard with his mouth full. He waved his spoon at Marie. 'Although it is the best I have tasted in a while.'

Marie accepted his compliment with a slight tilt of her head.

Pierre put down his spoon. 'Well, now we are all here I can tell you. Prosper is about to fall. I received a message saying many agents have been ambushed and arrested. I suspect that the Germans have control of their wireless and have been sending false messages to London for weeks.'

The news was greeted with horrified silence.

'We need to lie low for a while. No more meetings until I send word. After a month or so we will start up again. Sully, I want you to radio London and arrange for a Lysander to pick up Marie.'

'You want Marie to leave?' questioned Bernard. He dropped his spoon in his bowl, his appetite appearing to have suddenly disappeared.

'Marie is under suspicion. She needs to return home. As soon as London knows, they'll want her pulled out anyway.'

'How do you know she was not followed here?'

'We made sure of that.' He pushed his plate away, unsure if his own loss of appetite was due to Marie leaving or the bad news he was imparting.

Sully noticed. 'Why do I feel that is not all?'

'I can't be sure that we're not compromised either.'

The other members stopped eating too.

Raymond voiced what they were all thinking. 'That is quite an accusation, Pierre.'

'I know. I have no evidence for it. One explosive drop that went wrong, nothing more.'

Bernard looked at Sully. 'And which Sully mysteriously missed. Did you decide to search another area to make yourself absent?'

'Says the man who was arrested but was quickly released. Did you do a deal, Bernard?' As Bernard lunged at Sully, Sully retreated out of his reach with a tilt of his chair. 'Take it easy, Bernard. Not so much fun when the finger is pointed at you instead, is it?'

'Calm down, you lot,' ordered Pierre. 'It might be nothing.'

'You wouldn't have said anything if you didn't have concerns,' Raymond prompted. 'Tell us.'

Pierre continued to eat. 'If Prosper has been compromised for months, London has been unaware and has continued to communicate with them and send over agents. It appears they have unwittingly sent them into waiting ambushes. I just think we need to be cautious.'

Sully shoved his bowl away from him. 'You mean you want us to suspect everyone.' His eyes widened. 'Or just me, as I am the wireless operator?' All eyes turned to him. 'After all, there is only one person here who is half-German and it's not me.'

Bernard's jaw tightened at the implication that Pierre was involved.

'We won't be able to trust anyone soon,' continued Sully.

'He is right,' said Raymond, picking up his spoon again.

'It is how we have all lived since France fell!' ground out Pierre. He inhaled deeply to calm himself. There was no need to take his frustration out on them. 'Marie's neighbour reported her only a few days ago. Some people do not have the courage to fight.'

They all turned to Marie for confirmation.

'Pierre's right,' she said. 'I was arrested and interrogated, but they eventually set me free.'

'Which is why Pierre wants you to return to England as soon as possible,' said Sully, finally understanding.

Marie gave up trying to pretend she had an appetite and pushed her bowl away too. 'They have lost interest in me for now, but it is only a matter of time before they question me again. I don't want to go home, but Pierre is right to send me back. I'm recovered now and fit to travel. If they were watching me after my release, all they've seen me do is nothing more harmful than see the sights of Paris. We were careful we weren't followed today, but I can't guarantee I won't be in the future. If I stay much longer, it might compromise the whole network.'

Pierre smiled at her, glad she had finally accepted his choice. Her acceptance had lifted a great burden from his shoulders. He silently thanked her before turning his attention to Sully.

'Take this down. I want the message to say . . .' He turned to her. 'Remind me of your code name again.'

'Adele.'

He turned back to Sully who was scribbling it down. 'Pointer requests immediate assistance for Adele to return home.' He paused, appearing to consider adding more detail but finally decided against it. 'Best keep it short. They will know what I mean. I want you to send this message tonight.'

Sully immediately began translating the words into code. Pierre's order had shown the group he had confidence in him and Sully was eager to prove him right.

'Ideally, I'd like London to send a plane tonight,' he continued. 'Find a place that is far away from here. Wait for a reply, but don't stay in the same place longer than thirty minutes or they will track your signal to your location.'

Sully closed his case and shrugged into his coat. Pierre touched his arm as he made to leave.

'Good luck, Sully. Let me know what they say. Remember, ideally tonight.'

Sully nodded. 'I'll be back as soon as I can.' He looked around at the others, his gaze lingering on Bernard, before walking briskly to the door and slamming it behind him.

* * *

Waiting for Sully to return was tortuous. With no missions to plan for, they had little to do. Their guns remained hidden beneath the living room floor, their maps stacked under another in the hall. Bernard brought out the pack of cards again, and they began to play, each watching the clock between tricks and dealing yet another game. Marie retreated to the kitchen to wash the bowls and remained there, cleaning the cupboards as if she were making it her home. Eventually, Gérald and Raymond went outside for a cigarette, leaving Bernard as the only card player to remain.

'Is there something going on between you two?'

Pierre needlessly repositioned the cards in his hand. 'Between who?'

Bernard smiled humourlessly. 'You and Marie. I saw the way you two looked at each other. I saw the way *you* looked at her. I haven't seen you look at a woman like that before.'

'You haven't seen me look at many women.'

'Exactly.'

'I'm concerned for her safety, that's all. It's your turn to put down a card.'

Bernard did as he was told, placing it deliberately with a determined flick of the card's corner. 'Just because she has a pretty face and came straight from London, it doesn't mean she shouldn't be suspected too. She was released by the Gestapo. How do we know that she didn't tell them anything?'

Pierre placed a card on the table and gathered up the trick, positioning it in front of him with a determined calm. Was Bernard trying to plant a seed of suspicion in his head? If he was, he was too late. That seed had already grown and quickly withered.

He looked over his cards at Bernard. 'How do I know *you* didn't break under interrogation? You were arrested in the woods and subsequently let go. No one is above suspicion, Bernard. Not even you.'

Bernard pushed back his chair and stood. 'Or you. What are you today, Pierre? Half-French . . . or half-German.' He shook his head. 'I'm going out for a smoke.'

Pierre watched him leave, feeling regretful. He didn't like to fall out with Bernard. He'd always found him reliable in the past and had always trusted him before.

'Bernard.'

Bernard paused at the door. 'What?' he asked grumpily.

'You were right . . . about Marie and me. There is something going on between us. We are more than just friends.'

'I knew it,' he replied softly as he stepped through the doorway and outside.

Pierre watched him leave, angry with himself for doubting everyone and poisoning their trust in each other. Yet there was still the nagging concern that all was not well. He glanced at his watch, then the wall clock in turn. As soon as Marie was on the plane home, he would feel reassured of her safety and be able to focus on the future of Pointer. Until then, there was always the risk he might lose her. He had lost his wife in a bid for freedom. He didn't want to lose Marie the same way.

* * *

Eventually Sully returned, wide-eyed, a little breathless, excitable at his success and ravenous for something more to eat.

'Tonight. Midnight. The coordinates are here.' He dropped a small piece of paper onto the table with numbers scribbled on it. 'It's a good landing place. Eight hundred square. The ground is level and uncultivated. It's soft but not too soft. Free of wires and cables and there is enough airspace for a plane to turn.'

It was the good news they all needed to hear. 'I will go with her,' offered Raymond. Pierre was quick to decline it.

'No, I will.' He looked at his watch. 'We have three hours. The rest of you can leave. I will send word in a month.'

Sully didn't agree. 'I think we should all stay here until you've returned.'

Raymond frowned at the suggestion, but Bernard agreed. 'Sully is right. There might be a problem and we need to know about it. I'm not happy to sit around doing nothing for a month until you feel it is safe again. I would rather help at another network. And who will replace Marie?'

Pierre knew he was right — they had a lot to talk about. His role was to keep the group together — he didn't want them splintering off to work for other less coordinated groups.

'Okay, stay here. I'll be back as soon as I can.'

* * *

Pierre wrapped his arms around Marie to shield her from the cold night air. The sky was clear, which would be both an advantage and disadvantage to the pilot they were waiting for, but it had also caused the temperature to drop quickly as soon as darkness fell.

'What time is it now?' Marie asked for the third time. She rested the back of her head against his chest as she looked at the field and temporary landing strip in front of them. They stood on the edge of the natural landing strip, hidden in the shadows of a narrow strip of woodland, which had a country road boarding its far boundary. They stood alone under the branches of the old pines, with only the company of wild animals hiding in their branches or down hidden holes. It might have been only the two of them in the whole world, for all he cared. These moments together were precious as they would soon come to an end. He had the urge to nuzzle into the crook of her neck and kiss her, but instead rested his cheek into her curls.

'The plane should be here soon.'

'How late is it?'

'An hour.'

'I don't want it to ever come.'

He smiled into her hair. She must have felt it as she added, 'I'm serious. I don't want it to come. I might never see you again.'

'You will. When this is all over, I will come and find you.'

She turned into his arms and slid her hands beneath his coat to hold him close to her. He could feel her curves, her breasts and the warmth of her body.

'How will you find me? You don't even know my real name.'

'I'll ask every Englishman where the brave, stubborn, half-Frenchwoman with the sexy eyes lives.'

'If you ask random people in England that, you'll probably end up being arrested.'

'Let them arrest me. It will only make me more determined.'

'You fool,' she said smiling, and snuggled into his chest again. He looked up into the sky, desperate to spot, yet dreading it too, the silhouette of a plane flying low in the sky and circling to land.

Then he heard an engine in the far distance. Marie's body stiffened in his arms, indicating she had heard it too.

She turned to look up into the sky. 'Is it the plane?'

'I'm not sure. It doesn't sound right.'

Marie looked the other way. 'It's coming from over there.' He followed her gaze to the road beyond the wood and listened. The engine noise grew louder and came to a sudden stop. Boots landed heavily on the road surface as sharp demanding voices gave and accepted orders to begin a search.

They looked at each other and an unspoken message passed between them. In unison, they began to run, any hopes for a flight now firmly shattered. The trunks of the towering trees gave them temporary cover, but the ground was uneven and snared with roots, brambles and holes. Pierre reached for Marie's hand and encouraged her to run faster, fearful they would be parted in their hurry to escape.

A soldier appeared from nowhere and stood in their path, lifting his gun and opening his mouth to alert others to his find. Pierre let go of Marie's hand and barged forward, knocking the gun upwards and tackling him to the ground. They rolled several times, both not quite achieving the correct position to fight hand to hand. The soldier was about to shout to his comrades so Pierre grabbed him from behind, gagged his mouth with one hand while trying to strangle him with the crook of his other arm. They struggled for some moments, rolling again until the soldier was on top of him. He bit Pierre's hand and was about to shout for assistance again when Marie appeared above his shoulder and hit him in the chest twice in quick succession. The soldier immediately weakened, his body draining of all tension until it lay heavy and limp upon Pierre. He pushed him off, got up and saw a bloodied knife in Marie's hand.

'What took you so long?'

'I've killed him,' she whispered, in disbelief and horror.

He began searching the body, found the soldier's guns and began untangling them from their straps and holsters. He glanced up. 'Oh, of course . . . this must be your first time.'

She nodded numbly.

He began searching for the guns' ammunition. 'It may not be your last.' He exchanged the magazines of the soldier's machine-pistol and smaller gun for full ones and tossed her the latter. 'The Walther has eight rounds. Choose your targets carefully.' He stood up and slipped his arm through the strap of the machine gun and for the first time noticed that she hadn't moved, despite catching the gun he had tossed her. 'You saved my life. If you had not killed him, I would be dead now.' He added more gently, 'Come on. We'd better get out of here.'

They began to run again, breaking out of the woods further down the road and a short distance from the army truck which had brought the search party. Collecting their bikes from their hiding place — a pile of fallen leaves — they began the ride back to the safe house. They had been riding for several kilometres when Marie suddenly stopped, dismounted and ran off the road. Bewildered, he skidded to a halt, jumped off and followed her. He found her on her knees, frantically scrubbing her hands in a narrow rivulet of water.

'What are you doing?' he asked as he slowly approached.

Marie tore at the grass of the bank and used it to scrub her knuckles. 'I have blood on my hands. I have to get rid of it.'

His gaze slid from her concentrated expression to her hands. They were clean. 'You've washed them. We have to go.'

She shook her head. 'No, they're not!' She tore at another clump of grass and began scrubbing with renewed vigour. 'I have to clean them!'

He crouched beside her and watched in silence as she continued to wash. 'That's enough, Marie,' he coaxed. She continued her frantic scrubbing. He reached out, placed his hand on both of hers. 'They are clean, Marie. Trust me, they are clean.' Her hands stilled beneath his. 'You will make them sore if you continue.'

She stared at his hand shielding hers but remained silent.

'Look at me,' he coaxed.

She looked up with haunted red eyes, which twisted something deep in his gut.

'I know how you are feeling. I do understand.' He felt her hands begin to shake beneath his so he silently beckoned for her to come to him. She closed her eyes and sank against him, making it the most natural thing in the world for him to wrap his arms about her. They stayed like this, gently rocking, until the trembling in her body began to subside.

'I'm sorry,' she whispered into his shoulder. 'I should be stronger. I didn't think it was going to affect me like this.'

He stroked her hair. 'Don't be sorry for being human. I felt the same too.' He caressed her arm, unsure if she believed him. 'Tell me when you are ready to leave.'

She slowly withdrew from his embrace. 'I am ready now,' she said quietly, sniffing back the last of her tears. They silently got up, retrieved their bikes and held them upright ready to leave. She lifted her chin and stared ahead with a steely glint of determination in her eyes. He had seen that familiar look before and it gave him hope.

He smiled at her then dragged his eyes away from her face and tried to refocus on the mission ahead. As much as it pained him to see her so distressed, they both knew that there were more important things to do right now — to warn the others that the network had been compromised, their escape plan had failed, and there was, indeed, a traitor in their midst. He silently said a prayer of thanks that London had seen fit to send Marie to him, for she was far stronger than he had at first believed she was.

CHAPTER TWENTY-THREE

The sound of a gunshot brought them to a stop just before they rounded the corner to the house. Wordlessly, Charlotte followed Pierre's lead, dismounted from her bike and pushed it under the cover of the trees. He signalled to stay low and slowly approach the house using the hedge as a cover.

Charlotte made ready her gun, remembering her training to keep her finger off the trigger until she took aim. She followed, crouching low as she stepped across the pitted dry track. Dawn had yet to break and the visibility of the surrounding area was poor, but a glowing light emanating from the area of the safe house offered some guidance. A brazen light from an agent's safe house was also a sign that all was not well.

They took up positions which gave them a fine view of the front of the house but also provided adequate cover. It was as they feared — a German army truck was parked outside as soldiers searched inside and around the exterior of the house. Sully stood in front of one of them with his hands in the air. A shadow of a body lay crumpled on the ground at his feet.

'Someone's been shot,' whispered Pierre, needlessly.

'Can you tell who?'

He shook his head. He was about to speak again when Charlotte heard something and hushed him. It was Sully begging for his life.

'I'm the one who told you about this place! Please don't kill me . . . I can help you again.' He began to sob, desperate with fear. 'I'm your friend!'

'You are a traitor to your country so why should we believe you?'

Sully began to fervently deny it. 'I'm not. I'm—'

His defence went unheard. A close-range gunshot pole-axed Sully's body, killing him outright before he'd hit the ground.

Charlotte felt sick. Two of the group were dead, the other two were missing. A soldier came out of the building with a burning torch, its orange flames wickedly licking the air. Behind him, the light intensified to an angry glow as flames began to rage, unchecked, inside. The soldiers began to talk, their conversation made all the more sinister by their calm tone and laughter as they looked down at the bodies at their feet.

'What are they saying?' she asked, frustrated she could not speak their language.

'They think someone is hiding in the cellar but are not sure. They are making jokes about what is going to happen to them now that they have set the house alight.'

'Do you think they are? Should we attack and put the fire out?'

Pierre considered the option, but eventually he shook his head. 'There are at least ten of them, all with machine-pistols, grenades and possibly rifles. We are out armoured and outmanned, with no evidence that the others are still inside.'

Charlotte glanced at Pierre and wondered if he was thinking of her safety. If she wasn't here, would he still have attacked, spurred on by revenge for his friends and the destruction of his house.

She spoke her thoughts before she had time to censor them. 'Don't make decisions based on my safety.'

'How can I not?'

His eyes sought hers and she could see that they were filled with regret for his friends.

'If the other two were here to help fight,' he added softly, 'we might have a chance.'

At that moment, Bernard and Raymond burst out of the burning house, their limbs alight, spraying bullets blindly in an arc around them as they shouted 'Viva la France!' It was the diversion they needed. No need for words now. They stood and started shooting, too, with equal anger and revenge. Bodies fell all around in the chaos as ear-splitting bullets cut through the air. It was all over in seconds. No soldier survived their hailstorm of bullets. Only Pierre and herself, protected by their unknown position, remained uninjured. They wordlessly approached the battleground and walked among the bodies to search for signs of life. They soon realised there was nothing they could do. They stared at Sully's body lying next to Gérald's.

'He wanted me to believe you were a traitor.'

Pierre came to stand beside her. 'Did you?'

'He attempted to place doubt where none had been.'

'What did he say?'

'Nothing more than what was already known, but there was something about him, and the way he said it, that made me unsure of his motive . . .'

'War corrupts where corruption can be done. In the end, we all doubted each other but still remained together.'

They moved away and found Bernard and Raymond's burned bodies, both with a tale of their own to tell. Cornered in the cellar, they had little choice but to break through the flames to escape. They could have left through the back door, knowing they would probably die later from their injuries, but instead they chose to leave by the front door, using their last breaths to fight for the cause they believed in — the freedom of France for the generations to come.

Pierre guided her away from their sightless stares. 'I need to get you out of here. These soldiers won't be the only ones to know about Pointer. It doesn't end here. We have no wireless operator to request a plane to take you home. We only have one choice left.'

Charlotte knew what he was thinking. 'You want me to take a train back to the south coast of Brittany, to go to Doelan, and hope I can arrange a transfer from *the Emilienne*.'

'It's our only option. You know the crew and they have contact with London.'

'And I will no longer be your responsibility.'

He pointed to Bernard and Raymond, suddenly angry. 'Do you want to end up dead like them?'

'Do *you*?' she yelled back.

'Of course not!'

She inhaled deeply to calm the nausea rising inside her. 'Then come with me, Pierre.'

'I told you, I can't leave. I have too many responsibilities here.' He strode to their bikes and pulled them angrily from the undergrowth, passing the first to her. 'If we set off now, we will reach the station in time to catch one of the first trains of the day.' He slid the strap of his gun off his shoulder and discarded it on the ground. 'I can't be seen carrying that in a town. It will raise too many questions.'

Charlotte watched him in silence as he straddled his bike. He had just seen his friends murdered and, from his angry expression, now was not the time to continue arguing with him.

'You are right.' She mounted her bike and met his watchful gaze. 'The light of the fire will be attracting attention soon. We have already stayed too long.'

She watched his expression soften, relieved, no doubt, that she had accepted his proposal. Together they pushed off with a new destination in mind. The pungent fumes of smoke continued to claw in their nostrils for some time, reminding them of the colleagues they had lost and the duplicitous man who had betrayed them all. They instinctively rode faster, eager to leave — as if by doing so they could fool themselves that what had happened in the small house in rural France, with its picturesque setting and the adventurous stray cat on the steps, had never happened at all.

* * *

The journey to the train station had been fraught with problems. On several occasions they were forced to hide from passing military vehicles and trucks. Each encounter only solidified Pierre's determination to get Marie on board a train. Several hours later, they reached a station which had a direct link to the south coast.

'The less train transfers the better as it will mean less document inspection,' he explained under his breath as he searched the station's timetable.

The platform was busy with people travelling to work and they blended into the crowd, walking arm in arm as if they were a newly engaged couple. He chose a quiet carriage and pulled open the door for her, but she refused to step on board.

'I want to be the last to embark. I want to stay near the door and say goodbye.'

Pierre lifted his brow at her, their earlier argument already forgotten as far as he was concerned. 'Are you becoming sentimental?'

She remained composed in the face of his teasing. 'I am simply planning ahead.'

Her words dulled the smile forming on his lips as he realised any of her future plans from now on would not include him. She would be living a new life in London and perhaps would forget about him. Suddenly, he knew what he must do.

He cleared the choking feeling in his throat and pulled her away from the waiting train to an alcove. 'Before you leave, I want to give you something . . .' He surreptitiously withdrew a large envelope from the lining in his coat. 'Take this to London.'

Charlotte slipped it beneath her coat and manoeuvred it into her own lining. 'Of course. What is it?'

'Something I have been working on since I was in London.' Under the cover of a loving embrace, he whispered into her ear, 'It is the up-to-date coastal fortification of northern France.'

Her body stiffened in his arms, indicating she understood the significance of London receiving accurate defence information.

'Is it for an Allied invasion of Europe?' she asked quietly.

Pierre smiled. 'Yes.' He touched his cheek against hers. 'I haven't been able to send it to England before now. I didn't trust anyone enough to take it back. I couldn't even send a message that I had it.'

She glanced around her to ensure no one could hear. 'Come with me. You deserve the glory of handing this in, not me.' Pierre avoided her earnest plea but she would not let it drop and tugged on his coat. 'It is only a matter of time before they discover who owns the house they have just torched. They might already know.'

He shook his head. 'I will just have to risk it.'

'For what?'

'I have a hotel here. I have my connections with the Reich.'

'Do you think those connections will save you when they realise you have been a double agent and lying to them? See what they did to Sully.'

He wrapped his arms around her. 'I know you are afraid for me.'

She pushed them aside. 'I am not just afraid. I am terrified.'

'Don't be. I can look after myself.'

She looked up at him. 'My father used to say that, but words don't help in the end.'

A child ran to the alcove to hide, saw them and ran back to his parents. They watched him in silence as he was berated by his parents for running away.

He saw a small crease in her frown form as she felt for the child. He lifted her chin with the crook of his finger and made her look at him. 'You are one of the most brave and stubborn women I have ever met.'

'And you are one of the most brave and stubborn—'

Unable to resist the temptation, he kissed the last word from her lips. 'I'll never forget you, Marie Veilleux.'

Doors began to shut along the line of carriages, signalling the train was about to depart.

'You don't have to. Come with me,' she urged again. 'Your manager can look after your hotel until the war is over.'

He grabbed her arm and began walking her to the carriage, talking loudly as he did so to make himself heard. 'Do you think I could bear leaving you when the war has ended? By then, I will have got to know you even better. It is hard enough to part with you now when we have known each other for so little time.' He held the open door of a carriage wider so she could step in. 'I don't even know your real name.'

A man appeared, pushed between them and entered the carriage without a backward glance.

Marie flung her arms around his neck. It seemed he was not the only one to use an embrace as a way of communicating secrets. 'Then come to England and I will tell you. We can fight the war from London,' she whispered into his ear.

Her French perfume worked its magic, expelled the fumes of death and filled his mind with her. He held her tighter, his voice on the edge of breaking as their faux embrace became real.

'Don't make this more difficult than it is already,' he groaned. He kissed her hard, savouring the moment like a thirsty man, before breaking away suddenly as a whistle blew. 'The train is about to leave,' he warned, hurrying her up the steps. He shut the door as soon as she was inside so she could not change her mind. She turned, immediately pushed the window down and reached out her hand.

They held hands, their fingers barely touching across the gap between them. The noise of the train roared as his fingers broke away from hers.

'I can't bear to see you upset like this,' he said. 'Goodbye and good luck.'

He began to walk briskly away, the whistle blowing shrilly from the platform and drilling into his head. He glanced back once and saw her face only briefly, before another passenger pushed in front of her to wave goodbye to their friends.

He stopped, unable to take another step, memories of another time flooding back to engulf him. His wife and son's anxious faces disappearing in a sea of strangers, begging him to go with them on their journey to safety. It was all happening again, and he had done nothing different to prevent it. Last time he had not ensured they reached their destination. And this time he was doing the same.

The final whistle blew, igniting his feet with the power to move. He began to run, dodging several passengers and a luggage trunk, to jump onto the train. The door was slammed shut behind him by an irate platform guard, and for a moment, he stood quite still, surprised at what he had done. The train eased out of the station and as the sound of the wheels on the tracks slowly grew in momentum to rattle rhythmically beneath his feet, he began his hunt for the woman he could not say goodbye to yet.

He found her after several minutes of frantic searching. Her head was resting against the window as she watched the industrial landscape of the town morph into the open countryside. No one would ever guess that the solitary, pensive woman was carrying such important information inside her coat lining. He sat down next to her, but she did not turn round, choosing to ignore the man who was at risk of interrupting her daydreams.

He reached across her lap and took her hand in his. She lifted her head from the glass, stared down at his hand and a smile curved her lips.

'I couldn't do it again,' he admitted quietly.

'Do what?' she asked as she watched his fingers lovingly thread between hers.

'Send the woman I care about away, in the hope they will be safe. I did that once before and came to regret it. I realised I couldn't do it again.'

'The woman you care about?'

'Yes, the woman I care about . . . very much.'

She looked up at him, her smile broadening. 'I think you don't really trust me to deliver your envelope,' she teased.

He shook his head, returning her smile with one of his own. 'I trusted you. I just didn't trust myself . . . to be able to live without you.'

They hugged each other in silence for some moments, savouring the feel of the other's body against their own. Finally, they broke apart and settled to watch the countryside speed past their window, Marie resting against his shoulder, his cheek against her hair. Soon they would arrive at the town of Lorient, where soldiers patrolled the port and surrounding area, safeguarding their U-boat base against enemies, but at least they were still together — for the time being at least.

CHAPTER TWENTY-FOUR

They stepped onto the platform as soon as the train came to a halt. A group of soldiers were standing casually at the station, as if waiting for someone. Their disinterest in the train and passengers gave Pierre hope that they were not there for them.

'Wait here for the others to get off,' he said, preventing Marie from leaving. The remaining passengers spilled onto the platform and quickly surrounded them. 'Now we'll leave,' he said quietly as he allowed them to be swept along with the crowd. They gave the soldiers a wide berth as they passed them, but Pierre only began to relax once they were outside the train station.

'Let's get away from here as fast as we can,' suggested Marie. He nodded as they walked briskly away.

They headed northwest towards Doelan on foot, eager to put as much distance as they could between Lorient and themselves. Despite Allied bombing, Lorient's large bomb-proof submarine pens remained largely intact. This meant that the facility, and the surrounding area, would still be closely patrolled by German soldiers. Any unusual activity in the area was bound to raise suspicions and although they looked as if they were a married couple out for a walk, they were both aware that a stroll that lasted many miles would soon raise questions.

They took to hiding in the long swaying grass of the verge whenever a distant military vehicle was heard approaching and it did not take long before they had grown adept at distinguishing military transport from civilian. However, Pierre was aware that this tactic made the journey slow and it did little to sooth their nerves. Two hours into their walk, they became aware of increased patrols again.

Pierre watched a military plane take off in the distance. 'I should have taken the route we used when you first landed in France.' He pointed to the network of roads and buildings in the distance. 'That must be Lann-Bihoué. It's a military base. It appears the German air force has taken it over to protect their U-boat base at Lorient.'

Marie was more forgiving for his oversight than he was. She threaded her arm through his. 'Then we will have to keep away from the base and the roads until we are further west.'

They did as she suggested, and continued to make progress, this time westward towards the estuary river, Laita, where they hoped to cross by boat. The light was beginning to fade due to dark rain clouds gathering.. They came across an abandoned military motorcycle and sidecar on the verge. Pierre scanned the immediate area for signs of its owner, knowing they couldn't be too far away, as Marie looked it over. The sidecar was no more than a metal box with a curved front, it's rudimentary design perfect to produce large numbers quickly. The attached motorcycle stood upright, its front wheel casually tilted to the left.

'It doesn't look damaged. We could take it. It would shorten our journey.'

Pierre shook his head. It would have been better if it was damaged. An accident explained its presence. An abandoned working machine made no sense.

'No. Without the correct uniform, we'll be stopped and questioned.' He touched the engine. 'It's still warm.' He looked up sharply and scanned the nearby field. 'Whoever drove it here can't be far away.'

Marie touched his arm. 'Then we should leave.'

Something moved nearby and captured their attention. He quickly located its origin, lifted a finger to his lips and pointed towards a tree. Marie turned to look. Stretching out from the base was a pair of uniformed legs, slowly moving in readiness to stand. The soldier may have been sleeping but was now awake, preparing to reveal himself with a machine gun in hand. They barely had a chance to turn and run before he shouted his first command, loud and clear.

'*Bleiben wo Sie sind! Hände nach oben!*'

Pierre slowly raised his hands and hoped Marie would follow his lead. In what he hoped was a calming tone, he attempted to reassure the soldier in German.

'We were concerned for your welfare. It is not every day we find an abandoned motorcycle.'

'Concerned? It sounded like you were thinking of stealing it!' With a sweep of his machine gun, he indicated where he wanted them to stand.

Marie obediently stepped away from him as she was ordered to do.

'Who are you?' he asked, returning the point of his gun to Pierre's chest.

'I am Pierre Lesieur. This is Mademoiselle Marie Veilleux.'

'Where do you come from?'

'Paris.'

'Show me your papers!' His gun lowered to Pierre's stomach, then swung widely at Marie as if unsure which target to concentrate on. As they reached into their pockets, the soldier's agitation increased. 'Careful now or I will kill you both.'

'We don't want any trouble,' said Pierre, slowly withdrawing his identity papers using only his fingertips. 'We just want to be on our way.' The soldier quickly stepped forward, grabbed the document and looked at it.

'Why are you in this area?'

'Visiting family.'

The soldier quickly returned it and ripped Marie's from her hand.

'Why are you here?'

Pierre answered for her. 'She doesn't speak German. She is here visiting my family. We are—' he remembered that Marie had no ring — 'planning to get engaged. She is introducing me to her family.' The slip of his tongue made the soldier glance up at him. His eyes narrowed as beads of sweat broke out on his brow. The soldier knew he was out-numbered, but he still had a gun. His finger hovered over the trigger. Pierre realised it would not take much for the soldier to be spooked into shooting.

The soldier handed Marie's papers back to her with a flick of his fingers as he continued to stare at Pierre. 'Lift those hands higher. I want to search you,' he ordered.

Pierre did as he was told. Perhaps if he searched him and found nothing, he would leave Marie alone. He grimaced as the soldier's hands did a basic, hurried search of his body. The soldier turned to Marie.

'Hands higher!' The soldier began to roughly pat down her body for weapons, his gun aimed at Pierre as he tried to concentrate on both. Pierre's jaw tightened. He hated the thought of him touching her. He suddenly remembered Marie's concealed pistol in her belt, but the soldier failed to locate it and Pierre was unable to resist meeting her gaze in triumph over the soldier's bent body. The soldier stood and was about to push her towards Pierre when the lining of her coat rustled. He tugged her to a halt, his focus no longer divided between him and Marie, but at what was hidden inside her lining.

'Undo your coat!'

'It is cold,' suggested Pierre, calmly. 'She is prone to illness and will catch a chill.'

The soldier's suspicions grew. 'Open your coat now!'

Pierre stepped forward. 'Steady. She doesn't understand you. I will translate.'

The gun swung widely at him. 'Stay back!'

Pierre retreated a step. 'I meant no harm. I'm on your side. I'm half-German. My mother is—'

'Stand back or I will kill you!' screamed the soldier. He swung his gun at Marie, his hands now visibly shaking. She realised what he wanted and began to fumble with her coat, attempting to delay the inevitable.

Impatiently, the soldier shouted again, demanding that she hurried. Pierre took advantage of the moment, stepped forward and violently pushed the gun's barrel upwards and into the air. A short spate of bullets riddled the sky above Marie's head. She instinctively ducked as Pierre grappled for possession of the panicking soldier's gun. A single sharp pain burned in his arm as he wrestled with the machine gun, now raised high in the air above both their heads. The soldier was smaller, yet he appeared stronger. It made no sense — on any other day he would have easily torn the gun free.

Two single shots, in quick succession, brought the soldier to his knees. He stared up at Pierre, confused as to how he had been shot. After all, he had been on the brink of winning, yet now he had lost. As his confusion changed to fear, Pierre almost felt sorry for him. No one who could feel empathy could look into the eyes of a dying man and not feel something. Pierre pulled the gun they both held away from the soldier's weak grip and stepped back. The soldier's gaze wandered to Marie, in the hope she would help, but when he saw the small German pistol in her hand, he knew his end had come.

* * *

'You are turning into an experienced killer. You could make a living as an assassin after the war,' Pierre teased, as they dragged the soldier off the roadside and into the ditch. It was a poor attempt at a joke, but Marie's silence worried him. 'What's wrong?'

'Don't make jokes. He might be a Nazi, but he has a mother who loves him and who will be heartbroken.'

Pierre straightened, testing his painful arm with slow movements of the joints. 'Don't start regretting your actions. Regret is a heavy burden to carry for the rest of your life. I should know.'

She didn't appear to be listening, preferring to tear at the long blades of grass, but this time, instead of trying to wash her hands, she used them to conceal the body.

'Did you hear me, Marie?' She ignored him. He grabbed her elbow and turned her to face him. 'That soldier has been brainwashed since he was a boy to believe that Germans are a superior race. Do you think he would look at us and feel the same level of empathy as you feel for him? You know he would have killed us both and happily gloated over it to his friends.'

'I don't know that.'

'You *did* know that, which is why you killed him. It was either him or me. Us. Save your regrets for someone more worthy.' He felt the tension in her body drain away. He knew he was right and now he knew she knew it too. He dragged her into his embrace. 'I owe you my life.'

'Twice.'

He looked down and saw her tentatively smile, and it gave him hope. He kissed her soft curls.

'I owe you my life . . . twice. Come on, let's get out of here before someone finds out what we've done.'

It was as he was steering the motorcycle and sidecar off the road, that he realised something more serious had happened to his arm than just straining a muscle. Marie noticed it too when she saw him wince in pain.

'Let me see,' she asked as she circled his body. She saw the bullet hole at the same time as he did. 'You've been shot! Did I do that?'

He found himself laughing, despite the pain. 'No, it was from his gun.' He shrugged out of his coat and examined the bloodied shirtsleeve. 'It's only a graze.'

'How can you tell? Take off your shirt. It will need cleaning.'

'We don't have time. We are in the middle of nowhere and need to get to the coast.' He searched the motorcycle.

'What are you looking for?' asked Marie.

'A first-aid box. It might have a bandage.'

Marie began searching the soldier's body too. The sound of a military vehicle approached and they temporarily stopped to hide in the long grass as the vehicle sped by. The searching began again.

'I think I may have found something.'

He crawled over to her to take a look. Inside the soldier's coat, low to the right, was a long narrow pocket. He watched as Marie eased out two individual dressing packages. She pocketed one and tore open the other.

'Bandage over the shirt,' he said, offering her his bloodied arm while scanning the horizon. 'We don't have time for me to strip and clean it.'

She threw him a frustrated glare but did what he ordered. 'I hope you are right about it being just a graze,' she said, placing the wad of gauze over the area and winding the attached bandage firmly around his arm.

'I can move it, can't I?'

'Can you?'

He showed her that he could, clenching his jaw in an effort not to cry out in pain. 'You see . . . good as new. Come on. Let's get going. The further we can put ourselves from this body the better. Someone is bound to find him soon.'

They clambered back up the bank and onto the road. The body and motorcycle could not be seen from there and it gave them hope that there would be enough of a delay to allow them to escape. They continued their journey to Doelan, but Pierre soon began to fear that he would slow their progress. His blood loss had affected him more than he had first thought, and he was beginning to lack the energy needed for the hours of walking ahead.

A civilian truck driver passed them but then came to a halt not far ahead.

'What do you think he wants?' asked Marie. He could hear the concern in her voice and felt it himself. He approached everything out of the ordinary with a healthy dose of mistrust these days.

'I don't know. Just act normally and walk by unless he speaks.'

They had just passed the cab when the driver called out to them. 'Do you want a lift?'

Pierre realised he had no choice but to acknowledge his offer . . . an offer that might just help get Marie to safety.

He turned around. Marie's hand threaded through the crook in his arm to cover the bullet holes in his coat.

A man in his fifties, with a weathered face, wound down the passenger window further and smiled back at him across the empty seat. His greying stubble and stretched woollen jumper hinted at a single life, while his smiling eyes suggested his offer of a lift was genuine. If he was what he appeared to be, his single life went some way to explaining why he was seeking the company of two perfect strangers.

'Where are you heading?' prompted the man.

'To the coast.' Pierre felt Marie stiffen beside him, unhappy that he had given so much away, but the coast was long and although it answered his question, Pierre felt it was still vague enough to keep them safe.

The man lifted his beret and scratched his head with sharp, short movements. 'That's a long way to walk.' He looked up and down the road, leaned over the seat and opened the truck door. 'Look, I will come to the point. I drove past here five minutes ago. Back then there was a Nazi on a motorcycle and a young couple walking in his direction. Now there's only flattened grass leading off the road. So I had a look. Found the motorcycle . . . and a dead Nazi. Now I am no Einstein, but I can guess what happened. You can't hang around here. You need to get away.'

Pierre stepped closer and lowered his head to peer into the cab. He studied the driver, silently weighing up his options. The pain in his arm and the lightheadedness he felt suggested he had few to consider.

'We are planning to cross the Laita River near the coast.'

'How?'

'By boat.'

'And then where? I can tell from your accent you are not from Brittany.'

Pierre straightened. He felt uneasy answering so many questions.

'Listen. I am an old Breton who has lived here all my life. The German army value the Breton peninsula more than the rest of France has ever done. They use our harbours and dockyards as their main base to attack convoys ferrying supplies between North America and Britain. More soldiers have arrived in the area this week. I am warning you, it's not safe for a couple who are not from this area to cross the river alone. It raises too many questions.'

Pierre knew he was right. Anything out of the ordinary raised suspicions. 'What do you suggest?'

'I will drive you further inland and we'll cross the river by road. I can drive you to any small fishing harbour you want, cutting your walking time by hours.'

Marie had been silent, but suddenly she stepped forward and peered into the cab. She looked at him, weighing up in her mind what sort of man he was.

'What is your name?'

'Guellec.'

'Well, Monsieur Guellec, I have a feeling you have done this before.' Her shrewd suggestion turned out to be right.

The man nodded. 'I've helped four British and two American airmen return to England. I do what I can.' Monsieur Guellec's gaze fleetingly dropped to the bullet hole in Pierre's sleeve. 'And I think you could do with some help. I have some food and drink in the footwell. It's yours if you want it.'

Pierre realised they had not eaten in a long time. That wouldn't be helping his lightheadedness. He glanced at

Marie who gave a sharp nod of her head. If he still had any resistance to accept the offer, it drained away at her trust in the driver.

'Thank you, Monsieur Guellec, we will take up your offer.' He stepped aside so Marie could get in first, then climbed in to sit beside her.

'Help yourself to the food. Take any that is left with you for your long journey ahead.'

Marie opened the sack. Bread, apples, cheese and a small bag of fresh oysters lay in the bottom.

'Best eat the oysters first.'

Pierre took out the bag of shellfish and noticed an old army flask in the bag. From its weight, he could tell it was full.

'It has water in it. I brought it home as a memento of the Great War.' The shine in his eyes dimmed a little as he remembered the time. 'That water bottle and I survived a lot of difficult times together. Now it is time for it to carry water for you.'

Pierre turned the battle-worn bottle in his hand. The man had treasured it all these years and was now giving it away to two complete strangers.

'We can't take it. This bottle must hold so many memories for you.'

'Take it with my blessing and refill it whenever you can. The living are more important than the dead. My memories are safe in my head and nobody can take them away.'

Pierre wondered how he had ever doubted the man and knew, in that moment, he would remember his kindness for the rest of his life.

He swallowed down the emotion rising in his chest. 'Thank you,' was all he dared to say.

The next phase of their journey was strangely carefree as they enjoyed their meal of oysters, bread and cheese. Monsieur Guellec quietly chuckled to himself between amused sidelong glances as he watched them attempt to perfect their shell-opening skills. They quickly acquired a taste for the salty delicacy, sliding the oysters into their mouths in turns and savouring the meaty taste of the ocean. Those few precious moments, free of fear and worry, were what they both needed as it reminded them how carefree life could be.

They had just ended their meal when they saw the bridge that would take them over the Laita River. Their laughter and conversation died when they saw the soldiers ahead.

Monsieur Guellec straightened in his seat. 'They've set up a checkpoint. Our story is this . . . you are my nephew and have brought your girlfriend to visit me. You are staying for two weeks and I have just picked you up from Lorient train station. You have not visited me in years and know little about the region. You are my sister's child. My sister is called Fleur. What are your names?'

Pierre had no choice but to tell him as they were bound to look at their identity papers and compare. 'Pierre Lesieur and Marie Veilleux.'

The old Breton looked at them. 'Are you ready?'

They both nodded.

'Here we go.'

Their truck moved forward and was asked to halt. The face of a soldier, a battle-scar slash across his left cheek, appeared at the window. He asked the usual questions, but from his tone and delivery, he appeared jaded with his duties for the day. Pierre let the driver do the talking, instinctively aware that the slightest thing might raise the soldier's suspicions. Monsieur Guellec answered them in a friendly tone, but the soldier soon became bored. His eyes strayed to Marie and her legs, then to Pierre. The soldier's blue eyes studied him intently for a few seconds as he continued to ask pre-set questions and listened to the driver's reply. Silence fell and the tension appeared to rise in the cab. The soldier's nostrils flared slightly and, for the first time, he noticed the oyster shells at their feet.

Monsieur Guellec explained their presence. 'I knew my nephew would be hungry after his long train journey. Do you like oysters?'

The soldier ignored him and Pierre wondered if he had understood anything the old Breton had said. The soldier's nostrils flared again, so slight that one could have missed it if he had not been looking. A sudden urge to retch followed and he had to step back. Suddenly, he was waving the truck forward, a distasteful grimace on his face, eager to be rid of them. They were on their way again, thanks mainly to a bag of oysters and an unknown soldier's distaste for shellfish.

* * *

Monsieur Guellec dropped them off on the edge of the quiet port of Doelan and drove away. They entered the village under dark, black clouds and found shelter from the sudden rain in the disused basement where Pierre had previously hidden their bicycles all those weeks ago. It should have been a time to rest before arranging a passage across the sea, but as they entered the damp basement, Pierre began to feel unsteady. He heard Marie's voice by his side. It seemed unusually distant and full of concern, yet he could not understand a word of what she was saying. He looked at her. Her face multiplied, then blurred before him . . . and then the soft earthy ground of the cellar came up to meet his face.

CHAPTER TWENTY-FIVE

Charlotte touched Pierre's forehead with the back of her fingers. It felt warm but not overly so.

'Will I live?' he teased.

'It's not the time to joke,' she chided, softly tapping his chest. 'Why didn't you tell me you felt unwell?'

'I'm not ill.'

She tugged off his coat sleeve. 'You passed out on the floor. What am I to think? Let me look at your wound.'

He rolled up his sleeve to reveal a blood-soaked bandage.

She was horrified. 'It needs redressing.' She pulled out the other bandage from her pocket.

Pierre moved his arm away from her. 'It's not as bad as it looks.'

'Pierre, it *needs* redressing.' She tore at the packaging with her teeth.

'Okay. Okay. You can put another bandage on the top. If we take the old one off we might dislodge a clot. I don't want it to start bleeding again.'

Charlotte threw him a sceptical glance but did what he suggested. Her first-aid training had been basic. She could kill a man, but she didn't really know how to save the life of one.

'Don't ever pass out on me again. I thought you were dead,' she scolded.

'I'm just a little dehydrated, nothing more.'

Charlotte gave him the water bottle and urged him to drink. He did so as she worked.

'We have to get back to England as soon as we can.' She fastened the bandage and began to help him roll down his sleeve. 'If it becomes known you have a German bullet wound in your arm, we will be done for.'

He dragged his coat on and attempted to get up.

'Where are you going?'

'I'm coming with you.'

She pushed him back down. 'We aren't going anywhere. We'll stay here this evening and get an early night. When dawn breaks, I'll go and speak to the crew who brought me here. If they've been out fishing all night, they'll return in the early hours of the morning to unload their fish. I will be on the harbour waiting for them.'

She gave him some more water and watched as he drank from the bottle. His face was pale, and for the first time she wondered if he would be well enough to make the journey. He must have seen her concern as his arm came around her. Instinctively, she nestled into his one-armed embrace and closed her eyes.

'Don't worry about me,' he reassured her. 'I passed out, but I am fine now.' She said nothing, but as she rested her cheek against his shirt, she knew she had heard an edge in his husky tone. He might be trying to hide his pain from her, but she knew that he was suffering all the same.

* * *

Charlotte slept poorly. Long before dawn, she eased away from Pierre's sleeping body and left the sanctuary of the basement. Thankfully, the rain had stopped. Although her previous time in Doelan had been brief, she remembered it well and immediately made her way through the village to the harbour.

The village straddled both sides of the estuary river before it widened to merge with the sea. A strong harbour wall slanted across the entrance, protecting the boats from robust Atlantic winds. Rows of pretty houses lined the banks and on either side of the harbour stood two lighthouses — one near the water's edge, the other further inland and higher on the bank. In many ways the fishing village reminded Charlotte of Cornwall and it brought her some comfort as she thought about the perilous journey she was about to face.

In the hour before dawn, the horizon to the east changed to a deep magenta, with billows of indigo clouds spouting upwards like explosions of smoke. It was a dramatic backdrop to the assortment of boats moored in the harbour, some huddled together, others spaced further apart, all with the gentle sound of water lapping against their hulls.

Eventually the golden rays of the sun began to lighten the sky. As if waiting for the light to guide them in, a small flotilla of Breton boats suddenly appeared at the harbour entrance and entered the calmer waters within. Among the assortment of brightly painted hulls, Charlotte recognised the boat that had brought her to the fishing port all those weeks ago — the *Emilienne*.

She waited in the shadows as the trawler nosed itself between boats to the quayside. Mooring ropes were thrown onto the quayside, snaking through the air to be caught by waiting hands and quickly tied into place. As soon as the boat was made fast, everyone on board set about raising numerous baskets of fish from the hull by ropes and swinging them ashore to land straight onto a waiting lorry. The quayside was now lined by several boats, their crews busy unloading their hauls. A strong odour of fish began to permeate the air.

As the boats emptied, the activity at the quayside lessened. The trucks began to drive away in turn to take the catch to the main harbour wall of the port for sale, leaving the crews to tidy up. Each crew gradually returned home to their families' welcome of a hot meal and a recently vacated, but still warm, bed.

The skipper of the boat Charlotte was most interested in stayed on board. It was time to make her presence noticed. She pushed herself away from the wall she had been leaning on and weaved her way through the departing crew, her coat collar held high about her face and her gaze fixed on the ground just in front of her. Approaching the trawler, she jumped on board and brazenly stepped in front of the skipper, forcing him to stop coiling his rope and look up.

'Do you remember me?' she asked quietly.

His eyes narrowed as he searched her face. 'No.' He turned away, dismissing her instantly.

He may not remember her, but she remembered him. She stepped in front of him. 'I remember you.'

He stilled and looked at her afresh. A flash of recognition hardened his eyes. He knew what she was alluding to, even if he did not remember her in particular. He looked over his shoulder to the now deserted quay. Finding no one had accompanied her, he relaxed a little but was no more welcoming.

'Well, I don't know you so get off my boat.'

He retrieved a metal oil can from a box and began working the oil into the wheel of the net winch. She realised she had to be more specific.

'You picked me up from a British boat just off the Glénan Isles several weeks ago.'

He continued to work the oil into the wheel and she began to wonder if he had heard her.

She tried again. 'The last time we spoke you told me you named your boat the *Emilienne* after your sister. It made your wife angry and she refused to speak to you for a week. She was hoping you would name it after her.'

He carefully set the oil can aside and looked at her. His face reminded her of her father's, lined with worry, beaten by wind and scorched by the sun. His eyes carried decades of experience and wisdom. He had seen it all.

'What do you want?'

The tension drained from her body in an instant. 'I need to leave France. Can you help me?'

He shook his head. 'No.' He attempted to walk around her, but she sidestepped in front of him again.

'You have to help us.'

'Us?'

'I have someone with me. He's been wounded. We have to return to England as soon as possible.'

'I told you, I can't. It's not possible.'

'Please—'

'It's not that I'm unwilling. It's because the exchanges are only done by arrangement. A full moon and a clear sky are both needed. We need the light to see each other and the conditions won't be right again for several weeks. If the weather is bad . . . well, a meeting may not happen at all. If you are in a hurry, you need to find another way.'

His words felt like a blow to the stomach. 'Then take me all the way back to England.'

He began to laugh but quickly sobered when he realised she was serious.

'I can't take you all the way to England. I have a family here and can't risk sailing outside the permitted fishing grounds.' He attempted to pass her again. Once again, she stepped in his way.

'Then give me a boat.'

This time he did laugh. 'You are crazy.'

'I have never been saner in my life.'

He looked her up and down, taking in her size which was at least a foot shorter than his powerful frame. 'You can't manage a boat.'

'Trawling is in my blood. My father was a fisherman. I worked on his boat.'

Unconvinced, he ignored her and climbed down to the galley to check everything was in order. She followed him down the narrow wooden steps.

'Diesel engine isn't it?' she said when she reached the bottom step. 'Much better than steam. Less work. Cleaner. More reliable.' He pushed passed her and left. She followed him back up the steps into the fresh, salty air. 'Cruising speed about fifteen thousand rpm, I would guess. How many tonnes did you catch? From what I saw, the haul had a good assortment of nephrops and gadoids.' He threw her a glance. 'They all looked a good size, but I have always thought the fish caught in the Celtic sea grow bigger than in the waters of the North.'

He stopped and turned to face her. Once again she was under his scrutiny, but it felt different this time.

'I can't take you to England, and I won't give you my boat.'

She opened her mouth to argue again, but he stopped her by raising his hand.

'But I can give you my uncle's. He is ill. He's dying. Everyone knows it but him. The boat is smaller and older than this one. The engine is good but the wireless does not work.'

'That's not a problem. English fishermen have not been allowed to use their wirelesses at sea since the war started.'

He considered her reply. 'If you handle her firmly, the weather stays calm and the Germans don't blow you up, you have as good a chance as I would to get your wounded friend to England.'

Charlotte released the breath she had been holding. 'Thank you. Where will I find it?'

'I'll show you.' He walked to the stern and pointed to a boat in the distance. Its paintwork was worn, giving it a battered, forlorn air, but it was afloat, available and its name, *Presque à la Maison*, seemed the perfect omen for success.

'*Almost Home*,' murmured Charlotte. She couldn't wait to tell Pierre.

The skipper noticed her shoes and culottes. 'Do you have warmer clothes?'

'No.'

'I will leave some clothes and food for you both inside the boat. We are leaving this evening for another fishing trip. Come with us. Travel with our flotilla to the fishing grounds. By the time we reach them, it will be dark. You can head for the English coast under the cover of darkness. *Almost Home* might be a small boat, but she is tough. However,' he continued, looking up to the sky, 'if the weather turns bad you will need all the luck you can get too.'

Charlotte thanked him and returned to Pierre, buying some more food on the way. She entered the dark basement wondering what she would find and was relieved to see him sitting on an upturned crate, eating an apple.

He threw the core aside and slowly stood as she entered. 'What did he say?'

She dropped the bag of food on the crate and began searching inside it. 'He said there isn't another transfer arranged for several weeks.'

Pierre raked his hair with a hand. 'We will have to track down a wireless operator and ask for a plane.'

'And risk exposing ourselves for asking such questions?' She shook her head. 'We can't risk it. I asked him to take us to England.'

Pierre took the crust of bread she offered. 'I bet that didn't go down well.'

'It was worth a try, but it is okay, we don't need his boat. We have another.'

'We do?'

She bit into her own torn bread and smiled at him.

He raised an eyebrow as she chewed and swallowed it. 'How did you get it?'

'He's given us his uncle's small trawler. We are going to accompany them to the fishing ground and then we are going to—' she used her hand as a shark's fin — 'keep on going until we reach England.'

'Just us?'

She nodded.

He lifted his hand and grazed her cheek with his fingers. 'I don't know how to navigate the Atlantic, Marie. It's madness.'

She tore another piece of bread. 'Would it surprise you to know that I do?' she asked.

His eyes softened. He touched his forehead with hers. He felt warm, despite the cold basement. 'Nothing about Marie Veilleux would surprise me now,' he said so softly that only she could hear.

CHAPTER TWENTY-SIX

Charlotte stared at the wooden floor as she listened to the tidal harbour water gently lapping at the sides of the boat. Time had dragged in the abandoned basement, every sound outside setting them on edge and making it impossible to sleep or rest. Finally, they had decided to board the *Almost Home*, familiarise themselves with the boat, change their clothes and wait for the other trawler crews to arrive. However, they soon discovered that time dragged wherever you were if one was waiting to escape.

Charlotte got up, searched and soon located the first-aid box whereupon she set about redressing Pierre's wound. Although he always downplayed how much it was troubling him, this time he gladly offered her his arm to tend.

'It will help pass the time,' he said as he offered her a tired smile.

She carefully unwound the bandages and peeled away the original dressing to finally expose the wound underneath. She stared at it in disbelief. It was far larger than she'd expected, with red, swollen edges rolling in towards a mass of torn flesh and congealed blood. There was no doubt, even to her inexperienced eyes, that inflammation and infection had set in.

'I should have insisted on looking at it sooner.'

Pierre focused on some distant mark on the cabin wall. 'We had other things on our mind. The past cannot be changed now.'

She glanced up. Despite his words, his tone told her that he was as surprised and concerned as she was.

In a desperate attempt to halt the infection, she reached for the antiseptic and poured half of the bottle over the wound. Pierre's body stiffened against the stinging pain.

'I'm sorry. I should have warned you.'

'It wouldn't have lessened the pain,' he said through gritted teeth. 'Go on, do what you have to do.'

She continued to clean the wound as best as she could, but the first-aid pack was inadequate for his injury.

Finally, she gave up and applied a clean bandage. 'You need to see a doctor.'

Pierre examined the secure, white bandage. 'I will . . . when we get to England.'

She was about to suggest that she tried to locate a French doctor when they heard voices outside. Charlotte knew what that meant and voiced her thoughts. 'The crews are boarding their trawlers.'

'Then it's time,' said Pierre, standing up.

They went up on deck as several mooring ropes were untied from the quay and hauled onboard the various boats. The skipper of the *Emilienne* waved at them, confirming it was their time to leave. Pierre indicated the rope tying their boat to the quay and it was duly untied and thrown towards them. Charlotte caught it and carefully coiled it onto the deck. The *Almost Home* was now free.

Charlotte made her way to the mizzen sail and hoisted it, returning to the wheel to slowly steer it towards the small Breton fishing fleet. She edged the *Almost Home* between two Breton boats, mingling among the flotilla as if they had always done so. She followed as they took a well-established course between the prominent harbour wall and the rising bank on the other side. Soon they were out of the protection of the harbour and Charlotte set a course for the fishing grounds, where they intended to leave the fleet behind.

After several minutes, Pierre silently came to stand by her side in the wheelhouse to watch the rise and fall of the horizon with each roll and pitch of the boat. Charlotte was impressed he was not feeling nauseous, although he did look pale. When she suggested he went below deck to rest, he did so without arguing, which was even more worrying. She silently watched him leave before looking at the course ahead.

Bulbous white clouds filled the sky and she wondered what the weather held in store. Her father would know. The sight of Pierre's wound also played heavily on her mind. His health was deteriorating, she could tell, despite his reluctance to admit it. She looked about her. Despite being surrounded by men with the same experience of the sea as her, she felt quite alone in her worries. After all, she knew they would all think she was mad to sail for England if she told them that half of her crew was ill below deck.

They sailed for some time, the ocean deepening below their boats and turning the murky green waves to black. Eventually, the other boats began to disperse to different parts of the fishing ground, each skipper carefully positioning their trawlers so his crew could shoot their net down wind. Only the *Emilienne* and *Almost Home* remained on their journey, riding the mass of water that moved beneath their hulls like a giant restless animal.

The roar of German bombers caught Charlotte's attention and brought Pierre up on deck. They silently watched them pass overhead, cutting across the sky like giant prehistoric birds. The sight was a sombre reminder of the journey ahead and how they would not be out of danger until they reached British soil.

An eerie peace followed as the low rumble of engines disappeared into the distance, leaving the *Emilienne* and *Almost Home* alone again. A light mist began to form, bringing down a hazy curtain between where they were now and their journey ahead. Charlotte and Pierre agreed that the time had come to break away from their friends and head northwards on their own. They raised their hands in farewell to the skipper of the *Emilienne*. Understanding their meaning, he raised his hand in return. Charlotte set a new course and slowly increased their speed. Soon the skipper of the *Emilienne*, and his loyal crew of eight men, were fading into the swirling mist as they waved goodbye, leaving no evidence that they had ever escorted them at all. Pierre, Charlotte and the *Almost Home* were on their own. Good weather, skill and luck were all they could hope for now.

* * *

Charlotte decided it was best to hug the west coast of France for the first part of their journey. If they went too far westward, she explained to Pierre, they might attract attention from German reconnaissance planes. The first part of their journey was uneventful, but as they reached the latter part of the western coast of Brittany, bright searchlights lit up the sky, arcing between Ile Vierge to Le Trepied. As they swept across the inky abyss of space, Charlotte feared they would lower and search the sea. When she voiced her concern, Pierre was surprisingly calm.

'If they drop their beam, we cannot steer to avoid it. All we can do is keep to our course and hope that they don't.'

It was the logical advice she needed. With renewed determination, she increased their speed and continued their journey.

As they left the French coast behind, numerous silhouettes of planes passed overhead heading for German-occupied French ports. Several minutes later the faint muffled sounds of a bombing raid could be heard in the distance as another sinister hum of more Allied planes arrived from the north and passed overhead. Charlotte turned to look towards Lorient. The glow from the fiery explosions reflected in the sky, telling her Lorient was one of their targets. Knowing something of the port, she could clearly imagine the devastation being caused. The relay of bombing raids continued for more than an hour, providing a much-needed diversion for the Luftwaffe and the facade of protection for the *Almost Home*. Eventually the sky above became quiet again, with the only sound emanating from the small boat's engine as it chugged away like an elderly relative — determined, experienced, with the risk and inevitability that it could suddenly deteriorate. Fearing it may not last, Charlotte was reluctant to use full speed.

'I expect you think I am going too slowly, but I'd rather go steady and reach land than put too much pressure on it and risk breaking down,' she explained over the noise. She glanced over her shoulder when Pierre did not reply and found him sitting on a bench. He looked even paler.

'Perhaps you should go below deck again,' she suggested. He nodded, almost drunkenly, and left, stumbling at one point as the boat rose and fell violently by a rogue wave. She gnawed on her lip as she watched him go, torn between nursing him or nursing the boat.

For the next hour, Charlotte remained at the helm, the roar of the sea in her ears, the engine fumes in her nose and the salt air on her lips. She was dragging a tangled strand of hair from her eyes when she spotted a convoy of ominous shapes on the horizon. They were too far away to distinguish if they were enemies or allies, but she was sure that they were either battleships, cruisers or destroyers. She looked at them through her binoculars. They were strangely graceful, despite their bulk, and appeared to be moving so slowly it was as if they weren't moving at all. Reviewing her course, she decided to continue, hoping and praying that a single French fishing trawler would be difficult to spot, or if it was spotted, then it was perceived as not too much of a threat. Even so, she was still glad when they disappeared over the horizon, as she found their lurking and anonymous presence an impossible thing to ignore.

* * *

It wasn't long before her unease returned as she began to notice that seabirds were starting to head towards land. This coincided with a new north-easterly wind that was quickly gaining in strength. She knew, without any doubt, that a storm was brewing. She had three choices. First, to avoid it by sailing further out to sea. However, it would increase their risk of being spotted and place them in the wake of the convoy of ships. It was possible, but the engine was already tired and may not cope with the extra distance. The second choice was to head towards the nearest French port, which would obviously take them back to where they started — in occupied France and at risk of being caught. The third choice was to ride out the storm, which sounded as crazy as she thought she must be to navigate no-man's-land waters during a war.

She was about to go below deck to discuss it with Pierre when the wind suddenly picked up. The storm had arrived, spitting and snarling like a wild animal, and snatching any choice from her. She held on to the wheel, battling the sudden turn in events that had taken her breath away. Soon, the waves around her were "blowing smoke" as they tossed up water spray by the buffeting wind. Charlotte attempted to reduce the sea's impact by approaching each wave at an angle but made little progress.

The onslaught of the wind and waves were relentless, causing the boat to rise and fall at alarming speed and the compass to swing uselessly at 360 degrees. She checked the engine and saw that it was beginning to strain. Fearing that it would fatally stop, she made the decision to turn it off. She stared at it for a moment as the trawler began to drift precariously below her feet. It was time to go below. She had tried her best, she thought, as she made her way towards the hatch, now it was up to luck. Eventually she arrived at the hatch, flung it open and climbed below, her hair dripping wet, lips numb and fingers white with cold.

'Time to batten down the hatches,' she said cheerfully as she shut and locked the hatch above her head. 'The bad news is that a storm is brewing. The good news is we are less likely to be intercepted by hostile aircraft while it is here.' She stared at her stiff, cold, numb fingers and tried to move them to encourage the circulation to return. Who she was trying to convince that everything was all right, she wondered. Pierre or herself? She turned to find Pierre lying quietly on a make-shift bed on the floor.

'Pierre?' She slowly walked over to him and was relieved when he opened his eyes.

'It's all right,' he murmured. 'I am not as bad as I look.'

She ignored him and touched his brow. He was burning up. 'Bad case of seasickness?' she asked, knowing it was far from the truth.

He smiled, grateful that she was playing along. 'Something like that.'

She gave him some water as the boat lurched from side to side. Some spilled down his chin, but he was grateful and drank deeply until he turned his face away.

'I didn't want to strain the engine anymore, so we are sitting out the storm,' she explained.

'Then come and lie down with me so we can sit out the storm together.'

Pierre lifted his good arm and welcomed her into his embrace. She dragged off her wet coat and trousers, slipped beneath the blanket and snuggled up to his fevered body.

'Do you think we are going to survive this?' he asked quietly.

'Of course. We have to.'

'I have more faith that you will.' He smiled to himself. 'I think you can survive anything.'

'I don't want to survive without you.'

'Hush now. I don't want to hear you talk like that. I'm paying the price for not taking more care of my wound. I don't want you to pay a price for my stupidity.'

'You put yourself second. You wanted me to escape and did not want to slow us down. You were not stupid. You were selfless.'

'A selfless man does not lie on his back while the woman he loves is battling a storm.'

'The woman you love?'

He lifted her hand to his lips and kissed it. 'Yes, love.'

'Are you telling me this because you don't think we will reach land and I won't be able to hold you to it.'

'I am telling you this because I see no reason to not tell you the truth.' He inhaled a laboured breath. 'I never thought I would fall in love again, but I have . . . and I don't even know your real name. What is it, Mademoiselle Marie Veilleux?'

She touched his face, grazing her fingers across his stubble. They were on their way back to Britain. Did it matter now if she told him her name? Her mission had come to an early end and now she was on her way home. What did she have to lose?

'My name is Charlotte Bray.'

His heavy-lidded eyes lit up at her words. 'Charlotte,' he murmured, testing the name on his tongue. 'It's a pretty name. Are you married, Charlotte Bray?'

She smiled and shook her head. 'No, I'm not married.'

'That's a good reason for me to survive this storm and heal my wound, then.'

'Yes, it is a very good reason.'

'Tell me more.'

'There is nothing to tell.'

'Then tell me everything you can about this . . . nothing. Do you have a sweetheart?'

'No sweetheart.'

'Ever?'

'You are incorrigible.'

'I want to know my enemies.'

She rested her cheek against his chest and thought for a moment. 'You have no enemies to fight.'

'I don't believe there has been no one.'

She considered her life. 'There was one. A soldier. It was brief. He left me for another.'

'He sounds like a fool.'

'He was and I told him so.'

Pierre's low rumble of laughter felt good beneath her cheek. It was reassuring to know that, despite his fever, his humour had not left him.

'What about you?' she asked.

'There was only Odette before you.'

'Odette is a pretty name. Tell me about her.'

He sighed deeply.

'You don't have to tell me if you would rather not.'

'It is okay. I want you to know. If we are to survive this and start a new life together, I want it to be free of secrets. I am tired of secrets.'

'How long were you married?'

'Eleven years.'

'Was it a happy marriage?'

'Yes, very happy.'

She fell silent as she imagined him kissing the beautiful, never-to-grow-old, Odette. He took her silence as a cue to continue.

'We knew each other as teenagers. When we became adults it seemed natural that we would date and one day marry. We had a good marriage, but everything changed in 1940.'

'What happened?'

'I'd heard that the Germans were about to sweep into Paris. It was June. The nights had been cool but the days were warm, no different to any other summer's day. They came in their tanks, many marching through the streets with their chins held high and their bodies proud and straight-backed. Suddenly, it felt as if summer had ended. What they didn't know was that four-fifths of Parisians had already fled. My wife and son were among them.'

'They went without you?'

'I felt I couldn't go.' He teased her curls absently as he stared up at the ceiling. 'Odette didn't want to leave, but I said she must. I knew the German army was advancing and our city had no effective police or government to protect us. It was only a matter of time before Paris fell and we would be at their mercy. I thought Odette and Lucien would be safer away from the city.'

'How did they get away?'

'I took them to the station.' Pierre frowned, appearing to remember the day as clearly as if it were happening now. 'The platform was gridlocked with people attempting to leave. It soon became apparent that I was not the only one that thought it was safer away from Paris. It was by sheer chance that I got them onto a train heading south to Brive-La-Gaillarde. Odette had family there and I knew they would take care of them.'

'It must have been difficult to wave them goodbye.'

'It was, but I was relieved that they were leaving and would soon be safe.' He frowned. 'But as I walked away from the station I felt a sense of unease. Just as I did when I walked away from you.' He looked at her. 'I can't describe it. It felt unsettling, dark . . . as if I was about to die. Sometimes, when I think of that day, I still feel it.'

Charlotte eased herself on one elbow to look at him. 'You mustn't blame yourself. You did what you thought was right. Everyone who left thought they were doing the right thing.'

Pierre nodded slowly. He was with her physically, but mentally he was back in Paris, walking its broad streets.

'Paris was ill-prepared for the massive exodus. The roads were filled with people attempting to escape. Some families had cars, but many walked, rode bikes or hung onto carts loaded with their belongings. Few were prepared for a long trek. They didn't take enough food, wore the wrong shoes and either carried too much or too little. No one really knew where they were going or where they were going to stay en route. Desperate parents offered their children to strangers in the hope they would take them to safety. Some people even left their elderly relatives behind.'

He fell silent. They listened to the howling wind outside and the first waves of rain pelt the deck above.

'What happened to your wife and child?' asked Charlotte, eventually.

'I thought they were going to be safe but found out later that their train was bombed. I hadn't considered that Hitler's army would sink so low as to bomb fleeing refugees. I learned that the passengers on board died instantly. The news gave me little solace. I had sent them to their deaths and had to learn to live with the fact that if it wasn't for my decision, they would be alive and I would be with them now. Even now I wonder if that feeling of dying was really their deaths I was feeling.'

'You sent them away so they could be safe with her family. You cannot live your life blaming yourself for something you couldn't foresee.'

He reached up and touched her face with his fingers. 'It is hard not to when many who fled the city later returned. They are a constant reminder that if I hadn't . . .'

The tips of his fingers began to tremble so she pressed a kiss into his warm palm to still them. He closed his eyes. 'Lucien was beautiful . . . always happy . . . always smiling . . . or at least he was until he realised I was not going with them.' He sighed deeply, before his hand fell away. 'Then he looked upset and betrayed . . . and that is hard to forget.'

The boat lurched to the side and several objects fell and rolled across the deck above them, creaking and banging like sea monsters attempting to attack the boat.

'Tell me how you became a double agent?' she asked brightly, in an attempt to change the subject. She could see that the sad memories and the sound of the storm outside were draining him, and he needed his strength right now. He smiled weakly.

'I had just completed a reconnaissance of the fortification along the Brittany coast. I was arrested for suspicious activity and was . . . interrogated.'

She looked at him through her brows. 'You mean tortured.'

'Yes, I mean tortured.'

She lay on her back, rested her head in the crook of her arm and stared at the low-beamed ceiling above. 'When I was being tortured, I almost gave in, but then I heard more voices outside. I felt as if they were only just beginning the torture process. If you had not come when you did . . .' She turned her head to look at him. 'How did *you* survive it?'

He met her gaze, a faint smile on his lips. 'I thought of you.'

His confession silenced her.

'You don't believe me?'

'I am surprised. You had only met me twice.'

'You left a lasting impression.'

Despite herself, she couldn't help being intrigued and wanted to know more. He chuckled quietly when she asked how he had imagined her.

'You comforted me, encouraged me, supported me . . . and let's just say that our lovemaking at the safe house was not the first time for me.'

She rolled her eyes but found herself smiling despite herself. 'You are incorrigible.'

He grinned. 'You bring the worst out in me. I think, subconsciously, you gave me something to live for. I thought if you had been faced with what I was facing, your stubbornness, strength of character and determination would pull you through it. It gave me the motivation to try to survive it, too.' He asked for more water, which she gave him and they both settled back in each other's arms as before. She felt him shiver.

'Are you cold?'

'Yes, a little.'

She touched his brow. Torn between trying to warm him yet reduce his temperature, she told him the truth. 'You are burning up.'

'I know,' he said sadly. 'There is nothing to be done.' He returned to talking about his arrest. 'I gave nothing away at first, but then I heard that the main officer was transferring to Paris and I saw an opportunity to make things more difficult for them. I revealed my German connections and a deal was done. They would leave my hotel alone and I would feed them information.'

'What did London say?'

'I didn't inform them at first. I wanted to ensure the Germans didn't learn of my deception by intercepting messages. My previous network had fallen for that very reason. The German officers thought I was helping them, but in reality I was still loyal to London and fed them disinformation.'

'Tell me again, what sort of disinformation?'

He shrugged weakly. 'Potential attacks. Then they would divert their resources to the wrong places. I would drip feed snippets of information regarding an invasion, only it was for places far away from the intended area. Some information was correct but provided too late. It was enough to keep Kieffer hooked. I was living a life built on lies and trusted no one.'

'And then I arrived as your newest member.'

He smiled. 'Yes. Then you arrived . . . and I didn't want to lie anymore. For the first time I began to dare to look forward, rather than back. That day, when I promised to show you the Eiffel Tower, was the day I knew I was in trouble for sure.'

'Trouble?'

'Yes. For the first time I had not thought of my wife and son for several hours. I knew then that if it was possible for me to not only feel something for another woman, but to fall in love again . . . it would be with a woman like you.'

The boat rose and fell alarmingly, as the chill north-easterly wind buffeted the trawler, dragging it across the waves at an alarming angle. Several objects fell and clattered in the galley. Charlotte ignored them and Pierre closed his eyes, exhausted from the effort of being awake. She offered him some water and cradled his head as he supped. Eventually he eased the cup away.

He threaded his fingers through hers. 'Tell me about you. I want to know more.'

Charlotte drained the tin cup, placed it on the floor and settled into his embrace as it rolled across the floor with the next rise and fall of the boat.

'I went to work on my father's boat when I was thirteen, almost fourteen. Fishing is hard work. It's done in all weathers and a crew can be out at sea for days at a time. I had no brothers or sisters, my mother had just died, school no longer interested me and the neighbour who looked after me while my father was fishing had had enough. My father had little option but to take me to sea with him. He said I was causing too much trouble on land.'

A slight smile curved Pierre's lips as he listened.

'The crew resisted. It is a man's world and having a woman on board set them on edge, but they soon accepted me. I fished with my father on nearly every trip after that. Apart from his last.'

'Did you enjoy it?'

Charlotte thought for a moment. 'I enjoy being on the sea . . .'

He opened his eyes and looked down at her. 'But?'

'But not the actual work. It meant I spent time with my father and I felt I belonged there.'

'Belonged?'

'I've always felt different . . . restless. I was half-French and knew no one else like me. It always felt that something was missing. I'd lost my mother and I think I felt that I'd lost that part of me. Being on the sea felt like . . . a way of escaping.'

He brought her fingers to his lips and kissed them. 'And then what?'

'I began to embrace my French side and was going to teach French lessons.'

'How did that go?'

'It didn't go anywhere. I ended up being singled out as agent material and when my father died in a mine explosion, I saw no reason not to accept.'

'And now you have seen France and lived a French life.'

'And now I feel that I understand that side of me and have done my best to help. In a way, I feel at peace with myself . . . which sounds so silly when we are at war.'

'It's not silly to me.' Another bout of shivering temporary silenced him. When it receded, he released his fingers from hers and laid his hand protectively over hers as if it had not happened at all. 'I am half-German,' he said as he caressed her hand. 'It will be quite a while before I feel at peace with my ancestry. It will come eventually, I'm sure . . . when the war is over and we have peace again.' A shaky sigh escaped him.

'Are you tired?' she asked. Despite offering him a drink, his lips remained dry.

'Let me sleep a while,' he murmured softly, as his hand slipped from hers. 'I do feel so tired. Perhaps after a rest, I will be of more help.'

'You are a help to me now.'

He shook his head. 'Not at the moment, my sweet brave Charlotte Bray, but I will be . . . I will be.'

His eyes remained closed, too lethargic to offer her a smile or a glance. She watched his breaths deepen and his face turn boyish in his sleep. The only sign he was ill at all was the slight glistening sheen on his forehead and the warmth of his body beside hers. She lay down beside him again and immersed herself into the rise and fall of the boat, as the powerful waves of the storm passed underneath its battered hull and crashed onto the wooden deck above their heads. They were in luck's hands now, she thought, as she too slowly closed her eyes. Whatever happened now, good or bad, would happen to them both and she would rather be by his side in death, than alone somewhere else alive.

* * *

Charlotte opened her eyes to silence. The boat was still and the wind and rain that had raged all night, had finally blown itself out. She turned to Pierre to find him still asleep. She eased herself away from his side and climbed the steps to the upper deck, tentatively unlocking and pushing open the hatch to allow the dawn's bright, white light to flood in. She climbed up on deck, blinking in the light, to find a peaceful, flat sea all around her. Being her father's daughter, she immediately checked the boat just as he would have done. The previously saturated deck was almost dry — evidence that the storm had stopped within the hour. Some objects were missing. The mizzen-mast was broken and its flag lay damp and torn on the deck. A few objects had slid to the stern, but, on the whole, everything appeared relatively intact and where it should be.

She was trying to calculate how far the north-easterly wind had blown them off course, when she heard the engine of a plane. Shielding her eyes from the rising sun, she watched the German long-range reconnaissance plane approach, probably searching for convoys and U-boats in the Atlantic.

Could they see her small boat? She was far beyond the German permitted zone now and was bound to raise suspicions. Would they feel that her French trawler was significant enough to attack? She decided she couldn't take any risks and attempted to start the engine in a vain hope of putting some distance between them. The engine tantalisingly spluttered into life before falling silent. She tried again. Nothing. And again. Nothing. She began to lose the little hope she had, fast. She did a few rudimentary checks, including the level of the fuel, and tried again. Nothing.

She stared at the engine, unsure what to do next, then looked up at the sky and froze. A trail of bullets carved a frantic straight path through the water and across her deck, covering her in wood splinters as she ran for cover, shielding her head as she did so. She curled up on the floor, shaking from the sudden onslaught and thinking what a pitiful way this was to die. Another trail of bullets cut across the deck, showering her in splinters of wood again. She remained where she was, trembling, until the engine's roar in the sky began to fade.

She lifted her head and eased herself to standing. Her legs felt weak and she began to tremble, finally succumbing to hours of fear and fatigue — but she knew it was more than that. She had once boasted that she did not fear dying, but her body now screamed another story from its quivering muscles to the churning in her stomach. She still did not fear death, but she did fear not living, for if she died now so would Pierre, along with any future hours, days or years they might have together.

Charlotte inhaled slowly several times to calm herself, releasing each breath in a slow therapeutic sigh until her body stopped trembling. In her victory she allowed herself a smile, relieved that the overhead danger, and the one inside, had passed. But then she heard the familiar noise of a plane growing louder overhead again. She searched the sky and soon spotted the German plane heading her way.

As it drew closer another engine noise, higher in tone and with a distinctive purr of a single propeller, grew louder behind her. She turned, searched the sky and found the source — a lone British Spitfire approaching at speed. Despite its small size it appeared bullish and determined as it cut across the sky towards the German plane. The Spitfire spat out a round of bullets which peppered the larger plane from wing to wing, each successful hit exploding in a flash of flame and smoke. The German plane's heavy wings tilted in the air, but it remained on course, too large to change route and aim its fire at the nimble plane.

The Spitfire flew overhead, turned in the sky and returned to its target, spraying the back of the German plane with another hail of bullets. The plane could do little to escape the Spitfire's onslaught. Its tail-end exploded in a cloud of black smoke, leaving a trail of thick coils in its wake as it spluttered on. Suddenly, its engine fell silent and it began to lose altitude. With no power, its head graciously tipped downwards causing its great bulk to fall, rolling only once at an angle before slicing through the surface of the ocean in an explosion of white spray. As suddenly as it appeared, it had disappeared, its ending so complete that there appeared no wreckage marking its exit from the living.

Charlotte looked up at the cloudless sky and watched as the lone Spitfire flew away into the distance, seemingly unaffected by the encounter. If she had not seen it leave, she would have questioned if there had been a plane skirmish at all.

The small Spitfire's pilot had inspired her. Despite its size, it had attacked and destroyed the larger enemy plane and in doing so, had unwittingly saved her life. Somewhere out there, a vital convoy of ships supplying weapons and food would continue, possibly unaware of the courage of the lone pilot who had prevented them being spotted. She might be in the middle of nowhere, with a broken engine and the man she loved dying below deck, but she wasn't ready to give up yet.

Using the side of the trawler, she made her way to the engine again.

'Come on, Dad. What would you do?' Somewhere in the depths of her memory she retrieved a few rudimentary checks she had seen her father do. They were foggy, made little sense, but were worth a try. Several more attempts to start the battered engine followed and finally, to her relief, it spluttered into life. She lifted her face to the sky, thanked her father and laughed. Although the air reeked of fumes, the repetitive chug chug noise, in that moment, was the most beautiful sound she had ever heard.

Re-energised, Charlotte set a new course. The sea was relatively smooth, with only a mild north-west swell. The next hour brought her back on course and, for the first time since the storm had begun, she felt confident that she might make it home. Eventually a hazy landmass appeared on the horizon. She lifted her binoculars to study it and almost cried in relief when she recognised the Cornish coast. At the moment it was too far away to be detailed, but near enough to recognise it was home. Two Beaufighter planes approached from inland and circled above. Unsure whether they had come to escort her home or target her, Charlotte hurried down the steps, found a sheet in a cupboard and tied it to the broken mizzen-mast in the hope they would see that she came in peace. Although France were Britain's allies, there would always be a natural distrust at seeing an unidentified boat approaching the coast. Finally, the planes banked away, heading out to sea after, no doubt, reporting her presence.

She continued to navigate the trawler towards home, hugging the foggy coast towards the sheltered waters of Newlyn Harbour. Several Cornish fishermen silently watched her arrival as her boat limped past the harbour wall. One or two recognised her but there was no fanfare, no acknowledgement, no welcome or celebration as she jumped onto the quay and secured the Breton fishing boat. There was just a disbelieving raise of their hands or a nod of their heads. The villagers of Newlyn knew nothing of where she had been, what she had been doing, or the importance of what she carried in her coat pocket. And she would never be able to tell them the truth. It didn't matter. The *Almost Home* had got her home safely and Pierre, her love and best friend, now had a greater chance of survival than he had only a few hours before.

CHAPTER TWENTY-SEVEN

Autumn 1946

Charlotte stood on the old quay of Newlyn Harbour and inhaled deeply. To the left, the south coastline of Cornwall formed a natural shelter around the mystical island of St Michael's Mount, before stretching far into the distance to be swallowed up in the haze of the horizon. To the right lay the open sea, a treacherous, yet beautiful route towards numerous fishing grounds and the country of Pierre's birth. She had to decide about her future and the time to make that decision was now.

She'd hoped that by returning to Cornwall, she would find it easier to know where she wanted to make her home. She had loved Newlyn before the war, and as the fishing village had remained largely unscathed, she was surprised to find herself unsure if she wanted to stay. She watched the assortment of boats bobbing in the sheltered water of the harbour, waiting patiently for their owners to return and cast off. A few appeared neglected, their hulls dull and peeling, and Charlotte couldn't help wondering what story they had to tell as their souls and hulls seemed to grow heavy with the waiting. There were fewer Belgian fishing crews now, as many had returned to their home when peace was declared, the men and their families eager to salvage what was left of their lives. However, the harbour itself, with its hardworking fishermen, remained much the same as a century before.

On return to England, they had spent the remainder of the war in London. Pierre's detailed plans of the north coast of France had confirmed the information London already had in their possession and helped the greatest amphibious invasion of Europe to be a success. It was the tipping point of the war the Allies needed and, by smuggling the map in the lining of her coat and sailing back to England, Charlotte was proud to have played her small part. Now they were at peace and the new year stretched ahead full of promise and new beginnings. It was just the decision about where those beginnings should be which remained unanswered.

She heard Pierre's footsteps behind her and glanced at her watch. The hour of solitude that she had asked for had already passed and he was coming back for her. She turned to greet him, his beautiful face blurred as her eyes filled with tears. She rested her head against his shoulder as he came to stand beside her and wrap his arm about her waist.

'You look sad.'

She smiled sadly. 'Coming back here brings back so many memories.'

'The loss of your father?'

She stared out to sea, with its mystical dark shapes slicing through the water's surface. 'Yes. His body is out there somewhere, but I think he would have preferred the freedom of the sea rather than a burial on land.'

'I sense there is something more than that too.'

She watched a bird soar high into the sky. 'I feel I've lost the person I once was. I feel that so much has changed yet I find that, here, so little has. I can't decide if that's reassuring or terribly sad.'

'Sad?'

She shrugged, knowing she was thinking too emotionally. She had spent so much of her time lately trying to lock that side of her away, as it had little use when trying to fight a war.

'I saw my neighbour's cat earlier. She was eating some scraps of fish on the harbour wall. She never used to eat just any fish She always had a preference for the fish caught by my father's nets. I know life should move on, but it feels strange to see it happening.'

'Moving on can be a good thing.'

'I know and it is what I want us both to do. I think it's because there is nothing to acknowledge what has happened between the time I left and the time I've returned. To stay and live as I did before would feel as though I am discarding all those lives that did so much during that time.'

'You are not making sense, Charlotte.'

'It makes no sense to me.' She breathed in deeply and let it out on a sigh. 'I'm afraid . . .'

'Afraid of what?'

'That I may never feel a part of this place again . . .' She looked at him. 'And do I want to try?'

'You talk of people who helped change you and your fear of forgetting them. Do you mean Isabelle and Jeanne?'

Pierre was beginning to know her too well. She had hoped they were still alive, but when no one turned up at Wanborough Manor on the first Saturday in June, one year after the war had ended, she knew the news was going to be bad. Pierre used his former contacts at the Special Operation Executive department to find out what had happened to them. Their fate was as heart-wrenching as she had feared. He had been gentle and kind when he had told her, but he could not protect her from the pain the news had caused.

'Jeanne deserved a medal, not an execution at Ravensbruck Concentration Camp.' She wiped a tear away from her eyes with her sleeve. 'I should have persuaded Isabelle to return to England with me when I saw her.'

'And if you had persuaded her, she wouldn't have been able to warn her own network and all the others. She saved many lives, thanks to your message. She died a hero when she was eventually caught.'

Pierre slipped his arms around her waist and she rested her back against him, hugging his arms against her stomach. His protective, loving embrace told her more than words could say.

'You think I should not blame myself, don't you, Pierre?'

'You shouldn't. She was in danger the moment she set foot in France, as you all were. She knew what she was doing and what she must do. It is time for your nightmares to end.'

'It's hard not to have regrets. Especially at times like this.'

'Times like this?'

'When I feel guilty for feeling so lucky. But I only share my dark thoughts with you.'

'And I will take those dark thoughts,' he said, grabbing at the air, 'and cast them out to sea where they belong.'

She watched the wind carry her words from his open palm into the sky and away to the horizon. She closed her eyes as she felt him kiss the top of her head, drinking in the sensations of peace and calm to be resting in his arms. How lucky she was to be with a man she loved when Isabelle and Jeanne would never have that chance. Two ordinary women, in exceptional times, had shown remarkable courage. Their existence and feats of heroism would now remain a secret for decades, for those who knew about their bravery were muzzled by their own signature on the Official Secrets Act documents they'd signed. Yet secretly, she still hoped that the confusion, secrets and destruction of war had muddled their fates with someone else's.

'So many people have influenced our lives,' she mused. 'Not just Isabelle and Jeanne. If it wasn't for some of them, I would never have met you and be here now.' Her thoughts travelled back to the tearoom in Newlyn where it had all begun. 'The elderly gentleman, with a penchant for pouring tea so precisely, who attempted to recruit me in the first place.' She indicated the café overlooking the harbour and smiled. 'The building looks an unlikely place to recruit agents.'

'Which makes it perfect, of course,' remarked Pierre.

'The instructors who gave me the skills to survive were so dedicated. I'll never forget the last officer who gave me my mission.' She looked up at Pierre. 'He didn't really know me but was so kind and understanding.' She settled back into his arms as she stared out to sea. 'It must have been difficult for him, knowing where I was going and what I would face. But he did it well and it was what I needed.'

Pierre touched her cheek with his own, wordlessly providing comfort and support for her to go on.

'The British crew who risked their lives to transfer me to a French trawler. I wonder what they are doing now.' She smiled. 'The French skipper who risked his life and crew to transfer me to France, never believing for a moment that I would visit him again and ask for a boat of my own. His face was quite a picture when I told him I would sail it myself.'

'Bernard. Raymond. Gérald. All good men who are now dead.'

'Do you ever think of Sully? I wonder what drove him to betray us like that? Fear? Misplaced loyalty? Or something else that we'll never be able to understand.'

'I try not to think of him. However,' he said more brightly, 'there is one man who we should not forget . . . the truck driver with his bag full of oysters.'

'Of course! Monsieur Guellec! What a feast that was! It was so kind of him to give you his water bottle.'

Pierre patted the inside pocket where he always carried it. 'I will keep it forever to remember his kindness.'

She frowned as she remembered the Spitfire pilot who came out of nowhere and fought off the German plane. 'I wonder if any of them survived the war.'

'We shouldn't forget those who helped us when we arrived in England. I owe much to the doctor who saved my arm.'

'And the families who left pasties and cakes on my door-step until you were better. "For your French friend" they would say.'

Pierre chuckled. 'I think they wanted to prove that British food was better than French food.' He breathed in deeply behind her and slowly released it on a sigh of memories. 'And then there was the major who gave us a job at the War Office. That helped me a lot. I felt I hadn't abandoned my country . . . that I was still doing something useful to liberate France.'

'And all those nameless people who carried a message to Georges and were able to reassure you that he was well and your hotel had survived.'

Pierre nodded in agreement. 'There have been so many people. Some we came to know well, others we will never learn their names. But now it is time to move on from the war,' said Pierre, dragging her from her thoughts. 'Time for *both* of us to move on.'

He turned her in his embrace to face him. She wrapped her arms about his neck and looked up at him. He kissed her on the forehead and, as always, she instinctively found herself offering her lips for more. The kiss that followed promised her he would always be there for her, wherever she decided to live.

His lips softened and he slowly broke away. 'Have you decided, my love? Do you want to stay in England or leave for France?'

She gave him a shaky smile. Now it was time for a fresh start and to build a new life for themselves. What that life would look like had been a hard decision for her to make.

She turned to look down the empty road, still hoping, perhaps, to see her father approaching and exclaiming that the news of his death had all been a mistake. The road remained empty of his extrovert presence. Suddenly, she knew what she must do.

'Let's go to France,' she said, decisively.

He caressed her cheek with the back of a single finger. 'Are you sure? I think you'll miss Cornwall. We could try living in another village or town.'

'Yes, I will miss Cornwall, but missing a place . . . or a person . . . only shows how much you loved them. It is not a reason to stand still. I'm your wife now. My life is with you and your heart is in France.'

'But if life in France is not for you, tell me. I am willing to leave my country to be with you if I have to.'

'I know, but I see this next phase of my life as a grand adventure.'

He smiled. 'Haven't you had enough of adventures?'

She kissed his curved lips. 'Enough of adventures?' She shook her head. 'Never! We are alive and in love. Our adventure together is only just beginning.'

THE END

THE CHOC LIT STORY

Established in 2009, Choc Lit is an independent, award-winning publisher dedicated to creating a delicious selection of quality women's fiction.

We have won 18 awards, including Publisher of the Year and the Romantic Novel of the Year, and have been shortlisted for countless others.

All our novels are selected by genuine readers. We are proud to publish talented first-time authors, as well as established writers whose books we love introducing to a new generation of readers.

In 2023, we became a Joffe Books company. Best known for publishing a wide range of commercial fiction, Joffe Books has its roots in women's fiction. Today it is one of the largest independent publishers in the UK.

We love to hear from you, so please email us about absolutely anything bookish at choc-lit@joffebooks.com

If you want to hear about all our bargain new releases, join our mailing list: www.choc-lit.com

ALSO BY VICTORIA CORNWALL

CORNISH TALES SERIES
Book 1: THE THEIF'S DAUGHTER
Book 2: THE DAUGHTER OF RIVER VALLEY
Book 3: THE CAPTAIN'S DAUGHTER
Book 4: DANIEL'S DAUGHTER
Book 5: DAUGHTER OF THE HOUSE
Book 6: A DAUGHTER'S CHRISTMAS WISH

LOVE IN WAR SERIES
Book 1: THE PARIS AFFAIR
Book 2: WAITING FOR OUR RAINBOW

Milton Keynes UK
Ingram Content Group UK Ltd.
UKHW011833061123
432078UK00002B/5